LUCRETIA

or
The Heiress and the Dandy

A Regency Romance

by Rachel Carter

For Mum Dad
and Andy

CHAPTER ONE

Lady Rutland studied the letter with a disapproving frown. She was an imposing matron of indeterminate years whose considerable self-assurance was exceeded only by her haughtiness. In general of reserved mien, she was evidently much moved by what she read, exclaiming in severe tones, "A governess? No niece of mine will so demean herself! A Lanyon of Lanyon as a governess? Preposterous!"

Her husband, recognising that his participation in the conversation was required, sighed, lowered his paper, and regarded his beloved over the top of it. "Eh, what's that, m'dear?" he asked absent-mindedly.

Lord Rutland had chosen for himself an intelligent and cultivated bride, under the fond illusion that he would be able to enjoy with her rational conversation on the issues of the day. It was not long before he realised his error, for if his wife's understanding was superior to that of many of her sex, she had no notion of wasting it on the topics that interested her husband. And since he was singularly uninterested in such invigorating subjects as Lady Edgemont's shocking new hat or the odiously encroaching manners of that social mushroom Mrs Doughty, and since he was astute enough to realise that his wife's managing disposition meant that he was not expected to play any significant part in their exchanges, he had ceased, for the most part, to pay attention to her discourse. There were moments, however, such as these, when it obtruded irrepressibly upon his notice.

"My niece Lucretia, Charles. She writes, if you please, and alas! in the most execrable penmanship, to inform me that she has resolved to earn her living as a governess. I must say, if her script is anything to go by, it strikes me that she is as

1

entirely unqualified for such a job as the job is unsuitable!" Here the Countess held the letter some inches away from her face with a disgusted sniff before continuing, "She asks, most respectfully- anxious not to be thought of imposing upon our relationship, especially in light of the estrangement between myself and my brother- if I would be so obliging as to recommend her for any suitable position that may come to my notice."

"Really?" said Lord Rutland, laying his paper aside and displaying a tepid interest in the affair. "Why would she do that, I wonder?"

"My reprehensible brother's work, I imagine."

"Well, I know he's always been deuced queer in the attic, but you can't seriously believe him to be forcing the girl into such a life?"

"Of course I don't believe anything of the kind. He isn't forcing her to do anything. He's dead."

"Dead? Is he, by gad? Well, that's most unexpected," Lord Rutland mused.

"Unexpected? No such thing! I have lived in expectation of his being carried off by an apoplexy any time these last ten years!"

"Quite so, quite so," agreed the Viscount inconsistently, not from any want of intelligence but rather from the habit he had formed of naturally deferring to his wife's viewpoint, since she would listen to none but her own. "Nevertheless, devilishly eccentric fellow Lanyon. Daresay the poor girl's better off without him..." He broke off, realising the impropriety of voicing such unflattering views of a man only recently deceased. He hastened to turn his direction of thought, observing, "But if he's dead, I don't see what he can have to do with the matter. I know it's upset you, my dear, but Lucretia must be why... twenty years of age or thereabouts. So if she's set her heart on becoming a governess, there's not much we can do about it. If it's anyone's concern, it's the girl's guardian after all."

"Indeed! What *can* Horace be about to be letting Lucretia pursue such a course?" frowned Lady Rutland.

"Although to be sure, if there is a greater nodcock alive than Horace Fotherby, I have yet to meet him!"

"Though I must say," interposed Lord Rutland, steering his wife away from what would inevitably be a lengthy oration on the stupidity of the new Lord Lanyon, "I can't see why, in her situation, Lucretia could possibly want to pursue such a course. But no doubt she's as eccentric as her father. After all, must have been an odd upbringing, living with Hugo. Nevertheless, if it's the girl's wish to become a governess, it *is* her choice."

"How *can* you talk such nonsense, Charles? Of course we must stop the poor girl doing anything so foolish! If I'm not much mistaken, this situation has arisen because my brother failed to apprise the girl of the full details of her situation."

"Surely not?" exclaimed Lord Rutland, shrewdly reading between the lines of his wife's words and being genuinely shocked by the import of them.

"Exactly so," said Lady Rutland. "So, you see, it is essential that I see Lucretia and prevent her from doing anything bird-witted. I shall go and fetch the poor girl tomorrow. And she shall come and live with us. Naturally it is a trifle inconvenient to be obliged to make such a long journey at such short notice and when one has so much to organise for one's mourning. Although of course I do have my black bombazine gown, and the others I had made up after Aunt Sylvia's passing that will do for now..." she mused, distracted from the principal discussion. She continued in this vein some minutes for, after all, one must dress. Lord Rutland interjected noises indicative of agreement in suitable places and waited patiently for her to return to the point.

"... but I may have to let the waist out on that one a little. And I'm not sure that bishop's sleeves are altogether in keeping with the fashion this season... Nevertheless," said Lady Rutland, recalled to the main thread of her conversation unexpectedly, "I suppose I must do my duty and see the girl as soon as possible."

"Very well, Virginia. I'm sure you'll do as you think best," Lord Rutland said, not altogether without satirical overtones which were entirely lost on his wife. He accepted without a murmur the imperious addition of another member to his household and, anticipating that the hurried preparations for a sudden journey would be accompanied by just the kind of commotion that was most unlikely to add to his comfort, he hastily took himself off to his club.

It was a testament to her formidable organisational flair that Lady Rutland's smart travelling carriage set off on the morrow within an hour of the intended time. The journey was made in good time and, on the eve of the second day of travelling, the carriage jolted its way down the drive to Lanyon Hall, an approach that afforded an excellent view of the house and grounds. The Hall was an imposing rather than attractive building, built along grand lines but rather box-like in form. The late Lord Lanyon having been notoriously parsimonious, the upkeep of the house had been sadly neglected. But while his purse-pinching was evidenced in threadbare carpets, outmoded, shabby furniture and unkempt exteriors, it did not extend to his gardens, of which he had taken a rare interest and been inordinately proud. In the pale evening light, the gardens were gloriously alive with emerald hues and Spring's promise of blooms to come.

Lucretia was in the drawing room, which was situated at the rear of the house, and did not hear the carriage draw up. She was thus considerably taken aback when the footman announced the arrival of her aunt. Starting guiltily, she hastened to conceal the book she was reading, stuffing it behind her chair.

"Lady Rutland? I... I had no idea you would come to visit me," she said in faltering surprise.

Lady Rutland, sweeping majestically into the rather dingy apartment said, "But of course I must visit my poor orphaned niece. Especially when she writes me such a nonsensical letter. A governess? Naughty girl! Let us never speak of it again," she admonished.

"Lady Rutland I..." Lucretia began to say, but her aunt halted her with an imperious wave of her hand,

"My dear Lucretia, you must call me Aunt Virginia - I won't stand upon ceremony with you - you're my niece after all

- so silly to be calling each other Miss this or Lady that, eh? Especially when I mean us to become such good friends." Lady Rutland was not a warm-hearted woman but, to do her justice, she meant most sincerely to do her best for her niece, and to shower her with as much affection as her shallow disposition would allow.

Lucretia again tried to edge a word in, saying, "Very well then, Aunt..." but she was once again cut off by her aunt, whose invitation to address her as Aunt Virginia was, apparently, not a signal for Lucretia to actually speak.

"Do you remember me, I wonder?" Lady Rutland had interjected, evidently rhetorically, as she carried on speaking without pause. "It wouldn't surprise me in the slightest if you didn't. You must only have been seven years of age when we last met. Such an age as it has been since then! Needless to say, you've changed a good deal in that time. Well come here, come here and let me have a good look at you," she demanded, with a high-handed gesture, which directed Lucretia to stand in front of her.

Lucretia found herself being scrutinised by her aunt's critical eye, with acute embarrassment. She was an uncommonly pretty young lady, although not quite in the usual style, the fashion being for delicate, dainty beauties. Striking rather than shrinking, worldly rather than ethereal; there was nothing sylphlike about Lucretia's splendidly tall stature and buxom figure. And, although she had not as yet learned how to admire her own height or carry it gracefully, and was thus somewhat gauche, there was something undeniably magnificent in her looks of which her more insipid counterparts could not boast. Certainly, no fault could be found with her exquisite ivory skin, her twinkling dewdrop eyes, or the enchanting blonde ringlets dressed inexpertly but not unmodishly on the crown of her head.

"You look very well, my dear, very well indeed. You have the look of your mother, and she was a remarkably handsome woman, you know." Privately Lady Rutland prophesied to herself that Lucretia would take the town by storm. How green Mrs Doughty will look when I introduce her to the *ton*, so fond as she is of telling everyone that her Elinor

5

will be the most beautiful girl of the season when she comes out next year! Lady Rutland could not resist crowing to herself, her eyes gleaming triumphantly.

"Introduce me?" asked a bemused Lucretia.

"Certainly, when you make your come out."

"My, my come out?" said Lucretia faintly. "But ma'am, Aunt, I'm nearly one and twenty! Quite aged, in fact. There can be no thought of…"

"Aged? Pooh! You are not yet in your dotage! Of course you must make your debut into society. Naturally this is all coming about later than I had hoped. I did ask your father if I might bring you out for your seventeenth birthday…"

"Did you, Aunt?" Lucretia could not help herself from interrupting, astounded.

"Ah! I see he made no mention of that to you. Well, I own he wasn't taken with the idea, nor when I repeated my invitation the following year. I most truly felt for you, being so isolated out here in the country, and without even the smallest of amusements to pass away the time. But none of my arguments would move your father in the least. It was quite the height of cruelty, but sadly there was nothing more I could do about it. For a more obstinate, mulish man than your father I hope I never meet!"

"But, after all, it's not too late," continued Lady Rutland. "What good luck it is that Hugo had the sense to pass on when he did! For I would not put it past him to be quite disagreeable enough as to have persisted in his animate state any number of years, simply out of spite. I know I ought not to go on in this unseemly way and that we ought not to speak ill of the dead, but when I think of what he must have been saying about me these thirteen years, it seems most unjust to be obliged to be civil about him!"

This threw poor Lucretia into an agony of confusion, as she recalled the unflattering terms the late Lord Lanyon had used to describe his sister, 'meddling shrew' and 'damned pudding-brained busybody' being amongst the more complimentary. Thus Lucretia was relieved that Lady Rutland turned the subject before she was called upon to make any comment on her father's opinion of his sister.

"How he could have taken it into his head to hold me responsible for his wife's death I'll never know!" Lady Rutland disclaimed.

Lord Lanyon had come into the world as an eccentric and had left it in a similar temperament. Somewhere between these two states, however, he had had the good fortune to meet and marry a kind and beautiful woman of uncommon good sense, who had tempered her lord's leanings towards oddness and generally helped him to behave like a sensible, normal man. Sadly, she had died in childbirth, in the attempt to deliver of her husband a son and heir. She had taken the newborn into the next life with her, leaving Lord Lanyon at first bewildered and later conspicuously inconsolable and he swiftly talked himself into a degree of broken-heartedness which in no way matched his former affection for his wife.

Lady Rutland had, in her typically forceful way, insisted that it must be the fashionable and highly esteemed London physician, Sir William Knighton, who managed the care of her sister-in-law's health during her pregnancy. On the death of this lady, Lord Lanyon not only declared the doctor accountable for his wife's death, but also blamed his sister for recommending him, and somewhat obscurely held the whole of the polite world responsible for his bereavement. He subsequently packed up his life in the metropolis and retreated to his country house, eschewing the whole of polite society and forbidding his daughter from ever having contact with such a world or any of its culture.

"It is a relief to think that Hugo got his comeuppance at any rate," said Lady Rutland. "If it wasn't for the fact that he subjected you to his vagaries, I would have been so comforted by the vision of him condemned to live the life of a bored country gentleman with nothing but the sport of abusing his retainers to amuse him!"

Lord Lanyon had indeed been sadly unsuited to the life of a recluse and, unlike other retiring gentlemen, had not immersed himself in book reading, or indeed any useful hobby, with the one exception of overseeing the development of his gardens. Instead he had retired to his library, largely to stare at the four walls, becoming daily more cantankerous and odd, taking out his ever-increasing bad temper on his unfortunate servants and thinking up steadily more unflattering descriptive terms for his sister.

"But enough about my irascible brother!" said Lady Rutland with finality. "It seems silly to be talking about him when for once you are not obliged to be ruled by his eccentricities. Let us celebrate your freedom rather than bemoan your past. You had best go and begin your packing, Lucretia," she announced, as was her habit, in the form of a command, "for I mean us to set off first thing in the morning to get back to London in good time,"

"But Aunt, in my situation there can be no thought of my making my come out. You must know that there is the entail, and aside from that, my father left all his other worldly goods to Cousin Horace, without any mention of financial provision for me. Being quite without means, I'm obliged to find some way to support myself."

"Support yourself? Heavens, Lucretia, I must suspect you to have been reading novels," Lady Rutland accused, in evident disgust of this dangerous pastime. "Only families reduced to penury send their daughters out to work. Whatever you may think you know about your circumstances, I assure you that you would never be reduced to such a fate! Good God, a Lanyon in service?!"

"Indeed, you are quite right, Aunt, I have not been *forced* into such a life. Cousin Horace has been kind enough to offer to provide for me, and has assured me that I may continue to call Lanyon Hall my home as long as I wish. I, however, can think of no worse fate than to be forced to share a house with that blockhead! Let alone to be obliged to be grateful to him all my days!" While Lady Rutland disapproved of so much outspokenness in someone other than herself, and especially one so young as her niece, she could not disagree with Lucretia's assessment of this terrible prospect.

"But where is Horace?" demanded Lady Rutland. "To be sure he is uncommonly stupid, but nevertheless it is only proper that we obtain his permission for your removal to town. Not that I have the least expectation of a refusal." It seemed unlikely that Lady Rutland was in the habit of meeting with refusals to any of her demands.

"Oh, out with Mr Barnes, the steward you know, touring the estate, which he *will* call his populace and property," scoffed Lucretia. "He fancies he is being very clever in coming up with such a phrase, and you must know that, when Horace has come up with something he thinks clever, he must repeat the remark incessantly until it is reduced to sounding the very height of stupidity! It is to be hoped that he is faring better with Barnes than he did with poor Moyles. And to be sure I imagine that he will, for Barnes is very kind-hearted, and excessively patient besides. Moreover it is clear that he nourishes hopes that Horace may be encouraged to furnish him with the money for some much-needed improvement works, which indeed father could never be brought to do! Though Horace is so very deluded that he thinks he handled Moyles very well!" Lucretia unsuccessfully tried to stifle a snigger.

"What happened with Mr Moyles? Indeed, who, pray tell, is Mr Moyles?"

"Oh, the gardener. It was excessively diverting and of course it was too bad of Moyles, but you must understand that he was sadly provoked. But I must not repeat what happened for it would be most improper of me to poke fun at my guardian."

Lady Rutland's curiosity was roused. "Well, naturally, Lucretia, I could not encourage you to *poke fun* at anyone, and if we were in company I would, of course, recommend that nothing more was said upon the matter. But there are only us two good friends here and, after all, Horace is my relative, whatever the pity of it, and it is only right that I should know what is being said about him."

"Very well, Aunt, but you must promise me not to look too severely upon Moyles. What you need understand is that he is an *artiste*. To be sure, he is a little unlike what one would imagine of someone in the part, his being laconic and gruff – he is a northerner, you see - and very crotchety besides. But in his heart, you know, he is most truly the *artiste,* so it is not to be wondered at that he took Horace in aversion after his conduct. When Moyles accompanied Horace on a tour of the gardens and grounds, Horace could not but feel that some comment was due. He has become enormously puffed up since coming into father's estates and insists on putting all the servants' backs up with his patronising and supercilious airs. And he was so unwise as to condescend to Moyles that he thought that the flower borders were nicely colourful and that the garden would do very well when the trees were a little taller!" Lucretia paused, remembering these horrifying words.

"After having his life's work and masterpiece so slighted," she continued, "who could blame poor Moyles for muttering darkly under his breath that he must go and attend to his deadly nightshade, it being the best cure for stupidity that he knew of, and would no doubt be in great demand in future! Horace, not catching the remark but noting the tone, demanded suspiciously to know what had been said. 'Oh, nothing, sir,' said Moyles. 'It is only that I must be going, for Mrs Wallace' – our cook- 'will be needing the apples I promised her for her arsenic soup.' Only he pronounced it *arsenique* rather than arsenic, for all the world as if it had been the latest craze in gourmet cooking. 'For nothing but the best French delicacies will do for our new Lord Lanyon,' finished Moyles. Well, you know how grave a dislike Horace has of looking ill-informed? This has been greatly magnified by the pompous air he has adopted since becoming Lord Lanyon. 'Ah, *arsenique* soup,' said Horace. 'I am pleased to find that Mrs Wallace is up to cooking the latest dishes. I doubt her *arsenique* soup will better Lady Caulderton's French chef's, but we shall see.' Oh, I do not know how I managed to hold my countenance!" said Lucretia in amusement.

Lady Rutland strove to look disapproving but Lucretia was heartened to perceive a twitching at the sides of her mouth strongly suggestive of a smirk. "At all events," said Lady Rutland, who could suffer no longer the conversation being led by anyone other than herself, "I cannot but be glad that he is out, for it gives us the opportunity for a most comfortable cose."

Seated straight-backed and stiff in the chair she had chosen, it was hard to imagine Lady Rutland indulging in anything so casual as a *cose*.

"It was most ill-judged of your father to leave you in Horace's care. And it is no surprise to me that Horace has made a mull of the whole thing! For all we have had our disagreements, your father ought to have known that Horace was far from being a fit person to have charge of a young lady. Fortunately, there is no harm done. Horace cannot have the least objection to your coming to live with us, and we shall act as the guardians you ought to have."

"Of all the things father has done," said Lucretia with unusual heat, "to make Horace my guardian is by far the worst yet! We have never dealt well together, so I'm determined to earn my own keep rather than be dependent on him, which indeed I'm sure he would dislike as heartily as I would myself. And, if I don't mean to be a burden on Cousin Horace whom I have known all my life, I certainly have no notion of trespassing on *your* hospitality, Aunt. Why, it would be to foist myself upon you in the most shameless way and after all, although related by birth, we are practically strangers."

Lady Rutland was somewhat taken aback by this forthright obstinacy and was a little tempted to take the girl to task over it. But she was disarmed by the obvious gratitude conveyed in Lucretia's next words which made her realise that, however misguided the attempt, her niece was trying to do what was right.

"Indeed, it's so very kind of you to come and see me, considering all that has passed between you and my father. And to think of you considering me and my come out all those years ago... Oh, thank you, I would have liked it above all things!" For a second Lucretia paused and thought wistfully of the balls she might have attended had she been more fortunate in a father. She sighed sadly but, with resolve, continued, "But alas, it is not to be thought of."

"Well, well, all these very proper feelings do you credit, my dear," Lady Rutland allowed. "But I am happy to be able to tell you that you are most imperfectly informed about your circumstances. The truth of the matter is that your mother was a wealthy woman, Lucretia, a very wealthy woman indeed. And she agreed with your father that, after her death, all her fortune would be kept in trust for you until you came of age. Yes, you are to be a considerable heiress, Lucretia. And although I know we agreed not to speak ill of your father, I must say I find it most shocking in him not to have informed you of the fact. But it doesn't do to repine upon that. Now Hugo no longer has anything to say in the matter we shall go along very well."

"Naturally you shall come and live with us. And I'm sure it would make your poor mother so happy to know that, at last, you were living as you ought. Of course, we shall have to furbish you up a little," Lady Rutland remarked, taking in Lucretia's shabby, unfashionable clothes, "but without wishing to set you up too high in your own esteem, I must say that you are very pretty and I have no doubt you will take very well." Lady Rutland's mention of clothing could not have been more providential, for nothing was better calculated to make Lucretia's determination not to be a burden upon her family falter.

The book that Lucretia had pushed guiltily behind her seat upon her aunt's arrival had been an outdated edition of *The Lady's Monthly Museum*. She had found a pile of these bibles of fashion in one of her mother's cupboards many years ago, and had studied them with great pleasure until her father, coming across her engaged in this favoured activity, had snatched the magazine out of her hands. When she had, most unwisely, asked if she might have a dress made up in one of the pictured styles, he would not hear of it. Such clothing epitomised the world he had so passionately renounced, and her request put him in such a rage that he threw the book violently into the fire and forbade her from ever touching such a thing again. The damage had been done, however, and the fashions and finery she had seen filled all of Lucretia's daydreams. She rescued the remaining issues and, whenever she could, she pored secretly over the coloured plates, running her fingers reverentially along the beautifully cut seams on the dresses illustrated, and sighing that she would never wear anything half so ravishing.

12

As the years passed, her daydreams evolved. She pored most frequently over the plates of extravagantly dressed men, and it became Lucretia's most secret desire to meet one of a breed that was the embodiment of all she held most sacred: a dandy. The magnificently improbable attire which typified this group of fashionables was, to Lucretia, a touch of divinity, and she had sighed and longed as she gazed for hours on end upon their pictures.

Mixed amongst the dream of living in fashionable London which now, in light of her aunt's offer, seemed tantalisingly near, the thought that she might actually have the chance to come into contact with one of these exquisites flashed beguilingly before Lucretia's eyes.

"Yes," Lady Rutland continued without pause, "after the mourning period is over you will make your debut into London society as befits your birth as a Lanyon. And you will find it delightful, my dear. There will be balls and dinners and the theatre to attend. Oh, indeed, any number of agreeable entertainments. And you will become acquainted with many distinguished and estimable people - as a Lanyon, and my niece besides, you can be sure of an entrée into the highest circles - much beyond the very meagre set of nobodies your father has allowed you to know."

Lucretia was strongly attracted to this enticing plan, and it took considerable resolve for her to voice her objections to it. "But, Aunt," she sighed, wistful, "I've no notion how to go on in society! Collect how other girls, not brought up as I have been, have had an education that befits their station in life. I have learned nothing of the accomplishments and manners I imagine are necessary for going about in society. I don't even know how to dance! Oh, indeed, I do not think I am fit to for such a life," she lamented.

Lady Rutland recognised the justice of her niece's point and sat for a moment pondering this difficulty, barely listening as her niece continued to speak.

"In fact, I have been in flat despair about how to procure a post as a governess. I cannot help but think how unsuited I am to the position, having had no education myself. I did begin to

13

wonder if I might be obliged to settle for a post as a dresser or milliner's assistant."

These words brought Lady Rutland up with a jolt. The thought of her niece, and moreover one who was a Lanyon by birth, as a milliner's assistant shocked her so profoundly that had she been a lady of excessive sensibility she would undoubtedly have been reaching out for her vinaigrette. As it was, she was betrayed into railing, "A milliner's assistant! Good heavens, Lucretia! Do not even speak of such a thing! Only think how shocking! Why, just the thought of it has given me quite a turn. Do please try to remember what you owe to your family name. You are a Lanyon of Lanyon. No Lanyon could ever hold so menial a post. You will take your place in society like a sensible girl and give me no more of this nonsense. Now... we have only to think how best to go about things. But undoubtedly we will contrive."

Lucretia gave up arguing. It was so much easier, and so much pleasanter in this instance, to submit to her aunt's commands. She looked at her aunt expectantly, torn between the hope of a new life she so desperately longed for and fear lest, once offered, the beautiful dream now dangling before her eyes was to be snatched away. How much she longed to attend balls and be gay and happy and, above all, not bored by the mundaneness of her secluded life. How little she wished for the life of a governess which, she was well aware, would be little better than the life of a drudge. And most of all she dreamt of finery and fashion: modish outfits and all their accoutrements.

"Well, I suppose I could try to teach you how to go on myself, but it occurs to me how dull it would be for you to be living under my roof with little opportunity to make friends to help pass the boredom of your mourning period. What a curse it is to be obliged to forgo so many of society's pleasure's simply because one's relative, to whom one was never attached in the first place, most inconveniently dies!" Lady Rutland sighed at this sad state of affairs but Lucretia, tickled by the irreverence, let out a loud and distinctly unladylike crack of laughter. She was rewarded by an instant disapproving frown from her aunt.

"Gracious, Lucretia, do not ever let me hear you make such a noise again! So ill-bred! I beg you will remember that Ladies do not *laugh*. They may show an amused smile, but laughter, giggling or, heaven forbid, tittering…. All these must be avoided by ladies of our quality." Lucretia was mortified.

"There now, never mind. Let that be your first lesson in comportment. But you have interrupted my train of thought. Where was I? Ah yes… Well," she said, picking up where she had left off, "of course, one *can* go into society in half mourning. But one is obliged to wear such drab colours and dancing is strictly forbidden. That's no proper come out for a girl. I begin to feel that perhaps we should postpone your debut until next year when you'll be able to do it in style. We must only hope that no other relative is so disobliging as to pass away in the meantime. The question is: what are we to do with you until then?" Again, she fell to silent cogitation. Lucretia, waiting, breathless, to hear her fate, began finally to accept that her fortunes were indeed to change for the better.

"I have it! So simple, I can't think why it should not have occurred to me from the start. You shall go to Mrs. Trimble's seminary," she announced triumphantly.

Seeing Lucretia's look of anxious enquiry, she elaborated, "It's a finishing school, Lucretia. They will teach you how to comport yourself in society and I have no doubt that you will also make any number of unexceptionable friends there, for you must know that it is a very select institution. And then in a year's time you will come to us in London at the start of the season and we shall host a magnificent party for your entrée into society."

Lady Rutland's eyes sparkled at the very idea of entertaining on this grand scale, and for a moment she was lost in a reverie in which she hosted the party of the season. However, noticing Lucretia's nervous expression, she was recalled to her surroundings and reassured, "You will be perfectly ready for your come out then, my dear. At Mrs. Trimble's you will learn how to dance and converse and curtsey, and all the other accomplishments necessary to make your way in the upper echelons of society. And," she added as kindly as her somewhat aloof character would allow, "when you return to London I will naturally be there to guide you in making your curtsey to the polite world, so there really is not the least need for you to worry."

Lucretia's head was in a whirl of excitement mingled with confusion and nervousness. She was terribly afraid that, now she had consented to the plan, something would contrive to impede the delicious scheme. But, when Horace returned from his tour of the estate it was clear that he regarded Lucretia's removal from his care not only favourably, but with relief. And with nothing to stand in the way of it, Lucretia set off the next morning in her aunt's carriage to begin her new life.

And so Lucretia went to Mrs. Trimble's seminary for the daughters of gentlemen and learned how to be a Lady. And if it had not been for the very exceptional circumstances which brought Mr Horace Fotherby, the new Lord Lanyon, *post haste* to town to visit her and her husband in Grosvenor Square, it is very likely that Lady Rutland would have put Lucretia largely out of her mind until the following year.

CHAPTER TWO

In his haste to divulge his message, Fotherby arrived unseasonably early at the Rutlands' Grosvenor Square residence. Lady Rutland was naturally not pleased to have to deal with such an unwelcome visitor at such a premature hour. Moreover, she could not look upon Horace Fotherby without a pang of revulsion, especially when she thought of someone so contemptible assuming the title of Lord Lanyon. He had a distinctly amphibious countenance, with bulging eyes and clammy, moist skin. He was, in addition, possessed of the particularly unsavoury habit that when he was pondering a topic he had difficulty understanding (which his meagre intelligence ensured was a frequent occurrence), he would blow his cheeks out in a frog-like manner and then let the air whistle out loudly and in the most vulgar manner.

The unwelcome guest was ushered into the drawing room and met there by Lady Rutland who rose to perform mechanically the politenesses which were normally exchanged in such circumstances. Horace, however, was too agitated to listen to pleasantries and waved aside such conventions. "I come with the most shocking news," he began portentously, but was cut off immediately by Lady Rutland.

"My dear Horace, do please calm yourself, I beg of you. I'm sure your news cannot be so momentous as to necessitate your behaving in this peculiarly rude manner. If you carry on in this impassioned, half-witted way you will give me the headache, and at this shocking time of the morning too! Do pray have a seat and compose yourself while I call for some refreshments."

Horace was not unused to Lady Rutland's acid speeches but, having put himself to the trouble of journeying to London with the express purpose of informing the Rutlands, in person, of some information it would be a great advantage for them to know, such a harsh tongue-lashing left him feeling considerably ill-used. Conveniently forgetting that he was equally motivated by a desire to foist a thorny problem onto the shoulders of others, he was aggrieved that this selfless gesture met with so little gratitude. He was, moreover, since assuming the title of Lord Lanyon, becoming steadily more accustomed to meeting with sycophantic and assiduous civility wherever he went, and he was affronted by his hostess's supercilious tone. Despite his resentment however, he was somewhat afraid of Lady Rutland and so, rather than attempting any retaliation, he sat sulkily regarding the carpet and puffing out his cheeks while she rose to ring the bell.

The butler presently arrived to take her orders and disappeared unobtrusively to fetch the required refreshments. Before he returned, Lord Rutland entered upon the scene, where the frosty atmosphere was not lost on him. As this was a not unusual consequence of his wife's conversation, he was able to ignore it, and approached to shake Horace's hand. He was no more enthusiastic about their visitor than his wife had been. This was not due either to his lack of address or unprepossessing person (although he found these deplorable) but, rather, due to the fact that Horace was so far from needle-witted as to have the unhappy effect of irritating Lord Rutland with every mutton-headed utterance that left his mouth.

"Good day, Horace, I trust I see you well. To what do we owe this unexpected honour?"

Both men seated themselves but Horace was once again thwarted in any attempt to impart his news by the return of the butler with decanters of ratafia for the lady of the house and burgundy for the men. Waiting for the servant to remove himself, Horace became frustrated at having to wait so long to begin his narrative and squirmed in the most alarming way in his chair. Once he was finally free to do so, he maliciously decided that he would spin the story out at length to revenge himself on his hostile hostess who, he knew, had a hearty dislike of prattleboxes. He was very well pleased with his plan and impressed at his own cleverness and, licking his lips, relaxed into his seat and prepared for a lengthy exposition. "As I have already said," began Horace ponderously, "I come on important business."

Lord Rutland looked bored and his lady scornful, but they waited in silence for him to continue.

"It concerns my cousin Lucretia, who, I understand, is now living under your roof..." Here he interjected a significant pause. It was too much for Lady Rutland.

"You know very well that she's at Mrs Trimble's! If you cast your mind back, you will remember that I sent you a letter informing you of the fact only two weeks since!"

Horace visibly quailed at the look in Lady Rutland's eye as her impatience overcame her. His pompous eloquence quite forgotten, he hastened to continue his story. "You see, I was visited by a dashed peculiar fellow last week who claimed to be a friend of Hugo's. Yes... a very peculiar fellow indeed. If you ask me, he was a cursed rum touch but I'm aware that my uncle has not always been terribly nice in his associates. If you must know, I wasn't terribly keen on meeting with the fellow, for it was plain as pikestaff from my butler's face that he wasn't at all the sort of person anyone with the title of Lord Lanyon ought to be seen with. The devil of it was that the chap was deuced persistent. So rude that he quite put poor Lister's back up, but nothing short of bodily removing him from the doorstep would have answered, and Lister's not as young as he once was... Of course, I've no doubt he tried to stand buff like any butler worth his salt would've done, but by the looks of Ogleby when I laid eyes on him, I wouldn't have put it past him to tip poor Lister a settler, so I couldn't really blame him for not managing to turn away such a rough customer. In the end, he was over the threshold before the cat could lick her ear and he stood in the hallway insisting loudly that he came on urgent business. Well, then there was nothing for it but to see the man, which I did, in the library of course, can't have such people in the drawing room! But that is all by the by... In the end, it was a good job I did see him... because when I think about it, it *was* dashed important business, and that business, like I said, concerned my cousin. Cousin Lucretia, in fact."

Lord Rutland, his patience now tried beyond what he could contain, said with annoyance, "Yes, yes you've already said that. I wish you will get to the point, Horace."

"Well, I'd get to the point a good deal quicker without all these interruptions," snapped Horace peevishly, and was instantaneously diverted by an appreciation of his own quick-wittedness. He sat inflating his cheeks and whistling the air out between his pursed lips, making Lady Rutland cringe.

Recollecting that he had come in hopes that he could leave the issue in the Viscount's capable hands and be allowed to return to his country obscurity to deal with the combination of familiar problems and fawning staff which made him feel clever and valued, Horace continued, "Anyway, as I said, I was visited by this chap. Ogleby was his name. I remember it because it sounds dashed outlandish- never heard such an odd name before, who knows where he may have got it! Anyway, Ogleby, when he got to explaining the purpose of his visit, said that, being an India merchant, he had been out of the country managing his business concerns. In India, in fact.

He'd only just landed back in England the week before, whereupon he was met with a letter from Handle and Edmonds, a firm of solicitors previously unknown to him. Of course, I did not know they were a firm of solicitors until Ogleby explained this, which he did by and by. For before that I was quite in the dark. The letter he received, Ogleby that is, not the firm of solicitors, informed him that Lord Lanyon had died, which indeed we are all aware of." He looked round at his audience to confirm that they did in fact know this, continuing, "The letter went on to explain that as he had agreed to be a trustee for a certain legal document, he was asked to make contact with the firm. Mystified he was, Ogleby explained to me. Could not begin to imagine what the whole thing was about. Inclined to think it was a hoax. Mind you, not so much so that he did not call upon Handle and Edmonds. Expect he thought he might hear something to his advantage... lawyers, you know," said Horace somewhat obscurely.

"Well, when he did call upon Handle and Edmonds, what do you think he found? Well, he found that he had been appointed to be a trustee for Lucretia's Trust."

Lady Rutland interrupted this torturous exposition impatiently. "I do hope you are not come to tell us that Lucretia is so fortunate as to come into a substantial fortune when she comes of age. We have been aware of this for some considerable time. In fact, it was her mother who made me cognisant of the fact."

"No," faltered Horace, "well, not only that. You see, as it turns out, the situation is a little more complicated than I had previously thought. In fact, it is a little delicate."

"You begin to interest me very much, Horace," said Lady Rutland, leaning forward in her chair, eyes narrowing.

"What is it that you have been told about Lucretia's trust fund, Virginia?" hedged Horace, and secretly hoping to avoid the conversation he had come for the very purpose of holding. He prayed that they knew all about it and he could leave them in the peaceful certainty that they would deal with the issue, while he could wash his hands forever of the taxing problem of his cousin Lucretia. He gazed at Lady Rutland expectantly, which had the unhappy effect of giving his face the expression of a half-wit.

"Well, as you know, Lucretia's mother, Sophia, was an old and dear friend of mine," explained Lady Rutland slowly and clearly, careful not to tax Horace's intellect. "She was beautiful and possessed of considerable wealth; in fact, she could have chosen from any number of charming bachelors, but incomprehensibly she fell in love with my brother Hugo, and they were married. My brother had some very odd notions about his wife's money. He insisted that they should live off his own money - no great hardship as he was himself wealthy - lest he be deemed a fortune hunter."

Horace frowned as he tried to understand why a wealthy man would ever expect to be accused of being a fortune-hunter. Lord Rutland, equally at a loss to comprehend such an illogical idea, looked incredulous. Seeing her husband's expression and Horace's bafflement, she hastened to elaborate,

"I'm not saying it makes the remotest bit of sense. You were both acquainted with Hugo, he took some queer ideas into his head and would never let go of them! Naturally, when they were married, Sophia's money became Hugo's, but he stubbornly refused to touch any part it. 'What kind of a fellow would I be,' he said, 'if I hung forever upon my wife's purse strings? I am more than able to support my own family without being obliged to the Wrexalls for anything they have had any hand in!' Perhaps this was the very crux of the matter, since he had taken Sophia's family in strong aversion. Hugo, you know, had the gravest dislike of feeling obliged to be civil to anyone, let alone anyone he did not like. And gratitude was certainly not a feeling that he was at all in favour with! Furthermore, by refusing to touch Sophia's money, it provided a welcome excuse for his favourite pastime of penny-pinching. The money must have sat around being no use to anyone, so when Lucretia was born, the ever-sensible Sophia proposed to Hugo that perhaps a trust fund for Lucretia would be an appropriate use for the money. A suggestion to which he grudgingly agreed since, despite his best efforts, he could think of no reason to object to it. Of course, drawing up the documents was left to Hugo and his lawyers. I apprehend that his own particular, and no doubt reprehensible, genius has been at work in the settlement?"

Horace sat in silent cogitation, allowing this onslaught of information to be taken into his mind and shuffled into some semblance of comprehension. After a time, he said, "I see. At least, I think I see... Come to think of it, I've an idea that Hugo once told me that Lucretia would receive money from her mother's side. But I don't think he ever went into the details of it, which accounts in part for my forgetting all about it. Wait, now I think on, I do believe that when he told me about it, he asked me not to mention it to Lucretia. Of course, I did what he said for he could be deuced unpleasant when he was angry, could Hugo. Anyway, no mention of money for Lucretia was made in Hugo's will and I didn't think anything of it, because, as I've already told you, I forgot she was to have any money. And even if I had remembered, I naturally would have thought that Hugo must have changed his mind, which was not unlike him. "

Horace was obliged to pause after this considerable outpouring of eloquence and rearrange his thoughts. He fell into his habit of staring vacantly at the floor as if all understanding had abandoned him. It was therefore a little surprising to his audience that he persisted along the same train of thought.

"To continue where you left off, Virginia, we come to my part in the story," said Horace. "As it turns out, it seems that Hugo did not employ his usual law firm to draw up the Trust, he dealt instead with this Handle and Edmonds firm. And for some reason – I'm sure he must have had one - he appointed Mr Handle and Mr Ogleby to be the trustees."

"But surely Mr Ogleby must have been aware that he would be a trustee in the event of Lanyon's death? I mean, did Hugo not ask him to do so before appointing him?" asked Lord Rutland.

"Ah well, I did broach this subject with Mr Ogleby but it seems that he is not perfectly sure whether it was ever mentioned to him or not. I understand that much of his acquaintance with Hugo was pursued when they were both," Horace coughed, "top-heavy… that is to say, erm.. they were somewhat in their altitudes."

"I apprehend you mean they were drunk, Horace," said Lady Rutland.

"Exactly so," replied Horace, acutely aware that such topics should not be discussed in the presence of the fairer sex.

Lady Rutland thought his concerns ridiculous and said so. "I'm well aware of my brother's character. There isn't the least need to try to dress such things up in clean linen."

Horace stuttered and, eventually collecting himself, continued, "Mr Ogleby said that no doubt he may have agreed to be a trustee, in fact it is entirely possible he may have signed something to that effect, but sadly he has no recollection of it."

Continuing to be discomposed by having to impart this piece of the story, Horace once again puffed out his cheeks and stared blankly ahead. He was lost for some time in his thoughts, which centred around Mr Ogleby's comprehensive accounts of a number of convivial evenings that he had spent in Lord Lanyon's company, dipping deeply into blue ruin and cavorting with opera singers. There was certainly a limit to how much of this information it was necessary to impart to his audience. Lord and Lady Rutland stared at him as he sat in this vacant pose and eventually had to recall him to his surroundings.

"Ah, yes, where was I? Oh yes, so now we know that Mr Ogleby and Mr Handle are Lucretia's trustees. And as I am, and still will be for another month, Lucretia's guardian, Ogleby approached me to inform me of the terms of the Trust. Which I suppose, when you think of it, was rather civil of him. Anyway, to return to the terms of the Trust, well... Ah, um..." He ground to a halt, unsure how to continue.

"We are well aware that the fortune is considerable," said Lady Rutland, broaching what she apprehended to now be causing Horace discomfort.

"Yes, of course. But that's not it. You see it's as I said a little, er... delicate. The terms of the Trust are, erm, somewhat unusual, for want of a better word."

"Oh, come on, Horace, out with it man! You're among family here. No need to worry about delicacy: Virginia is quite capable of hearing whatever it is you have to tell us without having the vapours!" snapped Lord Rutland.

"Well you see..." stammered Horace, "the Trust states that Lucretia must marry someone who meets with Lord Lanyon's approval or, following his death, the approval of his trustees, or she receives nothing."

Both Lord and Lady Rutland stared at him in horror. But Horace was not finished yet; he gulped, resolving to pour out the unpleasant news in full as rapidly as he could. "And..." he continued resolutely,

"And?" exclaimed Lady Rutland, already stunned.

"And," continued Horace drawing in a deep breath, "the Trust also states that she must marry by the time she is two and twenty. If she fails to meet either of these two demands the money goes to ... to Hugo's gardener," he finished miserably.

A shocked silence followed, broken only by the whistling of air escaping Horace's cheeks.

"Oh, how wicked of him!" exclaimed Lady Rutland, breaking the silence. "How *could* he do such a thing? The gardener! It will create such a scandal if it becomes known. And two complete strangers to be given the responsibility over Lucretia's future, and both of them persons of no account whatsoever!" In this she underrated Mr Ogleby, as she would later find out to her cost. "To be forced to... to..." she was so appalled that she could not finish.

"But why would he do such a thing?" asked Horace, bewildered; this question had clearly been perplexing him for some time.

"Horace, you nodcock, isn't it obvious?" Lady Rutland snapped pettishly. "So that he could force her to marry whomever he chose. It must have occurred to him that if Lucretia had her own means at her disposal, he would lose the only hold he had upon her, for there could be no bond of affection the way Hugo treated his poor daughter. And if Lucretia came into her own money, there would be nothing to stop her from entering into society, marrying where she chose, or indeed making any number of decisions about her life: a state of affairs which could in no way meet with Hugo's approval, so managing and mean-spirited as he was.

He was most likely looking around for a suitable husband for Lucretia when death, thank heaven, got the best of him. I dread to think what his choice would have been for her. Some bumpkin who could be easily bullied by him, I have no doubt! And I'm sure that when he did have someone in mind, he would inform Ogleby and Handle of it so that they could push through the affair if he died before it came to pass. Hugo was determined not to let even the grave cheat him of pursuing his designs."

"By gad!" exclaimed Horace with an impressed whistle. "Then old Hugo was downier than I thought. Never suspected him of having the brains for playing such a deep game."

"Brains!" Lady Rutland spluttered indignantly, looking at Horace in deep disgust. "It is the most hare-brained, reprehensible scheme I have ever heard of! Even I had no notion

Hugo could behave so badly! Good God, isn't there something we can do about it?"

"Ah, if only one of us had been appointed as a trustee," lamented Horace, "but sadly that's not the case. So I don't see what we *can* do."

"No, Horace," interpolated Lord Rutland, infuriated by his slowness, "she means is it legal? Can we challenge it?"

"Oh, I see," said Horace, his slow wit catching up. "Mr Handle informs me that it is quite legal."

"Of course he does, he drew up the dashed papers!" said Lord Rutland, exasperated. "Didn't you consult someone impartial for a second opinion?"

Horace looked at Lord Rutland in admiration. "Now that's an idea, Charles. I should do that, shouldn't I? Yes, a very sensible suggestion."

"No, never mind, Horace. Leave it to me, I will make some enquiries. I trust you haven't told anyone else about this, have you?"

"No, I came straight here to discuss it with you."

"And what about this Ogleby, is he likely to spread it about?"

"I shouldn't think it at all likely, he didn't seem overly interested in the affair. Seemed to view it as a bit of an inconvenience. By all accounts, business is going well and he has little time to deal with such 'paltry sideline affairs'."

"Excellent," pronounced Lord Rutland. "What is needed here is discretion. The fewer people who know about it, the better. Where are you putting up in town, Horace? I will attempt to prosecute my enquiries this afternoon, and with some luck I can come and find you later to discuss my findings."

Horace's relief at having foisted the problem of Lucretia's trust into the hands of another was conspicuous. "I'm at the Clarendon. I have not opened the town house this season." He puffed up, imperfectly concealing his delight at his new-found wealth and position. He then took his leave more properly than he had made his arrival. He spoiled the effect, however, by almost breaking into a run on the Rutlands' doorstep in his haste to leave the unsavoury but bafflingly complex problem in the hands of someone else, leaving Lord and Lady Rutland in peace to discuss the revelations they had heard.

That evening Lord Rutland called upon Horace at the Clarendon, but with disappointing tidings. He had discussed the case in confidence with his lawyer but the news was not encouraging; it seemed likely that the Trust was indeed legal, although the lawyer could not say that with certainty until he had viewed the document. Not only that, but the lawyer had also raised another pertinent point: that the exercise of challenging the document in court would naturally draw attention to the infamous terms of the Trust and all discretion would be at an end. Lord Rutland could not think that the gossip this would naturally occasion would be pleasant for his niece to endure – it would bring just the kind of unwelcome attention that a girl making her debut in society, and her family, would be at pains to avoid. It seemed that the terms of the Trust must be borne.

Having by this time given the terms of the document considerable thought, Lord Rutland was inclined to be optimistic. "Although the girl will be close to two and twenty by the time she makes her come out," he said, "and to be sure seven months does not leave much time to arrange a marriage, she is an uncommonly pretty and taking young thing. We have no reason to despair of her making an eligible match and being comfortably married within the time. And furthermore, I see no reason why this Mr Ogleby or Mr Handle should want to exercise their right of veto over Lucretia's choice of husband. I expect that particular clause will turn out to be purely nominal."

"Having discussed the matter with Virginia," Lord Rutland continued, "we feel, with your agreement, that there's no need to trouble Lucretia with these facts. I suggest we let her make her come out as planned and I have every expectation that within a month of her debut, I will have any number of suitors banging down my door in the hope of becoming leg-shackled to the girl. She's a sensible young lady and will be guided by her aunt in forming an eligible attachment so neither of her trustees need have anything to say in the matter."

Horace agreed to all that was said, and was so delighted to have the weight of such a worry lifted that he was moved to invite Lord Rutland to dine with him. This hasty invitation was no sooner uttered than regretted for, on reflection, Horace could only imagine such an evening with gloom. Time spent in Lord Rutland's company was always time spent struggling to follow his conversation, feeling stupid in a way that quite cut up his comfort, and casting around to find some remarks which did not justify the contempt which Lord Rutland could not quite hide that he felt towards him. Thus it was a great relief to both parties that Lord Rutland was able to say with perfect honesty that he was engaged elsewhere and, after they had tossed off a glass of burgundy in each other's company, the Viscount made his departure.

CHAPTER THREE

Lucretia arrived in London in February in the midst of an unexpected commotion. The Honourable Arnold Rutland, Lord and Lady Rutland's youngest son, and officer of the –th Hussar regiment, had returned to the house only minutes before the carriage carrying Lucretia pulled up outside the door. He was on sick furlough, having taken a shot in the arm during the Peninsular campaign, and consequently had his arm bound up in a sling. His arrival was unanticipated for, despite the fact that a letter would have announced his coming in good time, his mischievous nature delighted in the prospect of surprising his parents. Lord and Lady Rutland were still greeting their unexpected arrival in the street when Lucretia's carriage drew up.

Lucretia was pleasantly surprised in her cousin Arnold who, as the son of a haughty mother and stern father, she expected to find arrogant and aloof. On the contrary, he was full of light-hearted merriment and not in the least high in the instep. Despite his considerable height and athletic figure, he was one of those men who would always resemble a mischievous schoolboy. Perhaps it was the impish twinkle in his eye, or perhaps it was the impertinent smile that hovered upon his lips, or maybe it was the irreverent laugh that escaped from his mouth when he was amused, as he frequently was. To him a joke was never far away and he was one of those happy creatures who was destined never to take either life, or himself, too seriously.

He turned to look about him at the familiar surroundings of home, and was the first to catch sight of his cousin descending nervously from the carriage. "Ho! Ho! And who's this ravishing vision?" he smiled. Lucretia found herself blushing, but looked delightful in the process.

Now noticing Lucretia, Lady Rutland moved towards her, saying, "Lucretia, dear, how charming to see you. As you see we have had another arrival today. Meet your cousin Arnold."

Arnold made his bow and took Lucretia's hand, raising it audaciously to his lips and planting a kiss upon her fingertips. "Enchanted to meet such a charming addition to the family."

"As you see, he is a shameful flirt," disapproved Lady Rutland. "Arnold really, the poor girl has only just arrived after a long journey and is no doubt exhausted. This is no time for your nonsense." Arnold did not look the slightest bit abashed and grinned at his cousin warmly.

"I'm delighted to meet my cousin, Aunt," returned Lucretia. "And I am never too exhausted to receive a compliment! If he continues to flatter me in this extravagant way, I have no doubt we shall be excellent friends, although I will become quite odiously conceited into the bargain, I make haste to warn you."

It was clear from this speech that Lucretia's time at Mrs Trimble's had been well spent. She had lost her nervousness and grown in sophistication. Gone was the gaucheness and awkwardness of her youth, she held herself well, straight-backed and dignified, and had evidently learned how to talk and act like a young lady of presence and refinement. Looking her up and down, her aunt observed these changes in her protégée with satisfaction.

The following day, Lucretia and Lady Rutland set out on a shopping expedition for the purpose of procuring all the clothes Lucretia would need for her first season and, walking past shops brimming with the latest fashions, Lucretia found herself in the kind of heaven she had previously only dreamed of. When they arrived at Madame Charabelle's establishment, her cup overflowed. Although her aunt had taken her shopping before, that was for schoolgirl dresses, suitable for wear at Mrs. Trimble's. She shopped now for outfits which would mark her out as a fashionable young lady of the first consequence. Lucretia could not believe how many outfits it was apparently necessary to own in order to pass oneself off as a lady of fashion. Morning dresses, walking dresses, carriage dresses, evening gowns, dinner gowns, ball gowns: Lucretia was to have them all, and many of each.

As they left the shop, Madame Charabelle personally accompanied them to the door of their carriage, which was brimming with bandboxes and parcels, curtseying obsequiously. "I'll have work started on making up the dresses *tout de suite*! The dresses will be ready oh, very soon, very soon, Madame!" she promised. Lady Rutland was a customer who was always accorded her personal attention, for she made many purchases at Madame Charabelle's establishment, and that lady was well aware that Lady Rutland was *somebody* in the polite world. Moreover, she was uncommon in being a lady who paid her bills, often after only the first reminder of her obligations. But on this occasion Madame Charabelle's sycophantic demeanour was even more pronounced, and was born of having supplied a full wardrobe to a young lady who was untroubled by any consideration of costs. Madame Charabelle was also shrewd enough to realise that when it became known that the prettiest debutante was kitted out in creations from her shop, it would spark a stream of business from all the match-making mamas desperate to turn out their daughters in a similar style, in the hopes they would look half so enchanting as Lucretia.

As they returned to Grosvenor Square, Lucretia was astonished to hear her aunt declare, "Well, we have made a good start on your wardrobe, but there is so much more still to buy."

"More dresses, aunt?" Lucretia asked in awe.

"Of course, more dresses; you cannot be seen to wear the same two morning dresses over and over. Gracious me, no! And though Mrs Charabelle's assistance has been invaluable, we must visit other establishments for riding habits, hats, boots, shoes, and pelisses. And then there are the accoutrements to finish your outfits: fans, reticules, stockings… not to mention feathers for your hair and also ribbons! But that will all have to wait for another day. Heavens, I never realised how exhausting it is to build up one's wardrobe!"

"We have done a good morning's work nevertheless," continued Lady Rutland, "and now that I know you will have something to wear, we can begin to think of plans for your debut ball. Would you like to help me with the arrangements this afternoon?"

"With the greatest of pleasure, Aunt," said Lucretia, excited about the novelty of this activity and keen to repay her aunt's kindness by giving whatever assistance she could.

"I chose an early date so that it would be the ball to launch the season, but I had no notion that so many people would be in town for it, or that I would receive quite so many acceptances to my invitations," said Lady Rutland, who was not above feeling some pride at her own popularity. "What a squeeze it will be!" She sighed in contentment, for clearly this was the aim of any hostess, that her ballroom would be so full of people as to ensure that none of them would have the space to be quite comfortable.

"Now... decorations..." mused Lady Rutland. "Do you think we should deck the ballroom with arrays of flowers, or blue silk sheets billowing down from the ceiling?" she asked rhetorically. "No, you're right, not original enough. Both those ideas were done to death last season. We need a fresh idea if we are to truly take the town by storm." She stopped and pondered and then suddenly exclaimed, "I have it! An Egyptian theme. For a truly exotic flavour!"

Lady Rutland had recently taken a most improving and educational trip to Bullock's museum in Piccadilly, and it was from this that she drew her inspiration. This recently opened and marvellously popular new sight housed any number of interesting curios from far reaching corners of the earth, ranging from preserved elephants to the vast armoury in the medieval hall. Its Egyptian-style architecture, decorative hieroglyphics and Egyptian friezes, and the artworks which included two magnificent statues of Isis and Osiris, offered great food for a ball theme.

"The foreign and outlandish are quite the thing nowadays," the Countess assured her niece. "Only think of the Prince Regent's passion for the oriental... not that I wish to emulate one I so heartily disapprove of. Although to do him justice, one must admit he has an eye for the eye-catching. Perhaps a statue or two. Yes, that would be the very thing. And what else…?" she wondered. "I will ask Gruby to call round from his emporium; he will know just what we ought to install for the event."

The afternoon was spent in vigorous planning on the part of Lady Rutland, although Lucretia, who had hoped to be of assistance to her aunt in the preparations, found that her role was merely one of agreeing with her aunt's judgements. She was therefore considerably relieved when her cousin entered the room and provided a distraction.

"Well then, mother," he said, "how goes the campaign?"

Lady Rutland looked up from her notebook, which she was using to jot down the details she had decided on and said, "Campaign...? Oh, you mean the ball planning? We are coming along very well, but you're interrupting us, Arnold. And I don't expect you to be the least use in the matter."

"A lucky escape!" he commented, although so quietly that Lucretia wasn't quite sure she had caught him saying it. It was accompanied by a naughty smile in her direction, however, which strongly suggested that she had not misheard.

"What's that?" queried her aunt, who evidently had also had trouble catching Arnold's remark.

"Nothing, mother!" he assured her. "I see you have Cressy here to help you, no doubt she is an invaluable assistant." He shot Lucretia a sympathetic look, understanding what her afternoon had been like but rather cheekily continued, "Have you had a good afternoon, cousin?" To her relief, Lucretia was prevented from having to reply to this by her aunt saying,

"Arnold, you are very much in the way. I do wish you would go away, this is no time for your chatter, so much as there is still to do!"

Arnold grinned. "I see that you are wishing me at Jericho. Very well, I will relieve you of my presence and take myself off for a drive in the park." Taking pity on his cousin, he said, "Perhaps you can spare Lucretia for an hour and she could come along and take the air with me. I do believe she looks a little peaky from the stuffiness of the room," he improvised. "What do you say, Cressy?"

"Of course I would like that very much. But one cannot help but wonder how you'll manage with your arm in that sling, cousin. I have no love of being thrown in the mud, I assure you!"

Arnold tried to look affronted, but undermined the attempt by grinning wide. "So beautiful and yet so harsh, cousin Cressy! Really, to draw attention to my injury, and not in a solicitous fashion. Have you no heart? And a very poor opinion of my driving skills you must have, if you think I cannot manage my pair with one hand. Why, who are you to snub one that the Four Horse Club don't turn their noses up at? I'll have you know that you are speaking with a man who once drove almost the full way through London's streets facing backwards. Now, would such a man be held back by so trifling a thing as an arm sling? I'm not such a paltry fellow!"

"*Almost* the full way through London?" Lucretia enquired sweetly.

"*Touché*, cousin. You force me to admit that I did find myself in a ditch before escaping quite out of town. Although I still maintain that it was the fault of a dunderheaded cit who stepped out into the road, and nothing whatsoever to do with my driving prowess! Nevertheless, I will engage to drive you out in the park and return you without mishap."

Lady Rutland smiled on this bantering indulgently, for the good understanding blossoming between Lucretia and Arnold had given her an idea which had not previously occurred to her: that they might become attached to one another. It would be a most advantageous match and would be a simple solution to the problem of how to marry Lucretia off before the Trust was broken. The idea pleased her so much that she refrained from condemning what she would normally declare nonsense talk, and encouraged Lucretia to accept the invitation.

It was that fashionable hour when one went to Hyde Park to bow to one's acquaintances, converse with friends, but above all, just to be seen. As they bowled along through the park in Arnold's phaeton, Lucretia turned to her cousin, asking shyly, "What is the Four Horse Club, cousin?"

"What is the Four Horse Club?!" he exclaimed. "You mean you don't know? Tare an' hounds Cressy, I knew you'd grown up in the wilderness but I never imagined you were *that* ignorant! What did they teach you at that silly seminary? Nothing useful obviously!" Her face fell and he looked down at her in pity.

"Have no fear," he said kindly, "we shall start your education at once. At once! The Four Horse Club," he instructed, "is an invitation-only kind of organisation that accepts only the best of the best into its elitist ranks. You have to be a first-rate whip and more before you're eligible."

"I see…" mused Lucretia. "And you are a… a first-rate whip, cousin?"

"I should say so! Can you not tell by the way I'm handling the ribbons? No mere whipster could control these horses; prime blood they are, but full of liveliness."

"I know nothing of horses or driving," sighed Lucretia. "But we do certainly seem to be going along at a spanking pace," she said in admiration.

"Oh, this is nothing! I'll take you out in my racing curricle one day with my team of greys. Then we shall see some sport!" Arnold's enthusiasm was infectious.

"Do you think I might be able to er… handle the ribbons? Do you think you could teach me, cousin?"

Arnold appraised Lucretia. "Perhaps," he said, "no harm in giving it a try, I suppose."

"And then I might be able to join the Four Horse Club," said Lucretia happily.

"You? Good God, Cressy! They don't let women into the F.H.C.," he exclaimed, deeply shocked.

"Oh," said Lucretia realising she had committed a solecism in suggesting such a thing. "And what do you do, in this club?"

"Do? You miss the point entirely, coz! It's not so much the *doing*, as the being a member. Well dash it, it says it all! We go on outings together and whatnot, and there's a uniform we wear, but that's all by the by. Anyway, if you're serious about wanting to learn how to drive, we can start our lessons tomorrow. I'll have a quieter team harnessed and we'll see how you fare. First thing, when the park's not too busy."

"If you please, cousin, I would like that very much," said Lucretia.

The rest of the drive passed pleasantly. Her cousin was a delightful companion and seemed to Lucretia, who had very few acquaintances, to have a hundred friends. He bowed left, waved right and pulled up any number of times. It did not escape Lucretia's notice that her cousin certainly seemed to have an eye for the ladies, and they for him. Lucretia was hugely amused to find herself eyed up jealously by any number of the ladies of Arnold's acquaintance.

It was clear, however, that driving and all things equestrian were his true passion and he passed the time between greeting acquaintances by pointing out all the best horses, the best and worst of the drivers and recounting all his favourite driving anecdotes.

The driving lessons progressed so well that it was only a few days before Arnold was inviting Lucretia to drive his phaeton, under his instruction, during the park's busiest hour. And if there had been a number of ladies who had looked on in envy as Lucretia was driven through the park beside her dashing cousin, the heart-warming sight of him educating her on the art of handling the ribbons set their bosoms afire with jealousy.

Lucretia fancied that one lady took particular exception to the friendly terms on which she stood with her cousin. This was Lady Scallonsby, a woman somewhat older than Arnold, and married. She had, several years ago, wed Lord Scallonsby to escape the ceaseless restrictions placed upon unmarried young ladies, and to ensure for herself a position of affluence and power. That her feelings towards her husband were tepid at best did not bother her in the least, for she was scornful of the notion of love, regarding with derision those sorry mortals who sacrificed position and wealth for such a nonsensical ideal. Her elderly husband was neither unkind nor possessive, but rather the opposite, which was worse. His genial good humour, coupled as it was with an uncommon degree of stupidity, began swiftly to grate upon his lady, becoming oppressive and stifling. Fortunately for his bride, Lord Scallonsby's stupidity meant that he had no need to overlook her extramarital dalliances for he failed to notice them at all, and she was able to conduct these with less discretion than was normally required by ladies more unfortunately shackled to possessive men. She had enjoyed many a light-hearted flirtation but she had eventually become the victim of that which she scorned, and had fallen in love with Arnold Rutland. She did not enjoy in the least the sight of him captivated by someone else.

Lady Scallonsby hated Lucretia on sight, threatened by her beauty and charm. These threw into sharp relief her own crumbling good looks and jaded soul. Coming across the two cousins in the park, she noticed Lucretia and Arnold long before they spotted her because, to her annoyance, they were laughing and joking together so much. This afforded her an excellent opportunity to take in Lucretia's attractive visage, and her eyes filled with jealous anger.

Arnold had, of course, mentioned Lucretia to her, but his description of his 'poor cousin, lately come from the country to make her debut, and so laughingly ignorant of London society' had conjured up in her head the vision of a plain, uninteresting girl, unlikely to attract much attention. Thus, the sight she was beholding made her suspicious of Arnold's motives in using such a description. Finally catching sight of his mistress, Arnold directed Lucretia, who was holding the reins, to draw up alongside Lady Scallonsby's phaeton.

"Ah, Maria, well met!" said Arnold to her cheerfully. "Lucretia, allow me to introduce Lady Scallonsby. Maria, this is my cousin, Miss Lanyon."

The hostile look in Lady Scallonsby's eyes was not lost on Lucretia, who smiled at her defiantly and said, "Delighted to make the acquaintance of any friend of my cousin. You have had a lucky escape, Lady Scallonsby, I managed to stop without putting so much as a scratch on your carriage!"

"I'm teaching Cressy how to drive," explained Arnold. "She's doing marvellously, as you can see. Just goes to show what a great instructor I am, eh coz?" he quizzed Lucretia.

"Indeed," Lady Scallonsby tried to interject dryly, looking at Lucretia with disdain. Lucretia caught the look, but Arnold had his full attention on Lucretia, who had just dug him painfully in the ribs.

"Ouch!" he exclaimed.

Pointedly ignoring Lady Scallonsby, whom she had taken in dislike, and well aware that there is nothing so likely as to make someone feel excluded as a private joke, Lucretia laughed to her cousin, "I see, so none of my progress is due to a natural talent on my part then?" She threw a radiant smile at him, partly to annoy his mistress, and continued, "In fact, I think I'm progressing so well that I will soon be able to set up my own horse club... since I can never join yours!"

"I'd like to see the look on my aunt's face when you tell her about your venture though!" said Arnold, continuing his conversation with Lucretia without a thought for his mistress, and he and Lucretia fell into fits of giggles as they imagined this sight.

"But I assure you that I would have the smartest of uniforms for all the members. They would quite shine down those of the F.H.C.," said Lucretia.

"Something tells me, cousin, that such an assurance would make very little difference to my mother's feelings on the subject. And anyway, trust you to be more concerned with uniforms than driving! So like a woman! That is exactly why they have no place in the F.H.C.!"

"I see you are busy with your lesson, Arnold," said Lady Scallonsby tartly, interrupting this banter. "Don't let me hold you up. No doubt I'll see you at the theatre tonight?"

She was feeling slighted and peeved, but was a little heartened by the saucy look Arnold sent her when he replied, "Naturally, could I bear to miss out on your company?" Nevertheless, this assurance did not stop Lady Scallonsby from falling under the same misapprehension as Lady Rutland in misreading the good understanding between Arnold and his cousin as the blossoming of love. Her jealousy inflamed and her competitive hackles raised, Lady Scallonsby drove off, determined to wrench Arnold from Lucretia's talons.

"Another of your admirers, Arnold?" Lucretia quizzed him as they drove away. "I fancy I have not made a friend there! Is she your mistress?"

"Hush, Lucretia! Have a little delicacy. You can't say such things! You're not supposed to even know of them! What if someone heard you?" he scolded her, but she continued to look at him piercingly and he had the good grace to blush.

"I see," she said, reading the answer to her question in his face, and she sat thinking to herself for some moments. "Ought I to have told her that I am not languishing over you?"

Arnold had regained his composure and, deftly avoiding a serious conversation, said jocularly, "You wound me, fair Lucretia! What have I done to occasion your disgust so quickly? Why, you have only known me but a couple of weeks… there's still time for you to learn to swoon in my presence!"

"You are very engaging, cousin, but you're not nearly so nice in your dress as I would like! Shabby, that's what I call your ramshackle style of appearance. It would not do for me at all!"

"Can it be that my cousin has a soft spot for dandyism? How frivolous!" He was joking with her, but she blushed nevertheless.

"Whatever my preferences may be, at least I'm not old and do not have cold, sneering eyes! My taste can only be said to be better than yours! Do you know, I do believe I wouldn't have told Lady Scallonsby I don't have a *tendre* for you, even if occasion would have allowed me to?"

"My, my, you have taken her in dislike, haven't you?" said Arnold, after which Lucretia turned the topic and it was not alluded to again.

The next few days continued pleasantly enough for Lucretia with endless shopping, driving out with her cousin and learning about the finer points of fashionable life from her aunt. After a few more days, the purchased dresses started to arrive and soon Lucretia had a wardrobe that would be the envy of all the girls in London, but still she had not made her debut. And although she had met a number of Arnold's acquaintances during their drives in the park, she remained hidden from the fashionable world at large. This was Lady Rutland's plan, to launch her niece in one magnificent swoop into London society so that her entrance could not escape the notice of anyone who was anyone.

She coached Lucretia on making her entrance at the ball, what to say, what not to say, what to do, what not to do, until Lucretia's new-found confidence began to falter and disappear. She grew more and more nervous as the day of the ball approached, terrified that she might disappoint her aunt and put herself to the blush.

On the day before the ball, when her cousin took her out for a driving lesson in his phaeton, Lucretia was so distracted by her cares that Arnold received not even a smile to what he considered a most amusing sally. Not, in general, an observant young man, Lucretia's oppressed spirits could no longer escape his notice, for he was unaccustomed to having his jokes unappreciated.

"What's wrong, my charming?" he asked. Lucretia sighed, but shook her head to indicate that it was nothing.

"Hipped, Cressy? It doesn't suit someone of your sunny disposition. You can tell your cousin Arnold all about it. While I naturally consider the most interesting topic to be myself, when the occasion demands it, I'm a surprisingly good listener, you know!"

She smiled wanly at this. "I..." she began, and then faltered. "What if I make a mull of it all, Arnold?" He looked puzzled. "Tomorrow... At the ball, I mean," Lucretia clarified.

"Ah..." said Arnold, understanding the cause of her disquiet. "Old dragon got you all nervous? Not surprised, the way she's keeping you in the dark, not giving you any practice at speaking to the types of dowds and buffoons you're likely to meet at the ball and expecting it all to go off right and tight.

Peagoose! There's really nothing to get you into the fidgets." He pinched her chin, assuring her cheerfully, "I'll keep an eye on you and make sure you don't do anything cork-brained. My sweet, they'll all be so bowled over by your beauty, not to mention the repute of your fortune, that you could insult everyone present and they would declare you an eccentric and love you all the more! No more frowning on that pretty face of yours, I beg! It is quite ruining my reputation to drive a woman who looks so sullen and bored. I will be held to have lost my touch with the ladies!"

Lucretia giggled at this and instantly felt better. By happy chance, only moments later she came across Miss Cecilia Pycroft, one of the girls she had met at Mrs Trimble's. Contrary to Lady Rutland's expectation, Lucretia had made few friends at the seminary. She was an oddity on account of her strange upbringing and her advanced age. Had she been less attractive, the other girls may have been more inclined to be sympathetic towards her and help her over these obstacles. But as it was, they were jealous of Lucretia's beauty and therefore mocked her for her poor understanding and knowledge of the polite world. Only Miss Pycroft, with a kind heart and experience of what it was like to be used unkindly, befriended her. A timid girl, on account of the constant criticism and cruelty she received from her mother, Miss Pycroft stood in considerable awe of Lucretia. She wondered at Lucretia's beauty, poise and ready wit, and the boldness of her character. But it was not in her nature to be jealous and an unlikely but firm friendship had developed between the two girls. Lucretia greeted her friend warmly.

"Ceccy, how lovely to see you!"

"Hello, Lucretia," said Miss Pycroft shyly; she had developed such a low opinion of herself that she never felt sure of a welcome.

"Finally I can boast of an acquaintance in London!" exclaimed Lucretia. "You cannot imagine how pleased I am to have come across you!" Miss Pycroft went quite pink with pleasure at her idol's obvious delight in seeing her.

"I do hope you'll be coming to my Aunt's ball tomorrow. I'm so desperately nervous. It's my first ball and the thought of not knowing anyone, save my cousin, is quite filling me with terror. Oh, do say you are coming!"

"Indeed I am. And I shall look forward to seeing you there," returned Miss Pycroft with a timid smile.

Having the support of her cousin, and knowing herself to have a friend in London, Lucretia began to feel very much better about things. She was able, the following day, to attend to the task of getting ready for the ball with excitement that was only a little tinged with apprehension. And nothing could dim Lucretia's delight in donning the magnificent ball dress Madame Charabelle had supplied.

All debutantes were expected to wear white or pastel shades, but not all were as complimented by such anaemic colours as Lucretia. The satin slip of palest blue that Lucretia wore became her colouring excellently. And the delicate sarsnet overdress, beautifully trimmed with spangled flounces and sleeves, had the effect of shimmering magically under the flickering candlelight. The elegant long kid gloves covering her arms and the bejewelled reticule which hung over her wrist finished the outfit to perfection.

In addition to the delights of her new garments, Lucretia had the thrilling pleasure of having her hair dressed by society's most famous stylist, Lady Rutland having felt that the occasion was sufficiently momentous as to warrant the employing of a hairdresser. Monsieur Armando (*né* Tobias Clegg), although possessed of a merely tolerable talent in dressing hair, affected a strong French accent and, by the employment of this alter ego had become the favourite hairdresser for the ladies of the *ton*; for who would choose to have their hair set by Mrs Tubb when the services of Monsieur Armando were available? To clinch his triumph, he naturally demanded three times the prices asked by Mrs Tubb, which reassured the *ton* that he must be an *artiste* of the first order.

When he laid eyes upon Lucretia, he threw his arms about in an exaggerated foreign gesture of excitement. She made a welcome change from the ageing matrons whose hair he normally had the doubtful pleasure of attending to. Upon hearing the theme for the ball, he clapped his hands in glee.

"*Mais*, but I have the idea most perfect! *À la Egyptienne*… assuredly it must be *à la Egyptienne!* It is fated!" he said enthusiastically. Without further ado, he set about his work. He coiled Lucretia's hair elegantly and caught it up in a high comb, allowing a few wayward soft wisps of hair at the front of her head to fall around her face. Taking blue and white beads perfectly matched to her dress, he wove them into her hair so they formed a trail across her forehead, marching right round to the back of her head. "*C'est magnifique, n'est pas!?*" declared Monsieur Armando, standing back to admire his own handiwork.

Lady Rutland, sweeping majestically into the room to check on her niece's progress, regarded the confection critically. It was a daring and unusual arrangement for a debutante but, after appraising the style for some time, she finally nodded her approval. "Delightful, my dear, you look beautiful. High praise indeed, for I do not use the word lightly."

She came over to the dressing table and placed a jewellery box in front of Lucretia. "There, a present for your debut."

"A gift, Aunt? After all the kindness you and my uncle have shown me? It is too much! Oh, how beautiful," she gasped, her breath momentarily taken away by the sight of the ravishing pearls nestled in the box.

She jumped up and gave her aunt a hug which surprised and slightly shocked that unemotional lady. "Thank you. I do not know how to thank you enough for all this. It is more than I ever dreamed of!"

"Now, now, Cressy. There's no need for all this," said Lady Rutland, discomforted. "It is only a small present from your uncle and myself. Really, we are delighted to be able to give you the opportunity to enter the polite world which is, after all, only your due. Come, finish your preparations, we must make our way downstairs and greet our dinner guests."

Lucretia clasped the pearls around her throat, checked her appearance over in the mirror and then made her way out of the room in her aunt's wake, with a strange feeling in her stomach that was experienced by every young lady setting off to attend her first ball.

CHAPTER FOUR

The guests who had been deemed worthy of attending the dinner held prior to the ball were already assembled in the drawing room when Lady Rutland and her niece joined them. Lucretia's entrance was everything Lady Rutland could have hoped. One lady was heard to gasp at the vision entering into their midst and conversation amongst the men ceased as they all turned to look at her. One fop reached hastily for his quizzing glass and openly ogled Lucretia, and Mrs Happerton had to nip her son on the arm to stop him staring in this most ill-mannered way. Lady Rutland smiled indulgently upon the group and proceeded to make her niece known to those present.

Lucretia's manners did her aunt credit. She curtsied as was proper to everyone she met, showing just enough self-consciousness for a girl making her debut, without excessive shyness. By the time the company had sat down to dine, she had already been pronounced a pretty-behaved young lady by even the highest sticklers who numbered amongst Lady Rutland's acquaintance.

"You have nothing to blush for in your *protégée*, Virginia," pronounced the severe Lady Castlereagh, normally the most censorious of the Almacks' patronesses, and one whom Lady Rutland counted amongst her intimates.

Lady Castlereagh, well aware of the signal honour she was bestowing and confident in the consequence of her own opinion, declared self-importantly to Lady Rutland, "A very pretty behaved, well-looking young lady. She may be somewhat past her prime to be making her debut but I have no doubt of you establishing her creditably. You can be assured I will send her vouchers for Almacks."

Almacks, known irreverently to many as 'The Marriage Mart', on account of the number of advantageous matches that had been arranged there, was renowned for its exclusivity. Only society's elite were allowed to pass its hallowed portals and there were many who, although they were granted an *entrée* to all other society events, were deemed unworthy of Almacks by its patronesses; no entry was allowed to those who had not first been approved by one of these powerful ladies. The low stakes at the club's card tables held no allure for any ilk of gambler, the strict rules were oppressive, the refreshments insipid and the desultory conversation often more so, but naturally nothing could exceed the pleasure of those in attendance.

At dinner Lucretia found herself seated between a diffident young man, Mr Harcourt, on her left and Lord Eversleigh, a man of immense proportions on her right. Opposite her, Mr Happerton tried to catch a glimpse of her fair profile but was foiled by the magnificently hideous silver epergne that graced the centre of Lady Rutland's table and obscured her from view.

Lord Eversleigh was as wide as he was tall and the whalebone corsets which strove to keep his corpulence at bay creaked alarmingly as he approached the table. The chair beneath him creaked still more alarmingly as he deposited his weight upon it. While it was customary for ladies to converse with the gentleman to their left, in the case of Lord Eversleigh, Lucretia found this dictate somewhat challenging. His moving passion in life, his *raison d'etre*, was food, and he applied himself to his repast with a fervour and reverence that precluded him from having dialogue with his dinner companions. Lucretia goggled with awe as he consumed a volume of food that could surely power a small army for a week. He had no conversation other than pronouncements on the food he was served, only being heard between mouthfuls to pronounce the *turbot a l'Anglaise* a masterpiece, the *fricandeau a l'oseille* beyond compare and the venison sadly marred by being overcooked. His gastronomic capacity survived the second and third courses, suffering no abatement with the sweetmeats.

"Gunter's outdone himself with these pastries," he remarked to no one in particular, directing the servant to place a further three onto his already heavily laden plate.

Her other companion was much more satisfactory for, although a nervous and quiet young man, under Lucretia's encouragement Mr Harcourt became almost loquacious.

"Oh, so you know my cousin Arnold?" said Lucretia upon discovering this fact.

"Yes, indeed, we have been friends for many years. Although I don't see half so much of him as I would like, on account of the war. Lucky devil, what I wouldn't give to join him in the action!"

"Could you not join up?" asked Lucretia innocently, having little knowledge of how one went about such things.

"I only wish I could! Sadly, can't afford a pair of colours. Besides which, mother wouldn't hear of it." This was said with a fatalistic finality from which Lucretia could divine that Mrs Harcourt ruled her nest with a rod of iron. Lucretia thought it a shame that Mrs Harcourt was so set against her son following the career he dreamed of, because it was evident that he was truly army-mad. His passion for the military exceeded even that of her cousin, and only the smallest encouragement led the young man to expound with huge enthusiasm, and at length, on the subject of the Peninsular campaign.

Lucretia, who frankly divulged that her understanding of current affairs left much to be desired, professed herself a willing listener. And though she could not advance an opinion on the shocking mistakes made by the over-cautious Burrard early in the war, the threat posed by Soult as an opponent, or Wellesley's skill as a tactician, she listened with patience to all Mr Harcourt's feelings on these issues. Nevertheless, she had to admit herself relieved that Lady Rutland's signal for the ladies to rise from the table and leave the gentlemen to their port saved her from a chronological history of the entire war, and a blow-by-blow account of its most famous battles, from *Roliça* to *Fuentes de Oñoro*. Mr Harcourt had perceived nothing but interest in her countenance and, having never before been called upon to exert himself as an educator on any subject, he reflected to himself, as he gazed moonstruck over his port, that the experience was decidedly enjoyable.

The gentlemen did not linger long over their port and soon Lady Rutland and Lucretia went to greet the ball guests as they arrived. With this office performed, they made their way to the ballroom, which was by this time teeming with guests.

Lucretia was at first somewhat overwhelmed to be a part of something so foreign to her. The exotic surroundings, crowds of guests and twinkling light from the chandeliers gave the evening an air of magical unreality. She had been introduced to so many people that her head was in a whirl and she was anxious about putting her dancing abilities to the test. To her relief, however, she soon found that she was able to converse naturally with the guests, and felt, moreover, that she had acquitted herself sufficiently well in the opening minuet.

By the time her cousin led her onto the floor for the second dance, Lucretia's nervousness had gone, and she was enjoying herself hugely, less because she knew herself to be admired but more because she was living her youthful dream: attending a magnificent ball in magnificent surroundings. As she looked about her while the movement of the country dance swung her around, she could see all around her beautiful fashions, and had the satisfaction of knowing herself to be likewise attired.

Conversing when the turns of the reel allowed it, Arnold quizzed Lucretia, saying archly, "you have made quite an impression on my friend Harcourt. I do believe it is the first time he has spoken to me for more than two minutes together on a subject other than the campaign!"

Lucretia laughed. "Then you fared better than me! Not two minutes did he devote to any other subject!"

"Poor Lucretia, what a trial for you! And poor Harcourt, I do believe he will have his heart broken."

"Nonsense, he may admire me for my listening ability, but if a plain-faced girl had but nodded and smiled in all the right places he would have liked her just as well. And if his mother would only let him sign up he would forget me in an instant!"

Arnold grinned. "You are an acute judge of character, cousin, and I'll give you one thing, you're not arrogant! You'll not have your head turned by the legions of conquests you've made tonight!"

"Conquests? My aunt is quite right, you talk a deal of nonsense sometimes, Arnold!"

"Ah, you relieve me. I thought my sudden popularity tonight, even amongst gentlemen I have barely even exchanged pleasantries with in the past, was on account of the fact that I have the power to introduce them to you. How gratifying to find it is not so!" Lucretia laughed again and shook her head. The dance had finished and they were walking to the edge of the room when Lucretia spotted her friend Miss Pycroft and rushed towards her saying,

"Ceccy, so you came. I'm so glad! I have been looking out for you this age but there are so very many people I have not caught so much as a glimpse of you until now." Miss Pycroft pinkened with pleasure at this warm greeting. "Let us find a quiet bench where we can have a comfortable cose... Oh but I am being so rude," Lucretia said, catching sight of a sour-faced lady stood beside Miss Pycroft. "I beg you will forgive me, ma'am, but I was so very excited to find my friend that you must excuse my poor manners."

"Oh, mama, this is Miss Lanyon, from Mrs Trimble's. You remember I told you of her? Miss Lanyon, this is my mother!"

"Mrs Pycroft, such a pleasure to meet you," said Lucretia. "There is no one in the world I think more highly of than your daughter, such a friend to me as she has been." Miss Pycroft blushed at this tribute but her mother raised an incredulous eyebrow. "I do hope you will not be offended if I spirit Cecelia away from you. We have such a lot of catching up to do!" Mrs Pycroft bowed her permission, although her face did not relax its bad-tempered expression.

"I'm so desperate to hear what you've been up to, Ceccy," Lucretia said as they made their way towards the side of the room. "No, Lord Gentsome," she said, turning to this gentleman as Miss Pycroft and herself seated themselves on a bench, "I'm afraid I cannot stand up with you for this dance. Now I have at last found my friend I mean to spend some time with her before she is once again lost to me in the crowds. Perhaps in the next set," she said kindly as the gentleman's face fell. He bowed and left the two girls to talk.

"Oh, indeed, do not feel obliged to turn down such an invitation on my account!" cried Miss Pycroft. "Lord Gentsome, Lucretia? It is such an honour to be asked by him, for you know he almost never dances." She lowered her tone whispering, "He is quite the most sought after and elusive bachelor. I'm afraid your aunt will be angry when she hears of your refusal."

"You widgeon, Ceccy! As if I would choose to dance over seeing you! Let us have no more on such a silly subject! Now tell me, are you enjoying the ball? Have you already been to very many?"

"Well, you know that the season is by no means in full swing yet, but, nevertheless, we have been to quite a few balls already; none of them, I make haste to assure you, as magnificent as this one. How beautiful the room looks!" said Miss Pycroft looking around her in awe.

"Oh, indeed, the sight of it as I entered quite took my breath away! No one in the Rutland household could be ignorant of the preparations for tonight, and everyone acknowledges my aunt's flair for organisation is prodigious, but all the same, one has to admit she has quite outdone herself. Indeed, the ball is more splendid than I could ever have imagined!"

They both looked around appreciatively at the room. Two huge statues of Sphinxes, a considerable talking point, stood guard at either side of the doorway. The ceiling was draped with sumptuous silks of the most exotic and indulgent hues and patterned with hieroglyphics and pyramids. The orchestra was discreetly ensconced behind a wall of lush ornamental shrubbery and further plants, housed in ornate earthenware pots, dotted the edge of the room.

"I was surprised not to see you at any of the other balls I have been to, Cressy," observed Miss Pycroft, turning to look at her friend.

"Yes, my aunt has been waiting to present me at her own ball. Nothing would do for her but to throw me in the deep before I had even had the chance to dip my toes in the water! In truth, I have never been more nervous in my life than tonight!"

"Nervous, you, Lucretia?" said Miss Pycroft with a hint of humour.

"Yes, even me! I was in a quake about doing something wrong and ostracising myself! When I was presented to Lady Castlereagh I confess my legs were almost shaking! But she has promised me vouchers for Almacks. Such a relief, for I don't know how my aunt would have taken it if she had not done so!"

"Oh, I'm so glad! I've been promised vouchers by Lady Jersey, such an agreeable lady. It seems so cruel of people to call her Silence just because she talks so much."

"Always so kind-hearted, Ceccy? I'm glad you haven't changed in that. But tell me, is it true that the patronesses of Almacks stand on the edge of the ballroom and look out for dancers who are not up to snuff? And that people have found themselves excluded simply because they bungle the steps of the quadrille?"

"Yes, indeed, and they have recruited Mr Brummell himself as one of their judges! My brother who is, in general, a most elegant dancer, was once made so nervous when he noticed Brummell observing his footwork that he lost all concentration and trod on his partner's foot! Fortunately, he has not found himself cut from the list because of it. He fancies it may be because the lady whose foot he jumped upon was Harriet Glasbrook. It is common knowledge that Brummell abhors her, so the whole incident may well have worked in my brother's favour. He swears Mr Brummell smiled in the friendliest way at him as poor Miss Glasbrook limped off the floor." Both girls laughed at this.

"And are the rules of the club really so unbending as everyone says?" asked Lucretia.

"Indeed they are. Even Lord Gentsome found himself turned away by Willis, the doorkeeper, you know, when he arrived in knee breeches instead of pantaloons."

"See how much I need you, Ceccy, to tell me how I should go on. Is it any wonder I am so nervous of putting a foot wrong when society's rules are so complicated and numerous! And I barely know who's who. What if I am rude to someone terribly important? Mr Brummell, for example," she breathed the name excitedly. "You had better point out these important personages to me now. And you know how much I have always dreamed of meeting a dandy in the flesh!"

"Well, there is Lord Alvanley," said Miss Pycroft pointing this gentleman out to Lucretia. "He is a great intimate of Mr Brummell and a famous dandy himself. And there," she continued, turning her head around the room, "is Mr Brummell. See, just to the left of Lord Eversleigh," said Miss Pycroft, nodding in the gentleman's direction.

Lucretia looked over to where Miss Pycroft had indicated. "Surely not?! Why his outfit is so plain!"

Lucretia's face had fallen in the most comical disappointment as she took in the understated colours Mr Brummell wore and his lack of eye-catching accessories. His dress was by no means what she had envisioned for a dandy. And Lord Alvanley, she noted, as she looked from one gentleman to the other, was also very plainly attired. The dandies that Lucretia had admired in the pages of the *Lady's Monthly Museum* had been clothed in the most flamboyant of outfits with splendid sparkling buttons, fingers dripping with dazzling rings, each and every item of clothing taken in every respect to its fashionable extreme. These magazines, however, were very out-of-date, and since their issue Mr Brummell had led the way in installing into society a new, plainer style of dress. Under his rule, gentlemen's clothes were now admired for their excellent cut and characterised by their simplicity, with over-embellishment sternly frowned upon.

"Plain? Don't let anyone hear you disparage Mr Brummell's attire," warned Miss Pycroft in shocked accents. "He is quite the acknowledged leader of fashion. And so very powerful that everyone looks to him to tell them what to think and what to admire."

"Indeed, is he really so important?"

"Yes, indeed, and although you must have heard very often how amusing he is, for he is a renowned wit, even his humour is to be feared, for when someone does not meet his favour he can be horribly disparaging. Last week he had only to lift his eyebrow disapprovingly to dash Miss Stapleton's popularity. And she had previously been thought one of the season's greatest beauties. After Mr Brummell's censorious remarks about her, everyone naturally found that they had been mistaken in their opinion of her. Now she has been consigned to the rank of wallflower, for no man of taste will be seen to go against Brummell's opinion!"

"Oh, how dreadful!" said Lucretia. "And so cruel."

"Yes, indeed. But you cannot let anyone hear you say so! Everyone thinks so highly of him. And his good opinion counts for everything."

"So my aunt has told me. Even my aunt, such a powerful society hostess as she is, has been anxiously telling me that I must at all costs earn his approval. So I must try to make a good impression upon him," said Lucretia anxiously. "Even if he *does* dress with such plainness," she whispered to Miss Pycroft, who giggled.

To both Lady Rutland's gratification, and Lucretia's relief, Brummell not only desired an introduction to Lucretia, but stood talking with her for nearly twenty minutes.

"Mr Brummell," Lucretia squeaked when she found him at her side as her aunt introduced him, her heart leaping anxiously. His outfit was not improved in Lucretia's eyes when he was closer to her, so Spartan as it was. Brummell was a further disappointment to her as she stood talking with him for, although she had indeed heard much of his wit, none of this seemed apparent to her in their conversation. He seemed to her a bore, odiously set up in his own conceit.

"Do you like peas, Miss Lanyon?" he had asked.

"Peas...?" she stuttered, taken aback at this unexpected opening. "... I...Yes, indeed I do," she had replied, painfully aware that to offend this man was to invite social ruin and struggling to find a reply that may not meet his disapproval.

"I do not like peas," announced the famous dandy pompously, and then paused so that everyone overhearing could have time to absorb his remark and prepare themselves for his next pronouncement. "If you too had disliked peas, then we would have been like peas in a pod." The eavesdroppers erupted into laughter in conspicuous appreciation of this quip. The thin joke drew a polite smile from Lucretia, who was working hard to appear honoured by his company.

Fortunately for her, Brummell perceived nothing amiss; he was too arrogant to imagine that anyone could find him a disappointment, and he took her quietness for shyness and awe in the face of one so exalted as he knew himself to be. Unbeknownst to that lady, he went away to crown Lucretia's success by pronouncing, when asked what he thought of the debutante, that she was a veritable diamond of the first water. With the approval of both the patronesses of Almacks and that arbiter of fashion, Beau Brummell, Lucretia could not have been launched into society more satisfactorily.

While Brummell had not recommended himself to Lucretia, she conversed with his intimate friend, Lord Alvanley with great enjoyment. Despite his disappointingly plain attire, he was nevertheless possessed of the charm and amusement that Lucretia felt Brummell lacked. And while he was obviously self-assured, he was neither vain nor self-important.

"So, this ball is in your honour, Miss Lanyon? I must congratulate you on its success, there is barely room to breathe! What more could a hostess hope for?" He twinkled at her. Lucretia smiled back.

"In truth, it is all my aunt's doing, she is a great organiser."

"Ah yes, the formidable Lady Rutland," returned Alvanley, looking over at Lucretia's aunt. "She would have made a great general, don't you think?" he mused. "I doubt Wellesley could have pulled off such a campaign as admirably."

"It is magnificent, truly magnificent. I've never enjoyed anything so well in my life. The fashions, the headdresses, the dancing..." she breathed.

"Now, now, Miss Lanyon, be careful. I do believe you look animated. You must be aware that it's not at all the thing to look like you are actually enjoying something! If you want to be in fashion you must strive to work upon your air of *ennui*. You must look thus," he said, pulling his face into a looked of studied boredom. A peal of laughter erupted from Lucretia which instantly drew a disapproving frown from Lady Rutland. Lucretia strove to stay her countenance, remembering how her aunt had chastised her for her laugh. But Alvanley was delighted, for the laugh had given her countenance a radiance that elevated her above a woman of considerable beauty, to one who was also possessed of charm and allure and beyond compare.

"No, don't curb your laughter. You look so charmingly when you laugh like that it is such a shame to tame it," said Alvanley smiling at her, captivated.

"But when you are not laughing," he continued, in mock seriousness, "I advise you to give the impression that you find life tedious, even exhausting. Otherwise you run the risk of seeming behind the times, and it is evident, from your obvious interest in fashion, that you plan to be most assuredly *à la mode*. Regard Miss Altringham, she has the look perfectly," he said nodding towards the lady. Lucretia followed his gaze and observed this lady's jaded, uninterested expression. "Although you'd be as well to try to look less like a dried prune in the process," he remarked with a straight face which belied the humour behind the comment. Again Lucretia let out a crack of laughter, this time untamed, since what Alvanley approved could never be wrong.

Observing the way this transformed her face, Alvanley mused, "But you look so delightful in your honest enjoyment that it quite suits you. Perhaps you could set a new fashion for manifest delight? Society is ripe for such a change, and you are so enchanting that I've an idea that you could bring it about." He looked down at her with a look so obviously admiring that she blushed.

Fortunately for Lucretia, who was so embarrassed by this comment that she had become tongue-tied and awkward, Mr

Silksley chose that moment to ingratiate himself into their conversation.

"Come now, Alvanley, you are monopolising the attention of the most beautiful woman in the room. I don't call that fair!"

"All's fair in love and war, friend," quipped Alvanley adroitly. "But allow me to introduce Mr Silksley to you, Miss Lanyon. And do tell him that I haven't been altogether selfish in keeping you all to myself. I have been doing Miss Lanyon the service of educating her on fashionable manners," he explained to Silksley. Turning to Lucretia he said: "I hope you won't take offence if I say that you stand in some need of my advice."

"Offence? Not at all. On the contrary I freely admit that you are being most useful to me."

"Useful?" interjected Silksley with amusement. "What a novelty for you, Alvanley!"

"Indeed, I do need his help more than you could know, Mr Silksley. For I have never attended a party or ball before in my life and see I have much to learn about fashionable society."

"Never been to a ball? But surely you jest? How can such a shocking state of affairs have come about?" exclaimed Mr Silksley.

"I have all my life lived in the country, and was not much in the way of er... attending social events," admitted Lucretia.

"The country?" said Mr Silksley with a shudder. "How ghastly! And no parties? Such cruel torment! You are a babe come in from the wilderness, what an escape! Indeed, we must help you to acclimatise. To do him justice, Alvanley is indeed the man to advise you on the subject of fashions. But you will be wanting to know who is who in this new landscape. I am eminently qualified for that task. I beg you will allow me to be of service to you in the matter," he said with a bow.

"It has to be said that no one can advise you better than Silksley on that subject, Miss Lanyon," interjected Lord Alvanley. He then lowered his voice and murmured, "It is truly a wonder his nose is so small, when it is most frequently used to sniff out information and gossip on people!"

Lucretia burst out laughing, affording Mr Silksley the opportunity to observe what Alvanley had seen with such delight: her shining beauty as she did so. Like Lord Alvanley he was captivated.

"Ignore Alvanley, he is merely jealous that I am so much better informed than he is himself! How trying to always be behindhand with the world; I confess I almost pity him." Mr Silksley grinned mischievously. "Anyway, enough on this topic, Alvanley is already talked about quite enough," he said with a wink. "Tell me, who else have you met?" Lucretia thought of the whirl of new faces that had passed her that evening and was at a loss to know where to start. "I see, such scores and more of new acquaintances, that you have quite forgot all of them!" said Silksley, understanding her difficulty. "Who did you sit next to at dinner, can you recall?"

"Indeed I can! Lord Eversleigh, a most memorable gentleman." She continued, somewhat naughtily and hence in undertones, by remarking on her dinner companion's marvellous appetite, "I have never seen a man enjoy his food so much. It must be his life's first love, for he is unlikely to find anyone to supplant it!"

"But surely you realise that you speak to the most incorrigible of gourmets," said Mr Silksley. "You must know that Alvanley loves his apricot tarts so much that he insists on his chef making one every morning for his sideboard, in case he should happen to fancy it at any time during the day." He was rewarded by a crack of laughter and, delighted to have drawn such a response and, in the hope of making her laugh again, continued, "Mind you, anyone will admit he gives the best dinners in town. You know, he once challenged his club to make the most expensive dinner they could dream up. No less than thirteen species of game birds went into just one fricassee!"

To his disappointment this drew no mirth from Lucretia, who looked instead disapproving. "I see you are not amused by such extravagance," said Mr Silksley. "Alvanley, you are quite in disgrace! But you must not be too harsh, Miss Lanyon, indeed it was considered a very amusing lark at the time. And nothing is so admired as a lavish dinner. Eversleigh is by no means the only person to take such things as seriously as the grave. The Prince Regent, too, takes pride in serving a very good repast, but sadly they are often marred by being cold. The dishes have such a protracted expedition from the kitchen to the table, they rarely arrive as they set off, as if they had journeyed from the heat of India to the icy expanses of Russia!" Lucretia giggled at this and Silksley was heartened. "That amuses you? I see you are whimsical. Ah, Lucretia, the incalculable, what will next make you laugh?"

Later in the evening Mr Silksley stood conversing with Lord Gentsome. "Have you met the fair Incalculable yet?" asked Silksley.

"Incalculable?" queried Gentsome.

"Miss Lanyon. Alvanley and I have discovered that she is quixotic, besides being the most beautiful vision I have ever beheld!"

"Good God, Silksley! Are you going to become a poet? I have never heard you use such terms. But what makes you think she is quixotic? I had not remarked upon the fact. Although assuredly she is very beautiful," said the ponderous Lord.

"Her laugh, it is her laugh. It lights up her face, the room even. But it must be surprised out of her. She is no simpering miss to be amused by every quip. But when one succeeds in making her laugh, ah..." he sighed. "It is a gift, a magnificent dream."

"Bah, a laugh?" said Gentsome, scathing. "I believe you have taken leave of your senses to get in such a taking over something so silly." But at that moment he looked over at Lucretia who was talking with her cousin. Although he had no notion what Arnold had said to amuse her, the sight of Lucretia laughing loudly made his jaw drop.

Mr Silksley smirked. "See! There is something almost magical, incalculable, if you will, in that laugh." Gentsome was too captivated, however, to pay Silksley's comment any notice. But 'The Incalculable' was whispered about the room until the Mr Silksley's epithet for her stuck. At all sides of the ballroom, men stood discussing the season's latest toast.

"Frowned you down, did she, Harcourt? Well, your wit is no match for mine," said Viscount Enderby, a foolish young greenhorn. "Lay you a monkey I can make the Incalculable laugh. Just watch me!"

"I never rated your wit above the ordinary," said Harcourt. "I'm happy to lay odds you won't succeed!"

So Enderby went off to try his luck with Lucretia, but for all his vainglory he returned unsuccessful. In truth, he was so in awe of her beauty that in her presence he stammered and became tongue-tied and stupid.

"Ha!" said Harcourt triumphantly. "You should have listened to me rather than making boasts and preposterous bets."

Mr Silksley, who happened at that moment to be walking past, stopped, sensing a juicy morsel of gossip. "Ho, ho! What's this I hear about a bet?" he asked the two young men.

"Oh, Enderby bet me a monkey he could make Miss Lanyon laugh," Harcourt, to Lord Enderby's embarrassment, told Mr Silksley.

"It is as I said. She has an appreciation of wit, but what will hit her fancy is a mystery. Assuredly she is the Incalculable."

Mr Samperton, who had been listening in and was well-known for his poisonous tongue said, "Incalculable? You have hit the nail on the head with that epithet Silksley. I hear her wealth exceeds £35 000!"

"Samperton," said Silksley disgustedly, "you have no class, do you know that?"

Lucretia, when she heard about her sobriquet from her cousin Arnold, was amused. "You men are very silly sometimes!" she said.

"Admit it, cousin," said Arnold, "you are secretly a little pleased to earn such fame!" Lucretia could not deny it. "It is a triumph to have earned yourself an epithet, and after only your first appearance. A triumph indeed! All the most celebrated belles of past seasons have 'em. Only think of The Incomparable, The Exquisite and The Enchantress!" he said, laughing appreciatively.

"Of course, no one could be a better authority on beautiful women than you, cousin," joked Lucretia. Arnold laughed heartily and displayed no shame at all in his reputation as a flirt.

"All the same, I cannot imagine that any lady of quality could have come to be addressed as The Enchantress," said Lucretia.

"Come to think of it, she wasn't a lady of quality. Barque of frailty, who was very much in demand at the time. Shouldn't have mentioned her to you," he said, looking a little stricken.

Lucretia grinned at him. "Have no fear, I will not put you to the blush by mentioning her again. You need not guard your tongue on my account."

"No, but I dashed well ought to!" he returned.

If the household had any doubts as to whether Lucretia had, indeed, made a hit at the ball, they were rapidly dispelled the next day. Lady Rutland, Arnold and Lucretia had only just retired from the breakfast table when Broome, his normally impassive butler's face displaying a hint of disapproval around his lips, showed Lord Enderby into the room.

"Good day, Lady Rutland, Miss Lanyon. Your servant, Rutland," Enderby said bowing formally. He was regarded in considerable surprise for his audacity in calling so early. Enderby manfully ignored Lady Rutland's evident disapproval of early callers and continued, "I expect you'll be wondering why I've come to see you at this time of the morning. Indeed, I beg your pardon, but I have brought you this recipe from my mother, Lady Rutland - she assures me you are most anxious to have it."

"Indeed," said Lady Rutland incredulously. "Funny, I have no recollection of it. And my memory is usually very good!" Arnold was grinning in amusement at Lucretia, who in turn was trying to hide her smile. Evidently Lady Rutland was not going to make it easy for the young admirer.

"Ah, well, it may have been some time ago," Enderby improvised, unable to tear his idolatrous eyes away from

Lucretia. "Now where did I put it?" he said, finally recollecting the pretext for his visit and digging around in his pockets. After a protracted but unsuccessful search, colour flooded into the young man's cheeks, and he muttered in mortified accents, "I seem to have misplaced the recipe after all. My apologies, Lady Rutland."

"How clever," said Arnold to Lucretia, not troubling to lower his voice, "now he has prepared an excuse to call again tomorrow!"

Even Lady Rutland was amused by this time. Feeling more indulgent than usual after the success of the previous night's ball, she took pity upon the young man and said, "Well, seeing as you're here, perhaps you'd like to take a seat, Lord Enderby."

Looking acutely grateful, he took the seat nearest Lucretia and began to engage her in conversation. He had barely got out the words, "And how do you find yourself after the ball. Not too tired, I hope?" when another visitor was announced.

"Lord Gentsome," said the butler. Arnold looked up in surprise at their visitor and Gentsome had the good grace to look embarrassed.

"I imagine you are surprised at my calling so unseasonably early, Lady Rutland…"

"Not at all," said Arnold archly, to Gentsome's great discomfort.

"… I have brought you this recipe from my aunt," the illustrious visitor explained. "She assures me you are very desirous of having it." To young Enderby's chagrin, Gentsome had outdone him on this occasion by actually having said recipe to hand.

"My, my, what a gourmet I seem to have become all of a sudden," remarked Lady Rutland, taking the recipe from Gentsome's outstretched hand. Arnold was now laughing openly and Lucretia's face was going red from the effort of trying to stop herself from giggling.

Arnold leaned towards Lucretia whispering, "Now do you deny your conquests!? To think of even Gentsome being so besotted as to actually flout convention and make a morning call before the afternoon!"

"Hush!" said Lucretia as Gentsome made his way to sit as near to her as possible. No sooner had he deposited himself in the chair, however, than the door was opened once again by Broome, whose eyes now had a twinkle of amusement in them. "Mr Harcourt," he announced.

"Ah, good day, Adam," said Lady Rutland to the latest arrival. "No doubt you have brought me your mother's recipe for apricot tartlets?"

Harcourt added confusion to his considerable embarrassment, stuttering, "Recipe? I... I had no notion you were expecting one from her. Of course, I will happily bring it to you this afternoon... Ah, Arnold. Just the man, have you seen today's papers? No? Neither have I but I thought there might have been news from the front."

"Indeed?" said Arnold. He raised a sardonic eyebrow. "And you did not think to read the paper before calling here to discuss it with me. How odd." Harcourt shuffled in discomfort. Having been invited to sit down, he was disappointed to find that there were no chairs near Lucretia unoccupied and made his way unwillingly to sit next to his friend.

"For shame, Adam! I thought better of you! But then I never would've dreamed that Gentsome would go so far in his admiration as to take such a detour from etiquette. Calling round straight after breakfast!" But Arnold was laughing as he spoke. Harcourt joined in, chortling heartily at himself. "You could at least have dreamed up a better excuse!" said Arnold. But Harcourt was prevented from replying by another visitor being announced. And so it went on for the rest of the day and the rest of the week until it was no longer amusing. Eventually, after a particularly trying round of guests, Lady Rutland instructed Broome that they were none of them at home to visitors, and enjoyed a blissfully uninterrupted afternoon catching up on her letter writing.

Unfortunately, when the cards that the callers had left were later brought to her, Lady Rutland discovered one from Lady Castlereagh amongst the pile. It was most unwise to snub this powerful lady and Lady Rutland hastened round to see her the next afternoon to apologise.

"Emily, so good to find you at home. I beg you will let me apologise for Broome turning you away yesterday when it was so evident I was at home," said Lady Rutland. "I meant no offence I assure you. Only the door knocker has not been still this last two weeks. If I have to endure one more mooncalf making excuses to see my niece…!"

"How trying for you," said Lady Castlereagh, sympathetic. "But then no doubt Mrs Doughty or Mrs Altringham would give their husband's ears to be in such a position. Such a hit your niece has made! Quite deservedly, I might add," she said graciously. "She remains as polite and unassuming as ever. A delight, Virginia."

"Why, thank you," said Lady Rutland, slightly taken aback by such uncharacteristic high praise from the haughty lady. "How kind of you to say."

"Yes, it is, isn't it," agreed Lady Castlereagh. "No doubt you've had a number of offers for Miss Lanyon's hand. Is it indeed true that Gentsome has come up to scratch, or was that rumour unfounded?"

"No, it is quite true, he called upon my husband several days ago."

Lady Castlereagh looked impressed. "Quite a coup! When are we to read the announcement in the papers?" she asked.

"There won't be an announcement of that particular happy event, Emily."

"You cannot mean that Lucretia has refused him?" said Lady Castlereagh in sharp disapproval. "I had not thought her so capricious!"

"Not at all. She understood what a signal honour it was and turned him down with polite gratitude. All done most properly. Charles and I have assured her that she need not rush into anything. And while Lucretia esteems Lord Gentsome very highly, she says she does not like him well enough to marry him."

"Foolish girl. She is very choosy then," said Lady Castlereagh severely.

"Ah, well she can afford to be. Lord Gentsome's is by no means the only offer she has had."

"I'm sure not, but no doubt the most illustrious? Really, Virginia, I cannot help but think that you did your niece a great disservice in not advising her to accept him. But perhaps you have other ideas?" Lady Castlereagh sent a piercing look at Lady Rutland. But if she was nursing secret plans for her niece's future, Lady Rutland did not betray the fact. Her attention was fully focused on her pride in all the offers of marriage her niece had already received.

"Alvanley proposed you know," she said with quiet triumph. This distracted Lady Castlereagh instantly from speculating on Lady Rutland's motives in supporting Lucretia's refusal of Lord Gentsome's offer. Her jaw dropped in amazement.

"Alvanley? Good God, you *cannot* be serious! Alvanley will never marry! He has always said so and I quite believe there has never been a more confirmed bachelor."

"You may be right. I too believe he will never marry. But he did propose nevertheless. My niece is a very good judge of character, however, and sensing his inherent dread of the married state, naturally she refused him. To Alvanley's great relief I have no doubt!"

"Quite an honour all the same," said Lady Castlereagh in continued astonishment. "Well, Virginia, it's all very well for Lucretia to be picky, but I hope you will not find that she falls for some very ineligible type. I have seen any number of them making up to her. To do the girl justice, she has not displayed any partiality that I have observed, but some handsome fortune hunter may yet be her undoing."

"I believe Lucretia has by far too much taste and refinement, and I haven't the least doubt that she knows a fortune hunter when she sees one. She has, I know, turned down Lord Maslebow. But then it is common knowledge that he's forever dodging the bailiffs, and that his family estate stands ever on the brink of being repossessed," reflected Lady Rutland.

"Poor Maslebow! I believe he has made up to three other ladies already this season, one was buck-toothed, one bran-faced and the other, God help him, smelled of trade!" Lady Castlereagh sniffed in horror that someone would sink so low.

"Even Mr Alleventon, who is undoubtedly too handsome and charming by half, has made no dent in Lucretia's affections," continued Lady Rutland. "Thankfully! Lucretia knew he was after her purse and not her heart. She is by no means stupid, Emily, no indeed! But all the same one cannot help but be a little relieved that Mr Morley has not put in an appearance in town this season!"

"Oh, indeed," agreed Lady Castlereagh. "He is quite the most dangerous of the fortune-hunters. His reputation! Undoubtedly deserved, but that hypnotic allure has been the downfall of more than one sensible young lady in the past!"

Lady Rutland allowed herself to hope that Lucretia's growing affection for her cousin Arnold was behind her refusal of all the very flattering and eligible offers she had received. As Lady Castlereagh had seen with suspicion, Lady Rutland showed neither impatience nor disapproval at Lucretia's throwing away of all these opportunities to find herself well established. But, while it was true that none of these suitors had made a dent on her affections, Lucretia was not impervious to all the gentlemen she had encountered, at least, not to one gentleman in particular; and it was not, as her Aunt so fervently hoped, her cousin.

CHAPTER FIVE

Happy as she never knew she could be, and unconscious that the terms of her Trust dictated that she needed to be married in six months to inherit her fortune, Lucretia had no expectation of falling head over ears in love at the very dawn of this new life. But so it happened, and only two weeks into the season, at the Poppleton's Ball. In truth, it was an unremarkable occasion: a success in the eyes of its hostess, since all that should attend such events did so, but for the most part a ball like any other.

Lucretia dressed with her usual care in a dress of lemon coloured silk trimmed with perfectly matching crepe, ornamented with pearls along the sleeves and set to form a pattern of flowers along the hemline. She still delighted in the feel of the exquisite material as it swished around her, and was still serious also in the modish setting of her hair, arranged on this occasion *à la Grecque,* – none of which joys had yet grown stale for her. Setting foot in the coach she looked forward to the evening ahead, hoped to see a good many of her new friends and was excited about showing off her new dress, which she knew to be a triumph.

Not long after she had entered the ballroom, she found Lord Alvanley at her elbow. They had now become firm friends, and he had the happy notion to compliment her on her new garment:

"I must say that becomes you very well, Miss Lanyon. You look delightful as ever. I had thought that the heart which wept so when you rejected it had mended itself, but I find myself once again inconsolable."

"Inconsolable? Doing it rather too brown, sir. I know relief when I see it on the face of another, and I have never seen it so apparent as when I refused you," Lucretia returned.

He laughed, acknowledging a direct hit. "I assure you that I would have been the happiest man alive. But as it is, I do believe you have had a lucky escape, Miss Lanyon. I do not think I would make a good husband. Though it pains me to admit it, I find I am too self-absorbed to give any woman the attention she deserves." This was said with some complaisance and without any hint of self-reproach, leaving Lucretia unsure how to reply; to agree seemed impolite, and she could not disagree for she knew it to be too true. They surveyed the room together as a most unaccustomed silence fell between them and thus overheard all the more clearly the conversation of a group positioned just in front of them. Lady Maslebow, an elderly lady, slight in form but with an immense presence, and an even louder voice, barked:

"She's here, is she? Well then, Julian, you must make me known to this latest heiress of yours. Though I hope she's as rich as you all tell me for it'll take more than a trifle to pull us out of the suds. By Jove, it's about time you made yourself useful by marrying money, you've spent enough of it!"

Mr Maslebow, to whom this embarrassing speech was uttered, caught sight of Lucretia and blanched. Lucretia had to look away to hide her amusement and, in the process, noticed a handsome gentleman evidently enjoying this exchange as much as she was. The sight of him made her stomach lurch, not altogether unpleasantly, and she felt oddly breathless.

He was only slightly taller than her, a few inches perhaps, but given Lucretia's height this did not argue shortness on the gentleman's part. Fashionable etiquette dictated a certain plainness in formal wear to which the gentleman had naturally adhered, being attired in shirt, coat, knee breeches and shoes; but there his restraint ended. From his exquisitely fashioned cravat, tied in the *Trone d'Amour* style, it was evident that he aspired to the dandy set. But, while he might adhere to the principles of excellence in the cut of his coat, he could not value the simplicity so crucial to the principles of modern style laid down by Brummell. His coat, made of blue superfine, was so tight that considerable effort had been expended by his valet in getting him into it. The tails of his coat extended far further down his leg than the requisite knee length, and his shirt points extended so high as to make it impossible for him to turn his head more than a little.

A dandy usually satisfied himself with only a signet ring garnishing his hand, but no fewer than six rings could be espied on this gentleman's fingers, several of which sparkled with magnificent jewels. A beautifully crafted ivory seal hung from his fob watch ribbon, which was weighted down by several ornamental fobs. Brummell, had he been asked to give his opinion on the young gentleman's appearance, would have severely censured him as a fop, for which criticism the gentleman would have cared not a jot as he failed to understand why all of London bowed to Brummell as the Monarch of Fashion.

Lucretia thought he was perfection itself. Her eyes met with his twinkling cerulean ones and he grinned at her, appreciative of the rude old lady's entertaining, indiscreet speech and Mr Maslebow's comical discomfort. Lucretia had been scornful of the idea that a person could fall in love on first setting eyes on someone, but after trading only one look with the exquisite gentleman, she knew she was lost, and whatever the outcome, her heart would never be quite the same again. It was just a moment, mere seconds, and then her beau looked away and she, with great effort, directed her attention away from him.

Mr Maslebow, meanwhile, had turned back to his grandmother, the lady who had made the offending speech, and was trying to convey the need for her to lower her tone.

"Eh, what's that?" Lady Maslebow demanded in strident tones. "How many times do I need to tell you not to mumble, my boy? And speak up, for surely you must know by now that I am very deaf, especially in that right ear." Mr Maslebow lent towards his grandmother's left ear to make his point.

"Don't you tell me to hush! I'll hush when I want to and not a moment before, you impertinent young whippersnapper," she said in affronted accents. "Your mother will hear what I have to say on this very displeasing lack of respect you show for your elders!" Mr Maslebow went up in the esteem of many bystanders for he most courageously did not quail at these words and, undaunted by the very evident displeasure in her eye, leaned forwards once again towards her ear.

"You fool, don't blow in my ear!" bellowed the old lady, "It's like being at the seashore on a windy day. And if that was what I wished for, I would go to Brighton… I almost wish I had rather than attend this very dull ball." Mr Maslebow, aware that more and more people were becoming privy to this already painful incident, was growing more discombobulated by the second and persisted speaking into her ear.

"Stood right behind me, is she? Well, what do I care if she overhears me? I'm too old to learn how to mind my manners now! I've no patience with all these modern fawning ways. Give me the leaf with no bark on it, that's what I say. If she's not born yesterday, she'll be well aware how the land lies with our affairs. And if she doesn't, rest assured Lady Rutland- a shrew of a woman- will enlighten her! You must exert yourself to be agreeable to her, Julian; else she'll not have you. I don't know what it was you did to give the other ones a disgust of you, but don't do it this time!"

It was clear that Alvanley was taking gleeful enjoyment from this scene but he chose to take pity on Mr Maslebow, turning to say quietly to Lucretia: "This has been most diverting but shall we rescue poor Maslebow, my sweet, before the eyes pop quite out of his head?" He chuckled and offered Lucretia his arm.

"Oh, by all means. I cannot remember when I have wished to make someone's acquaintance more," she agreed cheerfully, ostensibly meaning Lady Maslebow but, in fact, dreaming secretly of meeting the resplendent gentleman she had traded looks with moments before. She looked around for her dandy as they made their way towards Mr Maslebow's group but saw, with disappointment, that he was gone.

She caught sight of him later that evening at the far side of the ballroom. He had just that day purchased a quizzing glass, the use of which he had, as yet, not quite perfected. Managed artfully, this item could be used to depress pretention by regarding some unworthy through the glass with obvious disdain. Still a novice with this tool, he peered and squinted through his glass down at Mr Elsdon, who he had singled out for practicing the apparatus upon. Far from quailing beneath his gaze, Mr Elsdon thought to himself how very peculiar the man looked and, to the exquisite's great chagrin, asked kindly if he had some dust in his eye.

Slightly disheartened, he put away his glass for another day and decided to work on mincing, a walk much affected by dandies of earlier generations. It was a style of ambulation which, even when performed correctly, gave off the impression that the walker was in pain, but in this dandy's eyes it was an essential finishing touch to his appearance. So he teetered affectedly several yards, sashaying his hips, dangling his scented, lavender silk handkerchief delicately from his fingers; and he was very well pleased with the effect. Lucretia stood discreetly watching and admiring him from a distance.

A dance was about to strike up and she saw Mrs Poppleton looking about her for an unengaged gentleman to partner Miss Sedgely in the next dance. "There is Lord Prendergast without a partner," she said bearing down upon the object of Lucretia's admiration. "Yoo hoo, Lord Prendergast! You are needed for the next dance," she hooted, dragging Miss Sedgely towards him.

It was Lucretia's first experience of the painful stab of jealousy, but she could have spared herself from this. For no sooner had the gentleman noticed the approach of his hostess with a young lady in train, but he let out a noise that was a cross between a yelp and a squeak and, his mincing quite forgotten, hot-footed off to the card room. Lucretia wondered what he could find to dislike in poor Miss Sedgely, who she thought a most agreeable and pretty young lady, but not even this ungentlemanly conduct could abate the palpitations in her heart as she watched him go.

Lucretia did not see her dandy again that evening. She was disappointed but, while she could not put him quite out of her mind, she knew polite circles to be small and had every expectation of coming across him very soon at some party or other. She was not mistaken, and the next day spotted him mincing through Hyde Park as she took the air with her cousin in his phaeton.

"Arnold, who is that gentleman?" she asked gesturing in his direction with studied unconcern.

"But surely you know Mr Silksley?" Arnold asked. "Come to think of it, I'm sure I've seen you talking to him any number of times. Is not he one of your many admirers?"

"No, not Silksley, of course I know him!" she scorned, assured now in her knowledge of the world she had joined. "I mean the gentleman behind him."

"Oh him? That painted pup, he does look rather ridiculous, doesn't he? That's Topher Prendergast. He fancies himself a bit of a dandy, does Topher, but his taste in attire is somewhat erm... flamboyant."

The phaeton drew closer to Lord Prendergast and, catching a closer look at him, Arnold uttered, "Good God! I fancy those bottle green stripes are a mistake, especially against the purple. Where *does* he buy such shocking waistcoats? He's only a young cub though and we can only hope that his friends will encourage him to adopt a less remarkable wardrobe as he matures. Aside from his execrable taste in fashion, he's a very good sort of chap. He's got the most remarkable left hook and has a better eye for a wafer than any man I know."

This last was incomprehensible to Lucretia, who very naturally had no interest in male sports, but she felt herself bristle at the animadversions on the gentleman's dress. Lucretia saw in him her ideal, and thought the chastised outfit splendid. She could see not a seam, not a button amiss. But she saw that she could use her cousin's strictures to good account, observing casually: "Perhaps his wife will improve upon his wardrobe?"

"Wife?!" Arnold exclaimed with a crack of laughter. "Oh, no chance of that! Not in the petticoat line at all isn't Prendergast. How aghast he would look at the suggestion!" Her cousin chortled. "It's almost worth suggesting it to him just to see him squirm. Although I fancy he's had quite enough hints on the virtues of matrimony from his mother, she seems keen to marry him off. But mothers really have no greater joy than to set about matchmaking," he said ruefully. "I've had an earful of it myself so I sympathise with the poor fellow."

Lucretia did not pursue the topic further for she had no wish to advertise her feelings, and she quickly turned the subject.

Lucretia stored up what she had learned to reflect upon later. It did indeed seem that Viscount Prendergast was in no way disposed towards the company of females. And although she saw him any number of times over the following weeks, he was patently uncomfortable when occasion forced him to hold conversations with females, danced most infrequently (although very elegantly) and quite obviously did all he could to avoid interaction of any sort with the fairer sex.

While Lucretia was relieved to find herself without a rival, it did present problems in fixing her interest with her chosen beau. Wary of betraying her feelings to anyone, she was unable to orchestrate even an introduction to Lord Prendergast, for he naturally sought none with her.

Women of less resolution would have admitted themselves to being at *point non plus,* but Lucretia had a good deal of resourcefulness and, not content to wait patiently hoping for fate to take a hand in the affair, determined to make her own fortune. Although she had not succeeded in actually speaking with her object, she had contrived to subtly discover more information about him from Mr Silksley, that fount of all social knowledge. She learned that he was the eldest son of the Right Honourable Francis Prendergast, Earl of Godolphin, and had three younger sisters, and a younger brother not yet out of leading strings. Of the sisters, only the eldest, Lady Isabella Prendergast was out, and it was in this damsel that Lucretia saw her opportunity. She sought an introduction with her at the first opportunity.

"What a very beautiful headdress that lady is wearing, Arnold," she said to her cousin, pointing at Lady Isabella at Drury Lane one evening. "I must find out where she bought it. Do you know the lady? Yes? Then I beg you will introduce me, if you please."

"Ah, Cressy, have you never a thought for anything but your wardrobe? I barely know the lady but no doubt you will insist on the introduction nevertheless. What would you *not* do in the name of fashion I wonder? Because I'm quite sure that if you took a liking to the hat some notorious bird of paradise was wearing, you'd not take no for an answer until I presented her to you!"

"Well, I do know that if I was desirous of meeting some fair Paphian I could be sure that you would be able to provide me with the introduction!" she retorted.

"*Touché*," he said bowing at her with a grin. "We have all our little peccadilloes, I suppose," he mused, "And a frivolous obsession in fashion is at least blessedly harmless!"

They made their way to Isabella Prendergast's box. "Good evening, Lady Isabella," said Arnold with a magnificent bow that skated over all the awkwardness of hailing someone he had only a slight acquaintance with. "I trust I find you well and that you are enjoying Mrs Siddon's impressive performance as Lady Macbeth?"

From the coy look Isabella threw at her cousin and the flirtatious battering of her eyelids as she replied, Lucretia knew at once that she was not in the least the sort of girl she would normally choose as one of her intimates. "Oh, Mr Rutland," simpered Lady Isabella, rapping his arm with her fan playfully. "Is not the play too marvellous? I only wish I could live in such thrilling times! When one thinks of treacherous Thanes and witches brewing heinous potions and terrifying ghosts...!" she shivered in delight.

"Not to mention murder, suicide and a desperate descent into insanity," returned Arnold dryly.

"Oh, indeed," breathed Isabella mistily, entirely missing his sardonic overtones. "How very stirring it all sounds! I knew you would feel most earnestly, as I do, the passion and tragedy of the piece! Oh, how I wept when Lady Macbeth died! How deliciously poignant! Never have such tears poured from my eyes!"

Evidently, thought Lucretia to herself, Isabella Prendergast was an uncommonly foolish young lady full of romantic ideas and a good deal too much sensibility. She glanced at her cousin and knew he was having similar thoughts. Moreover, he was displaying telltale signs of being about to poke fun at Lady Isabella, so she nudged him in warning.

"Ah yes," said Arnold, recalled to his mission. "Allow me to introduce my cousin, Miss Lanyon. She is also a very great lover of tragedy. And no doubt you will have much to say to each other on the subject!" he added maliciously.

Lady Isabella eyed Lucretia with some hostility. "Ah, at last I meet the famous Miss Lanyon," she said with a titter. It was a habit with her to constantly compare herself to all the ladies she met. She delighted in pitying those who were less attractive than herself, and finding fault with any female who she feared may be in better looks or finer clothing than herself. And, as Lucretia was most definitely prettier than she was, this would normally preclude Isabella from accepting her as one of her friends. "You are quite as beautiful in the flesh as everyone says, and no doubt you have now repaired the deficiencies in your knowledge about the *ton*. Miss Altringham tells me that you used not to know the difference between Almacks and a teaspoon. How charmingly rustic!" she snickered.

Lucretia strove to bury her disgust of Lady Isabella's decidedly shrewish and jealous inclinations. "Oh indeed," she said, laughing good-humouredly at herself, "I was used to be so shockingly ignorant! I am grateful for any advice I receive on how to fit better into the world!"

To Lady Isabella's delight, she had been given access to indulge her predilection for delivering thinly-veiled, waspish insults. "If you are indeed keen for guidance, then allow me to drop a hint in your ear that perhaps you ought not to lean quite so close when you converse with men, as you do with Lord Gentsome. Of course *I* know you don't mean anything by it. But more jealous, backbiting women may delight in using it to censure you. And it seems just a little desperate, don't you think?" she smiled nastily. "Just a thought, no offence meant at all."

"None taken, I assure you," said Lucretia, fighting down her revulsion at such spite and striving to smile radiantly at her.

"How kind of you to give me your advice." Arnold looked astonished at this reply and would have said something, but the conversation was interrupted at that moment by the arrival of Lord Gentsome.

"Ah, Miss Lanyon, so this is where you have been hiding!" Gentsome said, laughing jovially. "Quite a business it has been to track you down."

All at once Lady Isabella resumed her coquettish airs, delighted to find herself in the company of such an eligible bachelor. "Oh, Lord Gentsome," she said with a titter, "how very droll you are!"

"Er, um…" said Lord Gentsome, unsure how to reply to such empty-headedness, and regarding Isabella with bored disdain. Lucretia was nauseated by Lady Isabella's airs but persevered in pursuing her acquaintance by saying, "Lord Gentsome, I'm sure you know Lady Isabella Prendergast, a erm… friend of mine".

"A friend of yours, Miss Lanyon?" he said, his countenance as he looked at Isabella altered into one of friendly interest. "Indeed? Well, any friend of Miss Lanyon's must be a friend of mine," he declared laboriously.

Lady Isabella began to see benefits in befriending Miss Lanyon. These were further highlighted when Mr Ovenstort arrived in the box hailing Lucretia with: "Miss Lanyon, you live up to your title as The Incalculable more every day, for no one was able to tell me where you'd disappeared off to! Tonight you have been both incalculable and intangible! I congratulate you on leading us all on a merry dance. Oh, but I am not the first to sleuth you down. Gentsome, you sly dog! Can't believe you beat me to it! Ah here's Alleveton!" Ovenstort laughed as this handsome rake entered into their corner of the box. "You are too late, Alleveton, you have been quite pushed out! Gentsome and myself have beaten you to Miss Lanyon's side, and now there is no room for you. You had best try again in the next intermission!"

"No, I think… yes, I quite think, there is a little room for me next to Miss Lanyon," said Alleventon. "Thankfully I am not half so stout as you, Gentsome… Besides which, Miss

Lanyon would much rather talk to me than listen to your prattle, Ovenstort! Confess, Miss Lanyon, is it not true?"

Lady Isabella had never before found herself in the company of so many attractive men all at once, and ones, moreover, that showed no disposition to be trying to get away. She realised that being friends with Lucretia would offer her access to all the gentlemen who followed lovelorn in The Incalculable's wake.

"Now, now, gentlemen, the truth is that Miss Lanyon has been taking advantage of this peaceful, secluded corner of the box to have a comfortable cose with her bestest of friends," she gushed. "Miss Lanyon, what a shame it is that we have been interrupted! I beg you will come to tea tomorrow. Mind, gentlemen, Miss Lanyon will be taking tea in Mount Street with me tomorrow and we don't want to be disturbed!" Having helpfully informed all these worthy gentlemen where they might chase Lucretia down the following day, she watched Lucretia retire to Lady Rutland's box. As she went, Lady Isabella managed to discover, to her relief, that Lucretia was a trifle too tall, her nose a little too pointy and her elbows a fraction too bony. Yes, altogether she would make an admirable friend, she told herself.

And so Lucretia began to spend as much time as she could in Lady Isabella's company, trying as this was. Lucretia found that Isabella was not improved by closer acquaintance. Her conversation was repetitive and vapid and she was, in addition, frequently ill-tempered. To be crossed in the slightest inflamed Isabella's ire. She also resorted to vapours and faints at the least provocation. This, Lucretia discovered, she had almost certainly learned from her mother, who was never seen without her vinaigrette close at hand. This was a mighty weapon, for if she was crossed she would resort to histrionics, tears and impassioned speeches on the depth of her sensibilities and the unkindness of whomever had upset her. Napoleon himself could have learned something from her methods, for these weapons never failed to win a battle for her, although they lost her respect and affection, even from her son. It was not difficult to locate where Christopher Prendergast developed his fear and dislike of women. Nothing could be so tiresome as the tirades, weeping and wailing he was subjected to whenever he did anything his mother did not like.

In no time at all, Lucretia found herself firmly ensconced within the Prendergast family circle. She proved to be as useful as Lady Isabella imagined she would be, bringing along a trail of interesting gentlemen wherever she went. Thus, Lucretia was frequently invited to spend cosy evenings at the Prendergasts' house.

This afforded Lucretia the opportunity to become known, as she most earnestly wished, to Christopher Prendergast who, although he had taken rooms in Duke Street, was very often to be found in Mount Street. He despised his mother's company, but he held his father in such affection and esteem that he was a frequent visitor on his account.

Christopher was naturally introduced to Lucretia but did not make any effort to talk more than commonplaces to her. He found his sister as boring and contemptible as his mother, and who Isabella chose to befriend interested him not a jot. Moreover, Miss Lanyon was a woman, and as such, Christopher naturally, albeit unconsciously, assumed her to be tiresome.

The Earl, however, did have occasion to talk with Lucretia and was surprised, for she talked like a sensible and good-natured lady, something he was not at all accustomed to meeting in his own home. He could not help but wonder, in a most unpaternal way, what on earth Lucretia could find to interest her in his totty-headed daughter.

It was not long before this mystery was answered for him. The group was sat around the fire on a cold evening, Isabella bent unconvincingly over her stitching, Lady Godolphin holding forth on the jangled state of her nerves following a visit from Mr Eagleton, a most disagreeable fellow by her account, and Lucretia sat trying to stifle a yawn and hide the boredom she felt. The Earl of Godolphin, hiding behind the folds of his paper, looked up as the door opened and his son entered.

"Hello, father; hello, mother," Christopher said, dropping a dutiful kiss on his mother's cheek. "Hello, Bella."

"Why, Christopher, so you have come to pay us a visit at last. How gratifying," Lady Godolphin said in sarcastic reproach.

"I was here only the day before yesterday if you recall, mother?"

"Alas! What did I ever do to deserve such an undutiful, impertinent son?" Lady Godolphin wailed tragically. "But," she shrieked, suddenly distracted from this very promising train of self-pity, "what on earth are you wearing? Good god, where did you get those trousers? If you can call them that! Why, oh why," she howled, "does the good Lord see fit to send such things to try me when I have been such a good Christian all my life! Really, Christopher, how can you? They look more like tents than trousers! Ridiculous! Utterly ridiculous! Oh, I'm coming over all faint. Bella, my vinaigrette, hand me my vinaigrette!"

Isabella ignored this demand and it was left to the Earl to pick up the vinaigrette, which was in Lady Godolphin's reach all the while, and pass it to her. She clutched it to her bosom dramatically.

Not to be outdone, Isabella added to her mother's tirade, "Please tell me that you do not intend to be seen abroad dressed like that, brother! No sane person could possibly dress in such a manner. Is it any wonder that Lord Gentsome has been avoiding me, if he knows us to harbour a madman in the family! You ought to think of your family before you choose such shocking legwear, really you should. I'm quite certain you go out of your way to upset my sensibilities, especially when you know how delicate my nerves are! Have you no proper fraternal feelings?"

Lucretia eyed critically the cause of all this hubbub. Resembling Cossack trousers, the innovative and unusual items were so wide at the leg that they billowed outwards until the ankle, where they tapered and were drawn in tight, giving the appearance that the legs were like big balloons.

"Well, I think he looks magnificent," said Lucretia defensively, looking up at her beloved with eyes full of hero-worship. Her words passed unnoticed by Isabella and her mother, who naturally did not listen to anyone other than themselves. But the Earl caught the words and the look which followed them, and eyed Lucretia piercingly.

"Do you indeed, Miss Lanyon?" he asked her, and then regretted it, for she blushed bright red and nodded. It was clear that Christopher and not Isabella was Miss Lanyon's object in visiting them. Lord Godolphin was amused and not a little surprised. He knew how to value his son and was very fond of him, but a lady's man he was not. The Earl could not imagine what a beautiful young woman, and one so courted as Lucretia, could find to attract her to his son when she could have a pick of all the bachelors in London.

Christopher would have been astonished to learn that he was the object of any lady's affection, let alone the toast of the polite world, and remained cheerful and unconcerned.

"Gammon!" he answered in the face of his mother and sister's diatribes. "These are the new Petersham trousers, dash it! He's only just designed them and I'm telling you they're going to be all the rage. Can't quite believe I've been so lucky as to steal a march on everyone else by having a pair already! What a bang-up and innovative chap he is, and what a stroke of fortune it was that I bumped into him at the tailor's when he was having them made up!" He looked down at the trousers in admiration and his mother scoffed. "I'll thank you not to pass judgement on what I'm wearing when you do not have the least idea what you are talking about! What do *you* know about the latest fashions? You wait for everyone else to be wearing a thing and pronouncing it to be wonderful before you'll admit you like it. They may be novel but, mark my words, you'll see every man wearing 'em before the season's out." He looked at his sister roguishly, "And I'll go bail that when you see Lord Gentsome in them, Bella, you'll declare he looks as fine as fivepence!"

The Earl heard Lucretia chuckle at this comment. Regarding her, he saw that she was looking up at his son, enraptured, and he felt sorry for her. His son had never shown the least disposition to be fixing his interest with any lady, and Lord Goldolphin could not imagine his son looking the way of a young lady for some time yet, if ever. He very much feared that Lucretia would find her heart broken, not by unkindness or inconstancy, but by indifference, which seemed somehow all the worse.

It certainly seemed that, despite all her ingenuity, Lucretia was making little headway in attaching the interest of her chosen beau, and it is hard to imagine how affairs between the two parties could ever advance. It is lucky, therefore, that fate chose to take a hand in the matter.

CHAPTER SIX

While Lucretia was thrown headlong into a dissipated life she had only previously dreamed of, Mr Morley, that notorious rake, arrived back in town. He had returned after a period of rustication made prudent by his pecuniary embarrassments and cut short by a fortuitous windfall brought about by the lucky fortunes of a chance outsider. The season was not so far advanced and he, naturally, had every intention of plunging himself back into his previous habits with optimism and a strong disinclination to learn anything from the circumstances which had, not so long ago, made necessary his expeditious removal from town.

He was a gentleman of medium height, slight in build, with chestnut brown locks and a strikingly handsome countenance. The perspicacious could discern a certain shiftiness in the darting of his eyes and a hint of ruthlessness as he pursed his lips, but the effect was so slight that very few remarked it. He followed Lord Byron's example in affecting a style of appearance that gave the air of a dark and brooding hero. Byron sported dishevelled locks and a seeming nonchalance of dress, which impression took many hours before his glass to effect. Similarly studious in giving this appearance, Mr Morley was dressing carefully on the morning after his return when he was visited by his old associate Mr Croxstowe.

"So, it's true that you are back then?" he was greeted by this gentleman.

"It would certainly appear that way," said Morley caustically, turning towards his friend. "Hello, Lucius, how goes the business of fleecing naïve young cubs of their money?"

"I resent your implications, Everard," Croxstowe said in affronted accents, but these were belied by a grin creeping slowly across his face: an unpleasant expression that was more a sneer than a smile. He sniggered malevolently, "The beginning of the season, you know, is always good for business. So many green young gentlemen desirous of acquiring town bronze fall in my way, who are ripe for the plucking."

"I see you are yet to develop a conscience, my friend. I congratulate you. There is nothing so tiresome as virtue!"

"I see myself as an educator," said Croxstowe, "supplying salutary lessons on misplaced trust and stupidity. In short, I provide a service which should earn the gratitude of my young acquaintances. Sadly, they are so rarely thankful for it." He released and unconvincing sigh. "In any case, who are you to preach morals when your own reputation is deservedly far from savoury? I ruin only purses: you, my friend, ruin also reputations. Miss Lyle, Everard? A beautiful young thing, no doubt? But alas, your lack of discretion is deplorable. I hope you do not find yourself an outcast because of it."

"Not in the least, dear fellow," said Morley, unperturbed. "It has been well hushed up. The family have seen to that, I assure you. I'm surprised it has come to even your ears. But then, you do have a nose for scandal like a pig for truffles. You might try your hand at blackmail when ivory-turning loses its appeal. But really, Lucius, you must surely appreciate that one must have some amusements to while away the tedium of the country. So interminably dull! In truth, it is good to be back in town."

"You have made a recover then? When last we met you were well and truly in the basket." There was a certain spiteful enjoyment in Croxstowe's tone as he referred to his friend's financial difficulties.

"Let us just say that I have enough to keep the wolves at bay," said Morley, noncommittal.

"Temporarily, I gather? You will soon find your pockets to let once again, I imagine," Croxstowe said with comfortable pessimism. "Do not look to me to bail you out. I find I too must retrench on account of my shocking bad luck."

"Faro again?" Morley asked sympathetically. "You ought to try the horses, they did well for me. Or rather, Light-hearted Lady did well for me."

"Was that the beast's name? How apt! But no, I learned some time ago that faro didn't answer. I thought hazard would be my salvation, and at first it did indeed seem that the luck had changed. Alas, it did not last!"

"It never does, dear friend," said Morley. "I will soon have to look about myself for other opportunities to keep myself afloat."

"But what of your well-juiced friends? I knew that their complaisant generosity had grown thin of late, but Mrs Hemmings, at least, was always wont to come to your rescue. Does she too refuse you an advance?"

"Ah, it is so. Her husband was getting ugly. And she had begun to tire me. I found that as the hold on her purse strings tightened, so my interest waned. Strange that it should be so," mused Morley.

"Strange indeed," said Croxstowe ironically. "Well, it had better be marriage then, Everard. You have skated on thin ice so long I think I see the cracks forming."

"Yes, sadly I begin to feel my toes getting wet," Morley agreed, sighing dramatically. "Marriage, it is such a bitter pill to swallow. But, alas, it does seem that matters have reached such a pass. There was a time I thought death preferable but, as it turns out, I value my life more than I supposed. Strange, when one considers how painfully dull it often is."

"No doubt you intend to try your hand with the fair Incalculable, London's newest heiress? I warn you that Maslebow and Alleventon have already tried and failed. Not but what you have more address in your little finger than the two of them put together," ruminated Croxstowe, with unusual charity.

"*Merci du compliment*! But how can it be that no mention of this lady has met my ears? Without doubt I have been in the wilderness too long. I beg you will enlighten me. No doubt she is bran-faced and insipid. They always are."

"You are wide of the mark this time, Everard. In beauty she is beyond compare, and in charm I do believe she is exceptionally well-endowed. And her fortune... well, they say she's swimming in lard. If rumour be truth she could buy an abbey and still have much spare."

"Well, well. Perhaps the luck has turned after all. I must seek an introduction with the... what did you call her?"

"The Incalculable. I gather it is on account of her fickle sense of humour or some such nonsense. Although Samperton insists it is on account of the incalculable immensity of her fortune." Croxstowe sniggered in appreciation of Mr Samperton's poisonous wit.

"Hmmm, the Incalculable..." Morley pondered, growing a slow smile. "I find myself strangely ready to fall in love."

"Love?" Mr Croxstowe lifted a cynical eyebrow.

"Well, do not you have an inordinate love of money? And if she be fair... that is all to the better," finished Morley.

Mr Morley's wish to become acquainted with Miss Lanyon was granted that very evening at the Ennerwick's ball. He was accorded a warm welcome from Mrs Ennerwick, for indeed he was a favourite amongst the women. He was a naturally handsome man, but the hours he had stood in front of the mirror perfecting his appearance had not been ill-spent. He looked artistically dishevelled and this careless appearance, allied as it was with a brooding countenance, gave him, as it was calculated to, an air of mystery and allure. Mr Morley was also blessed with a chameleon-like talent for being all things in all company, and was clever at reading the character of the women he met, tailoring his conversation and air to meet their desires.

"How delightful to see you, Everard!" gushed Mrs Ennerwick. "You have been gone this long age and have been sadly missed, I assure you." He bent over her hand and kissed it with a saucy look at his hostess. "This long time without your company has been desolation. Allow me to say that you look ravishing, quite ravishing," came Morley's playful reply. "I do not know when I have seen a more magnificent turban, are those grapes I see nestled within? An Eden in a head-dress. Remarkable."

"Tush tush, you silly boy," Mrs Ennerwick giggled, rapping him with her fan flirtatiously. "It is unkind in you to mock my outfit when you know I have taken such pains over it."

"I, mock? I assure you that it is no such thing. Fair lady, I am at your feet in that enchanting ensemble! Wait, I see a pineapple, I am quite sure it is a pineapple, situated just next to the plums. Alas no! It is just the folds of the material. Pity."

"I know very well I look like a quiz, but if one cannot be beautiful one must at least look interesting," she said prosaically, not in the least discomposed by this banter. "But come, there is a young lady I must introduce to you before they strike up the next dance."

"I am at your service, my dear. But do please make it a pretty young lady or I will have to flee back to the wilderness. I must be encouraged to stay, you know."

"Naughty boy! You will dance with whomever I say you will, that is my right as a hostess, and I am sage enough to know that young and beautiful damsels are not safe in your company. Miss Lisleham is a most sensible, good mannered and clever young woman, and you will like her very well because I instruct you to do so. She has but this season just come out."

"Then I beg you will put her back in again," Mr Morley exclaimed, catching sight of a plain and sullen-faced damsel within his hostess's sight line. "A bluestocking, ma'am, have you no heart?" But he allowed himself to be introduced with good grace, and invited Miss Lisleham very civilly to join him in the next dance.

Throughout the country dance he proceeded to make himself agreeable to her with talk on serious topics and compliments on her dancing. He managed with great skill to conceal that he was barely listening to her and would forget her the instant she was returned to her mother's side. His attention was engaged in identifying Miss Lanyon, which he very soon did, for it was not difficult to spot the prettiest young lady surrounded by a court of men all vying for her attention.

He took the earliest opportunity to make his way over towards the throng of admirers and insinuated himself into the press. He saw instantly that many had been waiting some time to capture the heiress's notice, and to stand waiting patiently in the hopes of being introduced to her did not appeal to him in the slightest. He looked about him to see if he could bring the thing about more quickly, and his shrewd eyes fell upon Miss Pycroft who stood at Miss Lanyon's side. Miss Pycroft was staring up at Lucretia, her worshipful eyes filled with quiet awe. None of the males present paid her the least attention as they clamoured for Lucretia's notice. Recognising Miss Pycroft as an old acquaintance, Mr Morley thanked fortune for smiling upon him.

He left the crowd in search of a particular gentleman, and to his relief soon tracked him down. "Hallo, Pycroft," Morley said, having made his way to this gentleman's side. Conscientiously he proceeded to make small talk with him.

"Is that not little Cecilia all grown up?" Morley said casually to Mr Pycroft after they had been conversing some time, gesturing towards Miss Lanyon's companion who, incidentally, happened to be Mr Pycroft's sister. "I remember her as a scrubby little brat, it seems only yesterday! Well, well. I beg you will introduce me so I can rekindle our acquaintance."

"Very well," agreed Mr Pycroft a little reluctantly. "But you must promise not to go breaking her heart. I am rather fond of her, she's a very good sort, is Ceccy. And I know your reputation. Lord only knows why, but the womenfolk seem to fawn over you! But then this badly dressed romantic style is very popular amongst them. It looks damned shabby if you ask me, but there you are. Here, Ceccy," he said, leading Morley over to the group, "here is Mr Morley desirous of making your acquaintance. Mr Morley, my sister Miss Cecelia Pycroft," he said making the introductions.

"Delighted to make your acquaintance, Miss Pycroft. No doubt you have forgotten but we were once firm friends. At least I used to wish to be your friend. You, as I recall, wished to see me fall into rivers and laughed most unkindly when it came to pass."

"Well, I don't know that I ever did anything so ill-natured, but I do remember you. You used to pull my pig-tails, and get me in trouble with Miss Reed by sending me home all covered in mud," said Cecilia shyly.

"Ah, the infamous Miss Reed! You stood in such awe of her, dragon that she was!" he bantered, with a friendly and amused glint in his eye.

Cecilia caught sight of this and, her normally timid nature emboldened by it, replied: "Dragon? Nothing of the sort, as you very well know! She was the kindest of creatures and really most tried by our high jinxes. I wish you might be forced to look after four rambunctious children and see how well you fare!"

"Heaven forbid! I call a truce, if you please," said Morley throwing his hands up theatrically. "Allow me to say that you look all grown up and very pretty too. How do you find your first London season? Are you bored? It is the fashion, you know."

"Bored? Not in the least! How could anyone be so?" asked Cecilia astounded, unaware that he was teasing her. "It is all so delightful. Although a little exhausting," she conceded. "We have attended no less than three balls this evening."

"Tired, my little imp?" Morley asked in an assiduously solicitous fashion. "Trotting too hard, no doubt. Then we must find you a seat and some refreshment."

Lucretia overheard this last. "Oh, Ceccy, are you tired? I wish you would have said. Let us find somewhere to sit at once and catch our breath. How very kind of you, sir," she directed at Morley as he led them away from the throng to an unoccupied bench and offered to procure drinks for them. As Morley had hoped, a young greenhorn, less adept at wooing fashionable ladies than himself, jumped at the chance to bring the object of his admiration a drink. It was a masterstroke and left Morley, as he planned, sitting between the two girls.

"Mr Morley, this is my friend, Miss Lanyon," said Miss Pycroft proudly. "Miss Lanyon, meet Mr Morley, a friend of my brother."

Carefully regarding Lucretia, Mr Morley calculated his next move. He felt that too much open admiration of her would be a mistake. He fancied that she may be one of those rare women who would be more appreciative of a man who paid attention to her oft-ignored friend.

"A friend of your brother?" he said to Miss Pycroft in wounded tones. "Oh, cruel lady! May I not also be called a friend of yours? If only for respect for our history?"

"History?" Lucretia asked.

"Yes, we played together as children," explained Cecilia. "Birchlands, Mr Morley's uncle's estate, neighbours Easterlay, and he was very often there visiting his uncle. How comes it, Mr Morley, that I haven't seen you in town before now?"

"I have been engaged in business on my estate," improvised Morley. "Father left affairs in no good state, and I have been trying to balance the accounts ever since, a lost cause I begin to feel. Morley Chase is a cursed Gothic pile that eats up money while yet remaining a ruin."

He considered it best to make a clean breast of his money situation, and endeavoured to make up any ground this may have lost him by demonstrating very proper regard for his family seat and his heritage. Proper family feeling... had he been alone he would have snorted out loud. What did he owe his cruel and extravagant father and his pathetic dab of a mother? But he would play any card in his hand that might further his cause with the heiress. His conversation must serve his business and not his pleasure.

Lucretia noted how quickly his thoughts turned to money and was suspicious. Without needing to be told of his reputation, she knew a fortune hunter when she saw one.

"Still, I'm very fond of the place," Morley continued, always economical with the truth if nothing else. "I will be very sad if it turns out I must sell it. It holds many cherished memories." He smiled sadly. "Even the ghosts and I have become old friends." It was masterly and he knew it. Miss Pycroft's response was just as he planned.

"Ghosts?" she whispered in thrilled tones.

"Of course, every house with a respectable history has 'em. I'm surprised to hear that you have none at Easterlay. At Morley Chase we have the headless monk who wanders amongst the ruins of the old abbey in the west garden."

Miss Pycroft gasped. "Have you really seen him, Mr Morley?" she asked, agog.

"But of course. He warbles hymns to the full moon – not terribly tunefully, but then he doesn't have lips so I fancy he would struggle in that respect," said Morley creatively.

"Oh, you are teasing me," Miss Pycroft said, disappointed.

"Not in the least, or only just a little bit," he said smiling. "I admit the singing headless monk is a piece of fiction, but I worried that the true tales may set you all a quiver. Now I see, however, that it is no such thing and that you are equal to hearing about them. There really is a white lady who whispers 'why, oh why?' as she makes her way along the corridors of the east wing. Rumour has it she was murdered by her husband on their wedding night and she searches for him desperately to ask him to explain himself." Cecilia's eyes were filled with wonder and fear. She shivered and whispered 'white lady' breathlessly.

"Don't listen to him, Ceccy," exclaimed Lucretia, looking at Morley reproachfully. "Ghosts? Honestly! He's bamming you. For shame, Mr Morley, you have scared the girl half to death."

"But only see how much she's enjoying it," said Morley. Lucretia saw, looking at the enraptured Miss Pycroft, that he was quite right, and shared an amused look with him that considerably heartened the fortune hunter.

"I see you have no taste for the romantic, but it is unkind in you to spoil the enjoyment of others," said Morley to her, confident that he was making a good start in his pursuit of his quarry. "But it shall be as Miss Lanyon desires, we will turn the topic. Now, Miss Pycroft, I believe I must have redeemed myself in your eyes from the days I sent you home covered in mud by rescuing you just now from that unruly mob of gentlemen. How tiresome it must be to have so many admirers?"

"Oh no, they are not *my* admirers! They come to admire Miss Lanyon. And who could blame them?" Cecelia cast a look full of youthful hero-worship at Lucretia. "She is so beautiful, and kind, and clever and droll." She sighed and admitted quietly, "I know it is very wicked to think it, but I cannot help sometimes but wish I was just *a little* beautiful."

"I fancy that there were a fair few amongst that throng for whom Miss Pycroft, and not Miss Lanyon, was the object of their attention," lied Morley. This earned him a look of fulsome gratitude from Lucretia. He felt he began to get the measure of her and calculated his next move to best forward his interests.

"You do very well, little one," he said, striving to look earnest and kind, while thinking to himself how plain she was. "Who could not but be captivated by your little button nose which, and I mean no offence," he said to Lucretia, "is more adorable than Miss Lanyon's more regal one. Furthermore, you have delightfully earnest brown eyes. I do believe there is the look of the cherub about you," he mused.

Morley shot a look at Lucretia under lidded eyes to check he was making a good impression upon her. The perspicacious Lucretia noticed this, but Morley was not conscious of the fact that he had betrayed himself and continued blithely on. "Altogether too charming by half! I shall warn your brother to keep a closer eye on you."

Conscious that he did not want Lucretia to fall under the misapprehension that Miss Pycroft was the object of his desire, Morley judged it time to bring his admiration of Miss Pycroft to a close and said: "But I don't wish to make you conceited, Miss Pycroft. It is your unconsciousness of your own prettiness that makes it all the more captivating. Let us speak, therefore, of something else."

Lucretia was not fooled by him. She knew how to value Miss Pycroft but, without arrogance, she knew instinctively that it was herself, or rather her fortune, and not Miss Pycroft, that Mr Morley was pursuing.

"What think you both of Mrs. Ennerwick's quiz of a turban?" Morley asked, turning the subject. "I have just now been remarking upon it to her. It is good enough to serve up at dinner, is it not? I thought, yes I quite thought, that I spotted a brace of pigeons amongst the fruit... but I may have been mistaken. Certainly I was mistaken in the pineapple," he mused in mock seriousness.

It was too much for Cecelia and Lucretia, who fell about in merriment. Catching sight of Lucretia's profile as she laughed, Morley understood why it had become a game to try and make her do so. She really was incredibly beautiful, and the laughter brought out something from within her that was mysterious and exquisite. If one must get leg-shackled, to marry such a prize would certainly sweeten the blow. Why, it may be weeks, even months, before one tired of her, he thought to himself.

And so began Mr Morley's calculated pursuit of the fair Miss Lanyon. Lucretia knew he was a fortune hunter but, even so, he was very droll and she could not but enjoy his company. Confident that her heart was in no danger, Lucretia saw no harm in talking with him and so was always pleased to see him. She met him with her accustomed disingenuous friendliness, occasionally looked out for him at parties, especially after having been subjected to a long and stodgy conversation, and her smiling welcomes upon him allowed him to hope she was falling in love with him.

On some occasions he would not approach her, in the hopes that this would pique her, and add to his mystery – a trick that had never failed him in the past. Lucretia noticed this ploy with amusement and, deciding to quiz him over it a little, remarked to him at the theatre one evening:

"You are quite in my bad books, Mr Morley. You did not speak to me once at the picnic yesterday! I quite thought I must have offended you, but here you are now so I see I must have been mistaken." Not perceiving the teasing note in her voice, and possessed of extreme arrogance, it did not even occur to Morley that she may be having a laugh at his expense, so he heard the words with a silent crow of triumph.

When, the very next day, she chose to wear the posy of violets he sent her for the Masterham's ball, he felt victory with the heiress was assured. In point of fact, Lucretia had only chosen to wear them because the blooms matched perfectly with her dress. Morley's supreme confidence, however, lead him to the misconception that the dress had been chosen to complement the flowers and not, as was actually the case, the other way around.

In Morley's mind, his conquest of the Incalculable was certain. It was time, he thought, to set about advancing their courtship further. The following evening, he insinuated himself into the seat next to Lucretia's in her box at the theatre where it was possible, by the employment of hushed undertones, to hold an almost private conversation.

"Miss Lanyon, you look very beautiful tonight. Quite in high bloom."

"As if I were a rose garden?" she laughed. "How can you talk such nonsense, sir?"

"But, my charming, I speak in earnestness. Fair nymph, with your golden curls, your eyes as deep and mysterious as the oceans, you are a goddess amongst all these mere mortals. You eclipse all others present," he waxed poetically.

"Now I know you offer me Spanish coin, and I will have none of it! A goddess, Mr Morley, how can you? You are in a funning humour tonight," said Lucretia dampeningly, in the hopes of making it clear to the rake that he would not win her heart.

Not heeding this hint, Morley continued passionately, "But I assure you I mean what I say. My regard, my awe in your presence, my feelings of unworthiness to be seated near you, I feel them most earnestly. Surely you must see how I have been slayed by cupid's arrow?" Glancing sideways at her, he found that Lucretia had turned away. Morley imagined that she was blushing in maidenly embarrassment (and pleasure) and, satisfied by how these more amorous attentions towards her had been received, was very well pleased with his night's work. He would give her time to consider the prospect of their future together, and chose not to press his suit further that evening. The next act of the play was just beginning so he took his leave of her.

"Oh, are you leaving, Mr Morley?" Lucretia said, a little preoccupied. "Very well."

Morley left in the comfortable conviction that he had made a very real dent in her affections. He was mistaken. Lucretia had not been distracted by Mr Morley's compliments, indeed she had barely been listening to the half of them, for her attention was quite otherwise engaged, as her next words would have illustrated had he stayed to hear them.

"Who is that most peculiar looking gentleman, Arnold?" she had leant over to ask her cousin, nodding towards a man of considerable embonpoint seated in a box opposite theirs. "He looks to be in pain."

Arnold chuckled, "Why, that is Mr Towford. He is forever seeking new and ingenious ways to halt the unstoppable growth of his form. If I'm not mistaken, he is trying out a new type of corset, which he has undoubtedly had laced so tight that it is constricting his breathing. And," here her cousin raised his quizzing glass to obtain a closer look, "ah, yes, it is as I thought, he is wearing an exceptionally tight pair of pantaloons. I expect he imagines they make him appear slimmer. Whether or not that is the case, I am thankful that we have already dined, else his appearance in them would surely put me off my dinner. I do believe poor Towford has tried everything to reduce his girth, save cutting back on his enormous repasts." They both laughed.

Arnold directed a sharp sideways look at his cousin. "Was that Morley I saw making up to you just then?"

"Yes. Alas, he was talking such fustian that I quite forgot to listen! He can be ever so droll but I am well aware that it is my fortune he has in his sights. It is such a shame that he now tries to make love to me, for it is really very tiresome and not at all amusing like his light-hearted banter."

"You should not encourage him, cousin," Arnold joked.

"Encourage him? No such thing! Only a fool could imagine that I had given him the least encouragement, or felt the slightest partiality for him."

But Mr Morley was just such a fool. Floating around in the cheerful certainty that he would soon become engaged to an heiress, he set out on an extravagant shopping expedition on the following morning, whistling as he proceeded down Bond Street. Should he buy her an engagement present, he wondered? No, he fancied his credit would not be sufficient until the notice of their engagement was published in the Gazette. Then there would be no limit to his purse, for no sensible tradesman would dun a man who was betrothed to an heiress, he thought with glee. He spent the afternoon at a prize fight, lost a good deal on the betting and, in no way discomposed, remarked to himself that the world looked very beautiful that day. But nightfall would bring a darkness that would later swamp that normally carefree gentleman in despair.

That evening he knew that Lucretia would be at Vauxhall Gardens with a party of friends. She was a guest of the Prendergasts although, to Lucretia's disappointment, Christopher had not put in an appearance with them that evening. Despite this, it was Lucretia's first time at Vauxhall and she was enjoying herself hugely.

It was a magical place, lit by thousands of lanterns hanging from the branches of the trees, some like many-hued stars, some like fairies twinkling beguilingly through the leaves, some reflected against revolving mirrors, all giving the place a fairytale quality.

"Oh!" gasped Lady Isabella as they walked to their supper box. "What a mystical paradise, a divine Eden! It is almost as if some sorcerer had cast a spell upon the place." For the first time, Lucretia found herself in sympathy with Isabella's romantical notions, such was the enchanted air of the place.

They dined on Vauxhall's famous wafer thin slices of ham. "They are so fine," declared Lucretia, "that we could watch the concert through one of these slices and not miss a detail on the musicians' coats!"

"Indeed, you are quite right, Miss Lanyon," said Lord Godolphin, smiling at her. He had come to like Lucretia very much for her ready wit and good temper. Her presence made the time he was forced to spend in his wife and daughter's company almost tolerable. "Most people declare you could read a newspaper through the slices, but what a waste of time spent at Vauxhall to read a newspaper. I had far rather see an orchestra in a brown haze than newsprint!" She grinned at him and he remarked to himself what a shame it was that Christopher had no interest in women. What a lovely wife she would have made him.

After the dinner, Lucretia and Lady Isabella, accompanied by Isabella's great friend Miss Altringham, set off to explore the maze of secluded groves and walks in the gardens. There the magical qualities of Vauxhall were magnified as they walked amongst the marble statues, the man-made waterfalls and grottos, and promenaded up and down romantically named alleys such as Druids' Walk and the particularly tantalising Lovers' Walk.

Here Morley was fortunate enough to come across his quarry, walking, he noted, with Lady Isabella and another lady - he had no interest in learning her name. He fell into step with the party, and leaning in to speak to Lucretia said, "Miss Lanyon, I need to speak to you. I have something of some moment to impart to you."

"Oh, have you, Mr Morley?" Lucretia said brightly. "Can it not wait until tomorrow?" she continued, trying to stave off the inevitable proposal. She was enjoying her evening so very much, and did not want to have it spoiled by being forced into the unpleasantness of rejecting one of her suitors. "As you can see, I am very much engaged with my friends this evening. Indeed, this place is so very magical I quite feel all worldly concerns must be left for another day."

Morley was a little surprised. He had expected her to welcome the opportunity to receive his advances. That she would reject him, however, was unthinkable to him, so assured of her regard did he feel. "Indeed, it cannot wait, I must speak with you now, tonight," he urged, worried that such a good setting for his proposal would not be repeated.

"Oh, come now, Mr Morley, I'm sure there is nothing you can say to me that is so important that it cannot wait one more day!" she returned lightly. "Let us walk in the gardens and enjoy this enchanting place." Morley told himself that her reluctance was born of the impropriety attached to being alone in a gentleman's company. He considered how best to overcome her scruples and get her on her own. He knew Lady Isabella through his pursuit of Lucretia and, understanding her to be a very silly girl with extremely romantic notions, very likely to be susceptible to the allure of intrigue, decided to use her as an accomplice, falling back to speak with her.

Isabella, like all romantic young ladies, was strongly attracted to the handsome and dangerous Mr Morley. She had, of course, been warned off all the well-known rakes, which naturally served to increase her desire to spend time in the company of one.

"Lady Isabella," Morley whispered to her in deliciously enticing undertones. Isabella shuddered in anticipation. Just then squeals of raucous enjoyment could be heard from one of the adjoining walks, undoubtedly the result of some wanton tryst.

"Yes, Mr Morley," she breathed back, very much inclined, despite her strict upbringing, towards having a similar encounter.

"I wonder if you could assist me in an intrigue… but no! I should not ask it of you…" Morley cut off after these tantalising words.

"Oh indeed, Mr Morley, when you look so earnestly at me I cannot refuse to help you," she said, leaning in close towards him to ensure he had an excellent view of her fair countenance.

"I need," he whispered, lowering his tone still more, "to speak with Miss Lanyon alone. May I count on you as my ally in the enterprise?" Isabella scowled, not at all pleased to be asked to assist such a fascinating specimen to woo her friend, when she wanted him herself. Morley saw her jealous hackles rise and realised he had erred.

"As improper as it is," he said, changing tack, "I mistakenly agreed to aid in arranging a liaison between Miss Lanyon and her lover. How much I regret it now, but I cannot go back on my word."

Isabella was once again all smiles and coyness. "Indeed, Mr Morley? How very shocking! It seems that the fair Miss Lanyon is not so pure as everyone seems to think," she said in spiteful enjoyment, dreaming of Lucretia's downfall should she be found out. "I ought not to help you, you know?" she said, waiting to be coaxed into her part in the enterprise.

"Oh, indeed not! And if you are too scared to be involved in such an impropriety, well, naturally I cannot ask it of you! How iniquitous of me to have even considered such a step! Why, you are a mere child, an innocent! You have not yet lost your naïveté, and it was wrong of me to try to steal it from you."

"Scared?" Isabella said, her chin rising defiantly. "No such thing! And I'm not naïve and missish, whatever you may think. I will help you, sir, since you beg me to."

"That's a girl, I knew I could count on you," he said. From Isabella's scowl however, he knew these words had undermined the delicious mystery of the scheme and hastened to add, with a suggestive wink, "You cannot imagine how pleased I am to find you are not such an innocent after all!"

Isabella caught up with Miss Altringham and Lucretia, who were by this time some way ahead of them. She drew Lucretia's attention to a statue of Artemis poised with her bow and arrow, meanwhile drawing Miss Altringham to the other side of the walk, declaring that she simply must get a closer look at a cascade they had just passed by. When Isabella looked over towards Lucretia, she saw that there was some distance between them, and that Morley had taken the opportunity afforded by this to stand at Lucretia's side and distract her by commenting on the sculpture.

"Ah, Elinor, is not that your aunt over there waving at us?" Isabella said loudly to her prune-faced friend. Miss Altringham looked set to spoil it all by answering in the negative, but Isabella nipped her arm and said, "Indeed, I'm quite sure it is! We must go and say hello to her. No need to accompany us, Cressy," she shouted over to Lucretia, "I can see you are quite caught up in looking at that statue. I'll not drag you away since we will be back in a trice anyway." She hurried Miss Altringham off down another walk leaving Lucretia and Mr Morley alone.

It was a deeply unsubtle ploy and Lucretia would have laughed at it had she not been dreading the inevitable proposal she was about to receive. Lucretia was not ignorant of the fact that she should not be caught alone in the company of a single gentleman, but she had long been expecting Mr Morley's proposal and knew enough of his resolution to know that he would certainly find another opportunity to get her alone should he be foiled at this attempt. She therefore did not hurry after the other two girls as propriety dictated she should have done, but instead allowed herself to be lead by Morley to a nearby bench.

Morley was feeling sure of himself, but then Mr Morley always felt sure of himself. He was very well pleased with his ploy and had only to give voice to his carefully worded proposal and all would be very well with the world.

"Miss Lanyon," he began, kneeling down before her and clasping her hand amorously to his bosom. "You cannot have but noticed my growing regard for you. What you cannot know is the strength of my feelings. They burst forth within my heart, threatening to engulf me. Now, I know," he said, taking pains to display a most touching awareness of his own lowliness and inadequacy, "that I am not worthy even to lay my head at your shoes, even to cast my eyes up at you while I genuflect before you." He had particularly liked this part of his speech when he had agonised over the wording of the proposal.

"Nevertheless," he continued, not wanting to dwell too long upon his inferiority, "when I am with you it is as if some bright star blinds me into forgetfulness. You swathe my eyes, indeed the whole world, in loveliness! Nightingales sing beautiful arias in my ears as I watch you walk, nay float, as an angel treads upon a cloud." Here he sighed tenderly. "Only the strength of my passion could overcome my conviction that I do not deserve you. Only you can be my salvation, only you can make me all that I can and should be. I assure you, with all my heart, that if you could overlook my sins, I would do anything, everything, in my power to deserve you, to cherish you, to protect you, for all my days!" Coming to the end of his monologue he breathed air in his lungs and looked in happy expectation at his bride-to-be. Surely Shakespeare himself could not have done better, he assured himself.

He was therefore surprised that his declaration of love and subsequent proposal of marriage met with a refusal that was peremptorily and summarily delivered.

"No, Mr Morley, I will not marry you," said Lucretia, adding dryly, "as you very well know."

He noted the decisiveness in her tone, but chose to delude himself that she spoke in maidenly bashfulness; it was expected, after all, that a woman would always reject a man's initial proposal, whether she planned to accept him later or not. So he continued resolutely, "But the strength of my passion... my heart, my hopes, they are all yours," he breathed soulfully.

"Come now, sir. You surely cannot think me such a fool?" she remarked tartly. "You are not in love with me and would not wish to marry me, or any other, if your circumstances did not make it prudent for you to do so. I am very sorry that your pockets are to let, but I do not have, nor will I ever have, the least desire to marry you," said Lucretia with unambiguous directness.

Morley recoiled as if he had been slapped across the face. He had underrated her. She was astute and, he now discovered, she could be forceful. He was at a loss for words; she had made him feel ridiculous and that made him first uncomfortable and then, swiftly on the heels of this, angry. Lucretia saw this, and knew him to be as calculating as she had suspected. But the flash of temper in his eyes frightened her just a little. She became acutely aware that they were alone, and she felt her lack of protection as she had never done so before.

She held out her hand in an effort to placate him. "My dear Mr Morley. It would be folly to fall out over this ridiculous affair. Let us forget that this incident has occurred that we may be able to return to our comfortable friendship," she forced herself to say lightly. "My aunt will be wondering what has become of us, so I would be grateful if you could now return me to my party."

There was a pause, a very brief pause, while Morley considered his options. He knew that there would be no changing her mind, and he felt the world close in around him. The thought of his debts, and his recent extravagance born of his expectations, filled him with a dread hopelessness. Never before had he felt so trapped, and it fed his anger. But he could do no more this evening, she was lost to him and he knew it. He must not add to this by giving vent to ill-considered wrath. He schooled his face, therefore, into a picture of rueful good-humour.

"Miss Lanyon, I beg you will forgive me," he said. "I have evidently been in error with regards to your sentiments, and have been justly punished for it. To remove your friendship would be to punish me more, I fancy, than I deserve, cur that I am! Let us by all means remain friends. And you are quite right, we have been too long absent, I will return you to your aunt forthwith."

Later in the evening Mr Morley stood talking to Lady Scallonsby, with whom he was great friends. He was trying to hide his bad temper at having been refused by Lucretia, but doing so imperfectly.

"So, you have tried your luck with the Incalculable?" sneered Lady Scallonsby. "Comfort yourself, Everard, many have failed where you have. While I do not deny your charm, I fancy Miss Lanyon is too clever to be taken in by you. She knows as well as everyone how the land lies with your finances." She stopped, looking over at the heiress across the dance floor; her eyes narrowed in loathing.

Lucretia was engaged in talking with her cousin and became aware of Lady Scallonsby's eyes on her. Mischief, and her dislike of that lady, overtook her and prompted her to begin to flirt with her cousin. Arnold Rutland was surprised to find his cousin simpering at him and rapping him coquettishly with her fan until he took in Lady Scallonsby's look and correctly interpreted Lucretia's unusual behaviour. He good-naturedly responded to her overtures but leaned towards her saying murmuring:

"Careful, Cressy. I know you have taken Lady Scallonsby in aversion but be warned, she would make a dangerous enemy. I cannot encourage you to flame her jealousy."

"Cousin, why do you like her?" Lucretia asked. "She is not worthy of you. I admit I find her repulsive, and fail to see how you cannot do so."

"A mere amusement, little Lucretia. Nothing more. You have no cause to worry your pretty head over such concerns, indeed you should know nothing of them! Come to think of it, I'd like to know what ninnyhammer told you all about it!" He broke off, recollecting that it was he himself who had as good as shared this information with her, and hastily continued, "I know what I'm about and will not find myself snared in her coils, have no fear."

At the other side of the room, animosity was patent on Lady Scallonsby's face, try as she would to hide it. "I fancy," she said to Morley, "that Miss Lanyon has her eye on a quite different prize. It may salve your pride to know that her feelings were otherwise engaged. Had they not been, you may have had more luck in securing her."

Morley, understanding her, said, "You are a fool, Maria." But Lady Scallonsby was not to be turned from her belief that Lucretia was planning to marry her cousin. She was jealous and it blinkered her to the truth.

"But oh, how I would love to do that hateful girl a mischief!" Lady Scallonsby responded with vehemence.

"You may yet have occasion to do so," said Morley darkly.

"Ah, you have some plot in mind? If I can be of assistance, be sure to ask it of me, for I will help to bring down the Incalculable with pleasure!"

CHAPTER SEVEN

The Hon. Viscount Prendergast, unaware that storm clouds were brewing over his future, set out early on the day following Mr Morley's proposal. He left the house with some surreptitiousness, for his errand was not one he wished to advertise. It was not, in fact, one that should cause the gentleman any embarrassment, but Christopher had worked hard to develop his reputation as a man for whom nothing mattered more than his attire. His destination was Jackson's saloon, wherein gentlemen and the lower classes rubbed shoulders in the ring, getting sweaty and dishevelled under the tutelage of Mr Jackson, and this pastime did not, in his opinion, add to his reputation as a dandy, whence the secrecy.

An early start in his pugilistic exercise would ensure that most gentlemen, as a breed not generally addicted to early rising, would not be present at the saloon, allowing Christopher's visit to go undetected. Few were privileged enough to be instructed by the famous Mr Jackson in person, but Christopher Prendergast was an exceptional exponent of the art, and was deemed worthy of that gentleman's time. Returning home from this exercise, Christopher considered dropping in at Manton's shooting gallery, for he was also an outstanding, and keen, marksman. However, the hour was now becoming advanced enough for gentlemen of the polite world to be venturing abroad, making it expeditious that he return home to avoid being seen, and to agonise over his wardrobe.

He was busily employed in front of his mirror when he received a visit from his great friend Mr Strangwald. Strangwald was a tall gentleman, so thin that he would have resembled a beanstalk had his features not been so pointy. There was something almost Slavic in his high cheekbones, apical nose and near-black, straight hair.

The visitor was evidently much discomposed; the eyes goggled out of his head in agitation and he paced anxiously around Christopher's dressing room.

"Hallo, Bertie, what's got you all in a passion?" he was greeted by Christopher.

"Napoleon!" yelped Strangwald almost hysterically. "He's back in town. Seen him at White's!"

"Ah, that's it then. What was I telling you the other day, never go to White's, bound to come across some earnest fellow you've been trying to avoid. Come to think of it, all the gentlemen's clubs seemed to be stuffed full of dashed dull dogs these days. Hardly worth going," Christopher mused.

Strangwald suffered from an affliction where he was never able to say exactly what he meant. It is unclear whether he actually lived in the fantastical world he described, or whether he was simply unable to find the right words to explain what he meant. It made it very difficult to hold conversations with him, as deciphering his meaning required some ingenuity.

Fortunately for Strangwald, his intimates had become quite accustomed to this quirk. And his two close friends, Lord Prendergast and Mr Castleton, were so used to this peculiarity as to enable them, almost always, to understand the import of his words. Indeed, it was peculiarity that united the three friends, for although in looks, circumstances and temperament they had little in common, they were each possessed of eccentricities for which the rest of the world mocked them, and which they overlooked in each other. For Strangwald this was his strange speech affliction, for Christopher: his taste in attire, and for Mr Castleton: delusions of literary genius.

Christopher, well informed enough to be sure that the great French general was safely employed in waging war across the channel, correctly interpreted his friend's impassioned utterance. "So the old man's back in town?" he said, referring to Strangwald's father.

Strangwald was the second son of Admiral Strangwald, Earl of Sheverton, who had very high, and very unrealistic, hopes for his son. The Admiral was also given to treating his offspring to imperious decrees, given in a naval manner, that brooked no argument. Strangwald was frankly terrified of him, so much so, that in discussing him, he struggled for breath and could speak only in gasping half sentences. He nodded with a gulp at Christopher's words.

"Well, what's he been saying to get you all jittery this time then, Bertie? I know his arrival in town never signals good news, but you seem mighty put out this time. Have a seat and tell me all about it, dear fellow," continued Christopher kindly.

Strangwald sank into a chair and sat for a few moments in utter dejection, his shoulders drooping in defeat. Having composed himself a little, he uttered, cryptically, "Slave trade," with a sigh.

"Ah, I see," Christopher replied sympathetically. "Insisting you find employment, eh? Bad luck, old chap, but then I suppose you always knew this day would come."

The Admiral made no secret of the fact that he strongly disapproved of the dissipated lifestyle lived by the majority of the *beau monde*. In rather controversial thinking, he was strongly of the opinion that all men, gentlemen alike, should be gainfully employed, even if they could afford not to be.

"What's it to be, army officer?" Christopher asked.

Strangwald shook his head. "Hangman."

"Hmmm... hangman... hangman?" Christopher pondered, repeating the word to himself thoughtfully, uncertain what this referred to. His brow cleared, "The church, Bertie?" he asked, thinking that no worse fate could overcome one, than that of being a clergyman.

Strangwald shook his head, adding in further clarification, "Hangman, in the asylum."

"Ah," said Christopher, enlightened. "The law. Working in the city. You must be bamming me! Surely he knows you'd never be able to make a go of it!"

"No choice," Strangwald moaned. "General's orders. Napoleon, you know. No defecting."

Christopher pondered over this. "It's no good, you know. Can't possibly go through with it. Tell the old man so. Why, Geraint's a younger son and you don't see his old man insisting he get a job! You'll just have to tell him, nothing for it!

104

Deuced unpleasant, but there you are." He caught sight of Strangwald's face at this suggestion and knew that it was more likely that the real Napoleon would be seen congenially socialising at White's than that his friend would be able to carry out this suggestion. He sat in silent cogitation considering Strangwald's difficulty.

"Tell you what, got an idea," said Christopher unexpectedly. Strangwald looked at him with near-watery eyes, feeling his cause hopeless. "What we need," Christopher continued, "is a plan."

Strangwald eyed him expectantly, waiting for him to continue, a glimmer of hope in his eyes. When Christopher did not do so he said, "What's the plan?"

"Well, I can't be doing all the thinking, Bertie!" said Christopher defensively. "Just saying, that what we need is a plan. Only can't at this moment see what it should be."

Strangwald's shoulders sagged once again, and Christopher sat thinking hard. It was then that Mr Castleton, most fortuitously, erupted into the room saying, "Can you think of a rhyme for Axminster?"

Mr Castleton imagined himself a literary mastermind and, determined not to hide his light under a bushel, poured out volumes of the most execrable verse which his poor friends were at a loss to save themselves from having inflicted upon them. "I confess I'm quite stuck and it's holding up my lyrical poem on Mrs Poppleton's new carpet mid-flow. I have never seen more marvellous floor covering in all my life! You must go and see it. That said, I'm near tearing my hair out over this dashed elusive rhyme, because otherwise it promises to be my best piece yet." He broke off as he caught sight of his two friends' faces.

"Hello chaps, what's this?" Castleton said. "Looking very serious for so early in the day. What's to do?"

"Just the man!" said Christopher getting up to greet his friend. "Hallo, Clem. Good to see you. You're a downy one, got some brains. Just what we need right now."

"I'm quite moved by your tribute, Topher," said Castleton. "As I wrote in my recent lyrical poem, you remember

105

the one… read it to you last week…" Mr Castleton's enquiry met with vacant looks. He was very fond of quoting from his own work however, so continued helpfully, "A noggin's worth will save from dearth?" His friends were still looking blank. "Well, it's quite true. And anyway, I can't but agree that I do, as you say, have some little intelligence. Glad to help. What's the issue?"

"Oh, Bertie's in a pickle. The Admiral's back in town," explained Christopher.

"Is he, by jove? My sympathy, Bertie. Thought he was away on the war effort. Shame. What's he done this time?"

"Slave trade," Strangwald repeated dolefully

"No, really? Stuck on that again, is he?" said Castleton. "What's he want you to do, or hasn't he said? I'm sure we can find you something to do that will keep him off your back."

"By Jupiter, that's it!" exclaimed Christopher, clapping his hand across his knee. "Knew you'd be just the man to get us out of the suds. Clem, you're a genius! We must find you a job you *can* do Bertie. There must be something you're fit for." He turned to Castleton. "Admiral wants him to learn the law. Solicitor, you know."

"Good God! Can't do it, Bertie! It's plain as pikestaff you can't!" cried Castleton horrified. "You'd be no good at it. Well, what I mean is, you've got plenty of talents, but the law… just not the thing for you. Must tell the Admiral so."

"Well, so I've been telling him," said Christopher. "But you know how scared of the old man he is. Started quivering like a blancmange when I even suggested it! Nothing for it. Have to come up with a plan. Find him a different job, like you said."

"Yes, but what job? That's the question." The three of them sat in silence for some time, pondering this question but could discover no answer to the quandary.

"Tell you what," said Castleton after some time. "I'll write an ode about it. Bound to help solve the puzzle," and with that he whipped out his pocketbook and began composing this doubtful artwork.

Meanwhile, in another part of town, Mr Morley had awoken on the tail-end of the morning. He was feeling a little delicate having, the previous evening, studiously drowned his sorrows over the Incalculable's refusal. He was not in the sunniest of humours. The despair, forgotten in drunkenness and fitful sleep, returned to him with force. The morning post, when he read it over a very plain breakfast of dried toast, brought no comfort. Bills and demands for payment, now couched in menacing terms, met him and he could see no way to redeem them. Far more worrying was the pocketful of vowels which he discovered in his jacket from the previous night's gaming. While tradesmen's debts could be put off, debts of honour must be paid, and paid promptly.

Marrying an heiress had seemed his only chance to save himself from a debtors' prison and, now Lucretia had refused him, he felt more desperate than he had ever before felt in his life. Giving it some thought he decided that, having failed by fair means to secure the heiress, his only option now was to employ foul ones. And so he set about his plans. Matters being in such a grave state, Mr Morley could not afford to wait for the ideal time to launch an offensive. He must put measures in motion as soon as possible.

It was only two days later, after some preparation, that he put his plan into action. Lucretia was, not unusually, at a ball, but what *was* unusual was that she was not enjoying herself. The ballroom was hot, Christopher Prendergast was nowhere to be seen and for the first time she found an evening of such entertainment insipid, and wished herself elsewhere.

Miss Pycroft was in attendance, but she was noticeably not in spirits. Mrs Pycroft had persistently followed them both around the ball all evening, taking pleasure in relentlessly chastising her nervous daughter vocally and severely on her looks, her manners, indeed anything she found fault with, and there were many such things. Miss Pycroft, always eager to please and full of dutiful regard for her parents, was so cast down by these strictures that tears smarted in her eyes. This had vanished much of the bloom from her cheeks, which her mother rebuked her for all the more. Lucretia sincerely pitied Cecelia but did not know how to help her, and the sight of her friend's pain banished all the last vestiges of her enjoyment in the evening.

Returning from the dance floor after a quadrille Lucretia found, to her surprise, Lady Scallonsby at her elbow. Her gallant dance partner had gone to fetch her a refreshment, which gave Lady Scallonsby the opportunity to talk privately with Lucretia.

Lucretia was at first suspicious, for she could not imagine what that lady could possibly have to say to her. But her suspicion was swiftly replaced by gratitude, so much so that she wondered if she had, after all, misjudged the lady.

"Miss Lanyon, I am sorry to intrude upon you but I feel sure that you can help me. I am looking for Miss Pycroft's mother. I am not acquainted with that lady and I am desirous of discretion in searching her out."

Lucretia looked around her and realised that neither Cecilia nor her mother was anywhere to be seen. "Why, what can you mean? Where is Cecilia? Has something happened?" she asked anxiously.

"It is nothing of great moment. It is merely that she has the headache and is desirous of leaving the party. She implored me not to draw attention to the fact, however, and was desperate to leave the party unnoticed. She seems to be labouring under the impression that her headache was more likely to draw frustration from her mother than sympathy, and that to leave without any fuss would be the most likely way to avoid recrimination."

"Oh dear, poor Ceccy, how wretched she must feel!" exclaimed Lucretia.

"I tried," said Lady Scallonsby, "to assure her that her mother would surely be more worried about her health than any other considerations, but my assurances fell on deaf ears. She is terribly agitated and looks as white as a sheet, poor dear! I very much feared that she was going to be sick. I understand that they came with a larger party and have not brought their own carriage, so I have called mine around and settled her into it. I must find Mrs Pycroft as soon as can be, so she can take Miss

Pycroft home and settle her into her bed. Only now I realise that I do not know the lady by sight."

"Oh, how kind of you, Lady Scallonsby!" Lucretia's animosity towards that lady was forgotten in her gratitude for the compassion she had shown her friend. "I must go to her at once! I'm sure you will not spread this information about, but her mother does not generally treat her with much kindness. Poor Ceccy, she must be feeling so miserable! Oh, I knew she was not looking well! How much I now wish I had taken better care of her! I beg you will allow me to take Cecilia home in her mother's stead, and I would be most grateful if you could add to your kindness by informing her mother, and my aunt, of what has passed. Please, I beg of you, lead me to Cecilia at once."

They left the house hastily, and Lucretia soon found herself stepping into an unfamiliar carriage in every expectation of finding an indisposed Cecilia within. It came as a very nasty surprise to find, instead, Mr Morley leaning leisurely back against the seat, a very ugly, self-satisfied look upon his face.

At Lucretia's arrival, Morley was startled into jumping up from his seat; Lady Scallonsby had extricated his quarry from the party faster than he had anticipated. He had planned on being at the ready near the door of the carriage to stop Lucretia from escaping when she stepped inside but, having no notion that she would arrive so soon, he had not yet got himself into position. He leapt forwards swiftly as Lucretia turned to step hurriedly out of the carriage, and Mr Morley just managed to grab her before she could put any distance between them. He caught her necklace as he lunged, breaking the wire, and the pearls fell about on the ground with quiet tick, ticking sounds.

They were just outside the carriage door now. Lucretia knew herself to be out of danger. "Get your hands off me or I'll scream and all these men will come running to my aid," she said, looking towards a number of coachmen milling in the vicinity. "What a commotion there will be if I should do so, and everyone will know what an odious man you are! If this incident becomes known, no one in the world will receive you. But if you let me go now," she bargained with him, "I will quietly return to the party and this matter need not be mentioned again. Now, sir, you must see you have no choice."

Mr Morley chuckled unpleasantly and with a smugness that made Lucretia's blood run cold. "On the contrary, my sweet," he said with a malicious smile, "you will find all these men have become unusually deaf this evening, while their pockets are unusually heavy, if you catch my drift. Come now, admit I am cleverer than you thought. It is a good trait in a husband, you know. Now step quietly into the carriage like a sensible girl, it is really much more dignified that being bodily flung into it, which is what will happen if you don't do as I say."

Lucretia appeared to concede defeat, and turned as if to get into the carriage. "Now, that's better," he said, shuffling her seemingly acquiescent form towards the step. "I know this is not what you would choose but you will come to like me well enough, and I have no doubt that when you forgive me we will deal extremely well together."

He broke off, letting out a sudden howl, for Lucretia had stamped on his foot with all her might. But despite the resulting throbbing ache in his left lower extremity he did not slacken his hold upon her. Lucretia winced in pain for his fingers were digging into her arms. Morley caught sight of the coachmen's derisive faces as they sniggered at Lucretia's retaliation. He did not like to appear ridiculous, and flushed in humiliation. He felt his anger begin to mount and tightened his grip on Lucretia still further.

"You are hurting me, sir," squeaked Lucretia. "I beg you will loosen your grip a little and I will go with you with good grace." This was said with a composure and courage she was far from feeling. She was a good deal frightened by this point, but she was also angry. So very, very angry that it helped her to bury her fear.

Neither of the two antagonists noticed a gentleman approaching along the cobbles. This was Christopher Prendergast, walking jauntily along the street, whistling to himself and quite forgetting to mince in his carefully practised manner. He was on his way to meet a party of friends for a convivial evening away from the restraints of polite society, and he was in a good mood, for he had just that day received his new boots from Hobey's, which boasted no fewer than five tassels apiece. He felt sure that they were a triumph and looked forward to showing them off. In expectation of this he had had them shined by Horeston, his excellent valet, and looked down appreciatively at them as he walked, in expectation of seeing his reflection in the polished leather.

As he turned the corner into the street where the scuffle was taking place, he heard Morley's cry and looked up, distracted from admiring his new footwear by this yelp. He could see the tussle up ahead and knew a gentleman's dislike of getting involved in a private scene. He could make out a tall woman with clusters of golden curls, in an altercation with a gentleman whom he knew only by reputation, and a most unsavoury one at that. It became very much apparent that the lady, and she was most assuredly a lady, was being forced into the carriage against her will, and he knew that it behoved him to intervene.

Mr Morley had just then loosened his grip on Lucretia's arms, feeling sure that she would now agree to go with him quietly into the carriage. He had once again underestimated his adversary, for, no sooner had she felt his grip slacken, than she wrenched one of her arms free and, curling her hand into a fist, landed a powerful punch across the side of Morley's face. Christopher was impressed at the power and aim of the blow. He had no notion that it was possible for a woman to show such talent. Indeed, most of the men of his acquaintance lacked the science and bottom that this lady had just displayed.

At the punch, Mr Morley recoiled, but did not let go of Lucretia, though he felt his face, and his pride, smart. He knew an ungentlemanly urge to slap her, but could not do so without letting go, which he was not prepared to do. Lucretia had put up a good fight but his strength was superior: she was overpowered and he was winning in his bid to force her into the carriage.

Christopher knew it was time to intervene. He sighed over the possible damage to his new boots, but it could not be helped. Coming up behind the two combatants, he politely tapped Morley on the shoulder and, when he turned round, sank a bruising blow to the other side of his face.

"I believe," said Christopher calmly and with deliberate formality, "that you cannot have noticed that the lady does not wish to go with you, sir. I feel sure that, now this fact has been pointed out, you will release her and discontinue this assault upon her person."

"Damn you!" bit out Morley, "this is none of your business, you meddlesome fool. Now go away!"

"I regret, sir, that as a gentleman, this unfortunate incident has now become my business," returned Christopher in unaccustomed dignified and haughty accents, which he very swiftly undermined by saying: "Now let go your hold upon her you damned cow-hearted dog! Or I will be forced to draw your cork, something which I am not in the least desirous of doing in front of a lady."

"Draw my cork? I'd like to see you do so!" said Morley, feeling nothing of the sort. He was no pugilist and the merest glance at the interfering gentleman made it clear that, even had he the least talent in the ring, he was no match for the athletic form of Viscount Prendergast. He feared that any attempt to engage him would result in far more than a bleeding nose. Furthermore, he was, despite all his bravado, a coward, and nothing filled him with greater fear than the idea of a physical fight with another man. He met Christopher's gaze, which he saw was full of scorn and determination. Christopher lifted a questioning eyebrow, daring Mr Morley to retaliate.

Morley hesitated for a second, and then his terror of physical pain, the reminders of which he could feel in his cheeks and foot, overtook his humiliation. "Oh, very well," he said pettishly, letting go of Lucretia's arm. He climbed into the coach, slamming the door, and shouted out of the window at his coachman, "Well come on, you idiot, set the horses to! Don't keep me waiting!"

Lucretia, now free, turned to see her rescuer and suffered a jolt as she looked up into the face of Viscount Prendergast. She could have screamed with mortification to be found, by her beloved, in such a situation. She would rather it had been anyone but him.

"Miss Lanyon!" exclaimed Christopher, recognising the damsel in distress with some surprise. He then waited for the inevitable faints, tears, and hysterics which he knew would follow. If his mother could find herself overcome in such a way by a burnt pigeon before a party, surely the extent of emotion this incident would provoke would be of monstrous proportions. But he was taken aback to find that Lucretia spoke in a voice which only shook a little.

"Lord Prendergast, I must thank you for rescuing me." She wiped a few tears from her eyes courageously, but showed no disposition to fall into hysterics. To his own surprise, he was rather touched by her fortitude and now sincerely wished to help her if he could.

"You must excuse my tears," Lucretia apologised. "Only I am so very angry. To be found in such a situation is mortifying in the extreme! What *must* you think of me? But I have been most shockingly tricked, I assure you. Which I suppose makes it all the worse - what a silly dupe I have been to have been gulled in such a way. You will give me, if you please, just a moment to compose myself and think what I must do now."

She took a few deep breaths, pulling her nerves together, and looked about her. "Oh, how vexatious!" she said stamping her foot. "My dress has been torn and it was so very beautiful, quite one of my favourites. And oh," she cried, seeing the pearls which were strewn about her feet on the street and glittered in the lamplight, "my necklace is ruined. What will my aunt and uncle say, for they gave it to me as a present? Oh, I cannot tell them of this, they will be so shocked! But what will I say if they ask where it is?" she gabbled on, her mind all in turmoil.

"Now, now, never mind the necklace. The veriest trifle to be sure, and it can be easily replaced. With the dress now..." he said, picking up his eyeglass and regarding the gown through it, "well, that is a different story. How *did* they get the skirt to hang like, that I wonder...? I have never seen anything like it.

Marvellous," he pronounced, entirely distracted from their unusual circumstances.

"But only look at your neckcloth, Lord Prendergast," exclaimed Lucretia in great consternation. "It is ruined beyond recognition and I'm sure it took hours to perfect. Your valet will never forgive me for such a tragedy!"

"My valet!" he expostulated. "I would never leave such a delicate operation to him, no matter how good at his job Horeston is! I tied it myself!"

"Oh! Of course," said Lucretia, mortified to have offended him. "Then that makes it all the worse! Oh, how will you ever forgive me for involving you in this sorry incident and reducing you to such a dishevelled appearance?! How terribly sorry I am!"

"There, there," he said much struck by Lucretia's understanding of the importance of dress, even at such a moment. "It is a shame, but after all, it is easily replaced," he added kindly, signalling his forgiveness. "And, after all, it isn't your fault we've ended up in this situation." This recalled him to the fact that they were standing in the street and why they were there.

He coughed self-consciously at having been distracted into bemoaning the injury to his neck tie, which indeed seemed to pale somewhat in importance when considered against Miss Lanyon's current predicament. "As important as it is," he said, "we cannot be forever standing here talking of the damage to our attire. I must think what to do with you...." he mused, while Lucretia looked up at him expectantly. "I'll have to take you home and then return to tell your aunt what has happened. Nothing for it. Naturally, it's not the thing for you to be unchaperoned in a gentleman's company, but I can't very well return you to the ball looking such a fright, can I?" It is not to be supposed that Lucretia would ever make any demure against her idol's opinion, so naturally she nodded humbly.

He hailed a cab and accompanied Lucretia to Grosvenor Square. "Been thinking about what you said," he announced as the cab set off along the way. "And well... you'll have to tell Lady Rutland about what's gone on. I mean... it looks dashed singular, your leaving the party and getting taken home by me. Can't expect her not to demand an explanation. Clever woman, is Lady Rutland, not one not to notice these things," he said sagely. "Thing is... no need to get in a pucker about it. What I mean is... she's not going to be angry with you. She'll be in a rage with Morley certainly... by gad he's a dashed loose fish! But I'd no idea he'd stoop to this!... But no reason to think she'll be angry with you. Not your fault after all," he explained to Lucretia, stumbling over the words but prompted by kindness to try and allay her fears.

"All the same," Christopher continued, "best not tell anyone else about this. In fact, the fewer people who know about it the better. I mean, *we* know you did nothing wrong, but there's bound to be people who'll say otherwise, given half the chance," he advised. It was a novel experience for him to be giving advice, he reflected to himself; he was not altogether sure how he felt about it. "And you've no fear from my quarter on that count, I'll keep quiet about it."

"Thank you, Lord Prendergast, you are very kind. And of course I'll do whatever you think best. I really cannot thank you enough for coming to my rescue. How marvellous you were too! How Mr Morley quaked in his boots!" she sighed in admiration. Christopher blushed. After this exchange, the earlier events were not alluded to again.

"What was the style of your cravat this evening, before it became so crumpled?" Lucretia asked. "I know Mr Silksley is much taken with the Waterfall, although I must say that when I look at Brummell wearing the Waterfall, Mr Silksley's version does seem to deviate on a number of points, but then that could just be my fancy, I'm no expert on such things... I know that Alvanley prefers the Mathematical, though he refuses to allow me into the secret of how it's done! For all I'm no authority in gentlemen's neckties, I do find them fascinating; they can be so intricate, so elegant. Or, in the inexpert hand, so poorly conceived!" she laughed. Christopher laughed too.

"I know! Did you see Cossington's the other day? It was more neck-mangle than necktie," Christopher chuckled. "But you do yourself an injustice; you have a good eye for such things. Silksley's Waterfall is not altogether up to the mark, although it takes a discerning eye to notice the imperfections in it. I favour the Intricate or the Oriental myself. Took me a deuced lot of time to perfect 'em, but now I flatter myself that I can pull them off rather well," he said with ill-concealed pride.

"Lord Prendergast," asked Lucretia shyly, "I was wondering if I could ask your opinion on a matter of fashion. Only you have quite the best understanding of dress and style of anyone I know, and I would value your opinion greatly."

Christopher was moved by this accolade, for he was not immune to flattery, especially when it concerned the talent he most prided himself on. "But of course, Miss Lanyon. Naturally, I am at your service."

"Well, it is about the ribbons on this dress. Madame Charabelle declares that they are all the rage, and my aunt thinks they look very well, but I cannot but help thinking that they are a little *deedy*. What do you think?"

He scrutinised the offending appurtenances seriously. "Why, I do believe you are quite right. They are a little *de trop,* I fancy. But only a little, certainly not vulgar."

And so they passed the short journey to Grosvenor Square. Christopher saw her into the house and then took himself back to the ball to inform Lady Rutland of her niece's sudden departure from the party. He had never spent so pleasant a ten minutes in a woman's company before. A very sensible young lady, that Miss Lanyon, he reflected to himself. Not quite in the common way of females. And although Christopher's restricted experience of the female gender somewhat reduced the force of this compliment, it was nevertheless the highest of praise from one who actively went out of his way to avoid the breed at all. He had never before been called upon to act as a hero in a piece and, though he tried to tell himself that it had been a sad inconvenience, marring his evening's enjoyment, there was certainly a part of him who had found the experience not altogether unpleasant.

He did not, however, relish overmuch the job of informing Lady Rutland of the night's events. She was a formidable woman, even to men who stood brave in the presence of such dragons as Lady Castlereagh. To men who were always nervous in the company of women, she represented a Medea, or some such formidable woman from mythology that one would never like to meet (Christopher had never really applied himself to classical learning). Nevertheless, he braved the interview and felt that he had brushed along tolerably well.

"Psst," he said, coming up behind Lady Rutland, making the unsuspecting lady jump a little.

"Lord Prendergast?" she returned in some astonishment.

Christopher's eyes darted around suspiciously, which served to draw attention to his conversation rather than effect discretion. He leaned towards her conspiratorially. "Er… um…" he stuttered, unsure how to go on, and acutely conscious of Lady Rutland's somewhat indignant regard. "Owing to some, erm… surprising events," he said in a whisper that was more carrying than he imagined, "I've had to take Miss Lanyon home." Most fortunately there was nobody within earshot. All the same, Lady Rutland drew him discreetly further away from the guests positioned nearest to them.

Christopher's eyes continued to flit around the room and, owing to his towering shirt points which prevented him from being able to move his head, it was necessary for him to wiggle his shoulders from side to side to gain any reasonable visibility. Lady Rutland, although far from famed for her sense of humour, could not help but be amused by the odd appearance he gave off. Christopher leaned in to whisper to her: "I'd go and see her if I were you. Only better do it discreetly, you know. Smoky business, best if it don't get about, if you catch my drift."

Lady Rutland lifted an eyebrow and regarded him piercingly. To his surprise and relief, however, she did not demand further enlightenment, made no demur and adroitly managed to leave the party without drawing the least attention to the act.

"Got herself into a scrape, has she?" she asked him as they left. Christopher shifted uncomfortably. "Well, no doubt she'll tell me all about it. I fancy I have you to thank for extricating her from it. I'm sure I'm very grateful, although I don't know what for just yet. At any rate, you are welcome to call upon us to find out how she is faring tomorrow, and then I'll be able to thank you more properly and knowledgeably. Good night, Lord Prendergast. Don't get too bosky or the watch will have you, you know," she said, demonstrating a superior understanding of the recreations of young gentlemen. But it was said with a wink and not the least severity.

Not a bad woman after all, thought Christopher. And certainly a knowing one. He had made a discovery that evening, a very surprising one in fact: that not all women were intolerable after all. And he set belatedly off for his evening's entertainment, feeling very well pleased with himself.

CHAPTER EIGHT

Lucretia was relieved to find that Lady Rutland, when she entered her niece's room, entered with a face that held neither reproach nor disappointment. "Well, Lucretia, what an interesting time you appear to have had. Perhaps you ought to tell me what has gone on," advised Lady Rutland.

"Oh, did Lord Prendergast not tell you?" asked Lucretia, fearful that when her aunt found out about the evening's events she would be angry with her.

"I fancy that advising me of your sudden departure from the ball used up all of young Prendergast's eloquence," said Lady Rutland dryly.

Lucretia felt her hackles rising in defence of her rescuer. "It is entirely thanks to the brave offices of Lord Prendergast that you find me safe and well, Aunt," she said, trying to keep the indignation out of her voice. For once she had her aunt's full attention as she explained the evening's events, skating over the more unladylike parts of the adventure.

"Good God!" said Lady Rutland, deeply shocked, when Lucretia had finished her narrative. "It is too bad! Everyone knows Mr Morley has a terrible reputation but to sink so low, so brazen and wicked, how could any gentleman ever do such a thing? After all, his antecedents are above reproach, so how he could have turned out such a villain I can't imagine. Did he hurt you?" she asked, recollected from her indignation and snobbery, and displaying an unusual degree of solicitude.

"No, Aunt, thankfully you find me unharmed and quite well. Though it would have been quite otherwise had it not been for the kindness of Lord Prendergast," finished Lucretia. But by this time her aunt was barely attending to her, ready now to impart her own musings on the events.

"As shocking as it is," Lady Rutland announced, "one cannot be altogether surprised at Mr Morley stooping to such things. I confess I'm surprised at Lady Scallonsby though! Such a poisonous woman! But I would never have imagined she would involve herself in such a plot!"

"I have been a silly fool, Aunt, I hope you can forgive me."

"Forgive you, Cressy?" said her aunt focussing once again upon her niece. "How can you be so silly? Of course you will be more careful in future, I'm sure. But enough said, let us put this sorry incident behind us."

She continued however, despite her assertion that the discussion on the matter had come to an end, but she was speaking more to herself than Lucretia. "The two of them would be well served if they were found out in their villainy. They would be entirely cut out of society for it. Nevertheless, there would be talk... yes, certainly there would be talk... No, I think it would be unwise to take such a course. Which is not to say that we may not see some benefits from the incident," she said cryptically. "Yes, it may well be that the whole episode will have very favourable repercussions."

"And it just goes to show," Lady Rutland said to Lucretia, after considering these issues, "how much young ladies stand in need of male protection. What you must do, Lucretia, is find a safe, protective husband who can shield you from such persecution in the future."

Both ladies sighed, one dreaming of Lucretia being led down the aisle to her second born, the marriage of the season; the other dreaming of a beautiful future with Christopher Prendergast as her life partner.

Lady Rutland made good use of the night's dealings by a recitation of the events to her son, which she had no hesitation in doing at the first opportunity. Watching his face as he listened, she thought to herself with satisfaction that it would certainly be the end of his deplorable association with Lady Scallonsby.

The next day, the two gentlemen who had figured in the previous night's piece awoke somewhat worse for the wear. Mr

Morley had once again been drowning his sorrows, and Christopher was suffering the inevitable consequences of a convivial evening spent in the company of friends.

Christopher remembered his invitation to call in on the Rutlands that day to find out how Miss Lanyon was going on and to receive thanks from Lady Rutland. He was very much inclined to shy away from the visit for, while he had made the discovery that not all women were repulsive, this did not predispose him to add to this discovery the wish to become more intimate with any of their kind. Nevertheless, an invitation from Lady Rutland was akin to a summons and to ignore it would lay him open to that formidable lady's censure, a danger which he was in no hurry to court.

He left the visit until the afternoon, optimistic that the ladies would be out. On his way to Grosvenor Square he came across Mr Strangwald.

"Where are you off to, Topher?" Strangwald asked.

"To call upon Lady Rutland," he answered airily. "I say," he said, struck with sudden genius, "why don't you come along, Bertie?"

"Delighted to accompany you anywhere, old fellow. Only, you don't think the General will be there do you?" Strangwald looked around with a hunted expression. "His spies are everywhere, can't be too careful," he whispered furtively. "Besides which, he's great friends with Lady Rutland... But," he stopped, suddenly arrested by another thought, "why are you going to see Lady Rutland anyway? Not at all the sort of thing you usually do. Shouldn't think it'll be much fun. Better go for a walk in the park instead. Watch the elephants, very amusing this time of year."

Christopher did not stop to unravel the meaning of this strange comment. "Can't do it. Said I'd look in at Grosvenor Square. Lady Rutland asked me to," he added in explanation, not wishful of expanding upon this. But Strangwald took this answer without demur and they set off arm in arm down the street.

Christopher, having hoped to avoid an interview with the ladies of the house, was foiled by timing, for they were just then descending the stairs. If he had arrived five minutes later, he thought ruefully, he would have missed them altogether and he could have left his card and be done with the whole thing.

"Lord Prendergast, how charming of you to call upon us," Lady Rutland condescended. "But I'm afraid you have caught us just as we were leaving. I am going to visit an old friend and mustn't be late. She is quite elderly and becomes greatly agitated if one does not arrive quite when one says one is going to," she said, stepping into the waiting carriage. "So I can't stop to talk to you. Lucretia's going for a walk in the park, but you see she is quite well. Anyway, mustn't be late," she said, having the horses put to.

"Hello, Lord Prendergast," said Lucretia shyly. "Have you come to call upon us? How very kind. I'm sorry that you find us going out, I should so like to have spoken with you. Perhaps you and your friend might care to accompany Miss Pycroft and me to the Park. We would be very glad of your escort."

Christopher did not know how to extricate himself politely from this invitation and was further frustrated by Mr Strangwald who, in addition to being very odd, added to this vice that he was incorrigibly polite, whatever the circumstances.

"Mr Strangwald," Strangwald said, introducing himself with a bow to the two ladies. "Very pleased to make your acquaintance. Naturally it would be a pleasure to accompany you anywhere," he continued, offering Miss Pycroft his arm.

"Be honoured, of course," agreed Christopher hollowly, squeezing Strangwald's other arm painfully in rebuke. Strangwald looked at him in some surprise but, aside from a reproachful look, did not respond to the gesture.

"Be an interesting trip," continued Strangwald loquaciously, having no notion of hiding his fantastical world from those he conversed with. "All the wonderful beasts escaped from the Tower yesterday and are wreaking havoc in the park. Should be quite a spectacle to see a tiger snapping at Lady Castlereagh's skirts." He grinned at the vision. Lucretia and Cecilia looked at him in considerable surprise. They knew that the Tower was home to the Royal Menagerie, for they had both visited the sight and wondered at the amazing collection of animals housed there. But they thought it most unlikely that the beasts would have been allowed to escape, let alone frolic unchallenged through London's busiest park.

Seeing this, Christopher felt that some explanation was due. "Ah, don't mind Strangwald. He lives in a different world from everyone else, quite a make-believe one, in fact. You get used to it after a time."

Lucretia looked amused. Cecelia giggled, not unkindly, and eyed Strangwald with interest.

And so the four set off towards Hyde Park, where it was the fashion to be seen promenading between the hours of five and six in the evening. It was a balmy day and it seemed that the whole of the *beau monde* had had the same idea. Cecilia, who was always a dawdling walker, fell behind, accompanied by the ever-accommodating Mr Strangwald who was divulging,

"I'm a foundling, you know. My real father was some sort of crown prince of one of those obscure European countries, forget which one... went into exile after some civil uprising... you know the lower classes, never happy with their lot... Anyway, he was hiding out here in England but had to go on the run again following some scandal or other. Now what was the story?" he mused. "Some say he murdered my mother, but I don't believe a word of it. Others say it was due to a duel over a lady, my mother having already been killed in the revolution. Whatever the truth of it, my father having been in such a rush to flee the country that he quite forgot me; I was left quite alone in the world. My nurse put me in a basket and left me on Napoleon's doorstep. He took me in, devilishly kind of him, I suppose... But he's not used me kindly all the same..."

Looking back, Lucretia saw Cecelia was listening, rapt. These were just the sorts of tall stories she most liked to hear about and she could not be better entertained had Mrs Radcliffe been expounding her latest plot to her.

Lucretia walked along at Christopher's side, feeling suddenly self-conscious. "I do hope you did not mind accompanying us to the park, Lord Prendergast. I fancy you may have had other plans, I would be sorry to have inconvenienced you."

This was said with such genuine concern that he could not but respond politely, "Not at all. Pleasure." He stopped, not knowing what to say next. He very much feared that she would start talking about the events of the previous evening, and he worried that time for reflection may have awoken sensibilities which she had not shown last night. He walked uncomfortably at her side, expecting every moment to be faced with tears and impassioned speeches. But it was no such thing.

"I say, Lord Prendergast, that's a very splendid walking stick! I have never noticed it with you before," Lucretia said, admiring this accessory. It had a silver eagle at its head with emeralds for eyes which glimmered as they caught the sunlight. It could not have been a happier remark, for Christopher had only that morning purchased this item and was giving it its first outing.

"I do think it's rather handsome," he said, flattered, letting out a sigh of relief at the turn the conversation was taking.

"The emeralds quite match the buttons of your waistcoat," Lucretia observed.

Christopher, having not yet noticed this, looked down and saw that she was right. "By Jupiter, they do as well! Funny, I hadn't noticed it before. I was quite right when I said you had a discerning eye." Lucretia blushed with pleasure at this tribute.

"Oh dear, do look at poor Mr Towford!" she exclaimed as they approached this gentleman on the path. "I see he has not been persuaded to loosen his corset, even for a walk in the park." Towford had most unwisely decided to take the air in his usual apparel. His form was really more suited to sitting comfortably at home and his chest heaved from the exertion of supporting his immense form on his legs, sweat dripping down his reddened face.

"Your... servant... Miss... Lanyon," Towford said as he passed them, taking deep gasping breaths between each word.

Christopher looked back at him after he had gone by and remarked, "Certainly, he is struggling in that corset but I must ask him where he bought his waistcoat. Really, an exceptional cut! And it takes an artiste to achieve that with such an uninspiring form." He seemed almost on the point of turning round to follow Mr Towford at that moment and put the question to him and then recollected how rude this would be. "Erm well, perhaps I can ask him another time."

Lucretia smiled at him saying, "But you have no need of such a cut for a waistcoat to become you, Lord Prendergast." Looking down at her he noticed for the first time that she was a very attractive woman.

The two fashion-lovers turned to a discussion of Christopher's cravat pin, which had a matching emerald and nestled most comfortably in his elegantly tied neckcloth. Thus they passed a very pleasant walk in the park, until they came across Isabella walking with Miss Altringham and accompanied, to Christopher's disgust, by Mr Morley.

It was a few moments before Lucretia, Christopher and Morley knew quite how to act. Isabella, unconscious of the tension in the air, stepped into the breach. "Well, is not this delightful to bump into such company?"

She looked at Lucretia exultantly, evidently proud to be found with Mr Morley in attendance. She had accosted this gentleman during the course of her walk and persuaded him to walk with her, exerting all her ingenuity to prevent him from escaping. She felt that she had triumphed over Lucretia in winning the gentleman's affections and was not above gloating, even to those she counted as friends. "Do all of you join our party, and let us walk together and enjoy this beautiful day!" Isabella exclaimed.

This was a suggestion that met with almost universal disapproval. It was doubtful whether Mr Morley or Lucretia was less pleased to be forced into the company of the other. Christopher felt the awkwardness of being in the company of one whom he had only the previous evening caught in the most reprehensible act and whom he had had cause to physically incommode. Even Miss Pycroft was unhappy with the arrangement because she heartily disliked Lady Isabella and, moreover, was very much enjoying the comfortable chat she was having with Mr Strangwald.

But none of them had any idea how to stop politely the merging together of the two parties. They were not helped by Miss Altringham, who had no opinion at all, or Mr Strangwald, whose naturally sociable disposition made him ever amenable to further additions to his party. And so, the two groups continued along together until excuses could be made for the unhappy companions to return home.

Lucretia avoided meeting Morley's eye. She was very angry with him, but could not express this without drawing suspicion from the others that something had happened. She therefore continued a studied conversation with Christopher. But to her annoyance she found that she no longer had the gentleman's attention. Christopher was not at all pleased to find his sister in the company of Morley, and he was trying to convey his disapproval to his sister by odd jerks of his head and significant looks.

"Why, Christopher, what can you mean by twitching your head around like that? Perhaps you have finally met your match in those shirt points? Or is your necktie, even more extravagant than usual, I note, tickling your chin?" Isabella asked sweetly, pretending not to understand him.

"Er, um…" stuttered Christopher.

Grinning at her brother's discomfort, Isabella turned to Lucretia to further spread her brand of unpleasant glee. "Ah, Cressy, Mr Morley was just telling me the most amusing story about a secret rendezvous." She lowered her voice conspiratorially. "To be sure, it is a little shocking but you won't mind that," she said with a wink. Lucretia looked at her in considerable surprise. Meeting Lucretia's eyes blandly, Isabella laid a possessive hand on Morley's saying, "Now, Everard, would not Cressy find it a most amusing tale?"

But she too had lost the attention of her beau who said vaguely, "Oh, er, of course," eyeing Christopher with dislike, while at the same time trying to steer himself so as to put as much distance as possible between himself and the exceptional boxer.

Strangwald most unfortunately fuelled the fire of Morley's anger by breaking into the conversation and commenting on Mr Morley's matching empurpled eyes. "Been in the dragon's lair, Morley?" Strangwald asked sympathetically. "I fear you have not fared well against your fiery opponent. Bad luck. Looks dashed painful!"

Morley's face flushed the colour of his bruises, and he glared at Christopher with enmity made all the more potent by his smarting pride. But he looked away hastily in deepening embarrassment on seeing the contempt that was very evident in Christopher's eyes. How much he wanted to make Christopher pay for putting a spoke in the wheel of his well-laid plans! How much he wanted to teach the impudent cub a lesson!

"I think it is time I took you home, Bella," said Christopher glaring at his sister's hand on Mr Morley's arm. "I seem to remember something about mother saying she needed you to accompany her to visit Aunt Lavender this afternoon."

Isabella sent her brother a deeply hostile look. "Nonsense! What are you talking about, Christopher? I'm quite sure mother said nothing of the sort."

"Perhaps you didn't hear her. I did. Said you needed to be back. I'll take you home now. No more fuss, Isabella, we don't want to upset mother, do we?"

Morley saw, with malicious enjoyment, how much his friendship with Lady Isabella annoyed her brother, and derived what small revenge he could from it. Without realising it, he saved the company from a nasty scene by delighting Isabella in suddenly flirting outrageously with her. So pleased was she that he seemed so amorous towards her, when he was previously somewhat reluctant to return her advances, that she was quite distracted from having a histrionic argument with her brother.

"Fair lady," said Morley, leaning over her hand and dropping a kiss upon it, "it seems our paths must here diverge, alas! And so soon. Every hour that we are apart will seem like a misery. I shall go to the river and stare in its waters that I might remember the blue of your eyes."

It was a small revenge, but he must use the full force of his ingenuity to extricate him from his financial difficulties and could not afford to get caught up in planning an elaborate revenge.

"Come on, Bella, Bertie, let's go!" said Christopher.

"Actually, Topher, I'll accompany Miss Pycroft and Miss Lanyon home. Not polite to leave them, you know," said Strangwald genially.

"Will you be dining in Mount Street tonight, Lord Prendergast?" Lucretia asked, as she took her leave of him, adding, "I am dining with your mother and sister tonight, before going to the theatre."

To his own surprise, Christopher found himself saying that he would be dining at home that evening, but he could not have articulated why on earth he should have done such a thing. Strangwald looked at him in surprise, as he thought they had made plans to dine together that evening. Christopher avoided his eye and Strangwald, not particularly a noticing sort of fellow, assumed that he must have been mistaken in their engagement.

And so the party took leave of each other, Mr Morley setting off on his own, Miss Altringham and Isabella accompanied by Christopher, and Lucretia and Cecilia accompanied by Mr Strangwald, who now seemed to be on the friendliest of terms with Miss Pycroft.

Having seen Miss Altringham to her door, Christopher took the first opportunity to give voice to his disapproval of his sister's intimacy with Mr Morley.

"Thunder and turf, Bella! He's not at all the thing! And it's dashed foolish to be seen walking around with him practically unchaperoned. As for encouraging his attentions, well, you'll put a stop to that right now! It's like I've always said, you've a damn sight more hair than wit. Take it from me, because I know about these things," he said rather self-importantly and, in an imperious manner which put his sister's back up all the more, said, "I forbid you to have anything to do with him."

"Forbid me! You've no right to forbid me to do anything! It's none of your business whom I choose to be friends with. And you don't know what you're talking about. You think I'm some pudding-brained know-nothing! But I'm not! I know more than you think. I know Mr Morley has a sad reputation. He's freely admitted to me that he's done some naughty things in the past, but he's very penitent and feels most badly about them. And now he's quite a reformed character, only no one will give him a chance to prove it. Which is most unchristian, and I will not be like that, no matter what you say," she said petulantly.

"What a goose you are, Bella!" scoffed her brother. "He is not at all the type of man you should be associating with. And if you'll not listen to me, you will listen to mama on this subject, for when she gets wind of it, she'll not like it any more than I do."

Had he been better informed about the psychology of women, he would have realised how ill-conceived his approach had been. For, in alluding to disrepute in Mr Morley's past, he only added to this gentleman's allure. And nothing could so flame the passion of a young lady who imagined herself to be in love, than to tell her that her love was forbidden. Ignorant of this, Christopher deposited his sister back into his mother's care feeling very virtuous, confident that he had acted above and beyond his brotherly duties.

"I'll be dining with you tonight after all, mother," he said as an after-thought as he left the room, and he heard the door shut on a tirade against ungrateful, rude, and disagreeable sons who make it their business to overset the sensibilities and nerves of their poor mothers by changing their plans every five minutes.

When he arrived that evening, Lucretia was already at the house and listening to Isabella enthusing about a thrilling new novel she had just read, which had launched its authoress into overnight fame.

"Oh, but you must read it, Cressy," she insisted. "It is quite the most exciting thing I have ever read! Only think, the heroine is kidnapped within the first three chapters, and by a very handsome but very wicked man who plans to lock her away in a dark tower and steal all her money. Just imagine how romantic and exciting that would be! It quite makes my life seem so very dull."

Catching this as he entered the room, Christopher was moved to interject, "Why, of all the cork-brained things to say! Trust you to think something so silly, Bella. You wouldn't find it exciting, you'd be terrified and scream and scream until the poor fellow threw you out of the carriage in disgust! Furthermore, such villains are never handsome, they're always craggy-looking unwashed fellows with crooked teeth and breath that smells of ale. And, if you thought about it at all, you'd consider that to be bundled unceremoniously into a carriage, even in the dead of night, as I've no doubt the heroine was, is a most undignified occurrence. Imagine what it would do to the skirts of your dress! Why they'd be irrevocably crumpled and any decent hairstyle would be utterly ruined," he exclaimed with a shudder. "There's nothing in the least romantic about being all dishevelled and shabby."

He caught Miss Lanyon's eye at this and she twinkled at him with an appreciative smile as they shared this private joke. The Earl caught this exchange of looks and was bemused. Something had happened which had brought about this special accord, and he would give a good deal to know what it was. Whatever, his son seemed to be in a good way towards developing a veritable tendre for the beautiful Miss Lanyon. He wondered where it would end. He would not have put the two of them together, but if that was the way the wind was blowing, he could have nothing to say against the match.

Isabella was scandalised by her brother's unromantic portrayal of the kidnapping. "Who could think of one's dress being crumpled at such a time, Christopher! Even you, with your obsession with your appearance could not show so much insensibility. There really are more important things in life than apparel!"

"You're in error, Bella, there is nothing that matters more," Christopher said seriously, noticing a speck of dust on his sleeve and brushing it carefully away. "It is what sets us apart from the milkmaid and the boots. And if you are ever the subject of a kidnapping attempt, I beg you will remember that or you will find yourself in more of a scrape than you bargained for." And with this sage remark he turned to talk to his father, leaving his sister open-mouthed and lost for words.

Further consequences of the failed kidnapping attempt were seen at the theatre that night. Lady Scallonsby was sat with her party across the auditorium from the Prendergast's box, and had an excellent view of the Prendergast party arriving. She suffered a jolt when she saw Lucretia, who she expected to be far away with Mr Morley by now, and a further jolt when she noticed Arnold Rutland at her elbow at just that moment.

"She looks very beautiful tonight, my cousin, does she not?" said Arnold into her ear.

"Yes," returned Lady Scallonsby faintly, as she caught Lucretia's eye. Lucretia bowed to her, with great pride and dignity, a mannerism that she had learned from her aunt and perfected admirably.

"You have been very stupid, Maria, and it has cost my cousin. I warned her not to make an enemy of you, but I had no idea that your spite would lead you to such lengths."

"Spite?" she said with a tinkling laugh. "Oh, Arnold, it was nothing of the kind! How could you think it of me? I thought I was assisting in an elopement: indeed, your cousin begged me for help and I could not be deaf to her entreaties. I know how fond you are of her and I knew you wouldn't want to see her unhappy. What could I think but that you would want me to help her? And, although Mr Morley is not what you or your aunt could wish for in a match, they are very much in love. Your aunt was so set against the match that they did not know what to do."

"Doing it rather too brown, my lady," said Arnold dryly, looking at her in disbelief, and vaguely disgusted. "And while my cousin is very forgiving, I cannot be so. I take my leave of

131

you now," he said looking very severe, all his habitual light-heartedness gone. "Enjoy the play, Lady Scallonsby."

There was a very meaningful finality to his words that were not missed by the lady, and tears glistened in her eyes as he turned to leave. She reached out her hand towards him, a gesture of penitence, but he was gone.

In the break before the next act, Lucretia, Isabella and Lady Godolphin visited Lady Rutland's box. Lady Godolphin stood making civil conversation with Lady Rutland, and Isabella had managed to corner Lord Gentsome who had been trying to reach Lucretia's side. Arnold Rutland had returned to the box and drew Lucretia to one side.

"I trust you are unharmed by last night's escapade, Cressy. I am very sorry that my friendship with Lady Scallonsby resulted in such unpleasantness for yourself. I feel very badly about it," he said, with unusual seriousness.

"You warned me not to make an enemy of her and I didn't listen to you. You have nothing to reproach yourself for, cousin. The idea was undoubtedly Mr Morley's alone, with Lady Scallonsby a mere pawn in his game. He was callously driven by financial motives, and he has used Lady Scallonsby as badly as myself. Her heart was behind her involvement, and I sincerely pity her that."

"You are too forgiving, cousin. You may be sure that my association with the lady is at an end," said Arnold.

"I am glad of it, cousin, for she's not worthy of you. And that will serve as adequate punishment for the lady's wrongdoing. I have no need to hold a further grudge."

Arnold pinched Lucretia's chin and drew her eyes up to his face. "You are too forgiving of me too, Cressy. Believe me when I say I am sorry. I will take better care of you in the future, little one."

Lady Rutland, with only half her attention on the vacuous conversation of Lady Godolphin, overhead this exchange, and saw the gentle way Arnold touched his cousin, and the intimacy between them, with satisfaction. Assuredly matters between them were marching very well. They would certainly make a match of it before too long.

She was not the only person to observe the intimacy between the two cousins. Christopher, watching her from the Godolphin's box saw it too, and for some reason he could not fully explain to himself, it made him feel angry. He was struck too, and for the first time, by the number of suitors for Lucretia's hand. Any number of gentlemen, having spotted Lucretia in the Rutland's box, sought her out there and clamoured for her attention, and then, pushing Christopher out of the way, followed her back to the Godolphin's box when she set off back there at the end of the break. Christopher wished for Lucretia's opinion on his new snuff box, and to remark on Mr Eldridge's peculiar hairstyle, but he had not opportunity to do so; this made him feel, unaccountably, rather sad.

And so, noticing Mr Castleton across the theatre, he went away to chat with him, outwardly cheerful enough.

"Your mother dragged you along to this cursed dull play too then, Topher?" Castleton asked him. "Personally, I think Shakespeare just a touch overrated. In fact, I think perhaps I should try my hand at a stage play, I couldn't make a greater mull of it than this! As if someone wouldn't spot Viola wasn't a man. I mean, if Katherine tried to dress up as a man I'd know it in an instant. And only imagine Bertie as a woman! Preposterous!" he said, so disparagingly that he missed the comic value in visualising Mr Strangwald in a dress. Sadly, Christopher also missed the humour; he was not finding anything funny that evening.

"What do you say we make an escape before the curtain goes up again?" continued Mr Castleton. "I can see James and Coleford over there looking equally bored. Why don't we make a party of it, few rounds of piquet at my place? Found an exceptional burgundy the other day, you must come and try it. Quite exquisite, I assure you."

Almost as a reflex Christopher looked towards Lucretia, but she was surrounded by admirers, laughing and smiling, obviously with no thought for him. "Couldn't think of a better idea myself, Clem," he replied defiantly. "Hold on, I'll make my excuses to my mother and we can get off."

Out of the corner of her eye, Lucretia watched Christopher leave, laughing and merry, with his friends. Suddenly the play, which she had previously been enjoying immensely, became dull, and indeed the whole evening seemed suddenly dreadfully insipid.

CHAPTER NINE

The Earl of Godolphin, having prosecuted a number of pieces of business in the city, stopped in at a local hostelry for some refreshment. He was the sort of gentleman who was never above his company, and was certainly not above rubbing shoulders with the city workers whom any lesser gentleman would treat with contempt. The inn was humble but served a very good ale and provided a tolerably decent repast, and the Earl was very much enjoying a quiet lunch away from the painful scenes so frequently enacted by his wife.

The strains of the conversation coming from the table situated just behind him were audible, although carried out in undertones. He had not the slightest inclination to listen in, however, until he heard the words "Miss Lanyon". These made his ears prick up.

The interlocutors were none other than Mr Ogleby and Mr Handle, the trustees of Lucretia's fortune. The terms of the Trust had so far remained a secret, save from the few who had become privy to it all those months ago. The conversation of the two gentlemen had evidently become rather heated as their hushed voices became more and more audible.

"You'll do as I say, Handle," Ogleby threatened. "I know you've been involved in some dashed havey-cavey dealings in the past. Yes, I know all about 'em, so you'll fall into line with my plans or I'll drop a word in Mr Edmond's ear, and you can be damned sure he'll be interested in what I have to say, eh?" Mr Handle turned as white as a sheet, and opened and closed his mouth soundlessly like a large fish.

Business was not going well for Mr Ogleby. His India trading company, once so prosperous, was suffering as a result of severe competition. His insalubrious trade practices, moreover, did not help matters, as they left many investors and associates unwilling to deal with him.   Revenues had been further damaged by the legislation abolishing slave trade, and by recent industrial advances, begun by Arkwright, meaning that cottons and muslins manufactured at home were often cheaper than the imported Indian ones. Ogleby had not acclimatised well to the new financial conditions in which he found himself; he had become used to a lavish lifestyle, which he was not prepared to relinquish, and his recent fall in profits resulted in a marked mismatch between his income and his outgoings. His nephew was likewise very costly, and for this Ogleby had only himself to blame, for he had taught his young relative extravagance, and the lesson was not easy to unlearn. Faced with the prospect of a folding business, he was forced to look about him for new business opportunities.

Being an avid reader of the society pages, it could not escape his notice that the notoriety of a Miss L. was worthy of many column lines. Much was made of this lady's fortune and marital prospects, and this brought to Mr Ogleby an idea. His nephew, Master Jesmond Ogleby, was a bachelor of marriageable age and, with some work and expenditure, could be brought to look presentable enough to rub shoulders with the quality. He was also possessed of no mean acting talent, which would be integral to Mr Ogleby's plans.

Ogleby's insinuations made Mr Handle squirm his discomfort. "Mistakes of my youth, Ogleby. I was under some pressure…" Mr Handle halted. At heart, he was an honest man, but he had made some missteps in his past, indiscretions which he would give much to have undone. He had married young and had, many years ago, found himself at low tide with no hope of salvation and a growing family to support. There was one instance, long regretted, which, brought to his attention, made him cringe with mortification: an incident involving the heavy overcharging of an elderly gentleman for services which he had performed for him. Mr Handle strove to pull himself together and present a bold and unconcerned front, saying, "I am not the only one, I fancy, whose business dealings would wish to avoid closer scrutiny, Mr Ogleby." It was said with a dignity which was undermined by the fear that could be identified beneath it. It was also largely a stab in the dark, for he had no particulars to fall back upon, only the nebulous idea that Mr Ogleby's business practices were not always altogether above board.

"Oh ho, so that's how you want to play it, do you, Handle?" asked Ogleby with menace. "I don't know what it is you think you know, but I fancy you will find your accusations difficult to substantiate. No, empty threats don't hold water with me. You may think you have some vague notions, but what you don't have is evidence. Unlike me." Here he waved a small wad of papers tantalisingly under Mr Handle's nose, snatching them away as that gentleman reached out towards them. "Yes, very interesting these papers... very interesting indeed! And what a terrible shame it would be for your family if they should find their way into the wrong hands." Ogleby leered and folded the papers with deliberate neatness, stowing them in his breast pocket.

Mr Handle's posture told its own story. His shoulders sagged, and defeat was writ across his face. He sighed and said, "Very well, Ogleby, I will do as you say. But on the condition that you return those papers to me once the transaction has been concluded."

"There now, that's better, old fellow," said Ogleby, clapping Mr Handle across the back. "I see we understand each other. And because of your speedy co-operation, I may even be persuaded to share some part of the earnings with you," he said, magnanimous, if unconvincing.

"Reluctantly, I have agreed to do what you ask of me, but to earn money from it? Every feeling revolts. I do not ask it."

"You weren't so damn moralising in the past, though, were you?" sneered Ogleby. He regarded the look of revulsion on Mr Handle's face and laughed, "All the more for me then!"

"I can't see how you will prosper in this venture, Mr Ogleby. The whole scheme is preposterous. As for my part, why, I am quite in your power and must do as you say, but it seems impossible. Tell me, upon what grounds I'm to deny my consent to Miss Lanyon's match, should I be approached to do so?" Mr Handle said miserably. "What possible reason can I advance for my refusal? And to Lord Rutland of all people! If he supports the match, how can I reasonably withhold my consent? Who could blame the Viscount for coming up ugly if I tried? He is not without power and influence and would, I very much fear, use any means against me. I just don't see how it can be done."

"Use your knowledge-box, Handle!" exclaimed Ogleby. "There'll be no need to refuse your consent, merely to give your whole-hearted consent to the match which I propose. For all Rutland's a damned stiff-necked fellow, the law is on our side. Think on that. So just keep your head and he'll have to swallow his spleen. No sense in his coming up ugly, doesn't have a leg to stand on." Ogleby took a large swig of his drink, draining his glass.

"What do you mean, the match you propose?" interpolated Mr Handle anxiously.

"Well, shut your bone box and I'll tell you about it!" snapped Ogleby. He slammed his empty glass on the table. "Where's the damn ale-draper?" he ranted, momentarily distracted from his plotting by his now empty glass. "What's a boozing ken coming to if a fellow can't get a blasted top-up, eh? Another Ball of Fire, inn-keeper," he demanded ungraciously of the long-suffering proprietor.

Turning back towards Mr Handle, Ogleby resumed his conversation, "Now where was I? Ah yes, the plan… allow me to enlighten you, Handle." Ogleby looked around him and then said, with some satisfaction, "Ah, here's the fellow now," gesturing vaguely in the direction of the inn's entrance. "Timed to perfection, I must say!"

Mr Handle looked towards where Ogleby was pointing, and perceived a man, a veritable vision, emerging from the crowd of rowdy lunchtime patrons.

"Bang up to the mark, Jesmond," Ogleby said to the approaching gentleman, "for once! Ye gads, you're a sight, almost didn't recognise you meself! Though I'll warrant those threads will cost me a pretty penny; kit like that don't come cheap," he muttered. "All the same, if it serves us well, it'll have been worth it."

Mr Handle found, to his great astonishment, the most magnificently attired gentleman he had ever seen at his elbow. He was every inch the grand gentleman and more, attired in clothing that was fit for royalty, but was reminiscent of the opulent style of the previous century, and would certainly have made Brummell shudder. He wore a wig, a fashion that had, in England, fallen out of favour following the tax on hair powder. His waistcoat, of yellow silk, was longer than was currently fashionable, and was elaborately patterned with leaves and flowers and worn over bright red pantaloons. Over this he sported a splendid crimson coat, which was collarless, with wide skirts, frogging at its edge, gold cording along the seams, and large turned-back cuffs. The voluminous ruffs of his shirt collar and cuffs could be seen cascading out of the coat at the neck and wrists. Snow white leggings with rosettes at the ankles, and shoes with inch-high, jewel-studded heels completed the startling ensemble. Mr Handle blinked several times in stupefaction at Jesmond Ogleby, overcome by the dazzling appearance he presented.

Mr Ogleby saw Mr Handle's reaction and smirked. "Allow me to introduce the Count Johann von Andermach, *né* Jesmond Ogleby. You see he is magnificent enough to win the heart and hand of any damsel."

Mr Ogleby's nephew made a splendid bow to Mr Handle. "Allow me to make to you my introduction, Mr Handle. I am Count Johann, of Austria, if it should please you." His words were clipped, and pronounced with just a hint of an accent, which characterised the speaker as highly proficient in English while still being markedly foreign. Mr Handle's amazement was obvious and profound. He was a clever man, but never would his imagination have conceived of such a plan. Had it been suggested to him, he would most certainly have averred that it could not succeed, but that was before he laid eyes upon the Count...

The Earl of Godolphin, with surreptitious gaze, also had the opportunity to catch sight of this vision, and had to admit that the effect was marvellous, and the plan cunning. If Ogleby's nephew had tried to pass himself off as an English gentleman, the scheme would almost certainly have failed, for the part of the English gentleman was one to which a man had to be born; it was subtle, intangible, and gentlemen could smell out those who were not of their kind, no matter how well they dressed the part. No, the choice to go foreign; it was clever, he had to acknowledge. This gentleman presented, in seeming flawlessness, the appearance of exotic nobility. Should anyone be suspicious, they could not, as in the case of British pretenders, make enquiries, they must take the Count at his face value. He would be accepted, or rejected, on the appearance he presented. And in face, indeed, he seemed most truly that which he purported to be.

If the Earl had not understood the complete terms of Lucretia's Trust from what he overheard, he had understood enough to realise that these two gentlemen were her trustees and that their consent was required to any match she should make. More would shortly be revealed to him, as he continued to listen in unobtrusively upon their conversation.

"In this get up," boomed Ogleby, having by now imbibed a large quantity of alcohol, "Jesmond is just the sort of chap romantic young ladies fall in love with. You'll win and marry the heiress, my boy, and then her fortune will be ours. It is so deviously simple. Sometimes I amaze even myself with my own cleverness," Mr Ogleby enthused.

"But what if she has already fallen in love with someone else? From what I can gather she is wonderful close with her cousin. Rumour has it that they'll make a match of it," observed Mr Handle.

"You leave that to me," said Jesmond Ogleby in a harsh voice which in no way matched his appearance. It was steeped in malevolent confidence. "I know how to charm a lady, I assure you."

"Good God," breathed Mr Handle quietly. Looking into Jesmond's cold eyes, he felt pity for Miss Lanyon. But suddenly the malice in Jesmond Ogleby's expression was gone; he was light-hearted, charming, exaggeratedly foreign, and Mr Handle saw how the plan could succeed. He had a daughter himself, and he suspected that she would melt as wax in the Count's hands.

He almost wished he wasn't so convincing. Poor Miss Lanyon, she had done nothing to deserve this.

"Mind, Jesmond," said Ogleby, "the Trust winds itself up in a few months' time so you've got to work quickly. But if she's not half-way in love with you by then, well then, the matter will have to be forced. No lady could throw her fortune to the wind, let alone the gardener." He chuckled. "When she sees her choice is between unmarried penury or marriage to my nephew, she'll soon come around. No sense in thinking of that now though, much better if she comes quietly. I rely on you, Jesmond, to get her down the aisle without needing to kick up a dust about it." He rubbed his hands together gleefully. "Good old spindle-shanks Lanyon! He'd turn in his grave if he knew what we're planning, damned proud dog that he was, for all he enjoyed sharing his cups with the likes of me. But he's well served for being such a blockhead! Ha! To pick his drinking partner for a trustee! No doubt he thought he could force me into line when the time came, more fool him! What a mad state of affairs. All we need now is for the gardener to make his bid for the fortune. I only hope he hasn't got wind of it!"

The Earl heard all this in some considerable surprise. He knew Lord Lanyon to have been an oddity, but the terms of the Trust took some believing. How could any honourable man serve his daughter such a trick? If Christopher and Miss Lanyon wished to make a match of it in the end, the Earl mused, such a Trust must be overcome. Furthermore, the Earl had developed a kindness for Miss Lanyon for her own sake, for she was a sensible and pretty-behaved young lady, and did not deserve to be forced to live with the consequences of the ill-advised machinations of her eccentric father. But what should he do with the information he had overheard, he wondered. He could drop a hint in Lord Rutland's ear. But there was an awkwardness attached to that, for he was not well acquainted with the gentleman. And for Rutland to know that a stranger was privy to the family's private affairs would certainly discompose him.

Then too, there was a question of motive. He knew Lord Rutland by reputation as an extremely knowing man; if he had marked Miss Lanyon's partiality for his son, Lord Rutland may think he was pursuing the affair for his own gain. That would not serve Christopher and would push greater notice upon matters between his son and Miss Lanyon; Lord Godophin was not yet convinced that anything would come of it. Christopher, he felt, was not ready for marriage. He was young and he was green, and had plenty of time ahead of him to enjoy bachelorhood. For all he was starting to display a marked partiality for Miss Lanyon, he may not be ready to pursue that partiality to the length of marriage. The Earl cogitated, and wondered how to proceed. In the end, he made up his mind, made a previously unplanned visit on his way home, and waited for affairs to take their course.

That afternoon a magnificent carriage pulled up at the Pulteney, London's most exclusive hotel, and out stepped Jesmond Ogleby, in his disguise as Count Johann, into the yard. Behind him another carriage pulled up, piled high with suitcases and furniture. He swept into the hall of the hotel, followed by the suitably dour-faced valet he had employed. Outside, the yard-hands had begun to pull down all Count Johann's belongings from the second carriage, marvelling that one man could possibly own so many suitcases. The host of the hotel gushed forwards all obsequiousness, and showed Count Johann up to his room.

On the staircase, the imposter Count passed Lady Erminsade descending towards the entrance, with her maid and granddaughter in her wake. He recognised the lady, for he had been diligent in preparing for his entrance into society by developing an excellent knowledge of all the important personages who made up the *haute ton*, and he bowed slightly to the lady in passing.

Lady Erminsade rivalled Lady Castlereagh in arrogance but, unlike Lady Castlereagh, liked to have her importance constantly reaffirmed by all she met. She had disapproved of both her son's and daughter's marriages on account of the fact that they had both married beneath them; of course, to marry at all for an Erminsade was to marry beneath oneself, for who could possibly be deemed worthy of such an honour. Unable to forgive them, she refused to stay with either of her children when she was in town and put up instead at the Pulteney, accompanied by her sycophantic companion and attended very often by her granddaughter Emily, who had not, as yet, alienated herself from the lady's affection.

The grand gentleman's haughty acknowledgement piqued but also intrigued Lady Erminsade. From his appearance, it was clear that he was *somebody,* but this did not alter the fact that anyone less than royalty must naturally bow down to her importance. Her favourable impression of the man was further affirmed by the bustle in the yard, where the volumes of matching trunks and cases were still being dragged from the smart coaches and carried into the house by the now exhausted yard-hands.

"Lucy," Lady Erminsade said to her maid, "Emily will accompany me to the shops. You stay here and find out who the new gentleman is, who has just arrived."

"He was very grand was he not, grandmamma?" enthused Emily.

"That's as may be, but until we know more of him I cannot say."

A few hours later Count Johann received a kind note from Lady Erminsade inviting him to take tea with her in her private parlour. Soon after, the hotel maid brought his reply.

"Is the gentleman coming to tea, grandmamma?" asked her granddaughter, watching her read the note.

"He says he is engaged for this evening but will gladly come to take his tea with us tomorrow. Hrrumph." Naturally Lady Erminsade was not pleased to have her gracious summons turned down, but she was impressed, despite herself, at the gentleman's audacity in refusing such an illustrious invitation. Count Johann knew very well what a powerful society personage Lady Erminsade was, and what a coup it was to receive an invitation from her. It would be a mistake, however, to jump at any invitation; he did not want to appear desperate.

The next day he joined Lady Erminsade and her entourage in her private parlour. "Delighted to make your acquaintance," said Count Johann, bowing magnificently over the old lady's hand. "I am the Count Johann von Andermach, recently arrived from Austria. I have not many acquaintances in London, so it is very much to me a pleasure to make new friends. Especially a lady of such importance, such illustriousness, as Lady Erminsade." He twinkled at the old lady engagingly and, to the surprise of everyone in the room, her craggy, stern face relaxed into a smile.

She bowed her head graciously at the Count. "My granddaughter, Emily," she said, waving in the young lady's direction, "and my companion, Miss Tinkerton." The Count bowed equally magnificently over both these ladies' hands, making Emily giggle and Miss Tinkerton blush in delight.

"Such joy, such happiness, to meet you all." He threw his hands up in foreign theatricality. "I thought to myself that I would be, how do you say it, sick for my hometown, all the way here in London. I find I have been mistaken. I have heard much of your English roses, but now I see that what I have heard, it is less than the truth. Such beauty, such wonderful posture! Is it any wonder that the poets of England are the greatest, when they have such inspiration?" The three ladies smiled and giggled, even the severe Lady Erminsade, and Count Johann knew he had made a hit.

After thirty minutes, the Count very properly rose to take his leave. As he made his farewell bow, Lady Erminsade, filled with a desire to know more of the gentleman, said, "My daughter, Mrs Saunderton, is holding a ball tomorrow evening. Perhaps you might like to attend, Count Andermach, and enlarge your acquaintance here in London? You are very welcome, if you do not have other plans for the evening?"

"Ah, you are too good to a poor stranger! It would be a most great pleasure, Lady Erminsade. How so kind you are to me. I must go away at once and work to improve my so terrible English that I will not tomorrow to you be an embarrassment." He bowed himself out of the room and returned to his own quarters where he poured himself a drink and could not help crowing at his own success.

And so Count Johann made his debut into London society at Mrs Saunderton's ball, and it was a success of no mean order. He played his part magnificently. Those who were first inclined to be suspicious were won over by his audacity, his confidence and the fact that the great Lady Erminsade vouched for him. He was the most sought-after gentleman at the ball and, when it was discovered that he was a bachelor, the match-making mamas rubbed their hands together with glee and rained upon him invitations for picnics, parties, balls, routs. He was even promised vouchers for Almacks by Lady Sefton. Before too long he was seen everywhere about town.

He kept up his part well, acting in a way that suggested he did not look for approval, inclusion or respect, but rather that he expected all these things. And then there was the money; he lived lavishly, put up at one of London's most exclusive and expensive hotels, clothed himself in the most costly of garments and accessories, and lost a good deal at gaming with cheerful unconcern. The women loved him, for he was flirtatious, audacious and mysterious. The men found him flowery and *de trop* but tolerated and accepted him, for he had an excellent seat upon a horse, gamed away a fortune without the least appearance of ill-humour, and could entertain a company with a varied repertoire of amusing stories unfit for the ears of women.

Christopher Prendergast disliked him immediately on setting eyes upon him, secretly jealous of the way he carried off his flamboyant style of dress, and the assurance he showed. Christopher did not like Count Johann any more after making his acquaintance.

"Quite a waistcoat you have there, Count Johann," Christopher said after he had been introduced, looking at the deep blue silk item, and impressed despite himself.

"Yes, certainly it is my triumph," the Count said, uninterested, turning away on the instant to talk to someone else. It had piqued Christopher no end for he had been hoping for some recognition of his own, he felt, far more glamorous waistcoat. Not only had such appreciation not been forthcoming, but he had been brushed off as a person of no account.

Christopher scowled at the Count, but the Count cared nothing for his disapproval and was not in the least discomposed.

Unbeknownst to Strangwald, he alone amongst all Count Johann's new acquaintances managed to rattle him. Strangwald was introduced to him at the same time as Christopher was. Count Johann, who was primarily interested in cultivating the acquaintance of the most important personages in London and the ones most likely to improve his standing with the Incalculable, was prepared to brush off young Strangwald with the same disdain as Christopher Prendergast.

But Strangwald's opening words brought him up with a start: "My uncle's an Austrian count," announced Strangwald to the pretender. "Thought you might know him, actually."

"Of that I doubt," said Count Johann uncomfortably, "Austria is not a large country but it is large enough, certainly, that not all the counts are with each other acquainted," he said, injecting a touch of mockery.

"All the same, doesn't hurt to ask. Very well known, my uncle. Odd chap, pretty memorable as a result."

"Ah, but I come from a part of Austria that very, now what is the word? Very obscure," fudged Count Johann. "In the hills, very few people live there. It is not well known."

"Really? Come to think of it, my uncle said something similar of where he comes from. Where are you from?"

Count Johann coughed on his drink, having never before been asked to go into such detail. "Lendewald, it is a tiny village, way up in the hills. Very few people have ever heard of it."

"Lendewald? Really? Dashed small world then, ain't it! My uncle's from Lendewald too. Schwarz Rittergut, that's the name of his place. Have you heard of it?"

Count Johann was looking distinctly uncomfortable. "Schwarz Rittergut?" he said. "No, I do not believe I have heard of it. I left my home village when I was very young," he improvised. "So it is not likely that I would remember the other houses of the village."

"You'd remember this one, I'm sure. Cast your mind back. Place has turrets with flags on all the corners. My uncle's very fond of flags. What do they call him? Ah, yes, a vexillophile… Flag collector, you know. Explained it by saying that he always likes to know which way the wind is blowing. Must introduce you to him and you can catch up on old times."

"That would be a great pleasure," stuttered Count Johann, "I think I see waving at me Lady Erminsade. I must go over and talk to her. Do excuse me, Mr Strangwald."

"Your uncle lives in Sussex, Bertie!" Christopher expostulated after Count Johann had walked out of earshot. "And I'm dashed sure you don't have another one, or if you do, you've kept him hidden away all these years. In Austria, no doubt." Christopher could not resist quizzing his friend. Strangwald shuffled about on his legs. "I know, you don't know you're doing it, old chap. Wouldn't worry about it, no sense in getting all worried about what that damn fop thinks of you, after all! Wouldn't surprise me if he's never been to Austria in all his life! Wonder where he got that waistcoat though…"

It was not long before the Count made Lucretia's acquaintance. She was introduced to him by Mr Samperton.

"To make your acquaintance it is a pleasure beyond compare, Miss Lanyon," said Count Johann, bowing flamboyantly. "Allow me to say that you look, now how is it you say it here in England? You look completed to a shade. Have I said it correctly?"

"*Complete* to a shade, Count von Andermach. When you say *completed* you leave me no room for further development, and I assure you that I always plan to improve. There is nothing so depressing as a finished article. Furthermore," she said with a laugh, "you must be careful not to suggest that I have reached an age where I have only dilapidation to look forward to."

"Careful, Count Johann, you don't want to offend the Incalculable," advised Mr Samperton. "She is quite the most powerful lady in London, for she has so many suitors who would jump at the chance to defend her honour that even Napoleon's army couldn't survive the onslaught. To insult the Incalculable is to incense them all! Tread carefully, my friend."

147

Samperton grinned, but it was not a pleasant look, more of a simper.

"Nonsense, Mr Samperton! Count von Andermach, don't listen to him. He's quizzing you! I'm not the least offended." She smiled at Count Johann kindly.

"I beg you will address me as Count Johann. My full name, it is so very cucumbersome."

Lucretia let out a crack of laughter at this. "I believe you mean cumbersome, although the thought of your name being weighed down by salad ingredients is too charming a vision to be forgotten! But certainly, I will address you as Count Johann if it is what you wish."

Count Johann cocked his head to one side, regarding Lucretia wearing a mask of confusion. "The Incalculable? Are you really with your mathematics so very bad? It seems to me very strange that people should be permitted to remark upon it when they address you. We would not in Austria do such a thing to a lady." Lucretia chuckled and Mr Samperton sniggered, storing up the remark to mock the Count at a later time.

"Alas, it is too true, Count Johann, I cannot add up my sums without error! It is most trying!" Lucretia exclaimed.

"But in Austria," continued Count Johann, "we do not judge our women on their ability to add and subtract. You would be, Miss Lanyon, on a pedestal the most high in my country. You are the most beautiful lady amongst all my acquaintance. It is like I look upon an angel, like in a dream." He looked at Lucretia warmly, bending to take her hand in his, "to kiss this hand it is a moment of magic…" He broke off, for he found the lady's hand elusive. Lucretia did not want Count Johann to flirt with her and had drawn her hands firmly behind her back, anxious from the outset to put the foreign cavalier under no illusions. Indeed, after her unpleasant experience with Mr Morley, Lucretia was so anxious that none of her suitors fall under the misapprehension that she was disposed to favour them, that she shied away from all flirtation, and endeavoured to either dampen down ardour in her suitors, or avoid altogether those whose attentions could not be repressed.

Count Johann glowered as he grasped air rather than her hand, and an uncomfortable silence fell between them. Lucretia was soon solicited to dance by another of her admirers, and she was relieved to get away. She had not missed Count Johann's ill-humoured scowl and he had gone down in her estimation because of it.

Count Johann watched her throughout the rest of the evening, and realised just how sought after she was. While he admitted that she undoubtedly shone down all the other damsels in any given room, the sheer abundance of her conquests surprised him. He perceived that he would have to work hard to win her, and, from that moment on, set about the task determinedly. He took every opportunity to woo her, but his steadily more elaborate and ostentatious compliments only served to alienate her further. Lucretia kept all of her suitors at arms' length, and Count Johann even more so. His attentions seemed desperate, artificial, and she could not forget that scowl when she had drawn her hand away from him. She began to suspect he was another fortune-hunter and sensed as well that, like Mr Morley, he was dangerous.

It was inevitable that Miss Pycroft and Lucretia, on their next shopping expedition, would fall into conversation about London's newest foreign arrival. Poring over the offerings on show in Grafton House, Lucretia gasped as she spotted and picked up a length of opulent sapphire-coloured organza ribbon. "Look Ceccy! How beautiful! Only see how it shimmers in the light."

"No doubt Count Johann would comment that it glistened like the waters of the Danube on a summer's day," giggled Cecelia. She had met the Count the previous evening and had been delighted by his now-famous strange sayings. "Do you know that he told Mrs Ennerwick that she would look a vision in lederhosen? Well, she didn't know whether to take it as a compliment or not. And even when the concept of lederhosen had been described to her, she was none the wiser!"

"I quite agree that it would be a vision indeed to see Mrs Ennerwick sporting lederhosen; whether a good one or a bad one though, I wouldn't care to say!" returned Lucretia, laughing.

"I'm told that Count Johann even remarked to Lady Castlereagh that her voice was as beautiful as Dietmar Horngacher's, Austria's most famous yodeller," said Cecelia, dropping her voice to a shocked whisper.

"Lady Castlereagh? You can't be serious!" said Lucretia, awed, imagining the severe lady's reaction to such a comment. "My God, I would have liked to have been there to see it!"

"He's very droll, isn't he?" said Cecelia.

"Yes, I suppose he is," said Lucretia unenthusiastically.

Cecelia looked at her in surprise. "Don't you like Count Johann, Cressy?"

"Of course I do," said Lucretia, a little too airily. "Everyone does so."

"No, you don't," said Cecelia, eyeing Lucretia. "You can tell me, I'm no gabster."

"I know you're not, Ceccy. It's not that I don't trust you, it's just that I don't have any real basis for my opinion. And well... it's not easy to describe, but there's something calculating about him, a certain ruthlessness... Maybe I'm imagining it. But, well... he reminds me of Mr Morley..." She broke off. Cecelia looked at her in horror and complete understanding. She was the only person, save her aunt, that Lucretia had told about the kidnapping attempt, and Cecelia had never been more shocked by anything in her life.

"Heavens!" Cecelia exclaimed inadequately. "I never imagined there could be anyone as villainous as Mr Morley, but even he seemed so very droll and charming at first sight. And, of course, my mother speaks very highly of Count Johann, and that must be a point in his disfavour- she's an exceptionally bad judge of character." Cecelia flushed after she said this, shocked by her own boldness in criticising her mother, something her upbringing had never before allowed her to do.

Lucretia laughed. "Well said, Ceccy!"

But Count Johann continued to be well regarded amongst the *ton* at large, and Lucretia came across him at most of the balls and events she attended. Christopher's sense of loathing towards Count Johann grew when he saw how often he was to be seen at Lucretia's side, constantly trying to capture her attention,

"Who is this dashed chap?" he near-ranted at Strangwald. "And who says he's a Count anyway? It's all a hum if you ask me! Come from nowhere. Who knows what his antecedents may have been? Too smoky by half! Can't think why everyone is falling over themselves to be agreeable to him. And those waistcoats he wears, well... I mean there's striking and then there's excessive."

Strangwald regarded Christopher in some surprise, directing a fleeting look at his friend's brightly-coloured, floral waistcoat. Catching sight of this covert glance, Christopher said defensively, "Well, what I mean is that I can carry it off, that style. The Count, if indeed he is a Count (which I am in no way convinced of) doesn't have the figure for it at all. Most ill-judged. And he's so irritatingly omnipresent. You can't go anywhere without bumping into the cursed fellow," he complained.

Count Johann's conspicuous pursuit of Lucretia was met with equal disfavour by the gossiping tabbies of the polite world. "I see Count Johann now makes up one of Miss Lanyon's court. She simply cannot resist stealing all the attention for herself. Conceited shrew!" said Mrs Doughty poisonously.

Lady Enderby nodded her head in agreement. "Men are such stupid creatures! She's had I don't know how many eligible offers and has turned her nose up at all of them, but still they fawn over her. It certainly seems that she revels in the attention, else what on earth is the girl waiting for?" Lady Enderby's severity had much of its basis in resentment, for she knew that Lucretia had repulsed her beloved son's advances. Since that time, he had moped tragically about the house like a cushion that had had the stuffing extracted from it. That she disapproved of the idea of her son marrying at all at his youthful age, and was well aware of the unsuitability of the match, in no way abated the animosity she felt towards Lucretia. "No doubt she is so set up in her own esteem that she is holding out for a Duke at the very least."

"Yes, it's clear that she's greatly picksome," answered Mrs Doughty, "for who could refuse an offer from Gentsome? So handsome and charming as he is. Not to mention his fortune." Here both ladies sighed at the thought of this engaging gentleman. "I hope she will not find herself on the shelf, having refused to entertain any of the very flattering offers she has received," Mrs Doughty continued, hoping nothing of the kind.

"Though it cannot escape one's notice that she is seen most often in the company of her cousin," remarked Lady Enderby. "She could do better than Arnold Rutland. But his scheming harpy of a mother must be doing everything in her power to promote the match, if only to swell the Rutland coffers. Insufferable woman!"

"If she wasn't so arrogant and superior about her family's standing she would see that her beloved Arnold is deplorably loose in the haft," returned Mrs Doughty. "The *on dits* about him are quite shocking. And the worst of it is that he lacks finesse. His affair with Lady Scallonsby is common knowledge to all, save her blockhead of a husband."

"No discretion, that *is* the worst of it," agreed Lady Enderby, shaking her head. "But rumour has it that their association has cooled of late. It may be that Arnold Rutland contemplates marriage after all?"

This had become Lady Rutland's greatest desire, and she was sanguine about the prospect. With every offer Lucretia refused, and every time she was seen radiant and happy in the company of her cousin, Lady Rutland's hopes for the match grew. Add to this that Arnold had broken off his affair with the appalling Lady Scallonsby, and Lady Rutland was very pleased with how matters between her son and niece were progressing.

Another week went by and Count Johann, despite making the most of every opportunity to woo the Incalculable, had to admit that he was making no headway. If compliments and charm were not winning the lady's heart, he must find another way to make her look favourably upon his suit, he thought to himself. He must somehow make her come to him, he mused. To make her feel grateful would be ideal, if only he could think of a way he could bring it about. And then the idea came to him, a simple one: he must come to her rescue, like a knight in shining armour. And since the time when valiant suitors could wrestle fair damsels from dragons' lairs was long past, he must orchestrate a situation from which to save her.

No such plan immediately presented itself to him, and he put the problem to one side, reasoning that no doubt something would come to him in time. Meanwhile, he turned his efforts towards nourishing the very lucrative friendships he had made during his time infiltrating the *ton*. Amongst the most promising was Mr Edgworthington, a young man half flash and half foolish, so foolish indeed that Count Johann was able to hang on his sleeve without Mr Edgworthington really noticing. This was invaluable, for setting himself up for the Season was costing the Count more than he had thought it would, and Mr Ogleby made it very clear that he thought the allowance he had made his nephew more than adequate for his needs. And indeed it might have been, had Count Johann not discovered a penchant for gambling. Things had come to such a pass that the Count was finding it necessary to purchase a new coat from his tailor almost weekly, to stave off his demands for payment. A wealthy young friend like Mr Edgworthington, who bled easily, was just what he needed to keep his head above water.

It occurred to Count Johann that Mr Edgworthington could make himself useful in other ways. His new friend had a decided *tendre* for Miss Lanyon. It was calf-love, and Count Johann recognised this. But the throes of youthful passion often lead young gentlemen to commit their greatest follies. And Edgworthington, furthermore, had an overly friendly disposition when it came to the fairer sex, which did not generally endear him to them. Nor were his looks more alluring, for he was slightly sweaty-looking, with bulging, rodent-like cheeks perpetually blotched with red.

The two gentlemen were standing at the edge of the ballroom at Mrs Moreton's ball. Edgworthington licked his lips as he looked at Lucretia, who was very prettily dancing a minuet, in a way that would have made her skin crawl if she had noticed it. He knew himself to be inferior in looks, intelligence, fortune and charm to many of Lucretia's suitors and never for one moment imagined himself a serious contender for her heart. In truth, he rather liked to admire from afar, as such a courtship did not involved putting himself out at all. Edgworthington's indolent disposition made him prefer to deal in lightskirts rather than troubling himself with the exhausting exertions demanded of serious courtship. However, he was also a suggestible fellow, and Count Johann saw how this could be used to good account. Through severe effort and the employment of some very creative versions of the truth, he managed to convince Edgworthington first, that Lucretia was secretly in love with him and, with greater difficulty, that he should do something about it.

"Bag o' moonshine, Johann!" said Edgworthington when the Count commented on Lucretia's partiality for him. "Girl hasn't got feelings for me, you must be dicked in the nob if you think she has."

"I assure you, my great friend," returned Count Johann, "that it is true. You obviously have about the fairer sex much to learn. Women, they are mysterious. They like to hide their feelings. This is true also of our Austrian ladies. They will often pretend not to notice the one they truly adore. But she was asking me about you, at the theatre only the other day. You remember how I was talking to her? And then she, how do you say it, brushed?"

"Brushed?" exclaimed Edgworthington, "At the theatre? Now I know you are talking fustian!"

"No, that is not the right word I have used. Alas, my so terrible English!" said Count Johann morosely. "How can I explain it? You know, when someone becomes red in the face. They are embarrassed, you see."

"Ah, blushed," said Edgworthington, enlightened. "Did she, by Jove? Well, I'll be damned! Can't think what such a lady would see in me. Are you sure you have it quite right, Johann?

Sure she wasn't talking about someone else? I mean, well, no can't be me!"

"But why not? You are a very eligible suitor, are you not? No, of Miss Lanyon's feelings I am quite certain. You should believe me, for I know about such things," said Count Johann with great assurance.

Edgworthington cocked an eyebrow at him. "No doubt you do, I'll be bound," he said with a ribald laugh. "How many Austrian hearts did you wound, Count Johann? That's what I want to know. And what scandal has brought you all the way across land and water to escape it? It must have been bad, for whatever it was you've been keeping it dashed close to your chest!"

"Not at all! You have it all wrong," protested the Count, deliberately sounding unconvincing. "Anyway, we move from the matter we were discussing. She is a very pretty lady, Miss Lanyon. You would be a fool not to ask her to marry you. Such beauty! Such a prize!" he enthused.

But this had brought Edgworthington to earth with a thump. For, of course, Miss Lanyon was no mere bit of muslin to amuse oneself with and then discard when she became tiresome or lost her comeliness. She was a lady of quality, and only marriage could be contemplated. And marriage was so damn final! Did he want to become a tenant for life? No, he thought, not at all, not even for a face as pretty as Miss Lanyon's.

Count Johann guessed what was going through his friend's mind, for he was in sympathy with his sentiments on marriage. He tried a different tack, which he hoped would make the thought of marriage more palatable to his sweaty friend. "And I believe she has a fortune not inconsiderable, is it not so?" he asked.

"So rumour has it," mused Edgworthington. But, unlike Count Johann or Mr Morley, Edgworthington was a man of means, so this consideration did not weigh heavily with him. On balance, he thought to himself, he would rather have his freedom than Miss Lanyon's money.

"I would like to see the expression on all the other suitor's faces, when they see she has chosen you and not them," said Count Johann, trying yet another approach to persuade Edgworthington to make a move upon Lucretia. "They will have very much jealousy, do not you think? I smile to think of their faces beholding such a thing."

This appeal to Edgworthington's vanity hit home. He was strongly attracted to the idea of stealing a march on all Lucretia's other suitors. It would be a not inconsiderable coup to be the envy of the gentlemen of London. His breast swelled at the thought of it. Yes, it would be very agreeable, very agreeable indeed, he mused. Perhaps he would make his bid for the heiress after all, especially now he knew that she was his for the taking.

Count Johann let Mr Edgworthington mull over these thoughts. "Thing is, though, Johann," said Edgworthington after a time, "Miss Lanyon may be in love with me, but I'm damned sure Lady Rutland ain't! Always been dashed rude to me in the past. Not going to favour the match."

Count Johann sighed in relief that Edgworthington reached these conclusions on his own, since presenting these ideas without offending the young man would be problematic. Now he had Edgworthington in just the frame of mind he wanted him. "It fills me with sadness, but that it is so is without the doubt. She is without the sense, that Rutland woman and has, I think, other ideas in her mind for her niece's future. You must get Miss Lanyon away from all persons and then make your proposal in the secrecy. When she has said yes to you, her family will have to agree also, is it not so?"

"Well…" said Edgworthington doubtfully, "I suppose you're right, but it's not so easy to get a girl on her own, you know. There are rules against such things, besides which, she's always surrounded by a hundred fellows dangling after her!" Edgworthington's resolve was wavering; perhaps the plan was altogether too much effort after all.

Count Johann saw him hesitate. "To do such a thing would be most easily achieved with a little help," he said reassuringly. "I will of course help you in the plan, of that you can be sure. If you allow me to, I will make it happen for you."

"Thanks, old fellow, you're a good pal!" said Edgworthington, all at once sanguine again about his prospects with Lucretia. He could continue in his indolence, waiting for Count Johann to deliver the beautiful heiress to him on a platter.

Count Johann smiled and clapped Edgworthington on the back. All the pieces of his plan were falling into place; now he could be sure he would be present when Edgworthington made his attempt. The Count crowed inwardly at his projected success in winning the heiress and, taking leave of his friend, he went off to attend a gaming hell where he lost a good deal of money with abandon, secure in the knowledge that he would soon be one of the richest fellows in the land.

CHAPTER TEN

While Count Johann was happily plotting, Mr Morley, following the failure of his own schemes, was utterly cast down. His finances were in dire straits and he could not see any way to make a recover. These worries were starting to take their toll on his usually carefree disposition. He had lost his appetite, and his cold eyes were beginning to sink into his head, seeping black rings beneath them. He was also drinking, a lot.

Calling in upon him one morning a few days later, Mr Croxstowe found him still in his dressing gown, slumped in a chair and already making inroads into a bottle of brandy. Croxstowe, deeply shocked by his friend's altered appearance, exclaimed, "Good God, Everard, what have you been doing to yourself? You look as sick as a cushion."

"It's damn low water with me," slurred Morley, looking grim. "In truth, I don't have sixpence to scratch together. "

"Ah, been dipping a little too deeply as a result. It's not the way, man," Croxstowe said, taking the glass out of Morley's hand and setting it down on a table out of his reach. "If you want my advice, steer clear of getting jug-bitten until you've sorted yourself out. Old Tom rarely helps affairs to prosper, only makes you more blue-devilled. Besides, looks like your constitution's taken about as much as it can handle." He looked at Mr Morley in some concern. "You don't look at all the thing, Everard. Sallow, that's how you look. Better start taking better care of yourself or you'll find yourself in an early grave."

"Well, maybe that wouldn't be so bad," muttered Mr Morley. "What good is health going to be to me in a debtor's prison?"

He was clearly in a bad way, thought Croxstowe, watching his glum friend get up to retrieve his glass and take a swig out of it defiantly. "Come now, it can't be that bad,

Everard. How's this all come about? I could've sworn that you had a plan brewing."

"I did," bit out Morley, "but it pains me to say that it didn't answer, fiend seize it!"

"Made a mull of it, did you?" sympathised Croxstowe.

"Well, it would have come off all right and tight if that damned young fool hadn't thrown a rub in the way. Damn and blast the impudent cub, why couldn't he keep his nose out of the affair!"

"Who? What happened? Well, don't keep me in suspense. Tell me all about it."

At this invitation, Mr Morley told Mr Croxstowe the tale of the failed kidnapping. His voice shook with anger when he told him about the part played by Christopher Prendergast. "Oh, how I'd like to wring that young imbecile's neck for his effrontery," Morley finished vehemently. His hatred towards the young viscount was growing out of all proportion, and being drunk only added to his sense of ill-usage.

"Well, there's always revenge," said Croxstowe. "Do you good, keep your mind off things planning it. Keep you out of the speakeasy as well. Must think of your health, dear fellow."

"Revenge? I can think of nothing else! But it's my finances that need my attention right now!"

"Well don't go flying into a miff with me. Only trying to help," said Croxstowe.

"Sorry," muttered Morley. "It's just I'm in a bad way, Lucius. I'm cleaned out and I don't know what to do. Say, don't suppose you could shout us a monkey. I'd be devilishly grateful. Wouldn't rescue me, but it'd make things a damn sight easier for a time."

"Can't do it, Everard. Haven't got it. Cucumberish myself," Croxstowe apologised. "Things have got to such a pass that I've had to play niceties with m'father. Degrading, I know, but I'd run out of options." He appraised Morley. "Still, you're a cunning one. If you've hit upon one plan, don't see why you can't hit upon another."

"Don't you think I've been trying to?" Morley snapped.

"All right, all right, don't bite my nose off! It's not my fault you're cleaned out! All I'm thinking is that I've seen you with Prendergast's sister."

"Can't shake the girl. She's a tiresome shrew but so persistent, let me tell you. Like a damned barnacle! But what of it?"

"Well, looking at Prendergast's face, I can tell he doesn't like her being seen with you above half," observed Croxstowe.

"Don't I know it? It's the only source of pleasure I've found recently, torturing him with the sight of it. Enough to make me put up with her mawkishness! But it's not solving my problems."

"Well…" said Croxstowe slowly, "seems to me that the Prendergast family are not without means. Could be the answer to your problems, especially as the girl seems disposed to favour you."

"Lucius, I do think you may be right. Been thinking the same thing myself and it seems like my only option. Only you can understand why I'm a little shy of elopements at the moment. But I've been trying to hit upon another plan for days and look where it's got me. Nowhere. At least running off with the girl would give me a chance to wipe that damned superior smirk off Prendergast's face. But to be shackled to such a girl! Well, the thought quite turns my stomach… Is it worth it? That's the question," Morley mused dubiously, looking slightly sickened.

"Occurs to me though, Everard," said Croxstowe, "that they're a devilish proud lot, the Prendergasts. Very proud of their family name and reputation. May not need to marry the girl after all. Just run off with her and then, when you refuse to go up the aisle with her, they'll pay out handsomely to hush up the affair."

"Good point. Yes, that might not be so bad after all," said Morley, heartened. He thought about it for a minute. "Yes, I believe I'll do it! God knows I have few enough options at this point. It's either that or flee abroad, and with the war, well…" He broke off, his instincts for self-preservation immediately

160

discounting the plan. Sighing, he knew what he must do and he jumped up from his chair calling for his valet to bring him his shaving gear.

"That's the dandy, old fellow!" Croxstowe encouraged.

It was a dream come true to Lady Isabella to find her erstwhile reluctant suitor disposed to be amorous towards her. She fancied herself head over ears in love with Mr Morley and hoped that she could win him.

Her brother was right in suggesting that her friendship with such a man would not meet with the approval of her mother, and she had had to endure a fine trimming down on the subject. But she remained adamant in her pursuit of Mr Morley and, with the optimism of youth, held no doubt that she could win over her parents' approval in the end. And if she couldn't... well, nothing could me more romantic than an elopement. After the knot was tied, they would certainly forgive her, if only for the family name.

To arrange matters, the doubtful couple must meet to discuss the finer points. Isabella found her mother keeping a prohibitively watchful eye on her whenever she met Mr Morley at social functions, so finding the opportunity to talk privately had become nigh on impossible. Thus it was that the two found themselves holding a secret meeting behind the Church of St Christopher. To Isabella a clandestine rendezvous was pure pleasure, and the gravestones surrounding them as they stood discussing matters did not abate her enthusiasm one jot.

"Oh, Everard, I have had to employ the most shameful of deceits to meet you here. We must be quick lest my absence be noticed," she breathed, enjoying herself hugely. Morley, in considerably less enjoyment, looked up at the grey clouds and remarked to himself that even the weather knew his mood.

"I don't think my father will ever agree to our engagement. You may ask it of him but I do not think your proposal will meet with success," said Isabella, imagining a stirring scene in which her iniquitous father vowed to blight the future of the star-crossed lovers, and Mr Morley fought violently to exact his consent. Casting herself in the role of Juliet, she was barely paying attention to her Romeo, which was fortunate since he wasn't the least inclined to direct rhyming couplets at her.

"Ask him?" said Morley, aghast, turning pale at the thought of it. "Good God, there's no way he'll agree to it," he expostulated.

"No," Isabella returned, reluctantly relinquishing the notion, since, whatever the outcome of such a confrontation, it would undoubtedly put paid to the entire play. If her father gave his consent, all the romance of the situation was lost, and if he refused Mr Morley, her parents would make quite certain that she had no opportunity to be in his company. "On balance," continued the would-be heroine, "I think you had best not try it, for it will only advertise our intent. Already they are suspicious and watching me like a hawk," she said with pride. "I know it to be very evil, and not at all the thing, and I hope I may not be shunned for it. But I really think our only option may be an elopement," she said dramatically. Morley sighed in relief at her ready acceptance of such a plan.

"Of course, I would wait for you until I came of age. I would wait for you, my love, until the end of time," continued Isabella soulfully. Morley gulped and he wished she would get to the point. Isabella, enjoying herself enormously, was in no hurry to do so, declaring, "Our love has been written in the stars. But to have to wait until I come of age, it is a lifetime! My heart could not endure it! And my mother and father would try to force me·into matrimony with another. What means they would use, I cannot imagine, but I do not see how I am to withstand them!" she wailed. Her father would be amused to find himself so cast as the villain in this piece, and would be at just as much of a loss as his daughter to imagine what dreadful means he could employ to force her into marriage against her will.

"Yes, yes," Morley said impatiently, never feeling less like playing the part of the romantic suitor. "Well, we must elope, nothing for it. Shall we set the day?" His curt matter-of-factness disappointed Isabella, but she was living a romantic dream and could overlook her betrothed's lack of sensibility by redoubling her own.

"An elopement, only think how shocking! I wonder if I should really consent to it? The shame it would bring upon my family!" she howled tragically, waiting for him to talk her into the plan. Morley was bored by these theatrics. He had the measure of Isabella and was fully aware that she was taking huge enjoyment out of the melodramatic value of this meeting. He was fed up and already beginning to draw back from the plan. Only a few minutes in Lady Isabella's company were enough to make him consider whether servitude in a debtor's prison may not be more acceptable than the trial of an elopement, however temporary the arrangement may be, with this tiresome female.

"Very well, Lady Isabella, if you do not think you can go through with the plan, then there is nothing more to be said on the matter," he said stiffly. Nothing could be more unlover-like than his demeanour, and he turned to leave.

"No wait, Everard," said Isabella hurriedly, alarmed that Mr Morley had reverted to addressing her in such formal terms. "I see that my words have wounded you," she excused his failure to press his suit. "Naturally such a plan must be repugnant to any gently-born maiden, but I see that it is the only way. Only we must plan how it can be contrived."

"Nothing could be easier," Morley declared, suddenly cheerful again. But, seeing how he had shocked Isabella with his prosaic attitude, he added hastily, "my sweet. Possessed of such ingenuity and cleverness as you are, I am sure we can arrange the matter easily enough. Meet me here tomorrow morning, at ten shall we say, and we can set off to Gretna in good time."

"Ten in the morning? Should not we leave at midnight, or at least at the very crack of dawn, to ensure secrecy?" Calmly entering a coach at a very sensible hour of the morning did not fulfil her expectations for an elopement in the slightest.

"I think you'll find that it is very much easier to sneak away in the bustle of the day than it is to creep silently out of a house at an hour when every floorboard creaks and can't go unnoticed. If you say you're going for a walk with your maid and then give her the slip, you can meet me here and no one will remark your absence for several hours. When they do notice it, they'll not know where to look for you, for naturally you will leave no direction. By the time anyone knows what has happened, we'll be too far ahead of them for them to catch us up. One always thinks that these things happen in the dead of night, but when you consider the practicalities, it really makes much more sense to do it as I have said."

Isabella's thoughts had been turned in another direction by his words and fortunately she was not struck by the fact that Mr Morley seemed to have a lot of experience in planning elopements. "Not leave any direction? But I must tell mama where I have gone. She would worry so. It would be dreadfully unkind not to warn her!" She scowled, for she had derived considerable enjoyment from composing just such a missive in her head. To be barred from this pleasure seemed terribly unfair.

Isabella's lip stuck out stubbornly and Morley saw the tell-tale signs of a tantrum brewing, which he hastened to stave off by saying, "Bella, you must see that elopements one hears about, which are naturally the unsuccessful ones, are always ruined by the parties advertising their intent. It's very ill-advised. No, leave letting everyone know until after the fact when they cannot upend the apple cart. That's the way to do it. You must promise me this, my angel, it is so very important. I understand your sensibility on this matter but it really is the way to do it, I assure you."

Isabella continued to look militant on the point and he saw that he needed to appease her.   "But naturally you can write to her in a few days when there is no chance they might catch us up. If your heart truly belongs to me, we must steel ourselves to some little unpleasantness, and causing some measure of pain to your poor parents is unavoidable. When the knot is safely tied, we'll make it up to them with our penitence. Come, my dearest, do not mar your beautiful countenance with frowning." He clasped Isabella's wrist to his lips amorously, hoping that this would mollify her.

"Oh, very well, Everard," Isabella agreed reluctantly, her wrist tingling from his touch. "But I can't elope tomorrow; I am going to the most delightful party at Mrs Sterling's house in the evening. It must be Wednesday," she said firmly.

Mr Morley was strongly of the opinion that elopements, like the pulling of rotted teeth, ought to be done as soon as possible, and was moved to expostulate, "But, my sweet, every hour I cannot call you mine is an age."

"I know, and I feel it too," Isabella sighed. "But after all, it is only one day, and I did promise Miss Sterling, she is quite a friend of mine, that I would be at her party. It would be too cruel to let her down. No, it must be Wednesday." With this Morley had to be satisfied, since it was clear that Isabella was immovable on the point.

Lucretia noticed that her friend was in particularly good spirits at Mrs Sterling's party, an event to which she had also been invited; but this did not spark her curiosity. Isabella was notoriously capricious and her moods swung more often than the tides. Lucretia was, herself, in spirits, for not only did Viscount Prendergast choose to escort them to the gathering, but he stood conversing with her for some time, a fact that turned her quite pink with pleasure.

Since the failed kidnapping, Lord Rutland had been keeping a closer eye on his niece. He had even put himself out to attend any number of social engagements he would normally have avoided, less because he had an unsociable disposition, and more because it forced him to be in his wife's company more than he cared. Previously disposed to be amused by the antics of Lucretia's suitors, the events forced upon her by Mr Morley made him determined to ensure that Lucretia was not further oppressed or incommoded by the attentions of the hoards of gentlemen who pretended for her hand.

It was in a fatherly spirit that he cast his eye around the ballroom to check how she was getting on and so he caught sight of Lucretia's pleasure in Christopher's company. He was considerably surprised, but he knew that the look betokened something highly significant. Having watched her over the previous weeks he had seen how she looked upon her other suitors, and he had never seen anything resembling the look he now saw in her eye. It was soft, worshipful, loving and, he shrewdly recognised, it was born of a lasting feeling. As he looked up he caught the Earl of Godolphin's eye, who had been observing his son carefully, following the progression of the understanding flourishing between Christopher and Lucretia. Lord Rutland and Lord Godolphin exchanged a knowing look tinged with a shared surprise at the turn of events. They nodded ever so slightly at each other in complicit agreement that there was nothing to dislike in the, albeit surprising, match.

Meanwhile, Mr Edgworthington was standing at the far side of the room from Lucretia, admiring her with a lascivious gleam in his eye. Having had leisure to consider what Count Johann had told him, he was a fair way towards considering Lucretia his own property, but he was still unsure how to complete the transaction.

Count Johann appeared at his elbow and whispered, "Have you asked her yet?"

"Not yet, it's a dashed sight more difficult than you think to get the girl on her own, as I keep telling you!" returned Edgworthington peevishly.

"If you allow me, I will make to you a suggestion?" said the Count, who had been doggedly following his friend over the last few days to ensure he would be present in case he should make his attempt on Lucretia.

"By all means, by all means," Edgworthington replied, and then listened intently to the scheme Count Johann expounded to him, nodding now and then to indicate his understanding. "By Jove," Edgworthington said when the Count had finished, "you're a clever chap, Johann! Yes, I really think it might work. Thanks!" He went off instantly to execute the plan.

To Lucretia's disappointment, her conversation with Christopher was cut short when she was solicited to dance with Mr Edgworthington, an offer that, much as she would have liked to, she could not refuse without seeming impolite.

During the dance, Lucretia found Mr Edgworthington marginally less repulsive than usual. He was never an elegant dancer but it was less this which served to give his partners a disgust of him and more the fact that he could not resist any opportunity to handle them more than was necessary. In this instance, however, his normally tactile nature was restrained by the fact that he was concentrating hard on implementing Count Johann's plan. He waited for his opportunity and, as the dance twirled Lucretia around, he managed to accidentally-on-purpose leap inelegantly upon her flounce, which tore with an unmistakable ripping sound. Nothing could exceed his apologies after the event. He was conspicuously mortified and keen to do everything in his power to rectify the problem, leading Lucretia off into the seclusion of one of the antechambers where she could effect a fix.

Lucretia barely noticed being led away; her full attention was on the extent of the damage inflicted upon her dress. Like any sensible lady, she carried pins in her reticule for use in just such a predicament, and she dug around in her bag searching for them. She could not be deaf to Mr Edgworthington's apologies, and his mortification seemed so extreme that, despite feeling somewhat miffed, she must, for politeness's sake, try to be forgiving towards him. No sooner were they alone, however, than such thoughts were expelled from her head by his far from chivalrous behaviour.

Jesmond Ogleby, still playing his part as Count Johann von Andermach admirably, had watched the incident with satisfaction and surreptitiously followed the pair, hanging back out of sight at the entrance to the room situated just off the ballroom. He was awaiting his chance to rescue Miss Lanyon from the unwelcome attentions that would necessarily follow when any pretty lady found herself in the sole company of the licentious Mr Edgworthington. Nothing, Count Johann thought to himself, could more readily win him favour with the Incalculable than to rescue her from such a predicament. Sadly for this gentleman, the turn of fate conspired to ruin his plans.

Christopher, now Lucretia had left, found himself, to his consternation, not only at a ball but also vulnerably positioned at the edge of the dance floor, rather than in the safety of the card room. Inevitably, it was not long before scheming mamas spotted prey in the form of an eligible bachelor unpartnered for the next reel. Looking left, he saw his hostess approaching with a young lady upon her arm and a predatory gleam in her eye. Gulping, he looked right and saw his mother approaching with a similar plan and a likewise determined look in her eye. She had Miss Wedderby walking in her wake and, having been subjected to many pointed lectures on the virtues of this lady, Christopher could not be ignorant of the fact that his mother favoured this lady as his future bride.

Desperate for escape, he realised how exposed he had made himself, for the card room was at the far side of the ballroom and could not be reached without coming across the path of one or other of these two hunting parties. They were still at some distance and if only some exit could be located, he could still make good his escape. Glancing frantically around himself he saw the entrance to the room only recently entered by Lucretia and Mr Edgworthington and recognised it as his only refuge. He had not seen them enter the room and ducked into it unsuspectingly. As he entered he passed by the Count and shot him a rueful look.

The Count, taken by surprise, flung out his hand as if to prevent the Viscount's passage, realising at the last moment that this was somewhat inappropriate. It was foolish, and it drew attention to the fact that he was lurking mysteriously in the doorway, a fact that Christopher would later recall. Christopher did not remark it at the time however and burst into the room to find Mr Edgworthington amorously clasping Lucretia.

Christopher halted and felt an explosion of anger and hurt within himself that was strange to him; his hearing was muffled by the thumping of his heart within his ears. Jealousy on account of a woman was such a foreign feeling that he did not recognise it for what it was, but it was sufficient to make him turn as if to leave until he noticed that Lucretia was struggling against Mr Edgworthington's embrace. She was red in the face and tears glistened in her eyes.

"Oh, let go, Mr Edgworthington!" she was saying, trying to repulse his attentions and feeling both frightened and mortified. "What if someone should find us in such a situation? You must not, really. Oh, please let me go!"

"Come, come, my pretty," Edgworthington replied cheerfully, in no way put off by her struggling. To him this was part of the game, well-born ladies must put up a show of resistance for propriety's sake. She would soon give in, he had no doubt.

Christopher's rage as he saw Lucretia struggling against such a man was terrible to behold. In two strides, he was across the room. He yanked Mr Edgworthington's arm violently and pulled him away, biting out, "Let go!"

Mr Edgworthington was inclined to be irritated by the interruption and giggled at Christopher's intervention saying, "Really sir, you are *de trop*, can't you see you have interrupted a private scene. There is nothing for you to do here. All is quite well, I assure you." But then he looked up at the interrupter's face and suffered a jolt as he perceived Christopher's murderous expression. The violence and enmity he saw there was unprecedented and he stepped back feeling himself to be in bodily danger.

Lucretia, previously so indisposed to close contact with males, fell upon Christopher, and he hugged her protectively, saying inadequately, "There, there, you are safe now."

Turning to the shuffling and uncomfortable Mr Edgworthington, Christopher said savagely and simply, "Get out." Mr Edgworthington looked briefly as if he may hold his ground but then thought better of it as he noticed Christopher's hand clenching into a fist. He hastened out of the room and out of the party, pursued by Count Johann who followed him, scowling and cursing the ruin of his plan.

"Oh, I am so mortified to be found in such a predicament!" exclaimed Lucretia. "You must think me the most tiresome of females to be always getting into such scrapes. I do not know how to thank you for saving me, once again, Lord Prendergast. You cannot know how grateful I am, I just could not repulse him, no matter how hard I tried."

Realising how improper it was to be hugging him, she stepped backwards. She patted down her hair and took a deep gulping breath. "And how am I now to fix my dress?" she despaired, looking down at the floor where all her pins were strewn. "Oh, how hateful it is to be oppressed in this way. I wish I were not an heiress and that everyone would leave me alone." She looked up into Christopher's face and saw that he looked very grim. "You are thinking this is all my fault, and it is. How could I let myself end up in such a position? You are right to look stern, I cannot imagine what you must be thinking of me," Lucretia fretted. To see Viscount Prendergast look so severely broke her heart. They had been going on so well and now she had given him a disgust of her.

"I will bring my sister to you," said Christopher curtly. "She will be able to help you with your dress. I fancy you will be quite safe now." He turned on his heel and left the room. Lucretia sank down upon a chair and felt very much inclined to cry her eyes out.

In truth, Christopher had been thinking nothing severe about Lucretia. Seeing her in pain angered him enormously and, with a jolt, he realised that her safety and tranquillity was becoming material to his own happiness. It was a feeling that frightened him so much that he felt he must escape and put some distance between these unfamiliar emotions and the cause of them. Jostling amongst this mesh of feelings, the ardent desire to plant a facer upon Mr Edgworthington and make him pay for the discomfort he had caused Miss Lanyon kept working its way to the forefront, try as he would to push it out of his mind.

Having led his sister to Miss Lanyon's aid, Christopher left the party resolving to forget that any of the evening's happenings had taken place.

CHAPTER ELEVEN

Isabella and Mr Morley's elopement did not get off to an auspicious start. Mr Morley arrived at the appointed spot on time and waited with a sinking heart for the arrival of Lady Isabella. Fifteen minutes passed, and then another fifteen, and still the young lady had not arrived. Morley began to feel somewhat peeved and not a little anxious. Had she changed her mind, he wondered. Had something gone wrong and prevented her from meeting him? Another ten minutes passed without any sign of the hopeful bride. For all Mr Morley did not relish going through with his plan, he recognised it as his last resort; if this failed he could think of no other way out of his pecuniary difficulties. After a further ten minutes he began to give up hope of her arrival and started to feel a growing sense of ill-usage. He had had to hire the coach and horses at considerable expense, an outlay which he could ill afford. He paced up and down the pavement, his anger brewing nicely, stubbed his toe on a loose stone, and swore vehemently under his breath. At that moment, Isabella arrived.

"I thought you were not coming," he said pettishly. "You are very late, my lady."

"I know, and I am sorry for it, but it really could not be helped. You have no notion how difficult it is for a young lady to escape the watchful eyes of her guardians. As it is I had to bring Betsy along with me since I couldn't give her the slip." Isabella looked resentfully at her maid, whom Morley could see in Isabella's train. This did not in the least fit in with his plans and he was very angry with Isabella for making such a mull of the situation. But Isabella was also feeling aggrieved. Sneaking out of the house was less fun than she anticipated, and she was very much inclined to think that the difficulties encountered could have been avoided had the elopement taken place under the cover of night.

"Now, if we had tried to make our escape late last night or early this morning as I suggested, we would not have run into these difficulties!" she muttered. "But you *would* insist that you knew best about these things. My departure may at any moment be discovered so we had best get underway, I suppose. Only I do not have even a toothbrush to my name for I could not, in the sober light of day, escape with baggage in tow!"

"Never mind that, we can sort out all those things later," said Morley, now more cheerful. "But you can't bring your maid along with us. She'll have to say her goodbyes to you here."

"Oh, very well," said Isabella who had been trying to shake off this faithful retainer all morning. She looked in the unwanted maid's direction. "You must go back, Betsy, but you're not to tell them where I've gone, do you hear?"

"Oh, but Miss, they'll be so angry with me for not stopping you from taking this step! They would blame me and give me *such* a scold," she wailed in great fear. "Really you did ought to reconsider, it ain't at all the thing, so it isn't. To be alone in a man's company... possibly overnight," she whispered in great shock. "Oh, at least let me come along with you, for propriety's sake, Lady Isabella!"

"Nonsense, Betsy, have I not told you any number of times this morning that Mr Morley is my betrothed? We'll be married very soon, so I count him as practically my husband already. You cannot tell me that any one could be shocked to find a lady unaccompanied in the company of her husband. Really, Betsy, you are being most tiresome. I wish you will go away."

"I would be failing in my duty if I did that, so I would," Betsy said stubbornly. "And," she threatened, "I would have no choice but to go straight to your mama and tell her what you have done. It goes against the grain with me, to do something which you would not like, indeed have ordered me not to do, but my conscience could not let me do otherwise."

Isabella stamped her foot, firing up at this. Morley saw that he must intervene. "Now, now, Betsy, it is really not so bad, I assure you," he said. "I'll take good care of Lady Isabella and treat her with the utmost respect upon our journey. Your concern is very natural and does you credit. And your employers could not be angered with you, for you've done all that you ought this day. But consider our situation, you cannot mean to stand in the way of your mistress's happiness. What you suggest would ruin both our happiness forever. Surely you cannot be so cruel-hearted as to blight such a love as ours? I beg you, support us in our hour of need," he implored the maid, wearing his most innocent and wretched of expressions.

It moved the young servant deeply. She wrung her hands together, saying, "If only I knew what I ought to do for the best." Morley saw, with frustration, that her better judgement was winning out.

"Well then, Betsy, perhaps you ought to come along with us after all, since your scruples will not let you do otherwise. But please do make haste, ladies, we've wasted too much time already." Morley bundled them into the waiting carriage. Bringing along a third, and particularly well-conscienced, person on this enterprise did not fit with his plans, but he knew he had no choice.

Isabella was looking militant, for the presence of a chaperone on her adventure seemed most inapt, and she opened her mouth as if to say so. Morley stayed her tongue, however, with an understanding look, and by whispering in her ear as Betsy alighted the carriage, "Have no fear, we'll soon leave her behind." With this Isabella had to be satisfied. She realised how late their departure had become and, very much fearing that her absence would be soon noted, she hastened to settle herself into the coach and allow the enterprise to get underway.

In Grosvenor Square, Lucretia was nibbling half-heartedly on a piece of toast and drinking her morning chocolate in bed. This was unusual for her, since she normally went downstairs to eat her breakfast but, after a sleepless night spent wondering what Viscount Prendergast must think of her, her heart aching terribly, she was in no mood for company. She looked tired and sad, and tried to wave away the rest of the breakfast that had been brought up to her on the tray. Her concerned maid implored her not to.

"You will waste away, Miss, so you will. You really did ought to try to eat something. And you're looking terrible pale besides, I very much fear you are coming down with something. Ought I to ask Lady Rutland to call the doctor?"

Concern was writ so clear on her maid's face that Lucretia, sorry to have inspired such disquiet, tried to rally and smiled wanly at her. "I feel quite well, I assure you, Martha. Only I did not sleep well, that is all. Really don't look at me so worried, there is not the least need!"

Martha scrutinised Lucretia as she leafed languorously through the morning post, picking up one invitation after another with little enthusiasm. Midway through the pile she came across a letter from Isabella and, slicing the edges open, she read it in every expectation of boredom. To be sure it was most unusual for that lady to put herself to the trouble of putting pen to paper, and a lengthy epistle such as the one Lucretia held in her hand was most unlike Isabella, but Lucretia had no expectation that it would contain anything of any moment. Within moments, however, she sat up straighter in her bed, thrust the breakfast tray off her lap and threw back the bed covers exclaiming, "I must get up now. I must hurry."

"Now, now, Miss, what's all this to do? You must try and finish your breakfast before you get up or you'll have no strength for the day. And you have that picnic this afternoon, not to mention the Mytchett's ball this evening. If you don't take care, you will be quite knocked up by all this gallivanting, especially if you don't have any fuel inside you to see you through the day."

Lucretia looked at her maid, barely focusing on her. "Breakfast? Oh, there is no time for that now! Please hurry and get me some clothes out. What clothes? Oh, it makes not the least difference. Anything, only please hurry!"

Her maid was deeply shocked by her mistress's sudden lack of interest in the choosing of her attire, and this concerned her more than her mistress's very evident agitation.

174

"Don't stand there gaping at me…" remonstrated Lucretia. "Quick, quick I must get dressed this instant!" Martha set about getting out the garments and Lucretia put on her clothes in a fever, talking to herself all the while, "Oh, what will he think?… I must save her… He will be so angry…. He will blame me… Oh, this is all my fault!"

Her maid did not understand these passionate outpourings and was deeply concerned about her mistress, whom she had never seen so discomposed. "Now, now, Miss Lucretia," Martha soothed. "What has got into you? Hold still while I tighten these corsets. Hush now, all will be well."

Lucretia was not listening to her. She was quiet now, but her mind was all a whirl, wondering what best to do. "Is my cousin Arnold in the house? Please go and find out immediately, while I set my hair." Seeing the maid hovering and wanting to do her hair for her, she said with annoyance, "At once, Martha, please go and check for me. I must see him, it is so very important." Lucretia carried on arranging her hair as quickly as she could and waited for the maid to return.

"Yes, he's still here, Miss Lucretia," said the maid coming back into the room. "Stokes says he talked at breakfast of attending to business all morning in the library. Lady Rutland has gone out, however," she added, coming to the dressing table to assist Lucretia, taking the pins out of Lucretia's shaking hands and placing them in her hair herself, continuing "and Lord Rutland has gone to his club, I believe."

"I don't care about that. I must see my cousin at once! Hurry up, are you finished? At last!" Lucretia swept out of the room and rushed down the stairs. She burst into the library, to her cousin's considerable astonishment.

"Cressy, a pleasant surprise," said Arnold with a cheerful smile. "You have saved me from these cursed sums. I have added up this column no less than three times and reached a different answer every time…"

Lucretia broke in upon these words. "Thank God you are here, Arnold. Something terrible has happened, you must help me," she gasped, out of breath from rushing down the stairs.

"Good gad, what's amiss? Naturally I'm at your service, cousin. But do calm yourself now. Deep breaths," he said, pulling up a chair for her. "Deep breaths, there's a good girl. Now tell me all about it."

Lucretia pulled out the letter with an unsteady hand. "Oh, the silly, silly girl, how can she have been so stupid? Oh, he will never forgive me... I must save her from herself..." Arnold was no more enlightened by these outpourings than Martha had been.

"Slowly, cousin. You must explain it to me. Calm yourself, little one, all will be well."

Lucretia took some gulping breaths, realising at last what a state she was in, and pulled her scattered wits together. "Oh, I am behaving like a widgeon. Sorry, Arnold, I will try to make more sense. It is Lady Isabella, she writes to inform me of her elopement with Mr Morley. See, it is all here in this hateful letter." She held the offending article out to him, which he took and read.

"*Dear Miss Lanyon,*" Isabella had scrawled. "*I know what I write here will shock you, for I know the step I am about to take is most drastic, shameful even. Only the most terrible desperation could lead me to do this.*" Isabella's veritable enjoyment in the writing of such a missive echoed in every melodramatic line she had written.

"*My love for Mr Morley is so pure, so eternal, so overpowering,*" the letter continued, "*But I know my family will never accept him, and will never allow me to marry him while it is in their power to prevent it. For myself, I could endure the torment of being parted from my beloved, of waiting and waiting until I came of age and we might be together. But I cannot bear to inflict such pain on my beloved Everard. He is so deeply in love with me, he says he simply cannot bear to wait,*" Isabella had finished the line triumphantly.

"*He avers that the agony of being apart would destroy his soul piece by piece, and so we are left with no alternative but to elope. I write so that you will know that you need have no anxiety about me. I will have no cause to regret this decision, whatever should happen after, for my love for dearest Everard*

176

is all that matters. I must beg your forgiveness, however, if his choice causes you pain. Oh, best of friends, I would not hurt you for the world, but I could not overcome my feelings, my love for my darling!" Lucretia could not be ignorant that Isabella's true reason in writing to her was not, as she protested, to save her worry or beg her forgiveness, but to crow over her in belief that she had won Mr Morley's heart from Lucretia's clutches. But Lucretia did not care, her worry was for Lord Prendergast and it didn't matter to her how poisonous his sister could be.

"Truly it was written in the stars", Isabella had continued, *"and who am I, a mere mortal, to fight that which fate decrees? We must elope because my father would never countenance the match, and because he would surely persecute me with demands that I marry another. Please, please forgive me dear friend, if I have caused you hurt. I only hope that I may still be able to call you my friend after all is done. Yours etc… "*

Arnold Rutland, having finished reading this epistle, looked somewhat nauseated. "Revolting girl! She is welcome to her fate," he said, handing back the letter. "I confess that at this moment I almost feel sorry for Morley. But I don't see what this has to do with us."

"But Arnold, we must go after her!" said Lucretia, shocked by his indifference.

"Nonsense," he said.

"What do you mean, nonsense?" demanded Lucretia aghast. "To be sure, she has been very silly, but we cannot abandon her to the clutches of that odious man, even if she deserves it. She is my friend, Arnold, I must help her."

"Lord only knows why you are friends with her, for a more irksome female I hope I never meet! Add to which, that she quite clearly would have no qualms about inserting a sharp knife into your back. Why, it's clear that she triumphs in winning Morley from underneath your nose, which would be amusing if it wasn't so malicious. No, leave her to it, that's what I say, and good riddance."

"But to let her marry such a man!" Lucretia expostulated, "it is too heartless, we must save her."

"Marry? God gad, I don't think so! Morley's a loose fish, but he knows what he's about. Won't marry the girl, stands to reason, she's a repellent shrew. Just running off with her, which is not the same thing at all. Probably hoping the family will stump up, out of pocket, no doubt. Best thing you can do for her is not mention the affair to anyone, make it easier for them to hush it up, you know."

"Not marry her?" gasped Lucretia. "Surely you cannot think it? Surely Mr Morley could not be so dastardly? But that makes it all the more important that we go after her! And if not for her, then for her family's sake. Her foolishness will put them, so undeservedly, to such pain. And after all that the Viscount has done for me! We must bring her back to them, before it is too late!"

"Nonsense," said Arnold again. "No need."

"What can you mean?" she said exasperated. "Hurry, cousin, we must go after her as soon as can be!"

"Nah, leave that to Prendergast, or the Earl. It's their job to look after their own. No sense getting in the way, which we would, I'll be bound. Leave them to it, and keep out of the affair. Don't worry your pretty head over it. Speaking of which, you'd best go and sort out that quiz of a hairstyle, and you look like you dressed all by guess. Not like you at all. Better worry about that instead."

"What do you mean, leave it to the Prendergasts?" demanded Lucretia. "What if they don't know anything about it? We must warn them at the very least. But that would waste time and she must be rescued as soon as possible. All this talk is wasting time! Oh please, cousin, let us go after her at once! I could never forgive myself if we were too late! Every second's delay could be vital."

"Don't be silly, Cressy. They'll know all about it. Stands to reason." Lucretia looked unconvinced. "Well," Arnold said, "that's how women are. First thing a woman does when she's sneaking off is write a bunch of letters telling everyone what she's doing. Always the way."

"How can you be so sure?" Lucretia asked, appalled that anyone could be so stupid as to write to advertise the fact that they planned to secretly run off.

"Well, she sent you a letter, didn't she? Stands to reason that she wrote to everyone else as well. Clearly enjoyed it, if you ask me. Stuffed full of sensibility, ain't she?" Arnold said in disgust.

Lucretia saw the force of his argument, but worried just the same. "But we can't be sure, Arnold, can we? Please can we go after her, just to be certain she'll be safe? Please, Arnold, you must do this for me. I would be so very grateful. Please," she begged.

"Oh, very well, if you insist, Cressy." He looked towards the window, "Nice day for a drive after all. And it'll give you the opportunity to see me put my racing curricle through its paces. You'll like that."

Waiting for the servants to bring around Arnold's curricle, Lucretia was in agonies. Finally, they were on the road. To Lucretia's relief, her cousin was driving along at a spanking pace. In truth, Arnold Rutland was enjoying himself. He always took pleasure in driving his horses at speed and, having been roused out of his indifference, was excited by the prospect of foiling an intrigue and paying off an earlier score with Mr Morley. The rake deserved to have his plans spoiled for what he had put Lucretia through, Arnold reflected to himself.

"Cousin," Lucretia said after some time, "how will we find them? If they are not, as you suspect, going to Gretna Green, they could be anywhere."

"I have a little idea," said Arnold, unperturbed. "We shall see if I am proved correct."

Some hours later, hot on the heels of their quarry, Lucretia and Arnold turned off the Great North Road. Enquiries at the toll pikes along the way had so far confirmed that the elopers had passed in that direction, and that they were, thankfully, not many hours ahead.

"Where does this lead us then, cousin?" asked Lucretia, noticing they had pulled off the main route.

"Well, if I'm right, Morley is taking Lady Isabella to his own property. I fancy he hasn't much money, especially after defraying the expenses of the journey. His seat lies not too far from London, so the cost of the whole scheme will be as small as he can make it. Once they reach Morley Chase, there'll be no expenses to speak of, and only his own servants in on the show, who will naturally assist him in preventing Lady Isabella from making an escape, should she try."

"Oh, what a villain he is! But surely Isabella could not be so stupid as not to notice that this was not the way to Gretna Green?" She stopped upon this thought, recollecting that there seemed to be no bounds to Isabella's stupidity.

Arnold pulled in at the first inn they came across to see if he could gain any further information on the runaways. It seemed unlikely that the pair would have stopped there, for The Kings Head turned out to be a ramshackle and dirty place, but, reasoned Arnold, someone may have seen the carriage pass by.

Arnold entered the taproom and approached the host, who came forwards, all obsequiousness to greet him. His humble hostelry had never before accommodated the likes of such quality as that he saw before him. "Good day, sir," Arnold greeted the inn-keeper politely. "I'm desirous of catching up with some relatives of mine who, I believe, may have passed this way. Have you perhaps seen a post carriage go by in the last few hours? It contains my two cousins, a young lady with mousy brown hair and her brother, a tall, handsome gentleman?"

"Ho, ho, an intrigue, is it?" snickered the landlord.

"Nothing of the sort," said Arnold, drawing himself up haughtily. "What you suggest is, of course, ridiculous. It is merely that they go off to visit friends and I have the unhappy duty of chasing after them to call them back to London because of the sudden ill-health of one of our family."

The landlord, not believing a word that Arnold was saying, nevertheless realised that he had caused offence, and so was quick to feign belief, all apologies for his *faux pas*. He did not want to lose such an esteemed customer. "Let me get you some refreshments while I think on it, sir? There have been several carriages pass this way today. Now let me think, let me think…"

Arnold recognised this as a ploy to keep them there. He knew their visit would be the talk of the establishment for many months to come, and did not begrudge his host this small celebrity. Furthermore, he was hot and thirsty, and the prospect of refreshment was appealing, although he could not but be a little dubious of the likely cleanliness of the tableware. "Yes, do, I beg of you, provide myself and my sister with some refreshments," said Arnold. "And while you're at it, consider what you can remember. Do you have a private parlour that we may use?"

"Very good, sir, very good. Alas, there is only this taproom! But I beg you will make yourselves comfortable here. You will be quite private. As you can see there is only one other person present, and I fancy," he said with a wink, "that the young lady will be able to assist you in your enquiries."

Sat at a table in the corner, sniffling and wretched, was Betsy. Recognising her, Lucretia hastened over.

"Betsy?" she said in surprise, handing the tearful abigail the handkerchief of which she clearly stood in need.

"Oh, Miss Lanyon, oh, I am so glad you are come! Have you come after her?"

"Yes, we have come to collect my cousins," Lucretia said, looking pointedly in the direction of the landlord, "our uncle is very ill and, they must return with us to town straight away."

Betsy was quick-witted and understood the need to acquiesce in this version of the affair. But she did not see how the events that had befallen her could be made to fit in with the story Lucretia had concocted, so she nodded but sat silent. Lucretia realised the maid's difficulty and turned to the landlord saying, "And be sure to bring a lemonade for this lady also."

Lucretia talked to Arnold and Betsy most naturally on indifferent subjects while the landlord prepared the drinks. When he had put them down on the table, Arnold said to him firmly and dismissively, "Thank you that will be all. I will call you if we need anything further."

181

After Arnold had secured the door closed behind the landlord (to the nosy inn-keeper's great disappointment) Lucretia begged Betsy to give them an account of what had happened.

Some hours previously the eloping party had been progressing well, if uncomfortably. The scorching weather, which may have been enjoyable to those driving in a curricle, was, in a closed carriage with three hot and bothered bodies within, oppressively hot, and tempers had frayed.

Their journey started out on the main northern post road but, after a time, the carriage turned off this road. This would not have evoked any notice from Isabella, who was not paying attention to such things, but Betsy, to Mr Morley's acute discomfort did remark upon their change of course.

"I think your coachman cannot know where he is going, Mr Morley," Betsy said. "We have turned off the northern road and are, if I'm not mistaken, going east now," she observed.

"Hush, Betsy, what can you know of such things, being born and raised in London? You who have probably never been out of the city in your life!" sniggered Isabella.

"But I do know of them, Miss," returned Betsy with quiet dignity. "My uncle owns a farm up north of London and I have been to visit him several times, so I *am* familiar with the northern route."

While this exchange was going on, Mr Morley was given leisure to come up with a convincing lie to cover the fact that they were not heading to Gretna Green at all, thinking to himself that the annoying Betsy was turning out to be even more of a liability than he could have imagined.

"Well, I'm sure Mr Morley knows what he is about at any rate, whatever you say, Betsy," Isabella said, turning to her beloved expectantly.

"I thought it prudent to take a more circuitous route just in case we should be followed, that is all," said Morley.

"See!" said Isabella to Betsy triumphantly. But the maid was looking at Mr Morley keenly and seemed about to say more. She held her peace, however. Morley perceived that she was becoming suspicious, and resolved to be rid of her as soon as possible. He saw that an inn was in sight up ahead and directed the coachman to pull up. It was not the kind of inn usually frequented by the quality and no welcoming ostlers bustled out to take control of the horses or to tempt the travellers in.

This suited Morley's plan very well. He turned to Betsy. "You make yourself useful and go in and arrange for some refreshments to be brought out to us," he commanded, handing her some change.

"Yes indeed, for I am very thirsty," whinged Isabella. "Do hurry, Betsy!"

The maid did as directed. When she was gone, Morley turned to Isabella saying, "Alone at last, my darling! What a tiresome female your maid is! Shall we be rid of her?"

"And when I came out of the door, the carriage was driving off. They had left me here and I did not know what to do until you came along!" said Betsy finished and promptly burst into tears.

"There, there, Betsy, never mind. All will be well now, I promise," said Lucretia, rubbing the distressed maid's arm.

"How long ago was this?" asked Arnold. "How far behind them are we?"

"Oh, I feel like I have been here for hours and hours. But probably it is not so long. Maybe not more than an hour. But I cannot be sure," Betsy returned, sniffing into her handkerchief.

Lucretia looked anxiously at her cousin, who reassured her, "An hour? Well then, we'll catch them up easily."

Having finished their refreshments and paid their shot, the three set off to continue their search. They had not far to look. A mere matter of miles up the road, a carriage came in sight. As they approached, it became clear that some accident had taken place, for the carriage lay leaning awkwardly upon a broken wheel. At the side of the road stood Isabella, in the company of one of the postboys. Morley was nowhere to be seen. Drawing up alongside the damaged carriage, Lucretia said, descending from the phaeton, "Well met, Isabella! We have come to take you back to London."

"Cressy?" said Isabella in astonishment. "Have you come after me? You really should not have done, I thought my letter made it all clear. Surely you could not be so jealous as to come running after me!"

"Well, there's gratitude for you," muttered Arnold to his cousin in an undertone. "Are you sure you want to go through with this? There's still time to leave her out to dry!"

Lucretia chuckled and elbowed Arnold in the ribs, whispering, "Shhh, this is no time for funning!"

To her errant friend, she said, with a warning look at the postilion, "Hush, Isabella." In a very deliberate manner she continued, "Your uncle is not well, we have come to fetch you back to his sick bed."

"Fustian!" exclaimed Isabella in irritation. "There's no need to make up stories, I'm not ashamed of what I am doing. And this postboy knows more about it than you do, so at least stop talking nonsense. And another thing," she continued, now rather heated, "I'm not going anywhere with you. Betsy, you were very wrong to tell them where I was gone to! I'm very angry with you!"

Lucretia was furious. "Now that's enough, Isabella! You are being ridiculous. How *dare* you blame Betsy for any part in what has happened today? Not only have you so lost all sense as to run off with a notorious rake, risking both your good reputation and your family's, and worry me half to death. But you have also been so heartless as to abandon your maid, without so much as a by your leave, in an out of the way spot, completely unprotected. You have been very, very naughty and very foolish. And now you'll listen to me and do as you are told. My cousin has been so kind as to bring me chasing after you, at considerable inconvenience to himself, and now you will get into the curricle this second and come home with us!" She stopped, having wrung this impressive peal over the uncomfortable Isabella, and waited by the steps of the carriage expectantly. Arnold looked at his cousin, impressed, experiencing a desire, which he was not so unwise as to indulge, to applaud the first-rate trimming down she had given the runaway.

"Get in," snapped Lucretia, gesturing towards the conveyance. Isabella looked stunned and, for a moment, as if she did not know what to do. Then her face began to screw up. But Lucretia was having none of it.

"Don't you dare start to cry or have hysterics, or I will be forced to deliver a slap across your face. And don't for a minute believe that I won't do it. I am taking you home this instant, young lady. This instant!"

Isabella had had a hot and bothersome day. Elopements, after all, were not half so romantic as she imagined, and her beloved, when she last saw him, had been bad-tempered and vexatious. On balance, she wished herself at home, ready to sit down to a comfortable dinner followed by an evening spent in light-hearted flirtation with any suitable beau. So, to everyone's surprise, she climbed into the curricle with very good grace.

"But where is Mr Morley?" asked the ever-observant Betsy.

"Gone to find someone to fix the carriage," explained Isabella, who then added defiantly, "I ordered him to go with the postboy, for you know such people always make a mess of things." Lucretia and Arnold grinned at each other, both thinking the same thing: that Mr Morley had volunteered to accompany the postboy so he could escape from his companion for a while. But since Morley was not there to deny Isabella's story, she was allowed her prevarication.

"But how are we all to get home?" fussed Betsy, worried she was once again to be left behind. "There is not enough room for four."

Arnold smiled kindly down upon her. "Now don't worry, Miss Betsy, we'll not abandon you, I promise. But it is a poser... I think Morley really does owe me something for the trouble he has caused me today," Arnold mused aloud to himself, after mulling the problem over. "Enough that he ought not to begrudge me the use of one of his horses. Lucretia, do you think you could manage the curricle as far as the nearest coach house where we can hire a chaise?" She nodded. "That's a girl! Knew you'd be up to it."

The postboy, now almost forgotten, was moved to expostulate, "You can't take one of these horses, sir. I can't let you. Bound to look after them, I am." But the postilion was distracted by admiration of Arnold's horses and his outburst was somewhat unconvincing. He was standing at the heads of Arnold's beautiful bay pair, stroking them reverently, and had barely been paying attention to the commotion around him until this moment.

Arnold walked over to the boy and slipped a number of heavy coins into his hand. "Don't worry, I'll make all right with Morley," Arnold said, and then he leaned down to speak quietly into the postboy's ear: "Tell him I overpowered you. You may as well, for if you try to stop me I'll be forced to carry it out for real." This was said with a cheerful grin and without a hint of malice. On the instant, the postboy decided that Arnold Rutland was a right'un.

"I will, sir, thank you, sir," said the boy, pocketing the change. "Although I feel I ought to warn you that they're not like these prime steppers o'yours. You'll find either horse sadly slow going, regular bone setters, if you must know."

"Know horseflesh do you, son?" he asked. "What's your name, boy?"

"Jimmy, sir. And yes, sir, horses is my favourite thing, sir. Never seen such a beautiful pair as your two though."

Arnold looked him over. "Well, if you're ever in need of employment, look me up in town. I feel I owe you." Jimmy was speechless at this tribute and took, with awe, the card Arnold handed him. "I could use a good tiger, is all," explained Arnold light-heartedly, seeing the looks of surprise of all persons present.

"Oh, thank you, sir," Jimmy stammered. "I will, sir... I mean... if you're serious, sir?" he asked hopefully.

"You know what?" said Arnold making a discovery, "I do believe I am."

Lucretia was just stepping into the carriage after Betsy and Isabella, and settling herself into the driving seat. Jimmy looked at her anxiously and then turned to Arnold saying in an anxious undertone, "Are you really gonna trust a mort to manage your bays? Do you think you ought, sir? Pretty high-spirited horses for a woman to handle!"

Arnold looked at him in considerable amusement. "Indeed I do, rascal," he said ruffling Jimmy's hair. "You don't know my cousin, she's at home to a peg. Well she ought to be... I taught her to drive myself!" Jimmy continued to look unconvinced, but Arnold's thoughts had turned away from the issue.

"Now, Jimmy, you'll tell our mutual friend Morley where we have gone?" he said to the postilion. "No, best write a note," Arnold mused. He dug out his pocketbook and scribbled off a message to Mr Morley, during the course of which his sense of humour got the better of him and he wrote, *Everard, I've taken Lady Isabella home. No need to thank me for coming to your rescue. Borrowed one of your horses so we'll call it even.* He made as if to fold up the paper and then, as an afterthought, added in an uncharacteristically selfless gesture: *Don't blame the postboy, he tried his best.*

CHAPTER TWELVE

Arnold had surmised incorrectly: Isabella Prendergast had not informed her family of her planned elopement. The effort of writing the one letter to Lucretia (although she enjoyed composing the epistle enormously) had exhausted all her literary talent and she had written no other. Before too long, her absence was noted by the Prendergast household. When she did not appear for lunch, her mother, whose memory was surprisingly elastic, recollected that Isabella had told her she was dining with Miss Lanyon and would spend the afternoon with her. However, when evening came and there was still no sign of the young lady, questions must be asked. When it was discovered that Betsy was also nowhere to be found, concern began to be felt for Isabella's whereabouts.

Informed of this remarkable fact, Lord Godolphin displayed some signs of consternation. He had no idea that his daughter could be so foolish as to embroil herself in an elopement, but she was a very silly girl, and he could not but fear that she had got herself into some manner of scrape. Her mother, in melodramatic accents, insisted that she could feel it in her bones that some terrible accident had befallen her most beloved of daughters. It was fortunate for the peace of the household, therefore, that the carriage containing this precious cargo pulled up outside the house just as this commotion was about to result in a fever pitch of hysterics which that would inevitably lead to the advertisement of Isabella's disappearance.

Isabella descended from the carriage and climbed the stairs to the house sullen-faced and tired, with every intention of hiding herself in her room. Miss Lanyon, still very angry with her, followed her into the house, insistent that her parents must know of her recent behaviour. In this she was supported by Arnold Rutland who, in mischievous expectation of enjoyment, resolved to be present at the scene of Isabella's confession, and very much hoped to have the pleasure of seeing Lucretia give her another fine trimming down for her actions. Betsy, tired and worn out, slipped unobtrusively off to the servants' quarters and hoped very much that the day's events would not result in her losing her job.

Opening the door to them, the butler, Staines, impassively took Arnold's hat and welcomed his young mistress with a bow. Lady Godolphin, unconscious of the party's arrival, had just then erupted into the hall in her husband's train wailing, "Oh, my beautiful little girl, what can have happened to you? I feel sure you are dead, it is too terrible..." But she fell suddenly silent as she caught sight of the would-be corpse. Having talked herself into the tragic role of a bereaved mother, the staid denouement was a sad disappointment. She had to blink several times at the sight of her daughter, to bring herself back from the melodramatic piece playing in her head.

"Bella, you are returned, and safely in one piece," Lady Godolphin said blandly, barely hiding her disappointment.

"Oh, mama, I'm sorry I'm late," said Isabella, trying for a voice of light-hearted unconcern. "Only, I was having such a delightful afternoon with Miss Lanyon and Mr Arnold Rutland that we quite forgot the time, and now we have given you such worry. I am very sorry for it. I beg your forgiveness, really, mama, I do."

Lucretia was looking stern and Arnold amused but, conscious of the presence of the servants, they kept their peace. Isabella turned to her rescuers and said, "Thank you for seeing me safely back. I'm sorry you'll be late home and hope that Lady Rutland has not been worrying after you. I beg you, do not feel obliged to linger here, you must go and reassure her that you are unharmed," in every hope of shuffling them out of the house.

"There's really not the least need. My aunt never worries, she knows that in Arnold's company I am always quite safe," said Lucretia, with no notion of being so easily fobbed off by Isabella. Most unfortunately, Lord Godolphin and his son, hearing all the noise, arrived in the hall to catch these words.

The Viscount took this assurance as proof of all he had been hearing about the intimacy between Miss Lanyon and her cousin, and disappeared back into the library forthwith. Lucretia blushed as she caught sight of him, and watched him leave with a look patent with longing and sadness. Arnold caught this look with some surprise. Ah, so that's the way the wind's blowing, he thought to himself, amused.

Lord Godolphin, remaining in the hall, said cheerfully, "Ah, Bella, I see you're home safely so there was no cause for concern after all. You must make haste to ready yourself for dinner or cook will be frantic with worry over the spoiling of the partridges! Your servant, Miss Lanyon, Mr Rutland," he said, nodding in the guests' direction. "Do you stay for dinner? No doubt there's plenty of food to go around. To be sure it is only a small family party this evening, but you are most welcome to take your pot luck with us, should you wish it?"

"That's most kind in you, sir, but we cannot stay," said Lucretia. "I don't wish to hold up your dinner but, nevertheless, I am charged with a number of important messages from my aunt and uncle which I must give you." Looking warningly round at the servants, she gave Lord Godolphin a look pregnant with meaning. Intrigued, Lord Godolphin bid Staines bring them refreshments and tell the cook to put back dinner, after which he civilly invited Lucretia and Arnold into the drawing room.

Isabella made as if to escape upstairs and Lucretia, unable to hide her severity said, "Not so fast, Isabella, their messages concern you also." She looked so fierce that Isabella felt sure that she would drag her bodily into the drawing room if need be, despite the interested eyes of the servants being upon them.

Safely inside, after Staines had left the refreshments and the Earl had poured his visitors a drink, Lucretia said, "I'm very sorry to intrude upon you in this way, Lord and Lady Godolphin, but I feel it is important that you hear what has happened today. Well then, Isabella, tell your mama and papa what you have done."

Isabella burst into tears, which very soon turned into hysterics and in the end Miss Lanyon calmly picked up her glass of ratafia and threw it on Isabella's face saying, "Enough, Isabella! You can cry all you like but you have been very wicked and your parents must know of it, in case there should be repercussions. If you do not tell them, then I will."

Lady Godolphin, swelling with indignation, rounded on Lucretia crying, "How dare you throw a drink in my daughter's face, and when she's so upset as well! Have you no heart?"

"Hush …" said Lord Godolphin. "Miss Lanyon, since my daughter is currently incapable of coherent speech, I beg you will add to your kindnesses this day and inform us of what has passed."

Lucretia told him of the day's events calmly and succinctly, and when she had finished her recital said, "We have brought her home safely, and as discreetly as possible. With luck, there will be no more heard of this unfortunate incident. I am sorry we could not have stopped her before things had gone so far. I feel very guilty, for it is my fault that such a man has had the opportunity to become intimate with your daughter. And, what is more, I ought to have predicted such an event and prevented it. For that I beg your forgiveness, sir. I cannot stay longer," Lucretia looked at the clock. "My aunt must by now be wondering what has become of us. I only beg that you are very kind to little Betsy; she tried as hard as she could to stop Isabella from doing what she did, and when she could not, tried to protect her by steadfastly refusing to leave her side. She was repaid by being abandoned most heartlessly and that, I think," declared Lucretia, throwing Isabella a reproachful look, "is almost worse than all the rest!"

With that she swept majestically out of the room, in a manner so poised and dignified that it did Lady Rutland proud. Arnold followed her, bemused, and accompanied her home. In the carriage, Lucretia felt her cousin's eyes upon her and turned to him, questioning, "Well, cousin, why do you stare at me so?"

He grinned. "You are quite remarkable, cousin. I have no love for ratafia but I would never have used it so! People rarely surprise me, but you have succeeded in astounding me. I congratulate you. I have never been more pleased to see someone treated so in my life." He chortled at the recollection of Lady Isabella's shocked face.

"Oh dear, was it too terrible?" exclaimed Lucretia. "I ought not to have done it. But she was so very trying!"

"Fudge! She never deserved anything more in her life. Really, Lucretia, you are so very remarkable I feel almost that I ought to do as my mother wishes and make you my wife." They looked at each other for a long moment and then both fell about in merriment, for the thought of marriage to each other was exquisitely humorous to them both.

After she had laughed herself out, Lucretia said, "I hope you will not be offended, Arnold, if I tell you that you are not at all the kind of man that I wish to be married to!"

"Not at all," he said politely, "if you will not take it amiss if I tell you that I have no wish to be married to you either. Although to be sure I must be the only bachelor in London who does not wish it! In fact," he said giving the idea some consideration, "I have no wish to be married at all."

Lucretia smiled at him. But then, after a time, said thoughtfully, "Does she really wish it, my aunt, that we should be married?"

"But of course, can it be that you had not noticed?"

Lucretia considered. "Oh dear," she said, and then fell into a pensive pose. Arnold studied her. I must cultivate my friendship with Christopher Prendergast, he thought.

Christopher sat disconsolately in the library, staring at a spot on the wall where two sheets of wallpaper met, and wondering how to overcome the painful sensation that had rooted itself in his stomach, when the sound of not one, but two, ladies having hysterics came to his ears. It was the last thing he wanted to deal with in his present mood, and he was very much inclined to sneak out of the house and dine elsewhere.

Just then, his father entered the room with a hunted expression and, seeing the grave look on his face, Christopher went to the sideboard and poured him a drink. The Earl wore an expression that Christopher had never seen before, somehow grey and sickened.

"Father?" asked Christopher, and then very gently, "father, what is it? What has happened?"

He looked up at Christopher, barely seeing him. "I have failed her, I have failed my daughter. I knew her to be absurdly silly and I should have tried to make her more sensible. The blame for all this rests with me. And it rests heavily."

"Gammon! Dash it, it's not your fault that Bella's so silly! And what can that signify anyway. What's happened?"

"Your sister," said the Earl with a disgusted snort, "is so lost to all sense of propriety as to have attempted to… to…" He stopped as if he could almost not bring himself to finish, "… to elope with Mr Morley. And if it were not for the kind offices of Miss Lanyon and Mr Rutland…" The juxtaposition of the two names caused Christopher another stab of pain, but he pushed it to one side. That was not important right now.

The Earl looked at his son sadly, as if pleading for absolution, and said, "Christopher, I knew her to be silly. But I had no notion she could be so wicked, so immoral. And the worst of it is that she isn't even sorry. Not really sorry."

Christopher had never seen him like this and the raw emotion on his father's face made Christopher acutely uncomfortable. He was not accustomed to thinking of his father as vulnerable in any way, and the realisation that there were times when his father needed support was an unnerving truth. He wanted to do his best to console him, but he wasn't used to such a role and didn't quite know how. He laid his hand on his father's shoulder and squeezed it in a way he hoped was reassuring, saying awkwardly, "None of this is your fault, father. No need to reproach yourself. What I mean is, well… Bella's always been addlebrained, there's nothing new in that! And dash it, I'm damned sure you've never encouraged her in it! And for all her mawkishness no one could've imagined she'd do anything so disgraceful. If this is anyone's fault it's…" His other hand clenched into a tight fist and his face was grim, "…it's that man. Morley. Hell and the devil confound him! Cursed loose fish and everyone knows it! But he won't dare show his face again after this, so at least we'll be rid of him." This brought his thoughts back to Miss Lanyon. He had been finding that most topics seemed to bring his thoughts round to Miss Lanyon these days. It was a development he wasn't sure what to make of, so he tried to put it out of his mind.

A further development of the story came to Arnold several days later. His valet padded hesitantly into his dressing room, cleared his throat with an embarrassed cough, and said, "Begging your pardon, sir, but Silchester informs me that there is a…" he cleared his throat self-consciously once again.

"Now out with it, man!" demanded Arnold. "What is there? Don't keep me in suspense, dash it!"

"He says that there is a young person here to see you."

"Young person? Good heavens! Get rid of her! Can't be having these women turning up at m'mother's house of all places! Really, Banson, you ought to know better. What do I pay you for, if not to sort out things like this?"

"It is not a young lady," said Banson with dignity.

"Just as I said, not a young lady, must be one of my ladybirds. Tell Silchester to fob her off!"

"It is not a woman at all," Banson informed his master blandly.

"Well then, I don't see who it could be," exclaimed Arnold in great surprise. "But I'm not expecting anyone, so it can't be anyone I want to see. And I gather from your tone that it's not someone you feel I ought to see. Get rid of him, man, get rid of him."

"Silchester has been trying to do so, sir. But he informs me that the young person, boy, in fact, is most persistent. He insists," Banson said, avoiding his employer's eye, "that you invited him to, erm, look you up in town. He told Silchester that you would be very angry if he turned him away, and that you needed him." Here the valet could not keep the incredulity out of his voice. "Of course, I said to Silchester that it was all a hum, and what could you possibly want with a boy, but," Banson's voice dropped to a whisper, "Silchester says he has your card, sir." In a normal tone, he continued, "The boy, it seems, insists that you offered him a job."

Arnold's brow cleared. "Did he, by Jove? Well, I'll be damned! If he's the chap I'm thinking of, I did offer him a job. But Thunder an' Turf, I never thought he'd take me up on the offer! Tell Silchester to send him to the stables, and to instruct Mrs Hickson to feed him there. I'll come along and see the boy later." He chuckled to himself saying again, "Well, I'll be damned," as he continued dressing.

The valet returned a few minutes later and tut-tutted over Arnold's carelessly tied neck cloth. "If you would just allow me, sir, to…"

Called before his new master some hours later, Jimmy was in high spirits. He had been fed better than he was accustomed to in the stables and had had time to make friends with those of Arnold's horses stabled in town. Never had he seen such a magnificent collection of horseflesh, and he had endeared himself to Arnold's coachman by instantly making himself useful in the care of the creatures, displaying considerable aptitude in his tasks.

"Well then, Jimmy," said Arnold. "So you are to be my tiger. I trust you know what the job entails?" Jimmy nodded enthusiastically. "Hickson gives you a favourable report and says he thinks you will do very well in your new role."

"Yes, sir, thank you, sir," said Jimmy looking up at Arnold with eyes full of hero-worship. "Regular prime-steppers you got here. Whole stable full of 'em and that's a fact. And the grub ain't half bad neither."

"Now tell me, urchin, what became of our friend Mr Morley after we left the other day. Am I quite in his bad books? Not that it signifies in the least."

Jimmy's eyes twinkled mischievously. "Well, he weren't above half pleased and that's for sure! Having come back with Fred, that's the other postboy, he brought along another cove to fix the wheel. Well, I didn't like to point it out to him, but he was a regular rum touch this cove. Gimlet-eyed, crusty fellow, he were. Took 'im hours to fix the wheel, and when he did finish the job, he demanded three times what the job were worth. Mr Morley reached into 'is pocket, to pay him

like, only to find that his purse was nowhere to be found!"
Jimmy chuckled at the recollection.

"Fred is a bit light-fingered, see," Jimmy elaborated,
"used to be a foot-scamperer afore he were a postboy. And, for
all he had the look of a well-breeched cove, Mr Morley wasn't
at all generous with the ready; so Fred thought it only right to
help hisself to a little extra. Course, Morley weren't none the
wiser – Fred, being right good with his fambles, had snaffled his
purse all secret like..." Thinking on this, Jimmy hastened to
add, "Not that I'm into that sort of lay, sir, so you've no need to
worry on that head. And Fred wouldn't have done it neither if
Mr Morley wasn't such a clutch-fisted fellow. Got his just
desserts, if you ask me. But anyways, being unable to pay the
wheelwright, who seemed ready to come up mighty ugly, Mr
Morley was forced to give him 'is watch in payment. On top of
the fact that the gentry mort had been swooped out from under
his nose, and that note you wrote, well, he was in a fair way to
blowing his top."

"Naturally, Fred and I had to ask him where he was
going to find the blunt to pay us off for the journey," continued
Jimmy, chortling, "seeing as how he didn't have enough ready
for the fixing of the wheel, let alone the rest of the trip. Alls we
could do is refuse to budge until he offered us one of his flash
pins as a payment of good faith. Quite mad as fire he were by
then! Funny, when you think on how Fred had his blunt in his
pocket the whole time." Jimmy grinned at Arnold who, unable
to hold his countenance, was chuckling.

"Add to which, of course," continued the loquacious
Jimmy after this encouraging reaction from his master, "with
only one horse, and a regular slug at that, it was right slow going
the rest of the way. Never seen a man more pleased to find
hisself at home by the end of it!"

Arnold was so delighted by the amusement that this
recital had afforded him, that he added to his favour with his
young employee by dropping a heavy coin in his hand and
ruffling his hair saying, "Well, you young scamp, don't be
trying those tricks on me or you'll find yourself soundly

whipped, be warned. And mind you listen to what Hickson tells you and do just as he says."

"Yes, sir," said Jimmy with a look of idolatry.

CHAPTER THIRTEEN

Mr Strangwald was not having a good time of it. The Admiral showed no disposition to leave town, or to desist from his plans to set his son up in business, and thus Strangwald now spent much of his time hiding from his father. Since he could not do so in the comfort of his lodgings (for his father would certainly seek him out there), he spent his days on various outings in the localities least likely to attract his father or, when called to go places where he might come across him, comporting himself with a surreptitiousness that made him look most peculiar.

That day, however, Strangwald was engaged in a shopping expedition on Bond Street which was so enjoyable that he had quite forgotten about the black shadow cast by the Admiral since his return to London. His contentment was soon shattered, however, by the appearance of his father further down the street. Fortunately for Strangwald, he spotted this gentleman before the Admiral chanced to catch sight of his errant son. This allowed Strangwald the opportunity to duck into the nearest shop, which happened to be Hookham's circulating library. No great reader, Strangwald found himself in unfamiliar territory but, most felicitously, he discovered that such places were enormously conducive to hiding oneself.

He could be safe behind the walls of bookshelves, and he ensconced himself behind a bookcase which permitted him, through the act of peeking round its corner, to keep the shop windows in his sight. This would allow him to make good his escape once he had seen his father pass by. Not surprisingly, he received some odd looks on account of this behaviour, and he endeavoured to make himself look less eccentric by feigning interest in the books on the shelves before him. Never before had he realised the wide range of topics which authors had chosen to make their lives' works. Momentarily distracted by this thought from his evasive manoeuvres, he was recalled back to this enterprise by the ringing of the bell on the door indicating the entrance into the shop of another patron who, Strangwald saw with a sinking heart, was his father.

Moving further into the shop to put greater distance between himself and his father, Strangwald found himself concealed behind a different set of shelves and, through the gaps between the books housed on these, he could see Miss Pycroft and her mother. Miss Pycroft looked miserable, and it was not long before Strangwald realised why. He recognised, with pity and understanding, the pain of a child subjected to the unkindness and brutality of a parent. Mrs Pycroft was talking and talking, every word a chastisement of her poor daughter.

"Cecelia, what are you looking at there?" she asked sharply, snatching the book Miss Pycroft was holding out of her hand.

"Novels? Really, Ceccy, what is this nonsense? Good heavens, it is one of Mrs Radcliffe's deplorable offerings!" (which of course she could not know to be deplorable had she not read them, as she had done with secret enjoyment). "How vulgar! No, don't screw up your face like that at me, it makes you look quite ugly. Do strive for a little countenance. You know I have only your best interests at heart."

"Yes, mama," said Miss Pycroft in a colourless voice.

"And stand up straight. I am ashamed to see a daughter of mine slouching in such an way. Really, you ought to know better! I have a good mind to talk to Miss Trimble about how little finishing of you she did at that so-called finishing school of hers, which we sent you to at such great expense. Although to be sure, the fault more than likely lies at your door. You are lazy, and no doubt did not apply yourself to your lessons. Always in a daydream, with no thought for your family, ungrateful girl. You must try to present a creditable appearance for my sake at least."

"I'm sorry, mama. I do try, mama," said Miss Pycroft, all wretched penitence. Poor Miss Pycroft, thought Strangwald, with strong empathy.

"Now hurry up, hurry up," said Mrs Pycroft talking all the while. "We must go to Price & Gosnell's to see if we cannot find a concoction that can improve your skin. Mrs Hennessy says their lavender water worked wonders on her daughter Caroline's complexion. At any rate, we must do something, no gentleman will have a thought for you looking as you do. No wonder you have not found a husband! And when I think of all the opportunities you have had this season. Not one single offer."

They were walking in Mr Strangwald's direction. Rather than removing himself from their path, a feeling of chivalry overcame him and he stepped out before them. "Good day, Miss Pycroft," he said, bowing deeply. "And Mrs Pycroft, what a lovely surprise. Book-hunting I see?"

"One usually does, in a library," said Mrs Pycroft tartly, who had no very high opinion of Mr Strangwald.

"Well, I hope you'll be reading Mrs Radcliffe's latest work," Strangwald said, picking up on the author that had been so censured by Mrs Pycroft. "I do not know when I have enjoyed a novel more," he improvised, having never read this or any other novel in his life, which soon became evident as he continued, "Of course, it is based on the true life-story of the marvellous King Olaf of Denmark, who took great pride in being a renowned apiarist. Speaking of bee-keepers, it was lovely to have met you, and looking in such high bloom, at Mrs Buttercroft's picnic the other day." Mrs and Miss Pycroft looked startled by this seeming *non sequitur*. In explanation Strangwald countered, "Oh, did you not know? Mrs Buttercroft is such a great lover of honey that she keeps her own hives in her attic. Quite marvellous, I assure you, and the honey, well you tried it, Miss Pycroft, a triumph! Anyway, I do hope you enjoyed the picnic, I do not know when I have enjoyed conversing with someone more," Strangwald added with pointed kindness.

Mrs Pycroft was regarding him with disgust, unable to decide whether he was amusing himself at their expense or whether he was touched in his upper works. Miss Pycroft, unused to compliments of any sort, went pink with pleasure.

"I enjoyed talking to you too, Mr Strangwald. Do you go to Almacks tonight? I do hope we will see you there," said Cecelia shyly.

"I…" Mr Strangwald opened his mouth to reply but at that moment felt a heavy hand on his shoulder.

"There you are, son, how lucky I am to have caught up with you," the Admiral said dryly.

"Father," squeaked Mr Strangwald in a small, scared voice. He made a slight jerk, as if he would escape, but found that the hand on his shoulder tightened painfully. Then his eye caught Miss Pycroft's and he saw she was smiling sympathetically at him. This helped him to find greater strength and, drawing himself up, he said in a more natural voice, "Hello, father. Nice to see you. I'm afraid we've missed seeing each other around of late. I'm glad to have bumped into you."

"Indeed," mocked the Admiral. He then turned to Mrs Pycroft saying politely, "Mrs Pycroft, how do you do? And this must be your daughter? Your servant, Miss Pycroft." The Admiral executed a little bow and directed his intense staring eyes at Miss Pycroft.

Cecelia looked at the Admiral and took in his fiery eyes overhung by dark, bushy eyebrows and quailed. His appearance and the gruff tones of his voice frightened the timid Miss Pycroft and she shook a little under his unwavering gaze. The Admiral had no time for nervous creatures; it was what frustrated him most about his son. He could not understand jumpiness, for it was an unfamiliar concept to him, and to see it in others bred his contempt.

"Well then, Bertram," he said, instantly dismissing Miss Pycroft from his mind and turning back to his son, "now we have had the good fortune to find ourselves in each other's company at last, perhaps you will do me the honour of escorting me home." It was politely said, but it was nevertheless an order and Strangwald recognised it as such.

"Yes, sir, of course, sir," said Mr Strangwald sadly, but he was heartened once again by an understanding look from Miss Pycroft as he left the shop in his father's wake. He heard

Mrs Pycroft continue her ceaseless infliction of censure upon the poor Miss Pycroft as he left.

"Don't stand there gaping after him, it makes you look even more of a widgeon than you actually are, Cecilia. Really you should not be wasting your time talking to such men as Mr Strangwald. I'll admit his father is a most estimable gentleman but that son of his... bees in her attic?! Bats in his belfry more like! Why the man is nothing more than a halfwit!"

Much to her mother's surprise, the invariably acquiescent Miss Pycroft disagreed with her mother at this point, saying, "He is not, mama, He's a most agreeable and kind gentleman."

Stunned by her own bravery, Miss Pycroft fell silent. Mrs Pycroft, recovering from the shock of her daughter's dissent, carried on as if Cecelia had not said anything at all.

Christopher was struggling with his own demons. The impression of closeness he had seen between Lucretia and her cousin hung like a cold, sodden hunting jacket on his shoulders. He wanted to see Miss Lanyon, converse with her, perhaps take her out in his carriage. He wanted to advise her on the subject of ribbons and reticules and to show her his ocean blue pantaloons and his very fine new handkerchiefs. He found he could no longer put these thoughts out of his mind. He had, at last, realised that the strange feelings he was experiencing meant that he was in love with her. He was an honest fellow and admitted it to himself with little equivocation.

Having conceded the fact, and being a man of action, he stood up out of his chair and began pacing the room. Dash it! he cursed, reaching the resolution to throw his hat into the ring and try to win the lady's regard. That she had many suitors he knew, but she had so far turned down all the offers for her hand, so there may yet be some hope for him. Certainly, she always seemed pleased to see him. There was, of course, the small problem of Arnold Rutland and whether Lucretia planned to marry him. But Christopher was a sporting gentleman and his feelings for Lucretia were such that he felt he must try for her hand, whatever the outcome might be.

Having reached this decision, however, he had no notion of how to go about wooing a lady. He battled with the problem for some time but in the end admitted to himself that he needed help. Casting his thoughts around, he contemplated who, amongst his friends, would be the most suitable to assist him in the enterprise. It was a subject which, naturally, he could only broach with his closest of friends, and so his choice lay between his intimate cronies Castleton and Strangwald. There seemed little doubt as to the decision, and thus it was that he set off to call upon Mr Castleton without delay to ask his advice.

"Hallo, Clem," he said, having been shown into the library at that gentleman's house.

Mr Castleton was seated at his desk and looked up as Christopher entered the room. "Topher, what a pleasant surprise!" He dotted a full stop on the paper before him with some energy, saying, "Your timing is excellent! I have just now finished my latest ode. You can be my first critic."

"Never mind that," said Christopher hastily, in no mood to hear any of Castleton's verses which, while not being characterised by being good, were nevertheless invariably very lengthy. "Come to ask your advice, don't know who else to turn to…" he broke off, suddenly struck with shyness, realising the difficulty in admitting his feelings to anyone else. He stood in silent discomfort, shuffling from one foot to the other.

Castleton was a perspicacious fellow, and noted his friend's embarrassment enough that it drew his attention from his throes of literary genius. "At your service, Topher. Only have a seat, dear chap, and tell me all about it. Can see it's got you in a regular pickle."

Christopher sat down but still didn't know quite how to begin. "Tell you what," said Castleton, "let's have a drink. Always much easier to talk things out over a drink. As I said in that villanelle I wrote a while back… you remember the one, on the subject of pies?" Christopher looked at him blankly, but Castleton was not to be put off his penchant for quoting his own work. "Well, anyway, the line went 'when it comes to pouring out your heart, a drink with a friend beats apple tart'. Seems apt for the circumstances, don't you think? Besides which, you've got to admit it's a damn fine rhyme, even if I do say so myself!" Christopher grunted and Castleton, realising that this wasn't a time for pursuing his own literary fame, got up and poured out two glasses of burgundy, bringing one over to his friend.

The distraction of having a drink in his hand seemed to make it easier for Christopher to start. "Thing is, Clem, well..." he stammered. "Well, you're good with the ladies." He ground to a halt.

"Ah," said Castleton, looking at his friend acutely. "Concerns a lady, does it? Well, can't say I'm not surprised, seeing as how you're not generally in the petticoat line. But these things do have a habit of creeping up on one. The itchy, itchy hand of fate will touch us all before too late," he said with aplomb. "I say that's a good line!" he exclaimed, impressed by his own genius. "I must use it in my next work. Beats 'out out damn spot' to flinders! Do you know, I'm thinking of writing a tragedy, what do you..." he broke off upon seeing Christopher's face, and remembered why he was there. "Sorry, old chap, got distracted. Take a deep breath and tell me all about it."

"See, the thing is, there's this lady. Well... I've become rather..." Christopher paused, blushed in excruciating embarrassment, and searched for the right word, "I've become rather fond of her. I'm not saying she feels the same way. I mean, I don't know whether she does or not. But well, I hope she does. And, well... I was rather hoping I could make her feel the same way. Ask her, you know... Only I've no notion how to go about it all." He stopped after this somewhat tortuous recital and looked at his friend hopefully. "I mean, well, you're good with the ladies, Clem, thought you might be able to help."

"Nothing could be easier, dear fellow. Have no fear! Ladies, God bless 'em, are simple creatures, easy to win them over if you only know how. We'll see you all right and tight, don't you worry."

Christopher sighed with relief. "Will you, Clem? Much obliged. Just tell me where to start 'cos I haven't the foggiest idea!"

"May I ask who the fair lady is?"

Christopher hesitated but took a deep breath and finally said, "Miss Lanyon."

"Miss Lanyon? The Incalculable? Good God!" Castleton exclaimed, taken aback. "Not a chance, Topher! She's the toast of all London. Above your touch, I'm afraid. Better pick someone more suitable." Christopher's face fell and Castleton realised how unkind and unflattering his outburst had been.

"What I mean is, well, not that you're not a top fellow. One of the best, naturally. But a lady's man you are not. And Miss Lanyon, well she's, she's…" he wasn't sure how to finish this sentence. Christopher hung his head unhappily.

"I know, Clem."

"And half of London's pursuing her. Some of the finest catches of the *haute monde*. Never was the battle more grand than that for some fair lady's hand. By gad, I'm full of inspiration today! But what I mean is…" said Castleton, seeing Christopher's miserable face and resolving not to be diverted again by his poetic vision, "You're up against the handsomest fellows, with practised address. I had it from Silksley that even Alvanley, quite the Pinkest of the Pinks, came up to scratch, and she turned him down! And Ovenstort! Samperton would have it that she's determined to live up to her title by keeping everyone guessing who she's going to pick, but she'll choose one of those Top of the Trees types in the end. I mean, can't expect yourself to stand up against them. In a shooting match, maybe, or in the ring, but not in this field. You're the best of good fellows, Topher, but can't be done, just can't be done. Tell you what, pick someone else. Plenty of nice girls out there. Not as beautiful as Miss Lanyon, I'll grant, but very pretty and agreeable. Pick one of those instead."

"But I can't pick someone else, dash it! I mean, you know me, Clem, have you ever known me to feel the slightest interest in a woman before? Quite so," Christopher said, observing his friend's expression. "Wouldn't pick anyone at all if could help it… but Miss Lanyon…" here Christopher hesitated, "Well, she shines everybody else down. Can't help how I feel; don't you think I've tried? I know I haven't much of a chance, but I want to try all the same."

Castleton thought this over. He saw that his friend was in earnest, and recognised the effort it took for him to admit his feelings. "My love is of a birth as rare as 'tis for object strange and high: it was gotten by despair upon impossibility," he murmured, for while Mr Castleton preferred, if at all possible, to quote Mr Castleton, he must at times retreat to the words of his literary forbears.

"Fiend seize it, Clem, you're not making any sense! You've lost me completely, besides which, you sound like a damned textbook, and we all know they're never a particle of use. Strange floating objects? Birth? This isn't a dashed exercise in medical science! Are you going to help or not?"

Castleton did not hold out much hope for his friend, but drew himself up and resolved to try his best for him all the same. "Of course I'll help, Topher. What kind of a friend would I be otherwise? But we must put our heads together; if we're going to have a chance at this, we'll need some kind of a plan." Christopher looked at him expectantly. "Naturally, we'll start with the traditional methods, flowers and gifts, all that flummery. And poetry, women love poetry. Makes them feel all romantic. Shakespeare says music is the food of love- not that I'm saying I agree with that, mind- but well, then poetry must be the beverage. Damned nice beverage at that, none of your meagre brews. Lucky for you, you've got me! I can help you in the poetry department, at any rate." Christopher nodded humbly.

"But that won't be enough," continued Castleton. "All the gifts in the world won't win her if you can't talk to her, stands to reason; no woman's going to fall for a gibbering wreck now, is she? No, it'll be bellows to mend with you, if you don't learn how to flatter and make love to the lady. Thing is though, you need experience at that kind of thing. No sense in thinking you can stand up against stiff competition if you go marching in without trying your hand at it first. I mean, when you started in the ring, you took a few punches and lost a few matches but you got better, and now you can win against all but the best.

Practice, that's the key," Mr Castleton mused. "Tell you what, practice on my sister, she'll oblige you."

Christopher made as if to argue. Castleton held up his hand to silence him. "Now, Topher, this is a difficult problem and one you've no experience with. You must put yourself in my hands and do as I say. You'll have to trust me or we'll not get anywhere."

"Oh, very well, if you think it's what I need then I'll do it. Since I haven't the first idea where to start with all this!" said Christopher.

"There's a good fellow. Yes, I begin to see what needs to be done. With enough planning, we may just succeed, who knows? Whatever, we'll give you the best chance we can." Castleton was enthusiastic. Having committed to the enterprise, he was resolved to give the problem his best efforts. And if the ladies of Mr Castleton's acquaintance would have been astounded to find him considered an expert in winning hearts, Christopher at least saw no fault with this assessment, confident that if anyone could help him, Castleton could.

"Now, where do we start, there's such a lot to do, and time's winged chariot is always drawing near…"

"Chariot? What the deuce?" Christopher's brow furrowed in confusion. But with great effort he calmed himself down, and forced himself to say evenly, "Thing is, Clem, no use winning a chariot race, Miss Lanyon likes fashion not Greek fustian!"

"Just an expression, old chap. Point is, can't expect Miss Lanyon to be single for long. Why, the season's drawing to a close, she must pick someone soon, stands to reason. Which is why we really must get a move on. Poetry, that's the first thing. We must compose a magnificent sonnet, one that would steal Helen of Troy from under the noses of both Menelaus and Paris. Now I know," he said, catching sight of Christopher's face, "that you're not addicted to poetry. And I'm not so blind that I can't see you don't relish hearing me read my verses," said Castleton somewhat reproachfully. "But trust me, ladies are all romantic and love nothing better than poetry, especially lines inspired by their fair selves. Here, I'll help you with the writing of it," he said, and then proceeded, as Christopher watched, helpless and bemused, to compose the poem, stopping now and then to count syllables on his fingers,

"Oh dear! Eleven!" he exclaimed at one point. "But what's one too many after all? No one will notice."

And then later, "hmm, another word for nose... beak?...bill? Or should I mention nostrils... no, sadly I think I must change the whole line. Shame."

At one point, reading over his friend's shoulder Christopher was moved to expostulate. "Ships' sails? Really, Clem, nothing of the sort!"

"Similes, Christopher. The backbone of all the greatest poetry. Besides which, must use sails, nothing else rhymes. And it's quite true, it *is* straight and pointy after all. Where's the dissimilarity?" Castleton did not wait for a reply, but directed his attention once more upon the writing of the poem, and Christopher, with nothing to do, paced impatiently around the room.

"There," Castleton said when he was finished. "Possibly my greatest masterpiece yet. Although, to be sure, it is a little on the short side. But, given the circumstances, a truly remarkable effort. Yes, all there is to do is for you to copy it out in your own hand, Topher, and send it to Miss Lanyon. Can't fail," the poet finished with confident optimism. "Now," he continued, "let's move on to the next part of the plan."

"Now?" asked Christopher, surprised.

"Of course now! Haven't I just been saying that time is of the essence? Must swoop on in there before anyone more engaging has the chance! Which means, got to get you up to scratch quick!"

He rushed the unwilling Christopher upstairs to the nursery. Castleton's father had died several years ago, leaving him at the head of a household which consisted of an invalid mother, and his three siblings: one sister and two lively brothers. Katherine, his sister, was sixteen, and had not yet made her debut in society, which would happen the following year. With little to distract her days, she divided her time between supporting her invalid mother and helping the governess in the care of her schoolboy brothers. She was a plain-looking girl, small in stature but big in heart, and even bigger in piety. She was, more often than not, to be found in contemplation of the scriptures, and, with good Christian feeling, she was always ready to oblige her older brother, of whom she was, in any case, genuinely very fond, in anything he should ask of her.

"Here, Katherine, we need you," said Castleton to his sister, as he entered the room.

Miss Castleton looked up from her Book of Common Prayer, which she was engaged in reading intently, blinking twice in surprise at her brother's entrance. Mr Castleton looked meaningfully at his two younger brothers who were also in the room, and then jerked his head towards the door, "Out! I want a word with Katherine."

"This is my sister, Katherine, Topher," said Castleton as he shut the door behind the boisterous forms of his brothers. "She's not yet out, so there's nothing to alarm you, won't see her at parties and such. And her looks are nothing above commonplace, so you won't be distracted by her appearance." Miss Castleton made no demur against her brother's assessment of her person, nor did she seem the least offended. "Just the ticket to practise paying your addresses. Katherine, you won't mind if Topher practises doing the pretty with you? He's not good with women, you see, stands in need of encouragement and rehearsal."

"Not at all," said the compliant Miss Castleton composedly. She put aside her prayer book, rested her hands in her lap and looked at Christopher expectantly.

"Right then, perfect. Imagine you're at a ball, or a party or some such thing," said Castleton, setting the scene. Christopher hesitated. "Come on, come on, Topher. This is no time to get all shy. It's only Katherine after all, nothing to get in a pucker about. How do you suppose you'll do this for real, if you can't do it here? Think of the prize, dear fellow."

Christopher thought of Miss Lanyon, and the conversations they had had, and how much he enjoyed her company, and it strengthened his resolve. If this was what was needed, then he would do it, he resolved. "Good evening, Miss

Castleton," he started politely, bowing to her. "Would you do me the honour of dancing with me in this set?"

"Good, good, it's a start!" said Castleton. "Now Katherine, agree but don't give him too much encouragement, need to make it all realistic."

"Very well, Lord Prendergast; I am very fond of dancing."

"Now, Topher, imagine you've led her out onto the floor, the chords have struck up and the dancing's started. The turn of the reel brings you in close to her, there, now give her a compliment, women like flattery."

Christopher blinked, as if in shock, and stammered out, "Allow me to say you look very becoming in that dress. An excellent sarsnet, you could not have picked a colour that becomes you better."

"Not the dress, you fool! Compliment her on something more sensible. Her eyes, or her dancing. Oh, dear me, this is going to be harder than I thought!" exclaimed Castleton, throwing his hands up in despair. "You look very becoming in that dress," he mimicked laughing. "No, no, good gad, no! Try again!"

"Doing my best, Clem! Dash it! Never said I was any good at this; if I was, wouldn't have needed your advice!"

"Sorry, sorry," said Castleton, penitent. "No need to look so cast down, old chap, we'll soon have you up to scratch. Only to talk of the material of a woman's dress, well...!"

"But Miss Lanyon is very fond of fashion," said Christopher defensively.

"All women are, but they don't expect their men to know all about silks and sarsnets," said Castleton sagely. "And you must understand, Topher, that it's not the clothing itself, but how it looks upon them that's important."

Christopher looked unconvinced. "Imagine, if you will," explained Castleton pompously, "that two women are wearing the same hat. If you pay tribute to the hat, is it a compliment to the ladies? No! Far from flattering both women, you have failed to compliment either, for your accolade goes to the item of clothing and not to either woman's natural charms." Christopher nodded, understanding the force of this argument, if still not wholly convinced that the argument held water in the case of Miss Lanyon.

"See?" said Castleton, feeling that he had got his point across. "Now try again."

"You're a very good dancer, Miss Castleton. My compliments," tried Christopher cautiously.

"Well, that wasn't so bad, but you're not exactly going to bowl her over with that, you know! Tell you what, I'll give you some phrases to use. Try these out." And so, having composed Christopher a poem for Miss Lanyon, Castleton proceeded to coach him in the exact parameters of a conversation. Christopher practised and practised until Castleton was satisfied.

"There now, that's better. What do you think, Katherine, better eh?" Castleton asked his sister.

"I think it's all nonsense!" said Miss Castleton, who had begun to conceive a very poor opinion of Lucretia. She eyed Christopher in kindly interest, saying, "God made you as you are, and so you should remain. And if the lady values pretty phrases above substance, well then, is she worth it, you have to ask yourself? It's all pride, and pride is the devil's work. No, it is as Shakespeare, under divine inspiration no doubt, says: to thine own self be true!" Miss Castleton had her brother's love of quotation but her motivation was godly rather than artistic. Christopher blanched slightly; he considered attendance at church about as much religion as any man ought to be forced to stomach.

"Fustian, my dear girl!" said Castleton. "When you've been around in the world a little, you'll understand better. Take my word for it, Topher, it's much better. Now to tackle the most important thing: the proposal. That's the real challenge! We must practice that above the rest. First you must clasp her hands, thus," he said, demonstrating by holding his sister's hands in his own, "and then here's what you must say…"

After he had finished explaining, Christopher did as he was told and practised his lines. "Here, Clem," he interjected after his second run through, didn't Romeo and Juliet meet a sticky end? Not sure it's such a good idea to mention them in the proposal. Don't want to make Miss Lanyon feel morbid."

"The point isn't how they died, but how they loved!" asserted Castleton, but Christopher looked militant on the point. "Well then, replace them with Othello and Desdemona, if you must!" said Castleton impatiently and sat back to listen to Christopher stammer through the new version. "Well done, Topher!" he said when Christopher had finished. "By gad, I wouldn't know you for the same man! Only look how far you've come on: you're like a regular Prince Charming. I think we're really almost there now. But then, it's not enough to do it when you're all comfortable with me in the room to support you. Tell you what, I'll pop off for a moment and you have a try on your own. Mind, Katherine, you're not to go talking any of your nonsense, just let him get on with it," he threw over his shoulder as he walked out the room.

Left alone with Miss Castleton, Christopher remembered his pact to do just as his friend said, and kneeled painstakingly down before the seated young lady, clutching her hands in imitation of what he had been shown. Gulping, he began, verbatim, to speak his lines, although studiously avoiding her eye throughout.

"Oh, fair nymph, you are Eve to my Adam, you are Cressida to my..." he paused trying to remember his line, "...Troilus, Othello to my Desdemona. Without you I am as empty as a cup. I beg..." he stopped, unable to continue, looking wretched and feeling acutely uncomfortable.

Miss Castleton pulled her hands away gently, saying, "I wonder if you can be quite sensible to be putting all your faith in my brother's advice on this matter, Lord Prendergast. He is hardly, after all, an expert in this field."

"He seems proficient enough in the art to me!" returned Christopher loyally. "Of all my friends, he seems to have the least difficulty in conversing with women. And, what's more, they never look disgusted or bored when I see him with them. Stands to reason he must be good with the ladies."

"Well..." said Miss Castleton slowly, "talking to women and winning their hearts are not quite the same thing. It may be very disloyal in me to own it, but I know that my brother has only proposed once to a lady, and that she did not accept."

"Oh, well there is nothing in that after all. Can't win every match, you know. Doesn't mean you're not good at the sport," said Christopher cheerfully.

"But in this game," returned Miss Castleton gently, "when one has found the perfect match, one rarely gets a second attempt." Christopher looked at her sadly, seeing the force of this comment.

"What do you suggest, Miss Castleton?"

"With flattering lips and a double heart do they speak," quoted Miss Castleton softly. "Do you want to be accepted because you can make pretty phrases? My advice is use simple words that convey true feeling."

Christopher nodded, "Perhaps you're right. And even if you're not, I have to admit that I don't think I can say the things Clem has told me to without looking green around the gills, or dashed uncomfortable! I can't be other than I am, no matter how I feel about a woman."

"Nor should you try to be!" Miss Castleton assured him. "We are all the work of God's hand and made in his image. It is arrogance to try to be other than yourself. Surely you must see that?"

But Christopher wasn't listening, years of being intimate with Mr Castleton had taught him how to pay no attention whatsoever to large chunks of his conversation. And Miss Castleton's voice shared that exact quality her brother's had which made it easy to disregard. Instead, Christopher was thinking furiously about his dilemma and the task ahead of him. To Miss Castleton's surprise, for she thought the Viscount would see no further need for practice, Christopher knelt down again, this time with greater confidence, took her hands in his, looked her in the eyes and said, "Miss Castleton, I am never happier than when I am in your company and, if you will have me, I would be very honoured if you would accept my hand in matrimony."

"That is very much more like it, and yes, I would accept your proposal," she sighed, for she was not without romantic

213

sensibilities. "Out of the abundance of the heart, the mouth speaketh..." she broke off from her sermon because at that moment the governess entered upon the scene and, beholding a man knelt amorously before her pupil, yelped and retreated hastily, displaying a most unprofessional disregard for her responsibility for protecting her charges.

Turning in the doorway, she almost collided with Mr Castleton, who entered cheerfully, saying, "Sorry I've been gone so long. I got caught up in improving the third stanza of our sonnet and quite forgot all about you being here, Topher! It was only when Bertie arrived that I remembered."

Christopher had jumped hastily to his feet, saying in an artificially hearty voice, "Hallo, Bertie, what brings you here?" He walked to the door of the schoolroom, ushering his two friends into the hallway and down the stairs without a backward glance at Miss Castleton.

"Almacks," said Mr Strangwald unexpectedly, when they seated themselves in the library. "Wondered if Clem might fancy toddling along there with me tonight?"

Christopher looked at Mr Castleton enquiringly. "Here's a queer start! Where do you suppose he means by Almacks?"

"I fancy he actually means Almacks on this occasion," said Castleton. Strangwald nodded in agreement. "Course I'll come along with you, old chap," said Castleton to Strangwald. "Although you know the Admiral might be there, he's dashed fond of the place. Forever meeting him there when I go. He's asked after your whereabouts a number of times too. Are you quite sure you still want to go?"

Strangwald looked briefly put off, but then drew himself up and nodded emphatically. "Well then, it'll be a pleasure," said Castleton jovially. "Can't expect Topher to come along though, he hates the place. Not in your line at all, is it, Toph?"

But, rather unexpectedly, Christopher said, "No, actually, I'd like to come along with you both."

If Strangwald's and Christopher's reasons for attending Almacks that evening were similar, they had no intention of sharing this fact with each other, and so the conversation turned to different topics.

Mr Castleton had been quite correct when he prophesied that Lucretia would be delighted with the poem. She had received countless gifts from her many admirers, but nothing had given her greater pleasure than this offering.

Leafing through her post she came across the sonnet, neatly written in an unfamiliar hand and, after reading several lines, a grin stole across her face. By the time she had reached the end of the second stanza, she had erupted into a most unladylike peal of laugher, which surprised her maid into dropping the hairbrush she was holding.

Finding her abigail looking expectantly at her, Lucretia said, "Oh, Martha, I have just received the most wonderful set of verses in my honour. Listen!" and she read out the sonnet.

The Face of Beauty

Oh fine Lucretia with hair in rings of gold
Bewitchingly they frame your fair visage
Your ears like wings I would never remold
Fly open to hear my humble adage!

Your nose so straight like the sails of a ship
A floating delight at the fore of your face
Your eyes like oceans my attention grip
Dreamy, placid and so perfectly spaced

Out of your mouth escapes a ringing laugh
So unlike a church bell it never does knell
It trills a divine song on heaven's behalf
And captures me in its beguiling spell

Oh! that the smile that quivers on your lip
Will beam upon my humble courtship

To her disappointment, Martha, who had no sense of humour and was in awe of the written word, said, "Very pretty it is, Miss, most flattering of you. And the rhymes are quite perfect."

"Pretty? You miss the point entirely! No doubt you also feel that my nose is…" Lucretia scanned down the poem to find the exact description, "a floating delight in the fore of my face?" Once again she descended into mirth. She read the full poem over a third time with enormous enjoyment and then said, "But who is it from? Alas, it is the greatest disappointment; I cannot thank my benefactor, for it is unsigned. What a shame!"

Mr Castleton had been insistent on this point. Women loved mystery, he asserted. Giving away the author's identity would detract from the lady's pleasure. Christopher did not question this, and it occurred to neither of them that, as exciting as all this mystery would be to the lady, all the gifts in the world would be unable to play a significant part in the courtship if she had no idea who had sent them. This was regrettable, for Lucretia had never enjoyed a gift half so much, and was still chuckling to herself as she descended to the breakfast table.

CHAPTER FOURTEEN

To Lucretia's great delight, Mr Castleton's poem was followed by a number of gifts from her mysterious admirer. These included a delightful bouquet of tulips, which Christopher had once gleaned from his sister's vapid conversation were one of Lucretia's favourite blooms. Attached was a note which said: *Helen's face caused many ships across the seas to zoom, but your fair profile launches all the flowers into bloom. Oh garden sprite of true delight, pray have a thought for an aching heart's plight!* This sent Lucretia off into peal of laughter.

A few days later she received the truly magnificent gift of a mechanical bird in an ornamental birdcage which sang out when the mechanism was wound up like a clock. She looked at the present in awe and put it in pride of place on her bedside cabinet. The note attached to the cage, which read: *Lovely Miss Lanyon as fair as straw, you are fodder to my heart,* made Lucretia laugh for almost a full half-hour, and she stowed it carefully away in a drawer in her dressing cabinet to re-read as a cure to cheer herself up, should she ever feel blue-devilled.

"Dash it!" Christopher had expostulated when Castleton had composed this note for him, "what's fodder got to do with a singing bird, Clem? Don't seem to go with the gift!"

"I thought we'd agreed, Toph," Castleton returned with infuriating self-assurance, "that you'd be guided by me in your courtship. Trust me, I'll see you right! Good to mention farms and such, shows you're down to earth, have serious intentions, you know."

"Oh, very well, if you say so. Just goes to show women are damned near impossible to understand. Good gad, I hope she won't be wanting me to talk about cows and geese with her, I wouldn't have the first idea where to start on the subject!"

Lucretia enjoyed all of these offerings enormously but, as Mr Castleton continued to be adamant in the need to keep the identity of the giver a secret, all the gifts came unsigned and so Lucretia could not thank her admirer or have the opportunity to fall in love with him. And so irrevocable had her feelings now become for her dandy that, despite the pleasure the mysterious gifts afforded her, no secret admirer, no matter how deliciously enticing, could supplant Christopher in her affections.

Relations were flourishing between Lucretia and Christopher despite, rather than because of, Mr Castleton's efforts on his friend's behalf. Christopher made only one attempt to follow Castleton's advice in his *vis-à-vis* interactions with Lucretia. But, after observing that her forearms rivalled the beauty of fair-armed Hera's and declaring her profile to be worthy of a Shakespearean sonnet, he received such a look of surprise mingled with shock that he hastily turned the discussion to his new sapphire tie pin. The conversation soon developed into discussion of his neckcloth and after pointing out proudly that he had just managed to perfect the tying of his cravat in the Mail Coach style, they had fallen back into their comfortable style of conversation. The awkward moment passed and was forgotten, and Christopher resolved never to make such an attempt again.

Following the cooling off of her friendship with Isabella, which the failed elopement had brought about, Lucretia was especially grateful for opportunities to spend time with her beau. While she in no way regretted the loss of her friendship with Isabella, Lucretia had worried that the resulting withdrawal of all invitations to Mount Street would mean that she scarcely ever saw Viscount Prendergast. To the relief of his admirer, however, and the considerable surprise of the hostesses of the parties and balls he graced, Christopher was seen more often in society than ever before. He was, moreover, unusually disposed to making himself socially agreeable, even to the point of dancing. The hostesses of Almacks even had the satisfaction of seeing him as a regular at their assemblies. But since Christopher was by no means one of society's well known figures, few people stopped to consider what may be behind this startling turn of events.

The months of the Season were nearly passed, and speculation about who Miss Lanyon would finally wed began to grow, a point which Lord Alvanley was not shy of quizzing Lucretia over when he met her at Almacks one evening. "Everyone is all at guessing who the lucky man will be, Miss Lanyon," he said to her with a twinkle.

"Lucky man?" said Lucretia.

"The lucky devil who will win your heart, of course! Bets are even being entered into the book at Watiers," Alvanley observed, fancying that this intelligence would tickle the Heiress's sense of humour.

He was not in error, and Lucretia laughed heartily. "Indeed? The silliness of men never fails to surprise me. What a subject to lay odds on; surely there are more worthy ways to spend money," she said lightly, for despite her amusement she was secretly somewhat embarrassed to find herself the subject of such gossip.

"I find my pride slightly salved by the fact that you've turned down everyone else who has proposed to you," continued Alvanley. "Nevertheless, you'll choose someone in the end, I imagine. Could there be the slightest hope that you've changed your mind about my proposal? No? Alas! Well then, at least give me a little hint on who the lucky contender may be. I know it's ungallant of me to ask, but I lost a deal at Hazard last week and I'm needful of a sure way to recoup my losses. I beg you, fair Incalculable, just give me the littlest of hints and I'll be forever in your debt. Is there someone who stands out above the rest?"

Lucretia blushed. "Ah, I see there is someone indeed," said Alvanley, observing the pink tinge that had stolen across her countenance. Lucretia had never been more relieved to be interrupted than at that moment, and she let out a thankful sigh as she was hailed by Miss Pycroft, who had just then arrived and had made her way to Lucretia's side.

"I do beg your pardon, Lord Alvanley, but Cecelia and I simply must go and talk fashion! I know you of all people understand the seriousness of the subject," Lucretia said hastily, ushering Miss Pycroft away.

In the clubs, betting on Lucretia's choice of husband was indeed rife, with Arnold Rutland the universally acknowledged front-runner. Gamesters willing to bet against his chances were offered very favourable and long odds. The friendship between Lucretia and Christopher Prendergast received little notice; the idea that Christopher could possibly be a suitor, let alone a credible competitor for Lucretia's hand, would have been laughable to the world at large even had they considered it. And there were very few that did.

Jesmond Ogleby, still persisting in his role as Count Johann von Andermach, was, in fact, one of the few that did remark Christopher's standing with Lucretia. Count Johann was still not making any headway towards winning the heart of the heiress. Bemoaning the failure of his first plan, and angered by Viscount Prendergast's interference, he stood scowling at Christopher with great dislike and, in the course of this recreation, noticed Lucretia's demeanour when she spoke to him. There was a certain softness in her expression, which was not obvious by any means, but was different from the way she looked at all her other suitors.

Observing Lucretia and Christopher talking together most comfortably, and looking at each other with quiet happiness, the perspicacious Count Johann understood instantly that here was the man who had captured the Incalculable's heart. Despite popular consensus, Count Johann had never believed that Lucretia favoured Arnold Rutland's suit, for why would he take such a long time in proposing to her, or, if he *had* proposed, why would she wait so long to accept him? It simply didn't make sense. For some time, he had been convinced that Lucretia wanted only friendship from her cousin, and that Arnold himself wished for no more. That is not to say that the Count was not surprised to find that it was Lord Prendergast who had captured the young lady's affection. He couldn't discover what Lucretia saw in Christopher that set him above all his rivals but, rather than considering this point, which may have helped to him understand better why Lucretia showed himself so little notice, Count Johann swiftly convinced himself that Lucretia's failure to favour his suit was because of her feelings for Viscount Prendergast.

Since no engagement had been announced in the papers, it seemed that Lord Prendergast had not yet spoken his feelings to Lucretia. Something must be done, the Count thought to himself, to make sure that affairs between them were not allowed to prosper. Furthermore, if he could only get Christopher out of the picture, Count Johann deluded himself, he couldn't fail to win the heiress for himself. No woman, his vanity asserted, whose heart was unattached, could resist Count Johann von Andermach.

But how could he put the Viscount out of the picture? That was the real question. And he must do it soon, for time was running out. He could not much longer support himself as a member of the *haute monde*; demands for payment from his tradesmen were becoming a daily trial, and they grew like a snowball. Noticing these demands, the hotel owner became nervous and began to hint that he himself would appreciate the payment of his guest's shot. Certainly, time was running out, and in another respect, there was also not much time, for Lucretia's birthday, and with it the trust fund's deadline, approached; in only two months she would be twenty-two.

Lord Rutland was considering the same point. He sat in his chair staring unseeingly at the newspaper before him, mulling over the issue of Lucretia's marriage prospects. His wife sat over her stitch work, humming absently, a pastime which she would have condemned in anyone else and which she would have strenuously denied having ever done herself. Finally, the Viscount looked over at her. Nothing for it, he thought, must broach the subject: unavoidable. "Virginia," he said to catch her attention.

"What is it, Charles?" she replied, looking across at him.

"Well, this is a topic we've long been silent upon," Lord Rutland said carefully, "but it strikes me that we must now address it. We're more than half-way through the month of June. Do you realise that in two months Cressy will be two and twenty?"

"Is it as soon as that? Good heavens, I had no notion that time had flown by so! But you are looking grave. What can there be in that to concern you?"

"Well, it strikes me that two months doesn't leave much time to become engaged and married. I wouldn't like the girl to miss out on her inheritance. Obviously, she must not be forced to marry for the wrong reasons merely because, should she not do so, she would find herself penniless. But if her heart should already be engaged..." said Lord Rutland slowly.

"Really, Charles, how can you think I haven't already considered this!" exclaimed his wife indignantly. "To be sure I have Cressy's welfare constantly in my heart, and I assure you that there's not the least need to worry. I have every expectation of her making an unexceptional match in the very near future," Lady Rutland asserted.

That, thought Lord Rutland with a sigh, is what I very much feared. He could not be blind to his wife's expectations and saw her descend into a daydream. Again, she was thinking of Lucretia and Arnold at the altar, with all her acquaintances watching in the congregation, all her enemies green with envy. Nothing could have worked out better, Lady Rutland was thinking. Lord Rutland, who knew that such an idea was in neither Lucretia's, nor Arnold's, hearts or hopes, wondered how he could dash his wife's hopes for the match without drawing her wrath upon his head. As it turned out, her reaction to the realisation that Arnold and Lucretia did not want to marry was the least of his worries; he must first convince her of this fact, and he could not do so.

"Now, Virginia," he said, "you know that it must be Cressy's choice, whom she marries."

"Naturally, Charles, who else's choice would it be? But, fortunately, she has very good taste and, as to choice, well there's no reason why she should not be guided in making hers...

222

She may well find it a comfort to be assured that someone very close to home will, after all, make the best match for her," returned Lady Rutland lightly.

"I cannot pretend not to understand your meaning. But are you quite sure that it is what Lucretia and Arnold wish for?" said Lord Rutland.

"But surely, Charles, you cannot have missed the intimacy so apparent between them? It has been remarked upon by any number of people."

"Intimacy? Friendship? Yes. But I am not convinced that it is love," he said gently.

"Love? Pooh!" scoffed Lady Rutland. "Such nonsense! No, what Lucretia and Arnold have is friendship, mutual esteem and respect, and that is so very much more a solid and lasting foundation to any union than mere love, as you and I know."

The Viscount sighed wistfully. He had long known his wife had not married him for love, whatever his sentiments at the time had been. "But perhaps Lucretia may develop something more for another gentleman. In short, perhaps she may hope to fall, or indeed may already have fallen, in love?" Lord Rutland hinted.

"No, Lucretia, I thank the lord, is a very sensible, stable young lady who does *not* cherish the silly notion that one ought to be in the throes of passion over a man," said Lady Rutland. "And she most certainly hasn't been in love, for she's turned down I don't know how many offers for her hand! It may be that all the while her affection for her cousin has surmounted any feeling she may have developed for any of her other suitors? I don't know. Whatever, it's a splendid and sensible match and they will both be delighted to make it."

"Even Arnold?" Lord Rutland asked her dryly.

"Of course Arnold will be delighted," said Lady Rutland, faltering only a little. "To be sure, he may not feel ready to marry just at the moment, but he undoubtedly cherishes an affection for his young cousin which in time would have led him to propose, only now we must make him aware that he cannot wait as long as he might have liked. When he knows the terms of the Trust, he will behave sensibly, I am sure. He knows he cannot remain a bachelor forever!"

"I'm not so sure that Arnold sees it that way. If you ask me he very much enjoys, sometimes rather too much, being a bachelor. I can't see him being sanguine about giving up the habit any time soon," observed Lord Rutland wryly. "Nevertheless," he continued in more serious tones, "I do think Lucretia ought to know about her circumstances. After all, we were both so censorious of Hugo for keeping her in the dark and, when you come to think of it, we've done exactly the same thing."

"Nonsense, Charles! It is not the same thing at all. We have Cressy's interests at heart," exclaimed his wife.

"No doubt Lord Lanyon also felt that he did," Lord Rutland returned, a little sardonically.

"Well, Charles," she said, unable to answer this, "you're being very disagreeable today, I must say. But I suppose we must tell her at some time..." Lady Rutland mused over this point, seeming to doubt the fact.

"At some time!" Lord Rutland was moved to interject. "Would you usher her down the aisle next week without explanation? Of course she must know, and I see no reason why she should not be told now, today."

"Well, I don't see what the urgency is. Lucretia will do as she's bid, and the terms of the Trust have nothing to say in that. But if you insist on telling her, Charles, I suppose I really cannot prevent you," Lady Rutland said coldly. "I do not, however, see the need for all this distasteful heat and passion. I can only suggest that you calm yourself before you embark on any other activity. Really, Charles, it's not like you to be so volatile!"

Lord Rutland let the matter rest, returning to his paper, and the matter was not alluded to for the rest of the evening. On the morrow, however, the Viscount addressed his niece across the breakfast table, saying, "Lucretia, I wonder if you could spare me a few minutes of your time this morning and come to see me in my library?"

"Certainly, uncle," replied Lucretia, surprised. She had never before been called before her uncle in private, and wondered what the matter could be. That he looked grave and serious could auger information of some moment, but then his face naturally fell into such an expression, so it may not be significant.

She entered his room a little nervously. She had learned to respect and esteem her uncle, but she had rarely been alone with him.

"Ah, Lucretia," he said, looking up from his desk, which was strewn with papers. "Come in, come in. Have a seat, m'dear. No doubt you're wondering what this is all about. Nothing to worry you, I assure you. It's just that your aunt and I, well, we've not been completely forthcoming about your situation. In retrospect, perhaps we ought to have told you all from the start, but there really didn't seem the least need and, after all, I don't feel that there's anything in it to concern yourself over," said Lord Rutland unconvincingly, trying to assuage his own guilt which grew the more he considered the matter.

Lucretia looked at her uncle. "My situation, uncle? What can you mean?" she said, sounding worried.

"Now, now, don't be uneasy, it's nothing terrible I assure you. It's merely that there were some terms to the Trust your father set up for you which you have not, as yet, been made privy to. I feel that the time has come to rectify that omission," Lord Rutland said, and then went on to explain about the two conditions to her fortune and the consequences should she fail to meet them.

Lucretia's reaction was a surprise and a relief to her uncle. "The gardener? Oh, how like father!" she said, upon a peal of laughter. "And poor Moyles, why he would have no idea what to do with such a sum!"

Lord Rutland looked at her in enquiry. "Our long-suffering gardener," Lucretia explained. "A lovely fellow, but one who truly delights in life's simple pleasures. He was never happier than when he was amongst his roses." She stopped, remembering this faithful retainer. "He was used to say: what need hath any man for more than the joy of simple flora," Lucretia quoted, and, unable to keep her countenance, she erupted in mirth.

She was joined in her merriment by her uncle, who also chuckled in amusement. "I see," Lord Rutland said, smiling at her. "And I must say that I'm most relieved that you don't seem cast down by these revelations and are not angry with myself and your aunt for withholding the information from you. Perhaps it was wrong in us, I don't know. But there seemed no need to trouble you with the information at the time and since then, well, it hasn't occurred to either of us that there was a need to tell you. Then time passed so quickly and here we are, only two months away from your birthday!"

"Angry, uncle? How could I be? You and my aunt have shown me such kindness. There's no end to my gratitude, I could never be angry with you."

"Well, I give you this information now, Lucretia, so that if there should happen to be a gentleman you have developed a *tendre* for," he said with a significant look at her, "it would be wise to encourage him to make his advances in the near future."

She returned his look with one of surprise. Could it be that he had discovered her secret? Or was he labouring under a misapprehension that she favoured one of her other suitors?

Lord Rutland soon made his accurate understanding clear. "Cressy," he said carefully, "if a lady should have developed a *tendre* for a man who is, perhaps, not a *seasoned* suitor..." He faltered and paused, but then continued, "A suitor who may not know his way in the wooing process, and may well take a long time, more than two months, to come up to scratch, even though there was no doubt that he would eventually do so... I trust you are catching my drift?" he looked at her to see if they were understanding each other. She was embarrassed but gave the slightest of nods.

"Well, in that situation," continued Lord Rutland diffidently, "I would be happy to help out that lady by dropping a hint into the gentleman's ear, should she wish it. I say this with the greatest delicacy and the lady could be sure of my absolute discretion in the endeavour."

"I do not pretend not to understand you, uncle, and I thank you for your kindness," said Lucretia awkwardly, "but I feel that your lady friend ought to be able to attend to such matters herself."

Lord Rutland looked at her kindly and with respect. "Very well, Lucretia," he said, "I won't mention this to you again unless you ask it of me."

"Thank you, uncle," said Lucretia, rising from her chair as if to leave.

"One final thing, Lucretia," said Lord Rutland, a very serious look upon his face. "You have said that you feel grateful to Lady Rutland and myself for taking you under our roof. There isn't the least need. Lucretia, I have come to esteem you very highly and it's a pleasure to have your company. You can always be sure of a place in my household for as long as you wish or need it. And you mustn't feel that there is any need to show your gratitude to your aunt and me by agreeing to anything you might not be otherwise inclined to do." He met her eyes and checked that she understood his insinuations before continuing. "Furthermore, should you be unable to marry before the deadline set by the Trust, rest assured that you'll not be destitute. We will naturally continue to support you. You are my niece, and your well-being will always be my concern, both in respect for our relationship but also because I have come to care for you for your own sake. Lucretia. My advice is always available to you and you may always count me as a friend, should the need for one arise."

Lucretia was lost for words. "That is all," said the Viscount, dismissing her.

"Th-thank you, uncle," Lucretia stammered, "such kindness… just… well… thank you!" And she left the room so moved that tears pricked in her eyes. Rushing upstairs she passed her aunt who noted the tears and took them to betoken that Lucretia was upset by the terms of the Trust. She was not disappointed to see this, for it suggested that she may be pliant in suggestions for overcoming the terms. Again she was lost in the daydream of St Paul's, Lucretia, escorted down the aisle by her uncle, Arnold waiting at the altar. Lady Rutland sighed blissfully at the picture.

CHAPTER FIFTEEN

Viscount Prendergast, Mr Strangwald and Mr Castleton were feeling somewhat stifled by their recent and unaccustomed forays into the stuffy world of polite society. They had attended a great many balls and assemblies where stringent rules made it difficult for them to find an outlet for the natural youthful high spirits felt by gentlemen of their age. They were in universal agreement that they needed a respite. The problem was that few activities presented themselves that evening to satisfy this need for less torpid amusements. It was this circumstance that led them, despite the fact that they were none of them especially partial to gambling, to present themselves at one of the gaming hells situated in the vicinity of Pall Mall.

They met a number of their friends there, and seated themselves at the hazard table in expectation of a comfortable evening. Unlike the other occupants of the room, whose bright-eyed fervour denoted them as hardened gamesters, and whose fortunes hung in the balance against the turn of the dice or card, the three gentlemen played within their means, lost small amounts with good grace and were pleased when they won, although none of these transactions made a great deal of difference to their fortunes. Such play was too tame for many of the patrons, for whom only the exchanging hands of huge fortunes met with their notion of an evening's entertainment. When the stakes at the table were, inevitably, raised beyond what the three friends were prepared to bet, they retired, with the similar minded Mr Albury, to a quiet table to enjoy a staid game of piquet.

Later that evening, Count Johann von Andermach arrived. This was one of his regular haunts and, in truth, he was greatly in need of winning a considerable sum: a bad frame of mind upon which to start an evening's gaming. Wise heads knew that it was a sad quirk of fate that desperate souls rarely prospered at the tables. It was not long before the Count began to lose, and lose badly. Scowling around the room, his heart in an anxious flutter over the evening's likely costs, he spotted Lord Prendergast comfortably enjoying his quiet game of piquet, without the cares of heavy debts, and this added to his ill-humour. He began, once again, to consider how he might do that gentleman a mischief.

The evening was advancing and more people were arriving. Christopher could not understand the allure of such places and was considering suggesting to his cronies that they depart in search of more promising amusements. All of a sudden, such thoughts were ousted from his mind, and his fingers froze in the act of selecting a card from his hand as he spotted a very unwelcome surprise. One of the new arrivals was none other than Mr Morley, entering with, to Christopher's mind, smug complaisance. How, Christopher wondered, could Morley dare show his face? How could he afford to, if he was as badly off as recent events had seemed to suggest? Christopher's blood boiled.

"Here, Topher, you can't play a diamond," protested Strangwald, who was not averse to sneaking a look at his opponents' hands. Christopher had mechanically laid down the first card he touched, his attention distracted. Strangwald's remonstrance caused the two other players in the game to look up from their cards, and to observe Christopher's suddenly flushed face and frozen demeanour.

"Oh no," murmured Strangwald, sensing trouble. Catching Mr Castleton's eye, he raised an inquiring eyebrow.

Christopher, angered beyond sense, was rising from his chair. "Wait," said Castleton, grabbing his arm, trying to pull him back into his chair. "Not the place, Topher, you'll draw too much attention…" But Christopher shook him off angrily, marching across the room with such violence in his eyes and determination in his stride that he began to draw notice.

Mr Morley was talking amongst a group near the entrance. "Thought you were dished up, old chap," Croxstowe was saying to him. "Wasn't expecting to see you back in town this season."

"I was, but by the greatest stroke of good fortune my great-aunt Jemima received her notice to quit last week!" said Morley who was, in fact, feeling decidedly sanguine.

"Not so fortunate for Aunt Jemima," observed Croxstowe.

"No," agreed Morley, shaking his head sombrely so as not to seem overly callous. "Poor Aunt Jemima, but she'd had a good run."

"Ah, thank the lord for distant great aunts!" exclaimed Croxstowe heartily.

"What's this about great-aunts? Cursed pain in the neck, my great aunt," said Samperton, arriving and joining in the conversation. "Always wanting me to write letters, and visit, and take tea," he continued, with great disgust in his tone.

"Ah, but we speak of the distant kind of great aunts," explained Croxstowe to Samperton, "the invaluable variety who time their deaths just perfectly, leaving behind them a fortune to brighten the lives of their indigent relations! Morley's just lost one, stroke of luck if ever I've heard of one!"

"Must have been a dashed distant relation, Morley! None of your close ones have sixpence to scratch together, and if they did they'd not leave it to you!" sneered Samperton.

"Not a fortune," protested Morley, not rising to Samperton's insinuations. "Alas, no! Not a fortune. But an independence, certainly."

"No doubt you'll lose it at the tables tonight! Or, if you don't fritter it all away at hazard, some ladybird will see more of the ready than you," tittered Samperton.

"At least my ladybirds receive me, be it for my money or my charm!" returned Morley. Samperton flushed angrily, but the other gentlemen of the group laughed immoderately at this sally. Christopher was almost across the room and seeing Mr Morley in such good humour did nothing to abate his anger. He pushed angrily into the group in time to hear Morley jeer at Samperton, "Heard you lost Sapphire's fair ankle to Cleeveland.

It seems even ready money cannot buy you what my charm can."

The group of men surrounding Mr Morley had fallen silent and Morley, surprised at the lack of response to his comment, was about to repeat the quip when he saw the cause of his companions' silence. The murderous face of Lord Prendergast appeared only inches from his own. So close was the angry young man that Morley could feel Christopher's hot breath on his nose.

"A word, Morley," said Christopher curtly. Then, seeing Morley hesitate, he barked, "Now!"

Morley quailed at the ferocity in Christopher's eyes. But, sensing the curiosity of interested bystanders, he said, "If you would excuse me, gentlemen," and walked aside to speak with Christopher. This distraction had given Morley time to calm himself and he was able to say, with tolerable composure, injecting into his voice a hint of boredom, "What is it you wished to speak of with me, Prendergast?"

Christopher was taken aback. When he had approached, he had had no clear idea of what exactly he had planned to do, or what he was going to say. But it seemed incredible to him that Morley would act as if he did not know what the cause of his approach was. An apology, at least, Christopher expected. Discomfort, certainly. But this smug indifference? It made the fury well up still more in his breast. "What do I wish…? How dare you! You know very well what I want to talk to you about, you damned impudent…" Christopher broke off, too angry to speak in full sentences.

Mr Morley regarded Christopher guardedly and saw the anger working upon him. Young hot head! But, Morley felt sure, Prendergast would not make a scene in such a public place. The Godolphin family had been fortunate to avert a scandal after his failed elopement with Lady Isabella. There had been, miraculously, no whispers of the incident. To cause a stir here would lead to questions, to the chance that the incident would become public knowledge. "Careful, Prendergast, you'll have people talking," warned Morley.

Mr Morley had misjudged the situation. Christopher was angrier than he had ever been in his life, and the smug disdain with which Morley spoke made him lose all reason. Somewhere in the back of his mind Christopher knew the sensible things that Morley was banking on to protect himself, but Christopher was too furious by far for them to prevent him from raising a scene. And Morley did not know that Christopher was enraged not just on his sister's account, but was driven also by his fury at what Lucretia, his beloved, had suffered at the rake's hands.

"How dare you!" bit out Christopher. Only then, as he saw that the Viscount's anger was such that he cared not for his surroundings, nor for the eyes of the interested onlookers, nor for the consequences of his actions, did Morley begin to feel frightened. He was a grand, bold talker but, at heart, he was a pusillanimous fellow, terrified of physical pain. The memory of the punishing blow that Christopher had dealt him came back to him and, to the young Viscount's scorn, Morley began to shake.

"Name your seconds, Morley," said Chistopher, marking his enemy's fear and smiling derisively.

"I.." Morley stuttered in terror. "I beg your pardon, Prendergast, but I fail to understand your meaning," he said, desperate to prevent the duel that he knew Christopher to be about to insist upon.

"I mean," said Christopher drawing himself up haughtily, "that you'll meet me for what you've done, curse you!"

By this time, Castleton had reached his friend's side and, trying to avert a scandal, said quietly in Christopher's ear, "Topher, careful, people are watching. Mustn't set them talking old fellow. This is folly, let's go."

Mr Morley looked at Castleton gratefully and himself leaned towards Christopher's ear, saying earnestly, "Castleton's right. There's no need for this. If you continue you'll make the elopement known, as it is, no one's any the wiser. Better for all if you kept it that way. Let it pass, you know… for your sister's sake."

Christopher's anger reached a new pitch. "Let it pass? No, Morley, I will not *let it pass*." He placed heavy stress on the last three words to emphasise his disgust. "I repeat: you'll meet me for what you've done."

Morley's fear increased as Christopher's anger intensified. The chance that he might receive another bruising punch from the notable pugilist frightened him, and the thought of a duel terrified him even more. He would avoid it at all costs. "There's no need for this, Prendergast..." Morley stuttered, almost incoherent with terror. "I'll... I'll not meet you. Please, Prendergast..." he finished, in pathetic entreaty. This drew a look of scornful disgust from Christopher, but it did not abate his anger nor his determination to seek retribution.

"Not meet me? You, Morley, are a coward," Christopher said, poking his finger into Morley's chest violently. Mr Castleton and Mr Croxstowe gasped at this insult, and Samperton grinned maliciously at Mr Morley's discomfort.

But still Morley steadfastly refused to meet the challenge. Never having before called someone out, Christopher was unsure of himself. He had no notion it would be so difficult to induce his adversary to accept. He looked to Castleton for help but received none: Mr Castleton remained firmly of the opinion that his friend was making a mistake in issuing his challenge in such a public place, and would not help him to finalise the folly. Strangwald had no such scruples; he was thoroughly disgusted by Mr Morley's spineless conduct and helpfully handed Christopher his half-filled wine glass. Christopher looked down at it, confused, until Strangwald's meaning dawned upon him. When the realisation hit him, he threw the remainder of the drink in Morley's face without further ado, and stood regarding him in grim satisfaction.

Morley's shoulders sagged. No gentleman could accept such an insult without demanding satisfaction. He wiped his handkerchief across his face in humiliation. "Oh, very well, Prendergast, since you insist upon this most unnecessary duel. Croxstowe will act for me. And..." he looked around in the hopes of finding some other gentleman ready to act for him. But his friends had shrunk back; they were ashamed of his conduct and would not meet his eye.

Count Johann saw an opportunity. He did not see exactly how he could use the events to his purpose, but he fancied, nevertheless, that here there may be some prospect of doing Prendergast a mischief, and he stepped forwards saying, "If I can be of some assistance to you in this matter, Morley?"

Mr Morley looked at him gratefully. "Yes, thank you." He turned back to Christopher saying, "And Count Johann will also second me."

"Bertie? Clem?" Christopher looked at his friends. They nodded. He turned back to Mr Morley. "Strangwald and Castleton will act for me," he said curtly, turning on his heel and stalking out of the club without a backward glance.

He was out on the street and pounding his anger out in heavy steps, striding out into the night, not noticing where he was going and completely forgetting his companions. "Hey, wait!" shouted Mr Castleton, rushing to catch him up. He and Strangwald had hastened out of the club after their friend. "Not wise, that," said Castleton to Christopher, as he fell into step beside him. He shook his head morosely, observing, "People will talk, you know." Christopher grunted, barely hearing him and caring little for his thoughts on the matter.

"Nonsense!" exclaimed Strangwald cheerfully. "Cowardly dog! Can't expect him to stand for such conduct. Teach the chicken-hearted villain a lesson, Topher, only thing for it! Here's a thought though, what did he do to occasion your displeasure in the first place?"

Christopher and Castleton stopped in their tracks and stared at Strangwald. "Bertie, do you mean to tell me that you've helped Topher into a duel without having the faintest idea as to why?" said Castleton incredulously.

"Well..." said Strangwald, considering. "Now you come to mention it, yes. But he's not a likeable chap, Morley. No doubt he had it coming."

It was perfect to lighten the mood. The three friends looked at each other and fell about in mirth.

"By gad, Bertie, you're an original, you really are!" said Christopher, clutching his sides. "Oh dear, there's going to be a deal of talk, isn't there? Father's not going to be above half pleased. Still, as you say, Morley had it coming. So I can't say as I really regret it."

The next morning Mr Strangwald set off to call upon Mr Croxstowe to arrange the projected duel, in accordance with the rules set out in the Code of Honour. It was the first duty of seconds to try to arrange a peaceful reconciliation in order to avoid the meeting taking place at all. Croxstowe had been given strict instructions by the craven Mr Morley to do his utmost to reconcile the parties without the necessity of putting his life at risk in a duel. Crowstowe had regarded his friend with contempt but felt, to do him justice, that he would feel very much the same in similar circumstances.

"Devilish good fencer is Prendergast, so I've heard," Croxstowe had pointed out unkindly to the obviously terrified Mr Morley as he walked home with him from the gaming hell. "Rumour has it he pinked Seberdon a few weeks ago, and Seb's accounted a master of the first order. Trained under Angelo, you know."

Mr Morley, whose face was already pale took on a greenish hue. "Best make it pistols if you can then," he said faintly.

"Ah well," said Croxstowe with morbid cheerfulness, "Prendergast's a damn good shot too, by all accounts. Farley told me last night that he saw him at Manton's the other day. Quite the best shot in the place. Never misses his wafer apparently."

Whatever the rules dictating the role of seconds in such affairs, Mr Strangwald had no intention of attempting a reconciliation. The three young friends had never been involved in a duel before and were anticipating it with excitement. They had no fear for Christopher who, as Morley and Croxstowe had learned, was an exceptional fencer and a crack shot. All in all, it seemed, to them, like a very good sort of lark.

So, when Crowstowe tried to broach the subject of apologies, Strangwald became amazingly deaf. "Can't stay long, Croxstowe," he interrupted. "My uncle's being beheaded today, must go and pay my respects." Strangwald caught sight of Croxstowe's look of complete bemusement. "Chopping off his head, you know," he said in explanation, misinterpreting the source of Croxstowe's misunderstanding. "They did it a lot in France a while back. Anyway, Wimbledon Common, first thing tomorrow," he said, returning unexpectedly to the subject of the duel. I'll arrange the sawbones. Know just the fellow. He's yellow but we don't hold that against him."

Croxstowe again looked understandably at a loss. "Jaundice," explained Strangwald. "Doesn't get a lot of business his way. Not a good recommendation of your medical abilities when you're the colour of a daffodil. Puts people off, you see." He nodded sagely. Croxstowe began to feel that the conversation had taken on the air of unreality and was unable to get out any of his carefully planned arguments.

"Pistols or swords?" Strangwald was asking, his conversation jumping back to the duel.

"Um... pistols," said Croxstowe weakly.

"Right then," said Strangwald nodding. "As I said, must go, beheading, you know. Poor chap, he only just got married. Charming young lady. Very short, mind, good head shorter than my uncle. Bit ghoulish to say, but they'll be of a height for each other by the time the day's out. Not keen on the sight of blood though, is Aunt Lillian, so I imagine she's dreading the event. Ah well, can't have everything." He was walking to the door with a wave. "Breakfast," he said suddenly. "I'll arrange a breakfast. No doubt we'll all be hungry after the duel, assuming we all survive it! Best if they don't make it a killing affair, devilish inconvenient these days, the law not looking too kindly on such things. Still... accidents happen and fate's a funny thing." He chortled, displaying, to Croxstowe's mind, a unnaturally blood-thirsty spirit. "Until tomorrow, Croxstowe!"

The door shut behind him and Mr Crowstowe gazed after him, bereft of words.

The affair was naturally the cause of considerable speculation and occasioned a good deal of gossip but, as the Earl of Godolphin was away on business for a couple of days, the duel was allowed to go forwards unchecked. Christopher woke up with a feeling of pleasurable excitement at dawn the next day, and was ready for Strangwald and Castleton when they came to collect him. It was a crisp morning with a promising clear sky overhead.

"Bang up to the mark, Topher," Castleton hailed his friend. "You look to be in prime twig."

"Of course! Slept like a log. Lovely day for it," Christopher said cheerfully, as he climbed into the carriage. "You must be the sawbones, I'm Prendergast, I'm the one who's duelling today," he said with a hint of pride in his voice.

"Chawbury," said the doctor, holding out his hand. "You seem mighty jolly for a man about to face his own mortality. Have you thought to put your affairs in order, just in case?"

"Cheerful chap, aren't you. Affairs in order? No need, Morley couldn't hit a target if it was right in front of him! Saw him trying once, at Manton's. Stap me if he didn't even know how to hold the gun, let alone fire it in a straight line! Got the pistols, Clem?"

Mr Castleton handed over a box containing his late father's duelling pair. Christopher opened the box and whistled, saying, "A pair of Manton's pistols! Whew! Magnificent! Have they seen any action?"

"Not that I'm aware," said Castleton. "Hope they shoot all right. Had an idea that m'father may have mentioned that one of them throws to the left, but I can't be certain."

Christopher took one of the pistols out and felt its weight in his hand with reverence. "Thing of beauty this, Clem! Looking forward to shooting it! Shame I won't really have a chance to put it through its paces, not planning on hitting the fellow after all."

"Tempting though it must be to shoot a bullet through Morley," said Mr Castleton, "best not. Would cause all sorts of fuss and bother."

"I know, Clem. Not sure I want a killing on my conscience anyway. But, by Jupiter, it'll be fun scaring the wits out of him a little! Did you see how he shook at just the thought? Cowardly chap… Paltry! Wouldn't be too surprised if he doesn't show."

"Not show up?" said Strangwald, startled into sitting up in his seat. "Good gad, d'you think that's possible?" He yawned. "But we've all got up so early, dash it! Horrible to think it may be to no account. Now I'm deuced glad I thought to bespeak breakfast!"

The atmosphere could not be more different in the other carriage approaching the common. It had taken some coaxing to persuade Morley to get into the carriage; he had come up with any number of excuses but knew that in the end he must go. It was utterly unacceptable for a gentleman to draw back; he'd never be able to show his face again.

Mr Croxstowe also wore a sombre expression. He was beginning to think seriously of the practicalities of the event and, recalling that he, like Strangwald's Aunt Lillian, very much disliked the sight of blood, began to regret that he had not thought to bring along his smelling salts. Count Johann was deep in thought, wondering why he had ever thought getting involved in this affair was a good idea. He could not even begin to see how he could use the event to good account. At best, he would be an audience to Lord Prendergast's shooting prowess, at worst he may find himself with an injured Morley to deal with. And in that eventuality, he very much doubted, having taken in that gentleman's pallor, whether Mr Croxstowe would be any use at all. How much he wished he had minded his own business and was still tucked up in his bed!

Christopher's party was the first to arrive, but Mr Morley and the others arrived soon after. They were greeted by the sight of Christopher being helped out of his coat, which was so tight that both Strangwald and Castleton needed to help him and, even with the two of them assisting, he was struggling. But they were all laughing in the attempt and their cheerful good humour jangled Morley's nerves all the worse. All very well to feel sanguine when you know yourself a marksman, he thought morosely.

Morley, who had been careful to choose a shirt with the most modest of buttons so that he provided no obvious target for his opponent, was disgusted to see that Prendergast wore a shirt with truly magnificent buttons, almost monstrously huge, which glimmered in the morning sunlight. Arrogant young pup, curse him! Morley thought. His annoyance served to rouse him somewhat out of his terror and he jumped down from the carriage and proceeded to remove his own coat in readiness for the meeting.

Strangwald called Mr Croxstowe over to examine the pistols as was customary. Croxstowe knew nothing of pistols and gave them the most cursory of glances, finding nothing amiss, well aware that he had not the least idea what he was looking for. After this brief scrutiny, he nodded to show his approval. Watching this exchange the Count saw his opportunity. It was a devilish idea, desperate and probably unwise, but he made the decision in seconds and strode over to Strangwald and Croxstowe.

"Mr Strangwald, I must raise with you an objection. My honoured friend," the Count bowed at Mr Croxstowe, "knows nothing of pistols. I do not think it is fair for him to check these weapons. With great respect to my friend, I do not think he knows what to look for. I beg you will allow me to examine the pistols to see if I can find any disparity between the two. In the interest of fairness, I believe you must allow this."

"Very well," said Strangwald uninterested, and he and Croxstowe went to count out the paces and mark the ground, leaving the Count alone with the weapons.

Count Johann bowed over the box. Glancing left and right he saw that neither Strangwald nor Croxstowe was watching what he was doing. He carefully emptied the shot out of one of the pistols. "No, it is as you say, there is nothing to choose between these pistols," he said loudly when he had finished, picking up the still loaded pistol and presenting it to Mr Morley. It was not exactly how it was normally done, the full box would normally have been offered to each of the combatants in turn, but Count Johann's actions were taken to be a foreign eccentricity and allowed to pass.

"Ready, gentlemen?" asked Chawbury.

"Of course," said Christopher with a grin, approaching the area chosen for the encounter.

"Of course," echoed Morley hollowly. His mouth had gone dry but his palms, unaccountably, had begun to sweat, and beads of perspiration were apparent on his brow. His heart beat most unpleasantly in his chest and then, every so often, swooped in terror: a rhythm which made him feel decidedly queasy. He wondered, with a quick glance at the sky as if appealing to God, if he were about to die.

He faced Christopher, and the two men saluted formally. Mr Morley looked into his opponent's eyes and saw that they showed not even a hint of fear. He knew his eyes betrayed his own terror and he looked away, mortified to heard Christopher snort scornfully. The doctor turned his back on the affair as, strictly speaking, it was illegal to be involved in such engagements, although physicians could generally get away with being present so long as they did not watch the duel.

The two duellers turned and walked the agreed fourteen paces. At the marked spots they stopped, saluted and then turned sideways raising their arms with guns cocked, waiting for the handkerchief to drop. For perhaps the first time in his life, Mr Morley prayed. He prayed for an interruption, for any act of God that could save him from this encounter. He was more terrified than he had ever been in his life. Christopher watched these thoughts play across Morley's face with amusement and satisfaction. This was what he had hoped to see, this was enough: he had no need to injure his target.

The handkerchief fell and Christopher, the experienced marksman with lightning reflexes, pulled his trigger instantly. But nothing happened. Morley hesitated, knew that he had hesitated, which made him hesitate still further, and then waited to feel the bullet hit him. When this did not happen, he was confused and then elated. Prendergast had missed! he thought with relief. He had missed! Morley had never had any expectation of putting a bullet in his challenger, and cared very little whether he did or not, but he now pulled his trigger to finish the affair. The bullet went ludicrously wide, but Morley didn't care. It was over, he thought, more thankful than he had ever been of anything in his life.

His comfort was short-lived however; suddenly he realised that something was not right.

"It didn't fire! My pistol didn't fire!" shouted Christopher angrily. "It wasn't loaded! I say, Bertie, didn't you check the pistols?"

"Of course I checked!" cried Strangwald, insulted. "We both checked, Croxstowe and I, and there was nothing amiss, I assure you. I'm telling you that both pistols were loaded and untampered with! And then..." And then he remembered that something else had also happened. "And then Count Johann also checked the pistols," he said slowly, a suspicion growing. Within an instant, they were all looking at the Count and they caught him unprepared, guilt written on his face. He opened his mouth to deny any wrongdoing, but his quick wits deserted him and he could not find the words.

"You tampered with the pistols!" accused Strangwald.

"I..." Count Johann stuttered.

"And you told him to," Castleton threw at poor Morley. "This is all your doing! You were so terrified of facing Topher like a man you resorted to this: cheating! Good gad, more ungentlemanly conduct I hope I never in my life see again! Why it amounts to attempted murder, or it would do if you weren't such a damned hopeless shot." Mr Castleton, hugely incensed was pulling off his coat ominously and Mr Strangwald seeing this, began to do so as well.

Christopher bore down on Mr Morley and punched him with great pleasure. "That's it Toph! Darken his daylights, damn coward!" shouted Castleton setting upon Count Johann. Not to be left out, Strangwald launched himself at Croxstowe, who was attempting to slink away unnoticed.

"Now gentlemen, really! Stop now," protested Chawbury, but his words went unheeded. There was quite a fray taking place with punches and kicks flying in every direction. Chawbury waded in, trying to pull apart the various combatants, and it was not long before he too was drawn into the brawl. All was a confusion of arms, legs, grunts and yowls which went on for some time.

Count Johann, managing in the midst of all this mayhem to disengage himself from the scrimmage, stole away unnoticed, released one of the horses, jumped on its back and was just setting off before he was noticed by Mr Castleton, who spotted him between the crook of Croxstowe's elbow.

"Oi!" Castleton yelled after him. "Oi you, how dare you! He's getting away. You swine, come back here!" He dragged himself from the brawling group and made as if to pursue the rider, but Count Johann was too far ahead of him and Castleton knew he could never catch him, so he gave up. But the event had served as if a bucket of cold water had been dashed upon the group.

"You, sir," said Christopher, getting up from the ground and straightening his shirt, "are no gentleman." He looked down his nose at Mr Morley haughtily, although his supercilious bearing was a little undermined by his dishevelled appearance.

"But I assure you, I knew nothing of it!" protested Morley truthfully, but he was looked at in disbelief.

"I don't believe you," said Christopher, a little childishly, and in a tone which clearly indicated that nothing could swerve him from his scepticism. "And as you are such a dashed paltry fellow, it's beneath me to associate with you further! Come on Bertie, Clem, let's go eat breakfast. Chawbury," he added as an afterthought, "you're welcome to join us." With that he retrieved his coat and hat, marched over to the carriage and got in, closely followed by Strangwald, Castleton and Mr Chawbury.

"Well," exclaimed Mr Castleton, "I knew Morley was a rum touch, but I never imagined he'd serve you such a trick!"

"By God, no!" returned Christopher. "I wouldn't have believed anyone could have done so! I'd ask for satisfaction from him but who knows what ungentlemanly deceit he'd put into our next meeting!" The young gentlemen all laughed, as shock gave way to amusement.

"Such a cow-hearted fellow! Have you ever seen someone more in terror than Morley before the fall of the handkerchief?" jeered Strangwald.

"And that was when he could be reasonably confident that Topher's gun wasn't going to go off," observed Castleton.

"Ah well," said Christopher, "seeing him so frightened was all the satisfaction I really needed, although darkening his daylights was a welcome bonus!" He fell silent, contemplating the events of the day. Then he grinned boyishly, "I packed some damned good punches into his face!"

"By God, it was quite a mill!" enthused Strangwald.

"He's right, Toph! In fact," remarked Castleton, "I don't know when I last enjoyed a morning so much!" The three friends laughed uproariously, in universal agreement with this sentiment.

"Hrumph," grunted Chawbury grumpily, his nose quite literally put out of joint. "You youths may enjoy such brawls, but I'm past an age when such things are amusing." His words were belied, however, by the unmistakable hint of pride that had crept into his voice. "I'm quite sure my poor old bones are going to be paying for this morning's work for some time to come. And who knows what the missus will say when she sees me in this state!"

For the first time the three friends took in their appearances. All their clothes were covered in dirt and mud, and ripped in places, some past repair. Castleton's hair stood out in wild disarray, blood dripped from Christopher's nose, and Strangwald's left eye was beginning to develop a gray ring around it.

"D'you think they'll serve us up breakfast looking like this?" asked Strangwald anxiously.

"I don't know, but I'm willing to give it a try! By God, I'm famished, aren't you?" exclaimed Chistopher. For once he didn't care what he looked like. It had been a magnificent morning and they were all in the highest of spirits. The young men whiled away the rest of their journey to the inn talking over the mill, the infamy of Mr Morley and Count Johann largely forgotten in their good-humour.

CHAPTER SIXTEEN

A few days later saw Mr Strangwald in abject misery following his first day at work. Instructed by his new employer to sit in a quiet corner of the offices and read the countless legal tomes with which he had laden him, Strangwald had seen his future stretching out before him and considered it with nothing less than dread. So miserable was he that, on leaving the offices at the close of business, he was desperate for a sustaining stiff drink. He called into the first hostelry that presented itself, and sat himself down in the darkest corner offered, to nurse his drink and his soul.

The inn would have been familiar to the Earl of Godolphin as it was the same one he frequented during his visits to the city. Mr Ogleby and his nephew had no idea that they had been overhead during their plotting there and thus continued to use it as a meeting place. Once again Mr Ogleby sat waiting for the arrival of his nephew, and he was in no very good humour. He had defrayed a considerable amount of money to fund his nephew in their plan for securing the heiress and as yet he could see little to show for it.

When his nephew arrived, he was once again Jesmond Ogleby and no longer the Count Johann von Andermach. Jesmond realised that his exploits at the duel made it impossible for him to show his face again in society, and he had put off his costume and acknowledged to himself that he had ruined the plan. The only comfort he could find in the whole escapade was the fact that the plan was admittedly already failing before he had made that ill-advised move. He knew his uncle would be angry, and steeled himself for an unpleasant encounter, but he was not frightened of him and had, moreover, put in place preparations for a further plot that he hoped would diminish his uncle's annoyance.

Mr Strangwald saw Jesmond Ogleby enter and sit down with his uncle at a nearby table. Indeed, all the tables were nearby each other, it being a cosy establishment. But Strangwald did not immediately recognise the gentleman, so different did he look without the garb he had worn as Count Johann. He had only the vague impression that the man looked familiar, but he could not place him and was caught up in his own troubles so his thoughts did not linger long on the issue. He preferred to be alone with his misery; even had one of his friends arrived, Strangwald would have shrank back further into his corner and hoped to be left alone.

Jesmond Ogleby looked furtively around the room to assure himself that no one of moment would overhear his discussion. Strangwald, in his dark corner, could barely be discerned and escaped detection from this cursory surveillance.

"Hello, uncle, how are you?" asked Jesmond Ogleby as he seated himself at Mr Ogleby's table.

"I'll be a good deal better when I hear some promising news from you, my boy! I've heard nothing from you this past month save ceaseless demands for further funds. And I'll tell you now, if it's money you're after, I'll not be giving you any more!" fumed Ogleby.

"No, uncle, nothing of the sort, I assure you."

"Well then," said Ogleby, slightly mollified, "tell me how our plan is going. Have you secured her?"

"I... well, no," Jesmond returned, deciding not to dress up the issue.

"No?" barked Ogleby.

"No. The plan has failed. She... well, she is in love with someone else. I could not make her prefer me."

"I see. So that's how it is? For all your flowery talking and grand boasts that there was not a woman you could not make one of your conquests! All the money I have put into your mad venture, and this is how you repay me!" said Ogleby, conveniently forgetting that the plan was largely of his own design.

"Sorry, uncle," Jesmond Ogleby said simply, and silence fell between the two.

Mr Ogleby was alarmed. He had been banking on this plan and financially he was now at breaking point. His mind whirled as he considered his options. After a time, he said, "Who is this man she prefers? No doubt some grand fellow, a duke or an earl, I imagine," expecting to hear his nephew justify his failure.

"No, actually he is a person of almost no account. The merest fribble," Jesmond added disdainfully. "Her choice is, well... surprising. But she is nevertheless firm in it."

"Well, if he's a nobody that makes things a little easier. We can arrange for him to disappear without causing too much of a kick up, and then she'll be yours for the taking," said Ogleby, heartened a little by the prospect of murderous designs.

"Ah," said Jesmond Ogleby. "Well, I tried that, and..."

"And you made a mull of it, did you?"

"Sadly, uncle, I have to admit that I did." He explained what had taken place at the duel. Nearby Mr Strangwald was listening to this exchange with incredulous interest.

"Young fool! How could you have been so stupid?" railed Ogleby. "Fiend seize it, I should never have let you talk me into this confounded idea! Nothing for it, we'll have to force the girl to marry you then."

"I have just been thinking the same thing," said Jesmond Ogleby.

"You will fix this, Jesmond!" Mr Ogleby demanded; it was said in the manner of a threat.

"I will, uncle. Trust me, I will."

"Trust you! You ask me to trust you? If I've learned one thing from this whole sorry episode, it is that I can't trust you to do anything! The way I see it, you are worse than useless! Now tell me your plan so I can be sure you're not going to botch it again. Trust you?" he repeated with a mirthless laugh.

Jesmond Ogleby outlined his plan and the preparations he had made. "And you have arranged everything?" asked Mr Ogleby sharply.

"Yes, uncle, I believe I have," replied Jesmond Ogleby, striving to inject a hearty dose of confidence into his tone.

"And when do you propose to make your move?"

"Tomorrow. Miss Lanyon, I understand, is to attend a picnic at Richmond - it will provide the perfect opportunity."

"Very well," said Mr Ogleby, slightly less displeased. "You must tie the knot as soon as possible. No dithering about it, hear!"

"Naturally," returned his nephew, now calmed.

"Well, you'll need a special licence, bet you hadn't thought of that, eh?"

"I have it here," said Jesmond Ogleby patting his coat pocket.

"Good," said Mr Ogleby looking no less severe but, from his tone, Jesmond Ogleby could discern that he was slightly appeased.

Mr Strangwald was aghast at these dark plots. Whatever his friends may have thought, for they considered him to be singularly undiscerning of things actually happening around him, Christopher's feelings for Miss Lanyon had not escaped his notice. Strangwald knew he must tell his friend what was planned. Shaken out of his self-centred pity, Strangwald would have rushed out of the inn on the instant, but did not want to be noticed by the plotters. With great presence of mind, he therefore waited for Ogleby and his nephew to leave, which they very soon did, before hastening out of the pub. He hurried in a frenzy down the street, thinking furiously, and, most unfortunately, walked straight into his father.

"Bertram, I have found you, good," said Admiral Strangwald. "I went to your offices but they told me you'd already left. I came to find out how you fared on your first day," he said with greater kindness and interest than he normally showed his younger son. He tried to take his son's elbow and steer him down the street saying, "Walk with me, walk with me, we can..." Suddenly he broke off. "Good God! What has happened to you?" he exclaimed, examining his son's countenance and taking in the bruise around Strangwald's eye socket, which had turned a purplish-yellow hue.

Strangwald waved this question aside. "Not now, father, I must go. Abduction... foul plots... dark machinations..." Strangwald gasped out.

"Now, son, stop with this nonsense! It was my plan that your new career would rid you of this very silly habit you have of talking absurdities. I'll be most disappointed if it turns out not to be so. Come now, compose yourself and try, if you can, to bring yourself to the real world and tell me how you found your first day of work," said the Admiral, with greater indulgence than he had ever before displayed in the face of his son's unlikely narratives. Admiral Strangwald was pleased with himself for finding his son this job, and was prepared to be pleased with him for submitting to this new life he had planned for him.

"I..." started Strangwald, "No, can't do it! Must go, tell them what is afoot! Kidnapping!" he said, almost hysterically.

"Stop this now! Now! I will not hear anymore from you on this subject," said the Admiral, angry now. "And you are not disappearing on me! You'll come home and take your dinner with your mother and me. Your mother has not seen you for some time and is anxious to hear how you are going on. There is to be no more talk of kidnappings, do you hear?" He was looking very severe, sterner than Strangwald had ever seen him before, and he quailed at the look on his father's face. All the terror he usually felt in his father's presence returned to him in full force and he was scared back into his customary submissive attitude.

"Yes, father, of course, father," he said hollowly.

The Admiral hailed a cab and ushered his son into it. "Brook Street," he directed the driver and then turned to his son. "Well then, how did you find it?"

Strangwald, obedient but distracted said in answer, without thinking, "Nightmarish."

This, not unjustifiably, incensed his father. "I find you rude and ungrateful, young man! You'll change your attitude, my boy! I'll not have you disappointing Mr Scrivenham when he has given you this opportunity. Moreover, I will not have you reflecting badly upon me. You will exert yourself to excel, and I am sure you are capable of it. Indeed, Mr Scrivenham had no fault to find with your work today. There now, isn't that encouraging? No doubt you'll go back tomorrow with greater enthusiasm now I have told you of it." Strangwald was silent; he was worrying about the planned kidnap.

"Well?" the Admiral snapped at his son, in expectation of an answer.

"Of course, father," said Strangwald absent-mindedly, but he was unconsciously shaking his head. His father began to be concerned about his son's commitment to his new employment, but chose not to broach the subject further at that moment. He was accustomed to his son falling into line and had no doubt that he would do so in this instance.

They arrived in Brook Street where dinner was ready to be served, leaving the two gentlemen no time to dress for dinner. But it was, after all, only a small family party, so Mrs Strangwald allowed them to sit down to table as they were.

"Wait," said Strangwald, still worrying about alerting Christopher to the plans that were brewing.

"I do hope you are not going to start up with your nonsense again, boy," the Admiral cautioned.

"I… no," said Strangwald, having an idea. "But I had other plans tonight, father. Just remembered."

"Well, you can cancel them," the Admiral commanded. "No doubt they revolved around spending time with those witless friends of yours. I doubt if they would think to miss you."

"Yes, father. But I must send them a note." The Admiral looked wholly unconvinced of the necessity of this.

"Rude not to," asserted Strangwald. The Admiral saw the force of this contention, for he was himself always punctilious in matters of politeness.

"Very well, but make it quick or you will hold up dinner."

So Strangwald scurried into the study where he dashed off a quick note to Chistopher. This missive was less effective in halting the kidnap than its author hoped for two reasons. The first was that Strangwald's notes were as obscure and fantastical as his conversation, and the second was that the Viscount was not at home to receive it. Nevertheless, unconscious of these two issues, Strangwald felt very relieved after he had sent off the letter, convinced that he had done all he could to save Miss Lanyon from the fate that was threatening her.

The next day dawned, bathing the world in gorgeous sunshine and warmth. The morning dew sparkled on the leaves of the trees and twinkled like gemstones in the sunlight. Lucretia sighed happily as she looked out of her window. It was, she thought, the perfect day for a picnic. She set off betimes in her aunt's carriage to collect Miss Pycroft, with whom she was to travel to the picnic, and before too long the two young ladies were on the road towards Richmond, in every expectation of a pleasant outing.

They journeyed to Richmond without incident and the picnic party was initially very enjoyable. But the sun beat down mercilessly and as the day wore on Miss Pycroft began to feel very hot and tired. Noticing how her friend seemed to be wilting Lucretia said, "Ceccy, you look done in. Shall we go home?"

"Oh no, I would not for the world cut your enjoyment short!" said Miss Pycroft who was, even after all this time, still somewhat in awe of her friend and ever anxious to please her.

"To be honest, I've rather had enough of this myself," whispered Lucretia in her friend's ear. "It is altogether too hot and Mr Samperton is a dead bore but I simply do not seem to be able to shake him. I would be glad to leave."

"Oh, yes then, if you wish it, Cressy," said Miss Pycroft, relieved.

Thus it was that the two young ladies made their excuses and left the picnic ahead of the rest of the party. The carriage bowled along back to town at a smart pace and the two girls reflected cheerfully on the day's events in comfortable contentment, until suddenly a loud crack outside the carriage met their ears and the carriage began to lurch around on the road. Miss Pycroft started in surprise, glancing out of the window.

Two masked men on horses had descended upon them, brandishing guns. Another shot whistled through the air and one of the ruffians shouted, "Stand and deliver!" his horse drawing ahead of the carriage and blocking the road. The carriage continued to travel but it was slowing, and veering most alarmingly around on the route.

"Highwaymen!" gasped Miss Pycroft, grabbing Lucretia's arm in terror.

"Hudson must have been hit," said Lucretia, observing that the carriage was behaving unpredictably. "I do hope he is not too badly wounded."

The coach driver had indeed been wounded, but not mortally so. The shot had taken him in the arm, he had lost the reins and, although he was losing blood, he was not grievously hurt. The quick-witted postilion reached out, grabbed the flying reins and yanked on them with all his might, drawing the horses to an abrupt standstill.

Inside the carriage, Miss Pycroft trembled in fear, clutching Lucretia's arm tightly. "Oh, Cressy, what are we to do? Oh, and there is no one here to help us." She was clearly terrified, but Lucretia was impressed to see that her timorous friend remained sensible, neither swooning nor becoming hysterical. She was herself quite calm, reasoning prosaically that there was nothing that she could do and, after all, though highwaymen may rob their quarry, they have no reason to harm those who cooperate and hand over their valuables. Lucretia prepared to surrender her reticule and jewellery to the robbers.

"There, there, Ceccy, don't be frightened. I'm sure they don't mean to harm us, merely to rob us. Hush now," she soothed.

A scuffle could be heard taking place in front of the carriage, between the highwaymen and the driver and postilion, Lucretia supposed. She wondered if she should descend from the coach to see if she could lend Hudson and the boy any aid, but thought, on reflection, that she would be unlikely to be of much help to them, while Cecilia clearly stood in need of support through the ordeal. So she stayed where she was and waited for events to unfold.

The noises outside the carriage stopped, indicating that either the highwaymen or the coachmen had been overpowered. The girls soon saw that the bandits had been the victors as one of them approached the carriage door. He was tall, hulking fellow and his brutish form moved clumsily. Lucretia expected him to stand outside and demand their valuables through the window but, to her surprise, he wrenched open the door of the coach and began to climb in.

"Get rid of the extra one," the other man demanded, appearing at the coach door and pointing at Miss Pycroft. He was smaller and less powerful than his accomplice, but he was evidently in charge. His voice wasn't one that Lucretia recognised but she was surprised to hear that it was not ill-bred.

The bigger man reached for Miss Pycroft, grabbed hold of one of her arms and attempted to drag her out of the carriage. Miss Pycroft was screaming, and gripped Lucretia's arm still tighter. "Oh! Don't let them take me!" she squealed.

"Hold tight, Ceccy," said Lucretia, wrapping her arms round Miss Pycroft's slim waist to stop her being pulled out of the carriage. A tug of war ensued, the man pulling and pulling on Miss Pycroft's arm but the two girls resisting fiercely.

Evidently impatient of this tussle, the other man drew out his gun and levelled it purposefully at Lucretia. "Let go of her."

Lucretia stared at the barrel of the gun, but remained impressively composed. "No, I will not let you separate us. Can not you see she is near paralysed with fear? She is in my charge and I will not leave her."

"She'll be quite safe," said the lead highwayman, not lowering the gun. "It's you we want. She'll be safer by far if you leave her behind."

"No, I won't let you take her, I won't, I won't, I won't," shrieked Miss Pycroft bravely, and she beat out with her free arm at the man trying to pull her away, admittedly somewhat ineffectually, but nevertheless courageously.

"Very well, we'll take them both. We're wasting too much time," said the man with the gun, looking at his watch. "Go drive the carriage, we must get a move on," he ordered his burly confederate. The brawny man left, and the man in charge climbed into the carriage, closing the door behind him.

Before long the carriage lurched forwards and continued on its journey. The highwayman held out a length of rope to Lucretia. "Tie up your friend," he demanded, pointing his gun once again at her. "And mind you make a good job. I'll be checking." He watched as Lucretia did as she was asked and, when she had finished, satisfied himself that the bonds were tight enough.

"Now, hold out your hands in front of you," ordered the man. Lucretia did as instructed and, after carefully putting his gun out of her reach, he bound her hands and feet. "That's better," he said when he had finished. "Now we can be more comfortable."

The highwayman pulled off his mask and lounged back in the seat looking smug. Lucretia and Miss Pycroft stared at him, like Mr Strangwald not recognising him at first. Eventually Lucretia realised his identity.

"Count Johann von Andermach!" she exclaimed in incredulous surprise. For a short moment, she wondered if the episode was an elaborate prank. But then she saw the malevolent, self-satisfied look upon his face, and reflected that the tightness of the knots constraining her hands and feet were certainly not part of any practical joke.

"Where are you taking us? What do you want?" Lucretia demanded, angry now despite her growing fear.

With an evil smile, Jesmond Ogleby looked towards Miss Pycroft, who was still shaking in alarm. "Miss Pycroft, is it? You may be the first to congratulate your friend on her upcoming nuptials," he said to her.

"Nuptials?" said Lucretia in bewilderment.

"Ah, but I have been remiss," he said unpleasantly. "I beg you will do me the honour of accepting my hand in matrimony, Miss Lanyon," Jesmond Ogleby said with derision, accompanying the words with another sneering smile.

"Of course I won't marry you! How can you think I would?" returned Lucretia sharply.

"I think you will find that you have no choice," drawled Jesmond Ogleby complacently.

"No choice? Of course I have a choice!" said Lucretia incredulously. "You can force your way into my carriage at gun point, and you can force me to stay here under restraint…"

"Evidently," he interposed dryly.

Lucretia ignored the interruption, continuing, "…And you may very well be able to force me to the altar, but no priest could possibly agree to marry me to you against my will. Do be serious, sir."

"I repeat, I think you will find you have no choice." He said it with such confidence that Lucretia faltered, unsure of herself. She looked at Jesmond Ogleby questioningly.

"Allow me to properly introduce myself. You see, my name is Jesmond Ogleby." He placed heavy emphasis on his surname.

"Ogleby?" said Lucretia. She knew the name was familiar but she could not recollect where she had heard it.

"I don't see what difference your name makes to things," said Lucretia acidly.

"Ah, what's in a name?" Jesmond Ogleby said with infuriating facetiousness. "I see you are still in the dark. Strange, I thought you had some intelligence. My uncle was a friend of your father's and is named as your trustee," Jesmond Ogleby explained in a patronising tone.

Understanding dawned across Lucretia's face. She thought for a moment and then said, in measured accents, "He may be my trustee but it is not within Mr Ogleby's power to force me to marry you!"

"No," Jesmond Ogleby admitted slowly, "but he can refuse to consent to your wedding anyone else. And, unless you marry, you will find yourself quite destitute. There now, surely marriage to me cannot be as bad as penury."

"I am quite sure that it would be immeasurably worse," Lucretia snapped.

"I do not think you can have considered," said Jesmond Ogleby unpleasantly, his self-satisfied good humour unimpaired. "Evidently you have never experienced true poverty. This world

255

is not kind to girls without protection or funds. I don't think you will like hard menial labour, and you are not fit for any other work. No, when you think about it, I'm sure you'll come around to my way of thinking that we two should make a match of it. Come now, be sensible." He tried to take hold of Lucretia's hands but she moved them away.

"You are in error," she said with hauteur, drawing herself up straight, "I am not without protection in this world. My uncle assures me that he will support me, even if I fail to claim my fortune."

"Is that so?" drawled Jesmond Ogleby in snide disbelief.

"Yes, it is," said Lucretia with dignity. "So you see you had better take us home at once and stop all this nonsense!"

Jesmond Ogleby fell silent, considering. He was not ready to concede the point. "He may say that now, but imagine the humiliation you will suffer when society finds out that you are no heiress after all... And I can easily ensure that they are not long in the dark about the fact," he menaced. "The *ton* will not soon pardon being duped, and it would disgrace your family, that's no way to repay them for taking you in and showering you in kindnesses. Lady Rutland, notoriously high in the instep as she is, could not forgive you for being the reason behind the slights she would receive as a result. Under such circumstances, Lord Rutland may be very much less sanguine about the idea of supporting you."

Lucretia faltered. She knew Lord Rutland would not abandon her, even in such circumstances, but she would be mortified to bring shame upon her aunt and uncle, to whom she did, indeed, owe a huge debt of gratitude. She considered her options and was silent for a few moments, thoughts revolving in her head. When she spoke, however, she was again defiant, for she had too much pride to let Jesmond Ogleby see how much his words had affected her. "That would be as nothing to the discredit my marriage to you would bring to the family. Why, marriage to such a person as you would be by far more mortifying in my aunt's eyes than a fall from grace a revelation about my true circumstances would bring about! I would do anything to protect my aunt and uncle from dishonour in the eyes of the world, but marrying you would be the last thing to bring them credit! No, your arguments do not weigh with me, sir. Now take me home at once!"

Jesmond Ogleby looked at her through narrowed eyes, and she forced herself to meet his gaze, unwavering. "Well, if you'll not marry me for money, you foolish girl," he said at last, "and if it is true, as you have asserted, that your good name means nothing to you, then we'll have to find another reason to make you want to marry me, won't we?" He smiled cruelly, in a manner that made Lucretia's blood run cold. He moved to the other side of the carriage drawing close to Miss Pycroft and, touching her cheek, said in her ear, "I'm glad, after all, that I brought you along."

Miss Pycroft flinched and trembled. "Take your hand off her!" shouted Lucretia.

"You want to ensure your friend comes to no harm?" He ran his finger carelessly along Miss Pycroft's jaw line, chuckling softly. Miss Pycroft shuddered, tears falling down her cheeks. "Well then, you had best marry me. Do so and you have my word that she'll come to no harm."

He's bluffing, Lucretia thought to herself. He *must* be bluffing. But he looked so truly evil in that moment she believed him capable of anything. And Cecelia was so very frightened, poor thing. Perhaps an opportunity for escape would present itself later, but, for now, taking steps to calm Miss Pycroft must be her first concern. "Very well then," said Lucretia, with a composure she was far from feeling, "It is as you say, it seems I don't have a choice. I will marry you. But I don't have to like you. And I'll thank you to keep your odious hands off my friend or I won't go through with it. Those are my terms."

"Come now, that's better," Jesmond Ogleby said, lounging back into his corner of the carriage, cold and indifferent. He closed his eyes and looked ready to drift off to sleep saying, before he lapsed into total silence, "Make yourselves comfortable, ladies, we have a long journey ahead."

CHAPTER SEVENTEEN

Christopher awoke with a sore head as Horeston, his valet, threw back the curtains. It was the morning following what had been quite a night. The sun streaming in through the window was bright and indicated that the day was advanced, as did the noise from the street below.

"Good morning, sir," said the valet.

"Oh, is it still morning, Horeston? Well there's a relief, I quite expected the day to have entirely passed me by. I've a feeling I may have been rather foxed last night. But by gad it was such a cockfight we saw though! And naturally I had to celebrate when I won a small fortune on it. Enderby was mad as fire, fancied his bird was a sure win, and although it did look the most likely candidate there was something about Sir Clucksalot which took my fancy. Dashed lucky thing it was too." He groaned and put his hand to his forehead as he sat up. "What time is it, anyway?"

"Nearly noon, sir."

"Is it really? Why didn't you wake me sooner? I've an idea there was something I was going to do today, although quite what it was, I cannot at this moment recollect. No matter, I'm sure it will return to me."

Horeston coughed before replying, "Actually, sir, I did twice try to wake you but was unsuccessful on both occasions. On the first I received only grunts and on my second attempt, when I tried to be rather more forceful, you er... picked up your shoe and threw it at me."

"No, did I really? How strange, I have no memory of it at all. I applaud your courage in trying again after that. Accept my apologies, not quite myself you know. Now what was it that I was going to do today? I really cannot remember," he said, wracking his brains. "I say, Horeston, you're a knowing chap, have you any idea what it was I had planned?"

"I believe," said the valet, "that you agreed to lunch with your mother today."

"Good gad, are you sure?" said Christopher, appalled. "Only it doesn't sound at all like the sort of thing I would have agreed to."

"Quite sure, sir. You mentioned that she had indicated that she wanted to discuss something important with you, and you were wondering what that was."

The fog cleared. "So I did. Well remembered!" exclaimed Christopher. "I do hope she isn't matchmaking again. Well, I suppose I ought to get up, she'll be expecting me soon, won't she?" Again he looked at Horeston in enquiry.

"Noon, I believe, was the agreed time," said the valet unperturbed.

"Oh dear, I'm going to be rather late it seems. No matter, if she knows me at all she won't be expecting me before one. Any post this morning, Horeston?"

"Yes, sir," he said handing the bleary-eyed Viscount a small pile of letters. "And this came for you last night while you were out. It is marked urgent. I left it on the table where I thought you would find it when you came in, but it seems that you did not perceive it."

"No, I didn't notice it. You would've been better to have left it next to the whisky decanter. No matter, I doubt it's of any consequence. Probably from mother reminding me of my appointment with her."

He broke the seal on the note and peered down at the writing. "Ah, it's from Bertie," he announced out loud, never one to exclude his valet from the goings-on in his life. "I wonder what he has to say that's so damned important? By God, he's got awful handwriting! I'm going to have quite a task making it out." He chewed on his lip as he read in heavy concentration.

"Kidnapping?" Christopher said, "Well, I don't know what he's on about but he comes across as mighty het up about something or other. What does that word say?" he asked squinting at the letter. "Is it lantern? Or longing? It reads as if it says tangon, but I don't think that's a real word. What do you think, Horeston?" he asked handing over the letter. His gentleman looked closely at it and then said, "I believe it says Lanyon, Master Christopher." The valet's countenance remained impassive, not betraying the slightest hint that the word held any significance to him.

"Lanyon?" Christopher exclaimed, sitting bolt upright in bed, snatching back the letter and concentrating even harder on deciphering it.

Dear Topher, the note read, *would have come to tell you in person but got cornered by Napoleon. Locked me away in the cellar and won't let me out so I'm penning you this note. Shocking news, had to warn you: Miss Lanyon is about to be set upon by a pack of trolls. They have every intention of kidnapping her and forcing her out to sea. When the pirate king gets hold of her, there'll be no hope of an escape. You must warn her before they attack. Best do it tonight, know you're not at your best in the mornings.*

Yours etc... Bertie. PS I've got scurvy but don't worry I'll be fine.

"Fiend seize it! I've no idea what he's on about! Have you, Horeston?" The valet shook his head.

"Whatever, it sounds like a damned havey-cavey business," said Christopher. He jumped up from his bed. "Only one thing for it, must go and see him and get him to explain it."

"But your mother..." remonstrated the valet.

"She can go to the devil for all I care!" exclaimed Christopher, taking his valet aback by the passion he had poured into this outburst. All Christopher could think of were the words 'Miss Lanyon'. He was worried. What can have happened to her, he wondered; various unpleasant scenarios revolved in his mind. Despite this, however, he was moved to expostulate when the valet hopefully laid out a cerulean blue coat and buff pantaloons. "Good God, Horeston, what do you think you're playing at? Not that blue abomination! Far too dashed plain! Can't think why I keep it... In fact, I thought I told you to get rid of it weeks ago? Get me out something decent to wear!"

Horeston looked sheepish. He occasionally made the attempt to dress his master in a more restrained style, and had hoped to take advantage of Christopher's distraction to curb his master's *penchant* for ostentation. He really felt that a style more akin to Brummell's would display his employer's form to greater advantage than the somewhat startling apparel he normally sported. Furthermore, to his chagrin, Horeston had an idea that Alvanley's man had sniggered at him on account of his master's appearance when he last passed him in the street. He reflected morosely that Christopher's appearance often reflected very badly on his abilities as a gentleman's gentleman. The valet went to the wardrobe and pulled out some of the Viscount's preferred apparel and watched glumly as he dressed.

Finally satisfied with his appearance, Christopher rushed round to Mr Strangwald's apartments, pounding very insistently on the knocker and demanding stridently to be let into the building.

"No need to bang the door down, Toph," protested Strangwald, "gave Evans quite a start. You must know his old heart can't take much more at his age!"

"Sorry, but the thing is, had to see you about this note! Doesn't make sense, you've got to explain it!"

"Explain it? Do you mean to tell me that you've not seen the fair damsel to warn her? Tare and hounds, Topher, I made it clear that it was important!"

"Clear?" expostulated his friend, "The only thing that's clear from this note is that you've terrible handwriting! Looks like a damned spider fell in ink and crawled all over the page... but never mind that now. Miss Lanyon, did you really mean to write about Miss Lanyon?" enquired Christopher, remembering that Mr Strangwald's conversation did not always convey reality.

"Yes," said Strangwald definitively, "isn't that what I wrote?" Christopher nodded. "Well then," said Strangwald almost offended by the original question. This moved Christopher to say sharply,

"But you also talk of pirate kings and trolls! You're not seriously telling me that's what actually going on." Strangwald shook his head. "Hell and the devil confound it, Bertie, what really is going on?" Christopher demanded.

"Pirate king, needs her to find the buried treasure," said Strangwald. He wanted to explain with less obscurity but found he could not do so. He had been so long afflicted with his conversational peculiarity that he could not shake it.

"Nonsense! Bertie, this is important, dash it! Just tell me what's really happening for once in your life!"

Mr Strangwald hung his head, muttering, "Stop the trolls."

Seeing his friend's wretchedness, Christopher was at once penitent. "Sorry, old chap, know you can't do it. Didn't mean to shout at you. Only I'm in the devil of a state as you can see. Can't bear the thought of Miss Lanyon in trouble. I'm sure you understand."

Strangwald nodded.

"Let me see if I can get to the bottom of this," said Christopher. "So it definitely concerns Miss Lanyon," he mused. "Now kidnapping, what could you mean by that? I say, you don't really mean that she's going to be kidnapped? Wouldn't be the first time after all, not so preposterous."

Strangwald nodded vigorously. "Good God!" exclaimed Christopher, his fists clenching. "We must save her! Who is going to kidnap her? Bertie, who?!"

Strangwald opened his mouth to speak but Christopher said, "Never mind, old chap, know you can't tell me. Have to work it out for myself." He looked down at the letter he had, in his agitation, crumpled in his hand. He smoothed it out to read it. "Trolls, now who could they be? No, I've no idea. But the pirate king, he seems to be at the heart of this. Pirate king. Hmmm…" he mused. "Is it someone I know? It'll be bellows to mend with us if I don't! Can't think of someone I can't think of, can I? Do I know this pirate king, Bertie?"

Strangwald nodded.

"Well, that's a start at least," said Christopher. "As I said, dashed awkward if I'd never laid eyes on the chap," he observed. "I take it it's someone I don't like, can't imagine any of my friends doing such a thing."

Strangwald nodded again, saying in clarification, "You don't like him at all. Nasty fellow. At war with him in fact."

"Had a run in with him, did I? Well, I fought Sheverton the other day at Jackson's. Displayed to advantage, but he wasn't a match for me all the same. Had a feeling at the time he wasn't above half-pleased when I darkened his daylights. Is he the fellow?" Strangwald was shaking his head.

"Wait, what a sapskull I've been! I know who I had a run in with: Morley, *must* be him who's the kidnapper. Why, he's tried it once already. Is it Morley, Bertie?" Christopher looked at his friend triumphantly. Mr Strangwald shook his head.

"Are you sure? Only I thought I must've hit upon it then. No?" Christopher was disappointed to find that his friend was quite firm in asserting that Mr Morley was not involved. "Hell and the devil confound it!" he cursed in frustration. "Well then, who else could it be? Who else have I had problems with lately."

Christopher's mind whirled and, as the memory of the duel drifted into his head, he fixed upon the true culprit. The Count's face floated before his eyes, and he remembered something else, something he realised vaguely must be connected: Count Johann lurking outside the door behind which Miss Lanyon was being assaulted by Edgworthington, and how he had started guiltily when Christopher passed him.

"It's that cursed Count, Count Johann von Andermach, isn't it?" bit out Christopher. Mr Strangwald nodded furiously.

"If indeed he is what he says he is," continued Christopher, hitting upon the truth of the matter. "Seems to me that he may be shamming it. All to win an heiress. Do I have it right, Bertie?"

"Yes!" said Strangwald emphatically. "Time to put your armour on, Topher! No time to lose, must go aboard and sink his ship! Happening today." He looked down at his pocket watch, "May already be too late."

"Well, what are we waiting for?" exclaimed Christopher. "Let's get going!" He jumped up and made for the door. "Time to save a damsel in distress! Good God, now you've got me talking like a dashed romantic book writer!"

"Aren't you coming?" demanded Christopher, reaching the door and realising that Strangwald had not followed him. "You've got to come, tell me where to go. You *do* know where they're headed, Bertie?"

Strangwald nodded, but made no move to follow his friend.

"Well then, don't see what the problem is. Come on," said Christopher, coming back to Strangwald's side and attempting to shuffle him towards the door. "Hang on a moment," he said, finding his friend wouldn't budge and momentarily distracted by another thought. "Why aren't you at work, Bertie? Thought you started this week."

"Yesterday," said Strangwald, nodding dejectedly. "Hangman's noose, couldn't do it. Couldn't go back. Napoleon's going to rip out my heart for drawing back. Treason, that's what he'll say. See, I've got my own problems, Topher. Thing is, love to help you out, but can't go gadding off now, I must think what I'm to do. You know what the price is for treason, don't you?"

"Well, of course your father's not going to be pleased. Fact is, he'll probably be mad as fire about it." Christopher moved on hastily from this train of thought as he saw Strangwald blanch, "But you'll just have to stand up to him. Nothing for it this time, Bertie! You've no choice now. Anyway, worry about that later. Come with me, it'll take your mind off things."

Strangwald still looked unsure but Christopher put his hand on his back and propelled his friend out of the room, overcoming Strangwald's scruples. "You do know where they're going, don't you, Bertie?" repeated Christopher anxiously as they rushed out of the building and into Christopher's curricle, which was waiting outside. His coachman was walking the horses as he had been commanded and climbed into the curricle at their approach.

Strangwald nodded, saying miserably, "The Americas."

"Going north are they? You'd best take the reins then, Bertie, you've a better idea where they're headed." Christopher found that hands were shaking in his anxiety to rescue Miss Lanyon, and felt that the driving of the carriage would be safer in Strangwald's hands. But, as they set forth, Christopher wondered at the soundness of this decision for he found that, without the distraction of handling the reins, he had nothing to do but panic at the thought of what Count Johann might do to Miss Lanyon.

Alarm was also being felt in the Rutland household. On account of the stifling heat of the day, the other picnic goers had set off not long after Lucretia and Miss Pycroft. The next coach to leave the event was Lady Maslebow's, and it soon came upon the injured Hudson and the postilion in the road. Spotting, from the window, the wounded man bleeding copiously at the wayside, Lady Maslebow, who was made of sterner stuff than her age-wizened form might suggest, directed her coachman to pull over so that they may offer aid to the wounded man.

"You fool!" Lady Maslebow said to the postilion, leaning out of the window to observe the scene. "Did you not think to bind up this man's arm, to stem the blood? Good God, he is bleeding half to death. Ellen, make speed and bandage the wound!" Lady Maslebow eyed the paling coachman as her maid went about applying a makeshift bandage to arm.

"Aren't you Lady Rutland's coachman?" she demanded of the wounded man. "I'm sure I've seen you before."

"Yes, my lady," said the coachman through teeth that were clenched from bearing the pain of the maid's ministrations.

"Where is your carriage then? And Miss Lanyon?" Lady Maslebow barked. But the coachman was in too much pain to reply. Seeing this, Lady Maslebow turned to the postilion. "You," she barked. "Tell me what has occurred here." She listened intently as the boy gave his account of the events.

She heard their story with astonishment. "Highwaymen? In broad daylight? How singular." If she felt any dismay at what she had heard, she certainly didn't display it. "But highwaymen do not kidnap young ladies! Assuredly there is something smoky going on here. We must go at once and inform Lady Rutland what has occurred. Help that man into the carriage, John," she directed her coachman majestically, gesturing towards Hudson. The injured man, bearing up with great fortitude, was assisted into one of the seats in the carriage. "Spring the horses to, John, we must get this man to a doctor. And we must alert Lady Rutland to the events with all possible speed."

The carriage set off at a smart pace but the jolting of the coach on the road caused Hudson such terrible pain that he could not stop himself from crying out, and Lady Maslebow was forced to instruct her driver to slow down. Nevertheless, they made good time back to London and Lady Maslebow directed her coachman to take them directly to the Rutland's Grosvenor Square residence.

The Rutlands' butler, Broome, was a good deal shocked to find Lady Maslebow pounding upon the door and even more shocked, when he opened the door, by the appearance of Hudson who was now as white as a sheet due to having lost a good deal of blood. The wounded man had held up magnificently despite his pain on the journey but now, arriving in the proximity of home, his injury overcame him and he fainted out cold upon the spot.

"Good day, Broome. I fancy you will need to call a surgeon for this gentleman," Lady Maslebow said with a wave over Hudson's inanimate form. With wiry energy she deftly stepped over Hudson's body and swept past the butler into the house. "Is Lady Rutland home?"

"She's not at home to visitors," said Broome faintly, somewhat overcome by the strange events unfolding before him. But Lady Maslebow ignored this warning and set off up the stairs to the drawing room, leaving the butler to deal with the situation before him. Pulling himself together, Broome decided to leave his mistress to deal with Lady Maslebow and set about helping Hudson into the house, calling for the housekeeper to deal with his wound.

"Hello, Virginia," said Lady Maslebow, sweeping into the drawing room. Lady Rutland looked up in considerable surprise from her seat in her chair where she had, in fact, been snoozing (although she would never have admitted to it). Coming round out of her sleep haze, she looked at the grey-haired octogenarian, affronted.

"You'll excuse my unceremonious entrance when you hear what I have to tell you," said Lady Maslebow. "I regret to inform you that your carriage has been stolen, with your niece inside it. I have brought back your coachman, who is injured, although, fortunately, I fancy not grievously. Of greater moment is that fact that your niece has been abducted, along with Miss Pycroft it seems. I've no idea why, and frankly I don't want to know, but someone must go after the men at once and rescue the girls."

She allowed Lady Rutland a moment to digest this before continuing. "The good news is that we've some idea where they are headed. Your coachman says he overheard the kidnappers mention a place called Little Ranglewood. I know it's not much to go on but at least it's something. You could attempt to question him further but, if I'm not mistaken, he has fallen into a deep swoon in your entrance hall. Broome is seeing to him."

"I tell you, Virginia," continued Lady Maslebow, while Lady Rutland stared at her speechless, "you're lucky I came across them and not Samperton, that paper-skulled gabster, else it would be splashed around town by lunchtime tomorrow. As it is, I have no plans to make the unsavoury events generally known. But I suggest you rescue her before it's too late to hush up the matter. I'll leave that to you. I suppose I ought to tell Mrs Pycroft too, but I simply cannot face that tiresome woman so I'll leave that to you as well. It seems to me that this is your affair."

Lady Rutland had pulled herself together by this point and said, "Helen, I can't thank you enough for all you've done. You'll understand me not stopping to offer you my hospitality in the circumstances."

"Naturally," said Lady Maslebow who was pleased to get shot of the affair and had no wish to stay any longer.

Elsewhere in town, Admiral Strangwald, while walking down the street, was accosted by a bellicose Lord Colton.

"Here, Admiral! I'll thank you to tell that madcap younger son of yours to have a care how he drives!" this gentleman exclaimed, quite obviously a good deal put out. "He damn near unseated me from my horse!"

"My son? Bertram?" enquired the Admiral in astonishment. "I fear you must be mistaken, Colton. Bertram is at present working in the city so he cannot possibly have done such a thing," pronounced the Admiral, drawing himself up haughtily.

"I saw it with my own eyes, and I know what I saw!" railed Lord Colton. "He was haring his curricle most dangerously and at a truly alarming speed out of town not thirty minutes ago. Young fools! With a bit of luck, they'll find themselves thrown in a ditch before they break their or anyone else's necks. Although quite frankly they deserve... Abominable conduct!"

"Impossible," said the Admiral, but he was less sure of himself now.

"It's true, I tell you!" asserted Lord Colton heatedly. "Young Prendergast was shouting at your son, mighty put out himself, I don't know why. And then Bertram suddenly, and in that very unfortunate way he has of coming out with peculiar utterances, said, 'I have it. Little Ranglewood!' He seemed so very pleased with himself that he stopped watching the road and that's when he nearly knocked me off my horse. And do you know what!" raged the irate lord, "stap me if Prendergast didn't clap him on the back in congratulation! They were crowing, I tell you. Crowing! I have never seen more shocking conduct in all my life!"

"If what you tell me is true, then I apologise for my son's disgraceful behaviour. Rest assured that I will be having words with him on the subject," said Admiral Strangwald. He had a bloodthirsty look upon his face that augured badly for Strangwald but seemed to satisfy Lord Colton. The Admiral turned on his heel and set off back up the street to his house looking grim.

CHAPTER EIGHTEEN

Following the duel, Mr Morley thought it necessary to lie low for a while. He did not want to actually go home yet in case he should be sought out there, he therefore found a quiet inn, located near his home, in which to retire and lick his wounds. He spent his days in the taproom drinking heavily and wondering how he had ended up in his current situation.

Mr Morley was thus engaged on the afternoon of Lucretia and Miss Pycroft's kidnapping. Dusk was beginning to fall when his hostess, Mrs Brown, ushered an uncomfortable-looking man into the room and thrust the gentleman into a chair. This was Reverend Stowe, the curate, who had a murine appearance with a snout-like nose, protruding incisors and wisps of hair on his upper lip, which gave the appearance of whiskers.

"Reverend, I'm so glad you could come," said Mrs Brown, having given the priest little choice in the matter. "Do sit down, do sit! Let me get you a drink."

"Dobbin!" she hollered in the direction of the bar, where her nervous husband appeared. "Pour the reverend a drink." Mr Brown went obediently to do so. "No, not that, the good ale! Merciful heavens above, oh sorry, reverend," Mrs Brown said, unsure whether this was a blasphemous phrase, and then proceeded to horrify the priest by continuing, "You can't serve a clergyman watered-down pigswill! If only divorce was not so unchristian," she added in explanation to the now scandalised parson.

"But what's this about? Why have you called me here?" Reverend Stowe asked, by now feeling very uneasy.

"Why, to perform a wedding!" exclaimed the inn-keeper's wife. "What else are priests good for? Now, make yourself comfortable, I expect them at any moment, but you never know but what there may have been some hold up along the way."

"A wedding? At this hour! Surely you cannot be serious?" exclaimed the priest faintly.

"Of course I'm serious. Wait, I hear a carriage, that may be them now."

A bustle could be heard outside, indicating the arrival of a vehicle in the yard. After a time, Mr Ogleby entered with a nervous-looking Mr Handle in his wake.

"Ah, good, I see you've got the priest here, Dora. Mr Handle, my sister Mrs Brown," he said, making the introductions. "Her husband owns this sorry place. Greetings, Dobbin," he yelled in the direction of the bar. "Any sign of my nephew yet?" Ogleby asked his sister. "No? Oh well, may as well have a drink while we're waiting."

No one paid any notice to Mr Morley who was by this time rather intrigued. A man of more delicacy may have chosen this moment to make his departure, but Mr Morley stayed in his spot in expectation of being a spectator to some interesting events.

Mr Ogleby sat slurping on his drink and waited for the arrival of his nephew. He passed the time in chatting convivially with his sister and laughing uproariously at her unkind tales of all the things her long-suffering husband had recently done wrong. When she ran out of these stories, she proceeded to recount classic tales of his stupid acts from many years ago. This pastime served to keep Mr Ogleby tolerably well amused for the next hour, after which time he became noticeably less relaxed. He glanced frequently at the door, hoping to see his nephew enter, but for some time there were no further arrivals and Mr Ogleby continued to fortify himself with liquor.

The events turned out to be even more interesting than Mr Morley had bargained for, as Mr Ogleby and Mr Handle's advent was eventually, some two hours later, followed by the arrival of Jesmond Ogleby, foisting an outraged Miss Lanyon and a terrified Miss Pycroft into the taproom before him. He had untied them both in the carriage and, though he had no concerns that Miss Pycroft would try to escape, he kept his gun digging into Lucretia's back; unlike Mr Morley he knew not to underestimate his captive.

Jesmond Ogleby paid off his unsavoury accomplice, who slunk out of the inn with hulking strides, and Jesmond turned his attention to his uncle.

"Ah, excellent, you're here!" said Ogleby rubbing his hands together. "Managed it all then?"

"Went off without a hitch," replied Jesmond Ogleby.

"So, this is the famed Miss Lanyon," said Ogleby, looking Lucretia lasciviously up and down. "A pretty piece, ain't you, my dear. Shame I can't have you myself, but sadly the courts look most unkindly on bigamy, more's the pity." Reverend Stowe looked appalled to the point of apoplexy at these sacrilegious comments. "Who's the other girl, Jesmond?" demanded Mr Ogleby, sounding a little anxious. "This wasn't part of the plan."

"Only one of Miss Lanyon's friends who was accompanying her today," returned Jesmond Ogleby in an off-hand manner. "Had difficulty shaking her and it didn't seem worth spending time in the exercise."

"Never mind, never mind," said Mr Ogleby jovially, with a whistle of relief. He was cheerful now that the plan had been carried off with so few problems. "Fortunate for you, Miss Lanyon, looks like you are to have a bridesmaid. Now you can't complain my nephew hasn't taken pains to make the ceremony pleasant for you."

"There won't be a ceremony," bit out Lucretia. "I haven't the least intention of marrying anyone today!"

"Ho, ho, feisty little thing, isn't she?" said Mr Ogleby appreciatively to his nephew. "Regular firebrand." He chuckled and then turned to Lucretia to say, "May as well marry him tonight, leave it 'til tomorrow and you'll really be in the suds. Think of your reputation girl – won't be able to show your face anywhere! No, marry him tonight or you'll be begging him to have you in the morning! Hardly dignified. See, we've got the priest all ready and everything." He gestured in the curate's direction.

Lucretia turned on the uncomfortable clergyman, demanding hotly, "Surely you cannot intend to agree to perform this ceremony?"

"I... er... well..." stuttered the curate disjointedly, unable to take his eye off the gun in Jesmond Ogleby's hand. He was frankly terrified. For all he was a man of the cloth, and could have a reasonable expectation of ascending rather than descending upon his expiry, he had no wish to be hurried out of this world. Fearing for his life, the clergyman uttered feebly, "If both parties wish it..."

Lucretia looked outraged. "I thought you, at least, a man of the church, could be trusted to call a halt to this outrageous plot!" Reverend Stowe was steadfast in his refusal to meet her eye.

Lucretia didn't know what to do. She couldn't see any means of escape, and her usual resourcefulness did not suggest any plan to her. Lucretia knew that killing her would not serve her captors' plans and felt little fear for her own life, but she could not be sure that her captors would have any scruples against harming her little friend, and was careful to give them no cause to do so. All she could think of was to buy herself some time before the deed was done, in hopes of hitting upon an idea in the meantime. "It seems," she said haughtily, "that you have given me no choice. But I would be very grateful for some refreshment before we proceed to the church."

"Well..." said Jesmond Ogleby, uncertain. "I'd as lief get the thing over and done with. Can't keep the reverend here waiting for ever."

Reverend Stowe was torn between the wish that he would have to wait forever rather than be forced to perform such a ceremony, and a desperation to get the event over and done with that he might escape the threatening presence of the gun.

"Nonsense, nonsense, my boy. Let the girl have a drink to fortify her! The church is only next door, after all. A toast to your wedding, you know!" bellowed Mr Ogleby in Lucretia's direction. He had become loquacious under the influence of the large quantities of gin he had imbibed in the last few hours; his cheeks had a telling red flush to them and he listed slightly on

272

his stool. "Then we can proceed to the church while Dora cooks up a wedding supper. Fine cook, my sister," he informed Reverend Stowe conversationally. The curate thought he had never felt less hungry in his life.

The men set about moving tables around in readiness for the upcoming supper, and it was during this exercise that Mr Morley's presence inevitably came to be noticed.

"You! Here!" cried Lucretia incensed. "I might have known you would have been involved. There doesn't seem to be a dishonourable intrigue you do not have your hand in."

"I… nothing of the sort, I assure you," stuttered the wrongly-accused Morley.

"Morley?" said Jesmond Ogleby sharply, espying this gentleman in some surprise and lifting his eyebrow in question.

"Do you mean to tell me that you really had nothing to do with this?" demanded Lucretia of Mr Morley hotly, looking from one gentleman to the other.

Morley looked at Jesmond Ogleby a good moment before recognition dawned upon his drink-ravaged countenance. "Count Johann? Good God, you are much changed!" he exclaimed.

"As, my friend, are you," said Jesmond Ogleby dryly, taking in Mr Morley's unhealthy appearance. "I do hope you are not planning on… er… interfering in this affair?" He looked meaningfully at the pistol in his hand. Lucretia looked at Morley expectantly, even a little hopefully.

"Not at all, not at all," Morley hastened to say.

"Do you mean to tell me," demanded Lucretia angrily, "that you are going to stand by and let this man force me into marrying him? And do nothing?" She saw from his indifferent expression that this was indeed the case. "I can't think why I'm surprised really, you have already shown yourself to be no gentleman! But I thought…" she stammered, not finishing.

"But really, Miss Lanyon," said Morley, slurring his speech ever so slightly, "it would be so hypocritical of me to stand in Count Johann's way now, wouldn't it?" He looked down at his glass, swilling its contents around before looking, with bloodshot eyes, back at Lucretia. "Unless, of course, you have changed your mind and would now, perhaps, like to marry me after all? No? I thought not. Count Johann, I raise my glass to your good fortune. Although I infer that perhaps the title is a mite inaccurate."

Jesmond Ogleby nodded. "My name's Ogleby, Jesmond Ogleby. That's my uncle," he said nodding in Mr Ogleby's direction "From the undercurrents between you and my fiancée..." Lucretia made a strangled squeaking sound at his use of the word. Jesmond Ogleby repeated, "From the undercurrents between you and my fiancée, it appears that there may be more than meets the eye with you also, Mr Morley. Apparently, you have some interesting tales to tell. Perhaps you can enlighten me later, although at present you can appreciate that I'm a bit engaged, ha ha." He laughed at his own inadvertent pun. "Expect you're probably pretty *au fait* with what's going on. Tell you what, you can be my best man, seeing as you're here. Well, this *is* turning out to be quite a party, I must say."

"Then you won't mind a few more additions," said Arnold Rutland, who surprised all the occupants of the room as he entered. The noise caused by the moving around of furniture had drowned out the sound of his carriage arriving. "And I'll tell you now that I take exception to you pointing this pistol at my cousin," he said into the stunned silence that had fallen in the room.

Like lightening Arnold crossed the room and pulled the gun from Jesmond Ogleby's unwary hand, and then ushered Lucretia and Miss Pycroft across the room towards the door. He firmly placed himself between the two young ladies and their kidnappers, as if to protect them. Miss Pycroft was shaking from the shock of everything that had happened, and Lucretia put her arm round her shoulders to comfort her.

"Cousin!" exclaimed Lucretia in amazement. "Oh cousin, you have no notion how pleased I am to see you. I cannot think how you came to find us, but I'm so glad!"

Although it had taken Lady Rutland and Arnold some time to locate Little Ranglewood on the map, Jimmy had once again proved his mettle by having the carriage ready to set off in a trice. And, because Arnold's impressive pair of match bays were far superior to the pair that had been pulling Lady Rutland's carriage, they had made up a lot of the ground separating them from the abduction party.

"Aunt!" squeaked Lucretia, catching sight of Lady Rutland in the doorway.

"Well, Lucretia," said Lady Rutland, sweeping majestically into the room on her son's heels. "You do seem to be falling into the habit of getting into scrapes, a pastime, of which, I tell you now, I cannot approve," she said with composure. "Heavens, what a lot of people!" Lady Rutland continued, looking at the other occupants of the room with disdain. "Who is the author of today's unfortunate series of events?"

Looking around the room imposingly, Lady Rutland's eye fell on Mr Morley. "Mr Morley, I congratulate you on your persistence. I'm afraid you will find it all in vain, however, my niece will not be marrying you today, or any other day!"

"You are in error, Aunt," interjected Lucretia, "Mr Ogleby, and not Mr Morley, is my captor, although, to be sure, Mr Morley has shown no inclination to help me in my predicament," she threw out reproachfully.

"Mr Ogleby?" said Lady Rutland sharply, her brow furrowing.

"Delighted to make your acquaintance, Lady Rutland," said Mr Ogleby moving forwards towards her. "I see the name means something to you." He chuckled unpleasantly. "I trust, now you understand who has orchestrated today's events, you will understand why Miss Lanyon is here, and why there isn't a damn thing you can do about it."

"I'll thank you not to use such language in my presence," said Lady Rutland haughtily, looking at Mr Ogleby as if he were nothing. "And I haven't the faintest idea why you have dragged Lucretia here, or why you should think there is nothing I can do about it. Furthermore, I do not care. Come, Lucretia, we will go home."

Mr Ogleby moved with the intention of barring her way. "Not so fast, Miss Lanyon! You are not leaving here before you marry my nephew."

"Marry your nephew? Gracious! *My niece,* marry *your* nephew?" Lady Rutland said, looking at Mr Ogleby as if he were something unpleasant she had found on the bottom of her shoe. "You are being ridiculous, sir."

"Ridiculous, am I?" said Ogleby colouring up. "I am Miss Lanyon's trustee, and it is my decision who she marries, and I say she will marry my nephew! And there is nothing you can say in the matter!"

"My dear sir," returned Lady Rutland, "there is a good deal I could say on the matter, but frankly I do not have the time or inclination to waste it in discussing the matter with you. Why on earth would my niece, a Lanyon, want to marry your nephew, a nobody? I fear you must be touched in your upper works!"

Arnold Rutland was grinning. This was his mother at her best, and he was enjoying Mr Ogleby's discomfort hugely. He caught Lucretia's eye and could see she too was appreciating the scene and struggling not to laugh. Mr Morley, not bothering to hold his countenance, was looking on in patent amusement.

"Lucretia, do you wish to marry this..." Lady Rutland waved her hand at Jesmond Ogleby disparagingly, "man?"

"No, aunt," said Lucretia, stifling a giggle.

"There you are then, let us leave," said Lady Rutland with finality.

Mr Ogleby was baffled to have found himself wrong-footed in this way, but asserted, "As trustee of the late Lord Lanyon's estate, it falls to me to decide who Miss Lanyon marries, and I say she will marry my nephew!"

"Nonsense! Lucretia is going to marry my son Arnold," said Lady Rutland. This pronouncement had the effect of wiping instantly the smiles off both Lucretia and Arnold's faces, and they caught each other's eyes in consternation. Battle continued unchecked, however, between Mr Ogleby and Lady Rutland. Miss Pycroft, who had a great dislike of raised, angry voices, was quivering.

"I will *never* give my consent to the match!" shouted Mr Ogleby. "And without it she'll be as poor as a church mouse. I'm sure your son has no wish to marry a pauper! There, what have you to say to that?"

"I find you ridiculous, sir," said Lady Rutland dismissively. "Of course you will give your consent. You will do as you are told!"

"I'm not a schoolchild to be ordered around!" blustered Ogleby, incensed. "I will not give my consent and that's final."

"We shall see what my husband has to say about it!" said Lady Rutland, becoming rather heated. "It cannot be lawful for you to withhold your consent to a match for no good reason."

"I assure you," said Ogleby, pleased to have shaken Lady Rutland out of her complacence, "the Trust is most explicit. Miss Lanyon cannot marry without the consent of her trustees or she'll lose her fortune."

"Well, that's as maybe," said Lady Rutland, determined not to be convinced by Ogleby's arguments, "and I'm not agreeing with you. But what it is *not* in your power to do, is force my niece, or anyone else, to marry against their wishes! And as my niece has no wish to be married to your nephew, that idea is at an end. In light of that, you can have no possible reason to object to her marrying my son!"

Arnold sent Lucretia a rueful glance, took a deep breath, as if he were about to dive underwater, and then leapt into the debate saying, "But mother, *I* object to that. I haven't the least intention of marrying Lucretia."

To Mr Ogleby's intense relief, this turned Lady Rutland's attention on her errant son, giving him a welcome reprieve from her onslaught. "Nonsense, Arnold, stay out of this discussion, it has nothing to do with you!"

Her son raised an eyebrow at her. "Oh, very well then," said Lady Rutland pettishly, "it does have *something* to do with you, I'll grant. But let us not discuss the issue here, in front of all these people. For now, let us just deal with this odious man and his preposterous claims! No, actually, I do believe I am finished talking to him, we had better just take our leave. The discussion will be better served in the comfort of our own home, which has the added benefit of being clean!" Lady Rutland ran her finger along the top of a shelf near where she stood and, holding up her glove which had developed a blackened finger from the exercise, turned to Mrs Brown, saying severely, "Landlady, you ought to be ashamed of keeping such a dirty establishment. Quite shocking!" She sniffed, adding to her son and niece, "I do believe that we should leave with all possible haste before we catch something!"

Arnold was about to fall silent on the issue and turned to take his cousin and mother home, when he saw that Lucretia's face was frozen and she was looking fixedly at something in the doorway. In the entrance, Lord Prendergast stood, as motionless as a statue, looking back at Lucretia. It seemed that they had forgotten everyone else in the room. Recollecting himself, Christopher smiled uncertainly at his beloved, and Lucretia's face at once burst into a radiant smile that was all the more dazzling for the love that shone from her eyes.

Arnold recognised that, given some little time, the two of them would finally speak their feelings to each other. This situation could serve as the catalyst needed to bring them to an engagement, if only given the opportunity to do so. But, to leave at this juncture, before the match was finalised, could set the young lovers back weeks. Arnold knew that the inexperienced Christopher Prendergast could take some time to gain the courage to declare himself, and, even then, would only do so then if a suitable occasion presented itself. Such felicitous circumstances as these would never repeat themselves, and Arnold was determined to assist the enamoured couple by nurturing the situation to its best advantage.

Therefore, in the spirit of one helping out a friend in need, Arnold chose to prolong his discussion with his mother to allow other events the time to flourish. He sighed and heroically drew his mother's full firing power upon his own head by announcing: "I think, after all, I will make Lady Scallonsby my wife. She plans to divorce Lord Scallonsby and take me as her husband instead."

Lady Rutland was dumbfounded. The room fell silent with all eyes on Lady Rutland, save Lucretia's and Christopher's (for they had eyes for no one but each other), all sensing that a dangerous explosion was imminent.

Mr Strangwald, arriving at this moment, proved as unconcerned by the battle about to rage between Lady Rutland and her son as Lucretia and Christopher were. He pushed past Christopher and looked round for Miss Pycroft. He spotted her shrinking behind Lucretia for protection, quivering and upset by all the shouting and arguing. Strangwald rushed to her side and nudged away Lucretia, taking her place in comforting the terrified young lady. Fortified by his presence, Miss Pycroft became calmer, and leaned into his sturdy form as if it were a haven in a storm.

Meanwhile, the uncomfortable hush continued to pervade the room as Lady Rutland's wrath seemed almost palpable in the air. As he had planned, Arnold's announcement had served to make his mother forget anything other than his words, and eventually she broke the silence by a tirade, brought down upon her son's head, of epic proportions.

Oblivious to this, Lucretia joined Christopher in the doorway. "Thank God you're safe, Miss Lanyon," said Christopher. "I've been in the devil of a worry about what might have happened to you."

"Well, it *has* been quite a day but, as you see, I'm quite unharmed," said Lucretia.

"That's a girl! *Quite a day?* Why, anyone else would be past swooning! You've pluck to the backbone, Miss Lanyon! I've never known such a girl."

"But you must be thinking me the most tiresome of females to be always getting myself into such scrapes! And you are forever having to jump in and rescue me, such a trial it must be to you," exclaimed Lucretia in embarrassment.

Christopher shook his head. "No such thing. I like it, in fact. Although on this occasion I see that I'm not needed." He glanced over at Lady Rutland and Arnold and then turned his attention back to Lucretia, saying shyly, "Like to spend time with you, Miss Lanyon, whatever the circumstances." He shuffled uncomfortably and then added light-heartedly, "Although the number of scrapes you get caught up in does seem to be becoming rather… er… incalculable." He twinkled at her.

Lucretia smiled back at him and sighed happily as she said, "You are very kind, but alas, it does seem to have become a regular chore for you to be obliged to come to my rescue, Lord Prendergast! I feel very badly about it, for I've no right to expect it of you."

"I rather hoped," said Christopher awkwardly, "that you may consent to making it my duty, even my right, to always do so."

She looked up into his eyes, to check that he meant what she thought he meant by these words, and saw that he did. "Oh," she said inadequately.

"Miss Lanyon," Christopher said after a short pause, "will you do me the honour of accepting my hand in marriage?" Contrary to what he may have expected in making his declaration, Christopher felt neither nervous nor embarrassed. He loved her, and it seemed very natural for him to say what he had said.

Mr Castleton would have been deeply disappointed by the manner of his friend's proposal, but Lucretia saw nothing amiss. "Oh, Lord Prendergast, of course I will!" she said joyfully.

"Then I think you'd better start calling me Christopher, Lord Prendergast sounds dashed formal under the circumstances."

Suddenly Lucretia felt shy again, but said, "And you must call me Lucretia… or Cressy rather!"

The two stood staring most happily at each other, as if they were the first people in the world ever to discover love, unconscious of the scenes that continued to rage around them.

"…So you will not marry that poisonous woman, do you hear?" Lady Rutland finished her diatribe.

"No, mother, of course I won't marry Lady Scallonsby," said Arnold Rutland humbly. "But you see," he said looking meaningfully towards the doorway where Lucretia and

Christopher stood with their heads together, "Lucretia has no intention of marrying me either."

Lady Rutland looked at the two lovebirds and then back at her son, and was thunderstruck. There was a long moment of ominous silence. The room at large expected another explosion, another terrible tirade from the lady. But to everyone's huge surprise, she let out a crack of laughter.

"Arnold Rutland, you rascal, so that was what it was all about! Well...!"

The newly engaged couple sensed that the eyes of the room were upon them, and looked round. Christopher met Lady Rutland's eyes and, with a newfound dignity that had been growing on him over the last few weeks said, "With the greatest respect, Lady Rutland, I inform you that Miss Lanyon has done me the very great honour of accepting my hand in marriage. I hope we may have your blessing." It was implicit that although he may like to have her approval, it made no difference to the result.

Lady Rutland looked at him for a long moment. Coming on the heels of the relief she felt that her son was not to ally himself with Lady Scallonsby, she was more disposed than she might have been to look favourably upon the match. Christopher Prendergast was young and green, and she would not have chosen him for her niece. However, he was heir to an impressive title and a considerable fortune and had, moreover, shown himself equal to the task of protecting her niece against the world.

"Lucretia, is this indeed your wish?" she asked of her niece.

"Yes, aunt," said Lucretia simply.

"Very well then," returned that lady graciously. "I wish you both joy." She smiled indulgently upon the pair and saw with satisfaction her niece's obvious happiness, a consideration than had become genuinely important to her over the last few months.

"Ahem," the almost-forgotten Mr Ogleby coughed. "This is all very touching indeed, but *I* don't give my consent to this marriage! You may have secured her ladyship's blessing, but you damn well don't have mine!"

Christopher raised his quizzing glass and looked Mr Ogleby disdainfully up and down. The effect was flawless; he had now learned to perfection how to employ this weapon and it resulted in making Mr Ogleby feel much diminished.

"Lucretia, who," Christopher said, drawing his eye away from Ogleby's person, "is this badly dressed man?"

Lucretia was much inclined to giggle at this. Ogleby coloured up, offended by the insult. "I'll have you know, you impertinent young greenhorn!" Ogleby said angrily, "that I am the trustee to Lucretia's fortune. And without my consent, her marriage will leave her without a feather to fly with! And hear this, young man, you will never, I tell you, *never*," he asserted menacingly, "have my consent to this match. There now, what have you to say to that?"

"Well, sir, if I perfectly understand the situation, I gather that although it may be within your power to withhold Miss Lanyon's fortune from her, it is not in your power to prevent her from bestowing her hand upon whoever she wishes. And although who she chooses to marry is, naturally, of the utmost importance to me, her fortune is a matter of supreme indifference. My fortune will amply support both of us. I would appreciate it, therefore, if you ceased to obtrude upon our notice any further." Having come to the end of this most eloquent speech, Christopher somewhat undermined the dignity of it by adding, "So push off, you dashed clodpole, before I'm forced to put your lights out!"

The Viscount had gone up immeasurably in Lady Rutland's estimation with his words, and she looked at him approvingly, saying, "Hear, hear! Well, then this has been a most interesting day, but I do feel that it is time we brought these affairs to a close. We shall go home at once," she added autocratically.

Once again the party turned to leave, but they were prevented from doing so by yet another arrival. A deeply impassioned Admiral Strangwald exploded into the room, shouting, "Where is he? Where is he?" His murderous eye fell upon his wayward son. "Bertram Henry Strangwald!" he bellowed. "Thought to escape your duties, did you? How *dare* you disobey me!" He loomed towards Strangwald.

Strangwald could feel Miss Pycroft begin to shake and looked down at her. She was desperately upset by the shouting and, coming on top of all that she had already borne that day, she was almost overset, tears begin to burn in her eyes. Once again Strangwald put his arm around her shoulders in a caring, supportive gesture. His fear of his father was cast aside by his need to protect the scared little lady beside him, and he rounded on his father saying, "Enough! Can't you see you're upsetting her? There, there, Miss Pycroft, you are quite safe." He looked back at his startled father and said firmly. "You may rage at me all you like when we're home, but I'll not have you do so here where you are distressing Miss Pycroft, who has the gravest dislike of raised voices."

Strangwald stared boldly into his father's eyes and the Admiral looked at his son in surprise. He had never before heard him speak so sensibly and so fearlessly. But his defiance did him no disservice in his father's eyes. Admiral Strangwald liked men to have the courage to say what they thought. His son's nervousness had bred his contempt but this new, forceful Bertram commanded greater respect from his father.

"Indeed," the Admiral said with a raised eyebrow. "Well, I'm glad you have enough proper feeling to admit that you owe me an explanation, but I can understand that this is not the place for the discussion."

"I do feel I ought to tell you, father," said Strangwald, wanting to make use of his new-found courage in case it should evaporate by the morrow, "that I will no longer be working for Mr Scrivenham. And I feel quite sure that, when I discuss it with him, he'll agree that the arrangement doesn't suit either of us."

"We'll see," said the Admiral noncommittally.

"In fact," continued Strangwald firmly, "henceforth I will have a new job: that of protecting my wife and attending to her happiness. That is," he said, looking down at Miss Pycroft, "if the lady will have me?"

Miss Pycroft, still very much discomposed and fighting back her tears looked confused. "What do you say, dearest," said Strangwald to clarify matters, "will you marry me?"

Miss Pycroft began to cry in earnest now, but it could be perceived that behind the tears she was smiling, and that they were tears of joy. She gulped and nodded her assent.

Christopher looked at his friend, impressed, exclaiming, "I say, I do believe that that's quite possibly the only sensible and intelligent thing you've ever said, Bertie!"

Mr Strangwald, not in the least offended by this, grinned at him saying, "Scurvy, you know."

There were no more surprising revelations to be made that evening, and the party turned to leave and squabble over who was travelling in which carriage. As they exited the inn side by side, Christopher looked down at his betrothed and said, "While I'm in a rescuing mood, Cressy, do allow me to rescue you from that truly horrible hat!"

"Oh dear, is it very ghastly?" she asked.

"Very," returned Christopher gravely.

"Of course, you know best about these things," she said meekly, removing the offending article from her head.

CHAPTER NINETEEN

Christopher was in his dressing room the next morning when he received a visitor in the form of Mr Castleton. Christopher had a strange floaty, happy feeling in his head, and was so distracted by this that he did not notice the severe look upon his friend's face.

"Heard the good news, Clem?" Christopher said. "Why, that's fast work! No notion it would get about so quickly; never ceases to amaze me how gossip travels like wildfire!"

"Good news? You've a nerve, Christopher!" said Castleton angrily. Christopher, engaged in the delicate matter of tying his cravat, didn't hear these words.

"Nice of you to come and give me your congratulations so soon," said Christopher. "I'm the happiest man alive, I assure you. There," he said, finally satisfied with the necktie.

"Happiest man alive? I ought to wring your neck for your impertinence!"

For the first time, Christopher took in his friend's indignant stance and tone of voice. "What's up with you, Clem? Thought you'd be pleased for me, especially after all the help you've given me."

"Fiend seize it! If I'd known what you were up to I'd never have helped you! How could you? It's utterly unsuitable," said Castleton severely. "She's not ready for marriage yet, and you should know it! Why, she's much too young!"

"Eh?" asked Christopher puzzled. "Miss Lanyon's nearly two and twenty. I don't call that too young. Why, the gossiping tabbies even had her on the shelf. I haven't the faintest idea what you're talking about."

"Miss Lanyon?" asked Mr Castleton, perplexed. "What are *you* talking about, Topher?"

285

"Miss Lanyon, she's accepted my proposal," said Christopher with unconcealed elation. "Who'd have thought I'd be first of us into the parson's mousetrap, eh?"

"Do you mean to tell me that you've gone and got engaged to Miss Lanyon?"

Christopher nodded cheerfully. "Thought you knew, old fellow. Thought that was why you were here. To wish me joy, you know."

"When did this happen?" Mr Castleton demanded hotly.

"Yesterday. Look, what's got you all in a pucker, Clem? You don't look pleased for me," he reproached, "and I can't think for the life of me why not."

"Oh, you can't, can't you!" said Castleton sarcastically.

"No, I can't! Don't look at me like that. I'm in such good humour I won't have you spoiling it!"

"You don't deserve to be in a good mood! Not when my sister's at home crying her poor eyes out!"

"Your sister? What's she got to do with anything?" said Christopher, taken aback.

"What has she got to do with it?" exploded Castleton, incensed.

"Now, don't go repeating everything I say. Just tell me what's got you all hot under the collar, without all these cryptic remarks. Can't you see I'm not following you at all?"

"You can't be engaged to Miss Lanyon, Christopher. Not when you're already engaged to my sister!"

"Engaged to your sister? No dash it, Clem! I've never been anything of the sort, I assure you. Can't be engaged to your sister, I'm engaged to Miss Lanyon. Just told you so."

"Ah, but you see, Christopher, you said you asked Miss Lanyon to marry you yesterday, but the truth of the matter is that you were already secretly engaged before that. So, whatever you say, you are not, in fact, engaged to Miss Lanyon. You are engaged to Katherine, who assures me that you asked her to marry you several weeks ago, and is now crying her eyes out because you haven't so much as called upon her since. She's worried you might have had a change of heart, which, indeed, it seems you have done. Whatever, you can't break off an engagement, as well you know! Breach of promise and, moreover, besides being illegal, damned ungentlemanly! So you will come to apologise to her and make wedding plans like you ought. I'm mad as fire that you didn't tell me about it sooner, dashed sneaky and underhanded. I thought you would have done the thing properly and asked for my permission to address her! But to be keeping me in the dark about it... well... not the actions of a friend!"

"But dash it, Clem, I've no idea what you're talking about! I never asked your sister to marry me... except..." He trailed off, struck by a sudden thought.

"Except?" Castleton jumped on the word.

"Except under your strict instructions to practise making my proposal. But it wasn't real, just practice, you know. I mean you set the whole thing up! So you know what I'm talking about."

"I told you to practise saying the lines I'd given you," said Castleton bitterly. "But Katherine says you couldn't do it, found the words weren't right for you. Then you had a good *tête-à-tête*, after which you proposed to her in earnest. The governess backs her up, says she saw the whole thing. Says there wasn't a doubt you meant what you said. So you see: you can't draw back now!"

"But Clem, I never meant to ask her to marry me for real. Good God, Clem, your sister!"

"What's wrong with my sister?" snapped Castleton suspiciously.

"Nothing, nothing," said Christopher hastily. "Lovely girl, just not the one I'm in love with, that's all. You know I never meant to ask her."

"Katherine's no liar, and from her account I'm inclined to believe what she says. And whatever was going through your head at the time, it doesn't really matter now. Thing is, Topher, you've raised expectations which you're duty-bound to fulfil. Katherine's very sure, and with the governess backing her up, well, you can't draw back, and you know it. I've tried to talk Katherine out of the whole thing, told her you're a frippery fellow and that you wouldn't suit, but she wouldn't listen to a word of it. Quite adamant, she is. Best go tell Miss Lanyon the bad news. I expect to see you to calling upon my sister this afternoon," ordered Castleton coldly.

It was a command, and Christopher was shocked by how forceful and peremptory it was. "But..." Christopher started to say. Castleton, however, had turned curtly on his heel and was walking out of the room.

All Christopher's happiness and peace of mind had evaporated. He knew Mr Castleton was right in saying that a man could not turn his back on an engagement. He had never meant to make the proposal but, with the governess's testimony, it meant two people's word against his own. He felt trapped and, after giving it some thought, could see no way out of the situation. As unpleasant as the job would be, and as injurious as it would be to his own happiness, he must go and tell Miss Lanyon and put their engagement at an end.

When he called at the Rutland's residence, Christopher found Lady Rutland and Lucretia in the drawing room, preparing to receive the usual round of morning visits.

"Lord Prendergast, what a surprise," said Lady Rutland a little ironically. Lucretia's heart fluttered in her chest at the sight of her betrothed.

"Good day, Lady Rutland, Miss Lanyon," said Christopher formally. He turned to Lady Rutland. "I wonder if I might have a word with Miss Lanyon in private?" he asked.

Lady Rutland looked disapproving but complied with the request nevertheless, sweeping out of the room. Christopher sank down on the sopha next to Lucretia, looking solemn. She reached out to slip her hand in his. He gripped it for a second and then, with resolve, pulled his hand softly away.

"What's wrong, Christopher?" said Lucretia anxiously. "Have you had a change of heart?" Christopher felt terrible to put her through such agony.

"No, of course not," he said. He could not lie to her. Lucretia sighed in relief at this. "But I...well..." he stuttered, unsure where to start. He gulped, "The thing is, well, I've got myself into the devil of a fix!" And he explained how he had been so nervous about proposing to her that Mr Castleton had made him practise proposing to his sister, and how this had lead to the day's events.

"And now she insists that we are really engaged. And, oh, I never meant to become engaged to her!" Christopher finished miserably, hanging his head.

"Oh dear, quite a pickle," chuckled Lucretia. Christopher looked at her in surprise, wondering what she could find in the awful situation to amuse her.

Lucretia saw his bemusement and said, "Well, you've got to admit that it's a little humorous. After all, it's not every man you meet who goes, in a matter of weeks, from fearing women to finding himself engaged to not one woman, but two at the same time!"

Christopher smiled wanly. He felt dejected and hopeless. To have finally won the heart of the woman he loved, to now find that he was bound to another was harrowing. "But what are we to do?" he asked desperately. "It seems I have no choice but to marry Miss Castleton. Nothing for it."

"Nonsense!" said Lucretia cheerfully.

"But as a gentleman I can't jilt her. Not the thing! You know that."

"No, of course not. But if she should draw back from the engagement..." mused Lucretia.

"Clem says there's no chance of that. Said he tried to talk her out of the thing, but she wouldn't hear of it."

"It seems it is now my turn to rescue you from a scrape then," said Lucretia who, having finally won her beau, had no notion of having him taken from her, especially by someone he did not love. "You will take Miss Castleton for a walk in the park this evening and leave the rest to me," she said firmly. Christopher looked unconvinced and Lucretia again slipped her hand into his. "Don't worry, my love, all will be well, I assure you," she said. Feeling a little heartened, he squeezed her hand then stood up to take his leave, daringly bending down and dropping a kiss upon her cheek before he went. After he had gone, Lucretia sat staring ahead unseeingly, thinking furiously, her hand touching the place on her cheek where the gentle kiss had fallen.

It was all very well, Lucretia thought to herself, to assert that one could solve a problem. But as she sat considering the issue, she could not think how to resolve the quandary before her. She chewed her lip anxiously, trying to hit upon a plan. Finally, she jumped up from her chair to go upstairs to her room so she would not be disturbed while she churned ideas around in her head. In the hallway, she came across Arnold Rutland bounding down the stairs in his typically energetic fashion.

"Cressy, well met! Do you care to tool around the park with me in my phaeton? I have just today purchased the most beautiful pair of matched greys from Lord Sutterham, who has lately found himself so out of pocket that he must needs retrench. If you're very good, I may just let you take the ribbons, so you can see for yourself how first-rate they are!"

"I..." said Lucretia, distracted, disappointed to have been disturbed in her ruminations. Then she looked up at her cousin and had an idea.

"Yes, cousin, I think I will come along with you after all."

"Excellent," he enthused. "Cressy, you've got to see these horses! The most beautiful steppers you'll ever see! Jimmy is in raptures about them. You'd best hurry and get ready; Jimmy's dying of impatience to see them put through their paces. You'll be in his bad books forever if you hold us up too long!"

"I can be ready in a trice," said Lucretia optimistically, and indeed was ready to set off after a mere half hour's preparation.

"What think you, Jimmy?" shouted Arnold to his tiger as they set off along the road. "Magnificent, aren't they? I told you you wouldn't be disappointed."

"That they are an' all, sir. Right sweet goers, they are," agreed Jimmy ardently.

"You're mighty quiet, cousin," Arnold noted, casting a sideways glance at Lucretia as they bowled along through the park. "Are you not impressed with my new blood cattle? You're so serious-faced I confess it is putting a bit of a damper on the experience. Perhaps you should not have come." He was sorely disappointed by his cousin's lack of enthusiasm.

"Oh, I'm sorry, Arnold," apologised Lucretia. "The truth is, I have a little problem that is exercising my mind a good deal."

"Well, never mind that now! How you could be thinking about some trivial problem when you should be savouring this moment. Such a bargain as this pair was! Really, Lucretia, I quite thought you shared my appreciation for good horse-flesh, and am disappointed to find I must've been mistaken!"

"Not at all, of course they make a marvellous addition to your stable, and if it was a trivial problem, naturally I could set it aside. Most unfortunately, my problem is neither trivial, nor can it wait. Perhaps I ought not to have accompanied you, only I had a notion that you may be able to help me out of my predicament."

Arnold sighed. "I see you are not to be talked out of your anxiety. Very well, what is it that I can assist you with?"

"It's actually rather funny, or at least it would be if it were not happening to me," returned Lucretia. "You see, the thing is, that it turns out that I am engaged to a man who is already engaged."

Arnold looked at her incredulously, his attention successfully diverted now, to the disgust of Jimmy, from his new pair of horses. "Prendergast? Really?" He asked in disbelief. "Do you mean to say that *Prendergast* is now engaged to two women? And him so averse to women... save yourself, of course," he added hastily. "Why, if that don't beat the devil! I thought he was an upstanding gentleman, only goes to show how mistaken one can be in people!"

Arnold frowned, considering the matter, and after a time said, "Perhaps I ought to take him to task over the issue. He deserves to be punished for upsetting you. Only you have to appreciate that I don't want to call him out, he's a damnably good shot, you know. Everyone at Manton's talks about his skill. Why, only last month..." He caught sight of Lucretia's face and realised that this was not the time for diverting stories that wandered off the point.

"He didn't mean to become engaged twice! It was... an unfortunate accident," said Lucretia.

"Accident? Ha! Coming it too strong, coz... no man gets engaged *accidentally!*" He gave the matter some consideration and then said anxiously, "I mean, if it's true, it's a lesson to be more careful!" He shivered convulsively; the thought of such a previously unsuspected danger as inadvertently finding himself betrothed filled him with blind fear.

"I assure you, it's quite true," said Lucretia.

"If you say so, then naturally it must be the case," Arnold returned, unconvinced. "I think you'd best tell me all about it." And so Lucretia explained the situation to him, and by the time she had finished her account they had both perceived all that was ridiculous about it and were in fits of giggles. This merriment heartened Lucretia, she knew she could always rely on her cousin to cheer her up.

After the laughter had worn off, however, Lucretia fell silent again, the serious look returning to her countenance. "What do you think, cousin, can you help me? Can you see any way out of this mess?"

Arnold thought the problem over and then said slowly, "I think I just might... If there's one thing I know about, it's women!"

"I've a notion that the things you know about women aren't fit for my ears, cousin!" said Lucretia naughtily.

Arnold laughed. "Perhaps not. But I may be able to put some of my talent to good use, it seems. So no more of your disparaging comments, girl!"

"Yes, Arnold," Lucretia said meekly. "Do you have plans this afternoon, cousin?" she asked.

"I... well, nothing that can't be put off. Why?"

"This afternoon Christopher, that is to say Lord Prendergast, and Miss Castleton will be going for a walk in the park."

"Ah, I see," said Arnold, understanding. "And your plan is that we can intercept them and upend the apple cart? And what, pray tell, am I to be doing during this exercise?"

"Only what you do best! Charming a young lady. I know you can do it, turn her up sweet, I mean. If you put your mind to it, you can make her forget Lord Prendergast within half an hour!"

"What a poor opinion of your future husband's charms you have," said Arnold roguishly. Lucretia blushed. Arnold pinched her chin and said, "Widgeon! I know you didn't mean it like that. Obviously, it is just that you rate my own hypnotic allure so very highly," he said with a grin. "I'll do my best to beguile the lady away from your intended, have no fear. And now we have concocted a plan of campaign for extricating you from your problem, I beg you will turn your full attention to appreciating these horses!"

"But it's starting to rain, we must make for home with all possible speed or I'll get wet!" exclaimed Lucretia, putting out her hand to feel the weight of the drops falling in her palm.

"Pooh! Surely you can't be meaning to let so paltry a thing as a spot of rain get in the way of this wonderful drive! You can have no objection to getting a little damp surely?"

"On the contrary, I have the greatest possible objection! Only think of what it will do to my dress, not to mention my hair! We must go home, cousin, on the instant!"

Later that day Lucretia and Arnold set off to Hyde Park to intercept Christopher and his party. It had been a dismal morning, and the drizzle had swiftly turned to a downpour which left the paths soggy and wet. It was followed by a dry but cold afternoon with a high wind that whipped Lucretia's hair wildly about.

"Oh dear, I do hope Miss Castleton and Lord Prendergast may not have been put off by the weather," worried Lucretia as they approached the park.

But Miss Castleton, a hearty young lady, had a high opinion of the value of exercise, which the less than ideal weather could not abate. She was in the process of extolling the virtues of a brisk walk to her brother and a miserable Christopher, when they came across Lucretia and Arnold in their path.

"Lord Prendergast, Mr Castleton, how nice to have met you," said Lucretia with studied nonchalance.

"Prendergast, Castleton," Arnold nodded at the two gentlemen in greeting.

"Good day, Rutland. Miss Lanyon, what a pleasant surprise," said Christopher heartily. Miss Castleton shot her intended a suspicious look and then eyed Lucretia with hostility.

Lucretia met Christopher's eyes and then looked meaningfully at Miss Castleton. Recognising the cue, Christopher said, "Oh, but where are my manners? Miss Castleton, allow me to introduce Mr Arnold Rutland and his cousin, Miss Lanyon." Lucretia and Arnold fell into step with the party and they all proceeded together along the path.

"I see you have not been deterred by this somewhat inimical weather from taking your exercise," said Arnold cheerfully to Miss Castleton, drawing to her side.

"Not at all, Mr Rutland," said Miss Castleton coldly, still eyeing Lucretia with suspicion. "There is nothing so bracing as a walk in the elements. It quite assists one to reflect on God's great authority, and our powerlessness against his might. A salutary lesson not to neglect our prayers, don't you think?"

"Er…" said Arnold, somewhat dumbstruck. As one who rarely contemplated matters of the divine, he had little idea how to respond, and no notion at all of how to attract such a sober individual.

Lucretia saw at once that her plan for Arnold to divert the young girl's attention away from the Viscount by engaging her in flirtation was doomed to failure. Clearly, Miss Castleton was of a serious and pious turn of mind and belonged, therefore, to one of the few categories of women immune to her cousin's charm.

Lucretia could not think what Miss Castleton had found in Lord Prendergast to suppose him a suitable husband when his mind leaned firmly towards the worldly rather than the heavenly. She soon realised, however, that the qualities possessed by her fiancé mattered not a jot to Miss Castleton, who had every intention of remoulding the character of whoever she married.

Silence had fallen upon the group and Mr Castleton broke this by addressing Arnold with enquiries about the Peninsular Campaign.

"Have you had news from your comrades of Wellesley's progress? From what I hear, he has had many successes."

"Less news than I would like, but the accounts I have received have been favourable. I expect he will make it to France soon. And, as Boney will be fighting on two fronts with the Russians and Austrians laying siege from the east, our prospects are good."

"Oh, are you an army man, Mr Rutland?" enquired Miss Castleton in a disapproving tone. She considered war, despite being a necessity, deeply unchristian.

"Yes, in the –th Hussar regiment. But alas, I took a bullet in the arm in one of our campaigns and have been home on sick furlough ever since."

"I expect you are glad to have a reprieve from all the violence and danger of the fighting. I imagine you must have seen some terrible sights," observed Miss Castleton.

"Not a bit of it! I wish myself with my regiment more than anything. What action they must be seeing now, and myself stuck here missing out on it all! I hope to get back to it soon. But the saw-bones says that the stiffness that is persisting in my shoulder means I must rest a little longer, curse him!"

"But surely you cannot mean it?" Miss Castleton was firmly of the opinion that, although men may be drawn into the war in support of their country, they certainly should not enjoy it. "This modern thirst for war can only sadden our great Lord, as Isaiah proclaimed: *nations shall not lift up sword against nation, neither shall they learn war anymore.*"

The conversation was interrupted at this point by a cry from Lord Prendergast. His interest in the military extended only so far as its influence on the fashions of the day, and he had been paying little attention to the conversation. Having just that moment stepped in a large puddle, he was looking down at his top boots in great consternation, stooping to investigate the damage and falling behind the rest of the party. The boots had turned down tops of shining white and the effect of his foot landing in the puddle was that their snowy perfection was now marred by a hearty spattering of mud.

"Oh no, they're ruined! And Horeston, for all he is a veritable genius with such things, will never be able to get the stains out. If they're not completely white they are quite hideous. Oh, no one should be so dashed foolish as to go walking on muddy paths in such weather! I was a blockhead to think of it! We must go back before there are further mishaps!"

"It seems so very paltry to be so concerned about a pair of boots when one considers how men are losing their lives over the waters on our behalf!" said Miss Castleton in sharp disapproval, walking back towards him.

"Paltry?" said Christopher, becoming angry.

Arnold Rutland jumped in, trying to stave off an argument by saying cheerfully, "Not at all, not at all. We fight so that we may protect such liberties as dressing oneself in the first stare of fashion..." He broke off with a sudden yelp, for Lucretia had stepped painfully on his foot.

"Hush," Lucretia whispered to her cousin. "Let them argue."

Just then, a strong flurry of wind blew, causing Mr Castleton, Arnold and Lucretia to clutch their hats to prevent them flying off. But Christopher, caught up in his anger, was not quick enough. His beaver, which was exceptionally tall, fell foul of the gust and sailed off his head into the mud. He swore and reached down to retrieve it.

"I beg your pardon," admonished Miss Castleton. "To use such language over a mere hat, sir; you forget yourself! This excessive concern over such worldly concerns does you no credit."

Christopher coloured up, incandescent with a rage which he struggled to swallow down. But Miss Castleton was not done with her censure. "You have clearly been encouraged in your disproportionate attention to your attire," she continued, with a meaningful and disapproving look towards Lucretia. "When we are married, however, I hope to turn your thoughts down more worthy avenues. After all, *wisdom is better than rubies*," she quoted.

"Fustian! When you are my wife," returned Christopher, who had lost his temper now beyond recall, "I hope you will dress yourself in a manner that does me greater credit than your current appearance!"

"Well then, perhaps we should not be married at all!" Miss Castleton retorted angrily.

"Perhaps not," agreed Christopher coldly. "It was you, Miss Castleton, who taught me to always be myself! Remember that the leopard cannot change his whiskers," he quoted imperfectly.

Silence fell, Christopher staring defiantly at Miss Castleton, who looked at him contemplatively, and cocked her head. After a long moment, she opened her mouth to speak but then closed it, staring at him a little longer. "Whiskers?" she said finally, choking on a giggle and unable to keep her amusement out of her voice. And then she laughed, a wholehearted, unrestrained fit of merriment. The tension evaporated, and Christopher laughed too, nervously at first but then as heartily as Miss Castleton.

"Oh dear, I fear I have been very unchristian," said Miss Castleton, gulping to control her laughter. "It seems abundantly clear that we should not suit, Lord Prendergast, but, I beg of you, let us not be enemies. As my brother's friend, and not as my husband, I shall know how to value you. Come, let us cry friends."

She held out her hand as a peace offering. As he grasped it and shook it, Miss Castleton leaned towards his ear and said, *sotto voce*, "And I think there may be someone who should suit you better than I." She paused, and then continued bravely, "Someone who is very dear to you." She smiled at him to show she held no ill-feeling. "It was very wrong of me to try to interfere. Only I did not think her worthy of you. But how evil of me to judge myself more worthy than another. I am so very sorry for all that I have put you through."

"Let us say no more on the subject, Miss Castleton," returned Christopher awkwardly. "All is forgotten." They returned to join the rest of the party in a relaxed attitude.

"Leopard's whiskers," said Miss Castleton as they walked, remembering his flawed quotation. They both chuckled.

Despite the recent unease, the atmosphere amongst the party was light-hearted and comfortable. They continued strolling on, but fell into two groups: Lucretia fell into step next to Miss Castleton, and the men formed another group, falling back to walk at a distance from the ladies.

"Thank you, Miss Castleton, for releasing him," said Lucretia. Miss Castleton looked embarrassed and penitent.

"It was the right thing to do. I am sorry for the trouble I have caused. Truly I am."

"You must have taken me in very great dislike to go so far to prevent Christopher from marrying me? I assure you, I love him very dearly and will strive to make him happy," Lucretia forced herself to say, despite the discomfort that talking about such feelings to a relative stranger caused her.

"You already do so, it is writ clearly upon his face," said Miss Castleton. They glanced round towards the men's party, where Christopher could be seen looking anxiously at the pair. "I had no right to dislike you, Miss Lanyon," she continued, "especially when I had not met you. And indeed, the main cause of my actions was far less honourable. I am not beautiful or witty or lively; I worry so that I will never receive an offer again. It is wrong of me, I know, to allow myself to get caught up in such worldly concerns, I, who have preached so at you all today for doing so! I despise myself for my hypocrisy."

"Peagoose! I feel quite sure that God does not begrudge us some small amount of vanity and insecurity," said Lucretia, smiling in genuine kind-heartedness at Miss Castleton. "Certainly, he doesn't begrudge us our love for one another. There is time and more for your looks to blossom, and for you to meet a man who will value your many good qualities as he should. Someone who will not forever be talking to you of his cravat or his topboots! And next year you will attend balls and picnics and enjoy yourself like any debutante should. For does it not say in the bible *eat, drink and be merry*?"

"Thank you, Miss Lanyon, you are very kind," said Miss Castleton gratefully.

"And I shall look forward very much to seeing and talking with you at those parties and balls, if you will allow me to?" added Lucretia warmly, slipping her arm through Miss Castleton's. They walked arm in arm for some few minutes, Miss Castleton asking Lucretia nervously about what it was like to make her come out and other unexceptional topics.

After a few more minutes the gentlemen caught up with the ladies, and Lucretia left Miss Castleton's side and made her way towards Christopher. The two of them drew back from the rest of the group.

"There now, did I not say that all will be well?" Lucretia said to Christopher with a gentle smile.

"Yes, my love," he agreed, "but I fear you lack my finesse in your rescue attempts! Perhaps we should leave the rescuing to me in the future."

Lucretia laughed immoderately. "Well... if you *will* get yourself into these scrapes..." she smiled impishly.

"Now listen here, Cressy! I'll not have you meddling in my problems in future. Naturally on this occasion I'm very grateful. But I'm to be your husband, and it's my job to do the rescuing! There now, tell me you've heard that!"

"Of course," said Lucretia sweetly. "It will be my job to hear everything my husband has to say."

Christopher gave her a suspicious look. "Hmmm..." he said. "I've a feeling all women pick and choose which of their husbands' words they want to hear. And you have a distinctly mischievous look in your eye that I mistrust!"

"I have it on good authority, Christopher," said Lucretia, pretending to look affronted, "that my ears are like wings that fly open to hear everything that is said. And, far from being filled with deviousness, my eyes are dreamy and placid and..."

"Perfectly spaced." Christopher completed the line without thinking. Lucretia stopped in her tracks and stared at him.

"Oh, was that you?" Lucretia let out a peel of laugher. "You should have told me! I have never enjoyed any gift so much in all my life! Your observations on my face are most truly original." She clutched her sides from laughing.

Christopher looked sheepish. "Oh dear. Cressy, I'm afraid I have to tell you that Clem wrote that poem, and the other verses. Please tell me you're not going to run off with him now in my stead! Sadly, I must admit I have neither taste for poetry, nor talent in the writing of it. I did choose the gifts, however," he finished, anxious to redeem himself.

"And they were beautiful presents," said Lucretia. "Don't think I'm not grateful. But all the same, I must thank your friend for his efforts on your behalf!"

"Mr Castleton," Lucretia directed at that gentleman. "I understand that I have you to thank for the most magnificent homage I ever received. You are a master of the verse, truly."

Mr Castleton blushed with pride. "See, Topher, told you it couldn't fail! You owe it to me to have me as the best man at your wedding. It's obvious that it's entirely down to my assistance that you've been fortunate enough to win this fair lady's hand," he said pompously. "I believe I will compose an ode to the happy event," he finished thoughtfully, "as a wedding present."

CHAPTER TWENTY

The next morning, Christopher, his peace of mind and happy excitement returned, called in Mount Street. He met his father in the hall, just about to leave to go to his club.

"Hallo, father," said Christopher.

Lord Godolphin was prevented from replying by a shriek, followed by shouts of, "My vinaigrette! My vinaigrette!" emanating from the drawing room. This commotion explained the Earl's haste to escape to his club. Father and son cringed at the noise.

"What do you mean, she has given notice?" Lady Godolphin's high-pitched voice demanded. A lull followed, during which some mumblings, presumably from some poor subordinate, could be heard. The words, however, were inaudible, and the Earl took advantage of the lull to greet his son.

"Christopher, what a pleasant surprise! It's not like you to make calls at this hour. To what do I owe this very early honour?"

Christopher opened his mouth to reply, but was drowned out by Lady Godolphin wailing, "Accused her of stealing? No such thing!" More mumblings followed. Lord Godolphin gave his son a pained expression as, upstairs, Lady Godolphin continued her tirade in the drawing room. "All I said was that it was mighty suspicious that one household could spend so much on candles, and beeswax ones at that! Just as if there were not a tax on all candles as it is!" More murmuring followed.

In the hallway, Christopher took advantage of the relative quiet to say, "The thing is, father, that I'd like a word with you."

Just then, the front door was closed with a firm click by the butler. Lady Godolphin, possessed, it seemed, of extraordinary hearing demanded, "Who is at the door? Francis, who is it? Staines, who's there?"

The Earl and his son blenched. "In private, father," said Christopher in hushed undertones, sending the butler an agonised glance.

Staines sighed, and proceeded up the stairs. "No one, my lady. Merely the wind," the long-suffering retainer could be heard saying to his mistress.

Lady Godolphin, seemed satisfied by the ruse, and returned to her earlier diatribe. "Well," she was shouting in affronted accents, "if beeswax candles are being used by the servants, I think I have a right to demand an explanation! And under such circumstances I have every right to drop a word in the housekeeper's ear. Why she should take offence at it, I do not know!"

In the hallway below, the Earl turned to his son, murmuring, so as not to be overheard, "Naturally, I am at your service, son."

Unfortunately, Lady Godolphin's excellent hearing was not undermined by her anger and, at her husband's whispered words, she broke off from her tirade. "Are you quite sure no one is in the hall, Staines?" she demanded sharply. "I thought I could hear someone down there."

"Quite sure, my lady," said Staines with conviction, displaying a good butler's superior skill in the art of mendacity.

Lord Godolphin, who was sporting a hunted expression, said very softly to his son, "Shall we escape… that is to say, *repair* to my study?"

"I should say so," said Christopher heartily. "Good God! What is afoot this time?" he asked once they reached the safety of the Earl's private study, Lord Godolphin shutting the door firmly (but quietly) behind them.

"Your mother thinks that Mrs Albury has been feathering her nest by over-charging on the accounts for candles. 'Deceitful lying wench' were, I believe, the words she used. Not unjustifiably, Mrs Albury took exception to the description. I gather she will not much longer be in our employ." He sighed. "That's the second housekeeper this year. May I recommend placidity and even temper as great virtues in a wife, when you come to be choosing one. But you didn't come to see me about such things."

"Well, actually, father," said Christopher with relief that the topic of his visit had already been broached for him, "it is exactly on that subject that I have come to see you."

"Really?" said the Earl.

"Yes. I have some good news. I dare say it'll come as a surprise, but I'm going to be married," said Christopher casually.

"Indeed," said his father, feigning surprise and eyeing his son in interest.

"Cressy, that is to say, Miss Lanyon, has done me the honour of accepting my hand in marriage."

"My congratulations, son," said Lord Godolphin, clapping his son on the back. "I wish you joy. She is a very estimable young lady. Shall I have my secretary draft a letter of notice to the Gazette, or do you need to alert the Rutland's to the impending nuptials first?"

"Of course not, I'll write it myself!" said Christopher, somewhat affronted. "And naturally I've discussed it all with Rutland, spoke to him about it yesterday, in fact."

The Earl looked at Christopher, fascinated, marvelling at the changes he could see in him. He had grown so much in maturity and dignity that his father almost didn't recognise him. It seemed love and commitment had improved his son, thought the Earl. "And how," he said, nonchalantly, "did they take the news?"

"Well, Lady Rutland gave her consent, although naturally I told her that I meant to marry Lucretia whether she gave it or not."

"Indeed?" replied Lord Godolphin, not batting an eyelid but thinking privately that it took a brave man to say such a thing to Lady Rutland. He would have given a good deal to have been present at the interview.

"And Rutland was most agreeable," continued Christopher. "He's a knowing fellow, the Viscount. Didn't seem at all surprised... very shrewd. Wished us well and all that mummery. Then invited me to dine with them, which explains why I didn't come and see you yesterday. Naturally, I had to accompany Lady Rutland and Lucretia to Almacks after."

Naturally," said Lord Godolphin sardonically, again wondering at the change in his son who, only weeks earlier, would probably have opted to have his eyes gouged out rather than attend such an event, let alone escort two ladies on the occasion.

"The thing is though, father..." said Christopher, hesitating for the first time. "Well, the thing is..."

"The thing is that..." said his father helpfully, seeing his son struggle.

"Well, I'll be needing an increase in my allowance. I mean, dash it, can't keep living in my lodgings when I have a wife to support! Been thinking about it all, and, well... Lucretia's been used to the best. Besides which, can't have my wife going about shabbily dressed, not the thing, you know. And well, what with clothing myself and paying for a house and stumping up to keep Lucretia kitted out in the first style of elegance, well, I'm going to find myself out of pocket, is all," Christopher finished, shuffling his feet beneath him.

"I see," said Lord Godolphin slowly.

"Well, of course when you've cocked your heels up, which I naturally hope won't be any time soon," said Christopher graciously, "there'll be no problem. What with the inheritance and all. But in the meantime..."

"I am very glad to hear you are not anticipating my demise joyfully," said the Earl, amused, not taking the least offence, recognising that none was intended. "And perhaps an increase can be arranged."

Christopher breathed out in relief. "Thanks, father, you're the best of good fellows! You won't regret it, I assure you. Lucretia looks beautiful as it is, but when I've got her dressed as she deserves, you know, with a bit of extra taste, you'll be blown away!"

"Blown away? I'm sure," said Lord Godolphin, regarding his son's flamboyant outfit with a small smile. "I was, however, under the impression that Miss Lanyon was possessed of a considerable fortune of her own." Not for the world would he let on to his son how much he already knew. For a start, he was very much interested to hear Christopher struggle through an explanation, watching this new version of his son in amusement. And secondly, a more kindly motive, he didn't want to embarrass his son by showing him how knowledgeable he was on the subject of his love life.

"Well, yes, she *is* entitled to a good deal of money. But it's bound up in the most stupid Trust. The terms are a bit complicated," he said airily, "but the long and short of it is that she can't get her hands on a penny of it without the approval of her trustees in her choice of husband."

"I gather, then, that they are withholding their consent to your marriage?" said Lord Godolphin.

"Not so much one chap," said Christopher, "he didn't seem to care either way. But the other, Ogleby his name is, well, he had something to say on the matter. If you could only have seen what the man was wearing, you'd understand in an instant. Looked like a damn ugly customer, if ever I saw one. There were gravy stains on his waistcoat... Looked like they'd been there a year or more! And his coat, if you could call it that, hung off him like a damp towel! Gave me a nasty turn when I saw him, I can tell you!" Christopher shuddered in horror at the memory.

"Says it all, really," Christopher continued. "Chap goes round dressed like that, must be a cursed rum touch, stands to reason! Anyway, he wanted to marry Lucretia off to his nephew, of all the dastardly plots! I gave him a good talking to, but he wouldn't hear of agreeing to our getting hitched. No getting round it, just have to kiss goodbye to the money, I'm afraid. Course, I told him I'd marry Miss Lanyon, fortune or not. Knew you'd approve, never been one to tell me to marry for money. Thing is..." he sounded uncomfortable again, "I love her."

It was all there in those three words given with such great embarrassment. The strength of his son's feelings could

305

not have been clearer to the Earl if he had said: *I adore her*, or *I worship the ground she walks on*, or *I cannot live without her*. The time for teasing was over. "Of course I'll increase your allowance, son. And I give you my most heartfelt congratulations on your engagement. I'm delighted to see you so happy. But perhaps this Ogleby will change his mind and give his consent after all?"

"No chance of that," replied Christopher. "Very set on his refusal, you know. Can't be helped. All the same, no sense moping about it. Best be off, shopping you know."

And perhaps, Lord Godolphin thought after his son had left, it's time that I paid Mr Ogleby a call.

Mr Ogleby's housekeeper was considerably surprised to find one who was obviously a member of The Quality on her doorstep. Nevertheless, she was not one to fall over herself with obsequiousness.

"What do you want?" she demanded.

"Good day," said Lord Godolphin, a little taken aback at this greeting. "Is Mr Ogleby at home? I am desirous of a few moments of his time."

"Are you now?" returned the inimical lady. "Well, who's asking?"

"My name's Prendergast, I'm the Earl of Godolphin," he said politely, executing a little bow. If he thought this would impress the crabby lady, however, he was mistaken.

"An earl, are you?" She hollered over her shoulder, "Josiah! Are you expecting an Earl of somewhere or other?" She couldn't hear his reply. "Wait here," she ordered and, leaving Lord Godolphin hovering on the doorstep, clomped into the house. Presently she came back. "He's not expecting you," she said, and made as if to shut the door in the poor Earl's face. He had to lodge his boot in the doorframe to prevent her doing so. She glared down at his boot, which was preventing the door from closing, and then scowled up at his face.

"I'd be grateful," said Lord Godolphin, grinding his teeth together and losing some of his politeness, "if you would send my card up to him."

The housekeeper looked at him for a long moment, very much inclined to refuse, but capitulated as she took note of the determination in his eyes. "Oh, very well," she said petulantly, taking the proffered card between two grubby fingers and stomping back into the house.

"Mr Ogleby will see you now," she said ungraciously upon her return, and led the Earl into a scruffy parlour, in a corner of which, Mr Ogleby was seated in an armchair.

Ogleby didn't rise to meet his visitor but said jovially, "Have a seat, Lord Godolphin. Come to talk about your son's upcoming nuptials, no doubt? I won't change m'mind, if that's why you're here. You'd be best served talking him out of the thing, if you want my opinion. He'll not see a penny of the money. And for all she's a pretty piece, there's no sense in marrying a pauper. Not when you're the heir to an earldom, stands to reason he can do better."

"That," said Lord Godolphin in warning tones, "is my future daughter-in-law you're talking about. I'll not have her spoken of in such a way. Ever."

"I don't know what you think you can do about it," returned Ogleby, chuckling.

Lord Godolphin ignored this sally and continued, "Perhaps I can make it worth your while to give your consent to the match?"

"Ho ho, so that's how it is, is it? Well, I can tell you now that my agreement won't come cheap! So you'd best name a pretty price. And throw in something for Mr Handle while you're at it." Mr Handle didn't need to know anything about it, Ogleby thought, planning to add his partner's portion to his own into the bargain.

"Oh, I'm not proposing to give you any money," said Lord Godolphin. "You see, the thing is, I've known about your involvement in Miss Lanyon's future for some time. And when I learned of it, having already developed a kindness for the lady, I made some enquiries into your career and dug up some rather interesting facts about you. Are you all right, Mr Ogleby? You are beginning to look rather green," said the Earl, somewhat smug. "I see we understand each other."

Ogleby struggled for composure and said defiantly, "I don't know what it is you think you know. But it sounds like a bluff to me and it won't hold water, I can tell you now!"

"Actually, I know a good deal," said Lord Godolphin, with unimpaired good humour. "I'm sure poor widowed Mrs Leech would like to hear about what you did with her husband's body. And I think Sir Hillsdon would certainly be interested in what I have to say. The name means nothing to you? Sir Hillsdon is a good friend of mine and, aside from that, he is also the magistrate for Swilditch, where, as you are very well aware, Mrs Leech lives."

Mr Ogleby's face had now drained of all its colour, but his unwelcome visitor was not finished. "It may interest you to know," said the Earl conversationally, "that around Swilditch, Sir Hillsdon is known as Hillsdon the draconian." Perceiving that Ogleby looked somewhat blank, Lord Godolphin added, "People in your line of work know him as Hillsdon the noose-happy."

The Earl saw, with satisfaction, that Ogleby had begun to sweat profusely. "So you'll give your consent to the marriage between Miss Lanyon and my son," ordered Lord Godolphin, "and you'll wind up the Trust as you ought. And in return I will er... stall... holding a very interesting after-dinner conversation with Sir Hillsdon. Are we agreed?"

Ogleby, swallowing in loud gulps, could only nod his assent. After a time, he pulled his nerves together a little and asked anxiously, "How do I know you won't inform against me after the wedding?"

"You won't know," said Lord Godolphin harshly. "And that is an uncertainty you will just have to live with. Now that I'm satisfied we understand each other, I will wait while you compose a letter appraising my son of the new state of affairs, after which, I'll take my leave of you. Then, you will send poor Mrs Leech all the money you can draw together. Believe me, I will be checking up on this fact. And then, if you're lucky, you'll never hear from me again. But I can't guarantee the fact, so watch your step, Ogleby!" And I, thought the Earl to himself, noting the malicious gleam in Mr Ogleby's eye as he left his lodgings, had better watch my back.

That evening Lord Godolphin was graced by another call from his first born. "Christopher, twice in one day? This is an unexpected privilege," he said jovially.

Christopher waved the pleasantry aside. "Good news, father! Thought you'd like to know, although you seemed to see it coming... Can't imagine how, but then you're a knowing fellow too. Always said so. Said so to Bertie the other day. If you need advice, go to Clem. If Clem can't help you, go to m'father, he's a dashed clever chap."

"You honour me," said the Earl in amusement, his eyes twinkling.

"What was I saying?" said Christopher, ignoring the interruption, "Oh yes, well Ogleby's withdrawn his objections to the wedding. Turns out I won't need that increase in my allowance after all, Cressy's going to be rich."

"I see," said Lord Godolphin, "That is good news. It may not be comfortable for you to hang on your wife's sleeve, however."

"Ah well," said Christopher with cheerful unconcern. "I'm sure she won't mind. We're a team now, share the money, we'll be married, after all."

"All the same, I will increase your allowance as we agreed," said Lord Godolphin.

"Will you?" said his son in some surprise. "Well, there's not the least need but that's generous of you just the same, sir."

"I wonder why Mr Ogleby changed his mind," said the Earl.

"I haven't the faintest idea," returned his son. "But it doesn't signify," he added indifferently. "I'm glad he did, that's all I can say. Anyway, thought you'd like to know."

Lord Godolphin thought of the afternoon he had spent ensuring his son's future and sighed. Sometimes being a father was the most thankless of tasks. "Will you stay to dinner, Christopher?"

"No, can't stop. Best go and tell Cressy the good news! Good evening, father," Christopher said, walking cheerfully out the door with a wave.

He went at once to call in at Grosvenor Square.

"Christopher!" said Lucretia, jumping up from the sopha as he was announced. Christopher grinned to hear his name upon her lips.

"Hallo, Cressy," he said shyly. Arnold Rutland, who had been keeping his cousin company since Lord and Lady Rutland were dining out, looked at the two lovebirds with a somewhat nauseated expression, and left the room.

"I've got some good news," said Christopher. "It turns out I'm to marry a very wealthy woman."

"Oh, has Mr Ogleby given his consent?" asked Lucretia. "Well, that's very good news."

"It is, isn't it?" said Christopher cheerfully. "Not that it signifies to me either way," he added hastily, anxious to make it clear that he was not marrying her for her money.

Lucretia patted his arm in reassurance. "If you're a fortune hunter, you're very good at hiding the fact," she smiled at him. "And I'd love you anyway, so it wouldn't matter."

It was a happy chance that Arnold had left the room, for this exchange would no doubt have revolted him.

"Got a present for you," Christopher said, drawing a box out from his coat pocket.

"Oh, how kind! But you really needn't have done so. I'm not the sort of girl to forever be needing presents. Not that gifts aren't very nice," she added, taking the proffered box. "Oh..." she breathed as she opened it. "Oh, how beautiful! Oh, and you remembered..." She broke off, staring down at the beautiful necklace of pearls nestled in the box. She flung her arms around his neck. "Thank you!"

"Nonsense, the merest trifle! But really, Cressy, have a care, my necktie, you know!" Christopher reproved.

"Oh, I am sorry," Lucretia said, penitent. "I can't think what I was about. I say," she said stepping back and patting down her hair, "is that a new way you have of tying your cravat? I haven't seen anything like it before."

"I'm so glad you like it," Christopher returned, making an attempt to repair the flamboyant composition. "It's my own design," he added with pride. "I call it The Incalculable." Sadly, the arrangement was not to survive Lucretia's next hug, but it was apparent that its owner was not unduly put out by the fact.

The End

Printed in Great Britain
by Amazon